SUPREME SUPERIOR HOTEL

Five–Star
FLEECING

Maura Stone

A WinS Publication

Published by Written in Stone
Astoria, New York 11106, USA
www.maurastone.com

FIVE–STAR FLEECING

Written in Stone/published by arrangement with the author.

PRINTING HISTORY
FIRST EDITION: November 2009

Copyright © 2009 by Maura Stone
Library of Congress Control Number: 2009941399
Edited by Lonnie Ostrow
Cover photo by Armando da Silva
Cover design, graphics and interior text design by Laslo Cheffolway

For information: Written in Stone at www.maurastone.com

PRINTED IN THE UNITED STATES OF AMERICA

Dedicated to three women who loved life:

My mother, Judith Iris Stone
Lucy Fishman
Patsy Blanks

*To Deb —
Don't let the
doctor know I
gave you this book!.
Keep on laughing.
Maura Stone*

"Between dishes and douches, I'm always in hot water."
—Rae Warren

Prelude
1995

Call it woman's intuition, but I somehow felt that this day was gonna be a humdinger. I came in ahead of time, expressly upon Mr. Ganiff's request for some godforsaken reason, and as usual it was his "do as I say, not as I do" situation.

Here I was, stuck in a dimly lit and empty hotel corridor at six forty–eight in the morning because Herr Ganiff had yet to make his matinal appearance. Otherwise, I would've been seated at my desk instead of standing in front of the closed and locked entrance to our offices at six forty–eight in the morning. The place gave me the creeps. I kept seeing fanged monsters in the shadows. While I searched in my handbag for the spare key, something took hold of my right shoulder and attempted to drag me towards the portals of a parallel universe.

I flailed my good arm to thwart off my attacker. At the same time, I dug into the plush carpeting using the four–inch heels of my Manolos as brakes. And, I let out a screech that could wake up the dead, or half... no, make that three–quarters of the guests in the Supreme Superior Hotel. Well, something succeeded because I was released the moment the dogs in the neighborhood howled in response.

I whirled around in a classic Kung Fu pose to confront my attacker, and in the process flung my handbag. It nearly beheaded a diminutive bellhop. Almost instinctively, I followed up with a one–handed chop while emitting a "Hiiiie–jha!"

"What the hell are you doing?" I screamed, "you almost gave me a stroke!" My right hand stung from the near–lethal blow.

"I almost gave *you* a stroke? Weren't ya tryin' to decapitate me?" he croaked. "Lady, all I did was grab yer shoulder, tryin' to get yer attention—" he broke off to clear his throat. Then he looked down and said under his breath, "To deliver yer newspaper."

I followed his line of vision. There, on the floor, was a crumpled *Daily Post* next to my discarded handbag. Right beside that, the key. I gave him a look that meant "Get it!" He gave it right back at me with a "Make me, bitch." Disgusted, I sighed and bent down. So did he. Clunk! That was the sound of our colliding skulls. I paused for a moment until the whorls of light and darkness subsided. But it didn't stop the little bastard's momentum. He snatched that newspaper right out from under my extended hand, purposely neglecting to pick up my personal effects. The joker then snapped to attention and produced the paper with a flourish. *What a fucking asshole.*

While he was doing whatever he was doing, I scooped up the key along with the handbag. I went to wrest the newspaper from his grasp except he wouldn't let go. When he finally did, my hand rebounded. Once again, I felt a clunk! This time, it was my very own hand holding all that crap smacking against my forehead.

I felt slightly vindicated when he eased his neck back into place from facing starboard. All at once, his arm trembled and his eyes bulged—primary indicators of mini–strokes of a vascular nature.

"Well, you certainly got my attention," I said.

"Sorry, Miss Linda," his voice quavered, "ya know it wasn't intentional." The bellhop looked sincere. In a matter of seconds he panicked and rasped, "Please don't tell Ms. Djorak. Please, I really need this job."

I considered his apology and did a mental tally of the damage: he hurt my forehead though I gave him a pretty good karate chop in return. Everything else was water under the bridge. So, I figured we were even.

"Okay, your secret is safe with me. Go! And don't come near me, don't even entertain the idea."

With restored grace and limited range–of–motion, I unlocked the office door and flicked on the overhead lights. I had scarcely a second to toss the *Daily Post* on the guest chair before the phone rang from across the room. As graceful as a gazelle, I lunged for the receiver and found myself the lucky recipient of a hale and hearty greeting.

"Good morning. Is Mr. Ganiff in? It's Jerry Orbach."

Yes, it was unmistakably *the* Jerry Orbach. The beloved actor best known for his role as Lenny the Detective on the television series *Law and Order.* *Oh great*, was my thought, *now a television homicide cop will interrogate me for nearly beheading a bellhop!*

"Good morning, Mr. Orbach. Mr. Ganiff isn't in yet. This is Linda, his assistant. Is there something I can help you with?" Cradling the phone receiver with my neck, I opened my handbag and retrieved my mostly completed *New York Times* crossword puzzle.

"Oh, a pleasure to meet you, Linda. Yes, I believe so. Mr. Ganiff and I, we met at a social function a while ago and he insisted that I call him should I ever need his services." While I waited with bated breath to hear what services he needed that compelled him to call a General Manager of a five–star hotel, I pulled out my lipstick, mascara, eye pencil, tweezers and dental floss. I proceeded to place those items in my top drawer.

He sighed. "Well, I have to discuss a situation that is very distressing for me," he said, "and weighs so heavily on my heart that I had no other recourse but to get up extra early this morning to phone Mr. Ganiff."

"Oh my! Are you all right?" Concerned, I stopped searching for a pen. This sounded serious.

He sighed one more time, this time deep from his soul. He waited a theatric beat before he responded, "My barber lost his lease."

5

What the fuck? His barber? Was he for real?

With utmost dignity, I refrained from blurting "Oy vey." I resumed my search and found my pen sitting right in front of me, on top of my desk. Despite the stinging in my hand, I carefully smoothed the rumpled puzzle and then proceeded to fill in one of the answers to a down clue.

Mr. Orbach continued, "You see, he's the barber I've used for twenty–five years. A very good man. I promised I would help him out and immediately thought of Mr. Ganiff and his kind invitation. Just like that, I figured the Supreme Superior would be a perfect venue for him."

I was flummoxed. This is *the* Jerry Orbach? And he's calling a five–star hotel about his barber? Perhaps I was concussed!

"Mr. Orbach, although we're truly sorry about your barber's plight, I don't believe we can accommodate him." This was the opportune time to recite the standard format response to all requests for installing vendor services in the hotel. I bent forward and read aloud from the little slip of paper taped to the side of my desk. "The Supreme Superior is in fact a small hotel. Every available square inch not used for guests and related guest services is delegated to hotel administration." For his benefit, I even threw in a little hotel logic at no extra charge. "Sir, our Lobby is so small that we don't even have a newspaper kiosk."

Undeterred, Mr. Orbach commenced a dissertation on the virtues of his highly regarded, yet displaced barber. Convinced that I was suffering from an auditory hallucination from my accident, I peered into a portable mirror dangling from the corner of my computer to assess the injury. A definite discoloration and swelling on my forehead. It looked like a facial baby bump that soon would attain mountainous proportions. I also noticed a little blood seepage from the serrated key incision. In the corner of my peripheral vision, I caught sight of Mr. Ganiff, shoes in hand, tiptoeing by. He stopped momentarily to snatch the *Daily Post* off my chair. Then he whisked into his office, making sure to slam the door shut behind him.

That slam set off all my internal alarms. Pain took hold of me. I could no longer concentrate. I couldn't even focus on my puzzle. Even more so, I was worried that soon my brains would seep out of my ears. Insofar as the conversation with Mr. Orbach, I no longer had any idea what he was saying. But if it were so, if he truly wanted to put a barber in our hotel, I'd have no other choice…

I girded my loins. Kissed my lucky charm. Invoked the munificence of the gods. I asked him point–blank, "Have you ever been here?"

"I'm in the Lobby as we speak," he said.

"Oh, you are!" *He's good. He got me.* "Okay, Mr. Orbach. Look around, please. Do you see the grand piano in the middle of the Lounge?"

"Yes, Linda, I do."

"Good, sir. Because that's probably the last available space we have." I waited a theatric beat. "But… Sor–ry. Wayne Newton beat you to the punch! Next week we're gonna remove it and replace it with a state–of–the–art chair for his shoeshine guy. Poor bastard lost his stand when his building burnt down. We, at Management, thought it would be a serious upgrade for this five–star hotel."

"All right, all right, I got it," he dryly said, "not in the Lobby. Maybe Mr. Ganiff has another idea."

"Well, speaking of the devil, guess who arrived at his desk?"

Mr. Ganiff would've gotten bent out of shape if I denied him the chance to converse with a celebrity, no matter the topic. I placed the call on hold, buzzed the intercom and informed him that Mr. Orbach was on the line. Then I left the office for coffee and an ice–pack and contemplated swiping a band–aid, or better yet, funneling vodka into my portable IV drip.

Using the employee staircase, I tottered down three flights to the in–suite service area located almost at the exit of the building near the loading dock. And encountered a mob scene. I had to dodge members of the uniformed waitstaff to get through.

Nimbly, I grabbed a large–sized carafe with my good left hand and filled it with the high–octane coffee of the day. With no time to spare, I picked up a tray and added a metal container worth of cream before heading to the pièce de résistance: one wall stacked with bins containing an array of ten varieties apiece of bagels, donuts and pastries. I skidded to a halt to scrutinize the morning's selection. Not the wisest move in a cramped work environment during peak breakfast room–service time.

As if on cue, one of my fellow employees smacked into me with pitchers in both hands and arms laden with pastries. The pressure in my head deepened. Others shoved past, hurling curses in Urdu, Punjab and Croatian. I had worked here long enough to know precisely what they meant. *Assholes.*

Ignoring my colleagues, I decided on my breakfast choice—a cream cheese and fresh pineapple stuffed croissant. Of course, I had to choose the only pastry located in the penultimate bin by the ceiling. Reaching that high up, even in my Manolos, proved useless. So, I pursued the crowd, searching for someone, anyone among the bustling waiters to assist me.

"Achmed, Achmed, here!" I bellowed at one of the regulars closest to me. For some reason, he dashed like a madman towards the exit. Out of desperation, I wailed for assistance. My plaintive plea struck a note with one of our newer employees. With something like pity, he put his coffee carafe down and fetched my breakfast. "You're a life saver," I gushed.

When I turned around, an army of scowling faces greeted me. Hastily, I made my way towards the exit, not without snagging a forlorn and dusty muffin perched on top of a pile of dirty plates, a little morsel for the boss. Then back to my office pronto via the staff elevators.

I set up my coffee and breakfast treat and was about to plunge in when

I spotted the staccato blinking of the hold button. With trepidation, I picked up my phone. Mr. Orbach said "hello" three times in succession.

That fucker, Mr. Ganiff, did it again! He didn't even bother to answer his call. "Mr. Orbach, I'm sorry," I said. "I did notify Mr. Ganiff that you were on hold. Give me a few more seconds. I have the stick with one nail right beside me, should he not pick up this time."

"Not a problem, Linda," he graciously responded. "I was hoping to hear the good word. That, during this interminable wait, you found a spot for my barber."

So, I hadn't imagined that conversation! Or I still was! I placed him on hold once more. For the first time since I accepted this godforsaken job, I pounded on Mr. Ganiff's doorframe with my bruised right hand which hurt like hell. "Pick up line one!" I shrieked while thinking *you sonofabitch scumbag motherfucker.* I guess that did the trick because the repeated flashing of the hold button ceased.

I shook off the pain in that hand. Time to pour his coffee and blow the dust off his muffin. With aplomb, I arranged his breakfast on the tray. With my bum, I pushed his office door open. He was prattling amiably on the phone and avoided eye contact. I dropped the tray on his cluttered desk, spun on my heels and left, making sure to firmly slam the door behind me.

The stuffed croissant on my desk called to me, so I plucked it up and licked the excess fresh cheese and pineapple oozing out of one of the sides. At this inopportune moment, the phone rang. Annoyed, I threw my treat back down to pick up the receiver.

"Mmmph, Mithhter Gonfff hummm," I said, my mouth full of cream filling.

"Oh, Linda, I'm glad you're there. Do me a favor, okay?" said one of the front desk clerks, "no one's in Sales yet and there's a major complaint from one of the VIPs at Ford Motor Company. He's expecting someone senior to come talk to him."

I glanced down at my croissant and coffee. They eagerly begged me to eat them. How could I not oblige? I mustered my strength and ignored my hunger and pain. There was work to be done. I bade my breakfast a remorseful goodbye, not without missing the chance to lick some more of the creamy center.

Soon, I descended to the ground floor. Just my luck. The one and only person in the center of the Lobby—Jerry Orbach. He was still on the phone with Mr. Ganiff discussing the imminent eviction of his barber. I made a mental note to get myself checked out later today. In the interval, I enjoyed the performance. What magnificent stage presence! His voice resonated with the same fervor attributed to false prophets, spewing declarations tantamount to changing the fabric of the universe as we know it.

I glanced over at the front desk. Robbie, the overnight clerk, rolled his eyes. I guessed that the executive had not yet arrived.

"Ms. Linda, what happened to your head?" he asked.

"Slight accident," I responded while gingerly touching the bump that now appeared larger than Mount Rushmore. "You should see the other guy!"

"You mean a certain bellhop?" Robbie responded. "You know, the one with the matching bump?"

Exasperated, I spun around to return to my office when I was hailed once more. "Psst. Ms. Linda, he's here," said Robbie. He turned his eyes in the direction of a gray–haired man who now stepped into the Lobby.

Courageously, I walked up to the man who didn't appear too happy. "I believe you're looking for me? I'm Linda from the Executive Office." The man shook my right hand with vigor and I fell to my knees from the onslaught of pain. In my anguish, I observed that he was oblivious to my strangled intake of breath. And to the fact that I was suddenly two feet shorter. He rummaged in his pants pocket and handed me a lint–laden business card with the Ford logo. It read "Jim Jonas, Director of Automotive Efficiency." No longer in a crouched position, I gestured toward the sofa in the center of the Lobby across from Mr. Orbach where we soon sat down.

"Thank you very much for meeting with me, Ma'am. I had a very unsatisfactory exchange with your front desk a few minutes ago." He seemed wound up in attack mode.

"How exactly may I help you, Mr. Jonas?" I had to commend myself for having the discipline to suppress the immediate impetus to strike him, the insensitive lout. It wouldn't have quelled the resurgence of stinging in my right hand. Au contraire. But I would've felt a mite better.

He inhaled and leaned forward. In a hushed voice he asked, "Say, isn't that Jerry Orbach?" I nodded, grateful that the celebrity across from us had no idea who I was. Even more so, that the celebrity across from us was real and not a figment of my imagination. Now, if I could only reconcile the matter of the barber conversation. Anyhow, Jonas was impressed and settled back into the sofa. In lieu of launching right into his complaint, he made a radical departure. "Looks like you've been handling a lot of the rough trade that the Supreme Superior attracts."

"Funny that you mentioned it, Mr. Jonas. Let me tell you that we, at the Supreme Superior, are hands on. As you can see, too many complaints, they send me, 'The Enforcer' and wham! You should see the other guy!" I could tell that the guest was unprepared for my comeback.

Right at that instant, the bellhop walked by. I winked at him. In return, he tipped his hat, hitting the bruise on his forehead. His whimper reverberated off the Lobby walls. Mr. Jonas did a double–take. Then a triple–take. He whipped his head over at me, the bellhop and even at Jerry Orbach.

In a lower pitched voice I said, "Don't you get the impression that we're smack dab in the middle of a *Law and Order* episode?" The look on his face was priceless.

He said, "Please excuse me. I've been flying non–stop for a few days visiting the domestic Ford facilities, so I'm already a little tense. All I wanted was my Continental breakfast. Instead, I got Miso soup. I phoned room service and, to my surprise, no one spoke English anymore. I mean, they did earlier this morning when I placed my order. At any rate, I don't want to get anyone in trouble, but this turned into such a fiasco." Once again, he changed tactics. "By the way, what's with the Miso soup? Who the hell eats that in the morning?"

I smiled. "Mr. Jonas, the Supreme Superior Hotel is Japanese–owned. As such, they try to retain some of their culture by offering a Japanese–style breakfast which is essentially Miso soup. You'd be surprised at how many Japanese guests we have at the hotel. It's a big hit."

He remained unconvinced despite the element of truth.

I continued, "At any rate, let me have your bill adjusted. I'm sorry for the mix–up. Have you eaten yet?"

"No, I have to run to a meeting. No more time."

"Once again, I apologize for the situation which is highly irregular. We'll conduct an investigation on our side. To compensate for your inconvenience, we would like to offer you a complimentary room service meal for each day of your stay. How long are you staying with us?"

"Another two days."

"Great. I'll inform my Front Desk and we'll take good care of you. Should you have any further questions, feel free to contact me at the General Manager's office." He gave me a bright smile as we shook hands once more. I squelched my yip. That counted as the fourth time in succession a sensory overload had flooded my nervous system. In less than ten minutes.

I wondered, after our guest left the Lobby, whether he enjoyed the results of Hotel Efficiency. When all was said and done, he did receive two freebee meals from "The Enforcer" and the opportunity to rub ankles with a celebrity. Either way, Mr. Jonas got a good dose of the five–star life.

Back at the ranch, I sat down to my lukewarm coffee with curdled cream spilt on top of my crossword puzzle. Evidently, faxing the puzzle today was not in the stars. Then I noticed crumbs where there was once my croissant. *Damn!* Nothing was sacred here.

Oh no! I forgot to pick up the ice–pack! My forehead throbbed like the dickens. The swelling reached critical mass. A headache formed behind my eyes and traveled down my neck to the dreaded lumbar region. My hand exponentially expanded and contracted with each beat of my pulse. So far, no brain matter spilled out.

Then the phone rang.

During my absence, someone who I ascertained as Mr. Ganiff, had left me a gift: a foot high stack of papers strategically positioned on my desk to block access to my phone. Without any warning, the fax machine behind me whirred and chugged. In rapid fire, it spat out page after page, causing a steady cascade of paper that quickly covered the carpet.

As delicately as possible, I waded through the papers on the floor and hoisted them onto my chair. I added the papers from my desk as well. Standing, I answered the first of several flashing phone lines when the intercom buzzed. Mr. Ganiff took precedence over all calls—a fact he had made eminently clear from the outset. I had no other choice than to hang up on an unidentified caller. I hit the intercom speaker button. A resounding thud echoed through my office. *Damn!* "Mr. Patience" had hung up on me.

I debated dialing him back, yet decided not to because the outside lines kept ringing. I hit line two and grabbed the receiver. Precisely at that moment, "Mr. Persistence" intercommed me once more. I hadn't even said hello to the outside caller when I hung up again to grab the intercom. This time, Mr. Ganiff timed it perfectly: the moment I said yes, his receiver slammed down with a bang.

Was this some kind of a game for him? I couldn't be sure. I went to buzz him back but hit another incoming line in error.

"Is this Linda? Jerry Orbach gave me your number." I recognized that voice as one of our frequent guests. *Oh no*, I realized, *it was Wayne Newton!* He continued, "What is this about my shoeshine guy?"

I said, "Hold that thought," and hung up because Mr. Ganiff and that pesky little intercom finger intervened once more. With the speed and agility of a frighteningly terrific tic–tac–toe player, I dove for the intercom. And knocked into the chair which tipped over, dumping all its contents onto the floor. All this, simply to receive another eardrum puncturing "k–tunk."

This game could continue the rest of the day. Or to the end of time.

My nerves were shattered by yet another source. "Goddammit!" shrieked Mr. Ganiff. That shrill and irritating voice succeeded in penetrating through the office door. More than likely, it could penetrate through steel because it easily pierced through my brain. He persisted in shouting like a maniac, "What the hell is her problem? Why won't she answer the phones?"

I groaned.

Another day in paradise.

Chapter 1
September 1994

It has been nearly fifteen years since I had the dubious pleasure of working at the Supreme Superior Hotel. And, it was two years before that, when I had left my very high paying, senior–level banking job out of sheer boredom and pre–menopausal—ahem peri–menopausal blues, to the consternation of my parents who worried endlessly about my life, or their belief of my lack thereof.

Okay, so I'm full of it.

I quit my prestigious job because my psychotic and vindictive boss, a highly respected member of the international banking community, scared me shitless. Unfortunately, I discovered that the man was up to no good. Major league no good.

He was one of a triumvirate of managers who ran the New York subsidiary of GermBank, one of the world's leading financial institutions at that time. Legend had it that he had a collection of shrunken heads in his desk drawer. Let me restate that. Legend had it that he had a cache of folders containing juicy reports on current and former employees. He reminded me of a modern–day J. Edgar Hoover with a guttural accent. The most distinctive feature of his personality was the way in which he performed amazing feats of revenge. "Sadomasochist" was his name and destruction was his game.

All I knew was that due to my discovery of my boss's misdeeds, I felt I had no other recourse but to leave my job. Or face certain retribution at his hands. I approached the remaining two–thirds of the bank trio with information about his questionable activities. To no avail. Those guys knew about that desk drawer and what was contained therein. Or perhaps… they were guilty of even worse.

This was uncharted territory for me. I was out of my depth. Also out of my mind. I faced the distinct possibility that I might be involved in legal action of some form from the Federal government. The only viable alternative I could foresee was whistle–blowing which everyone knew was the kiss of death. I ended up paralyzed about what to do, given my finite options. In other words, I chose the easiest way out. Admittedly, not the best way. Nonetheless, it was what I did.

I walked away.

Forget about explaining all this to my parents. Like my time at the Supreme Superior—if it hadn't happened to me, I would've assumed that it was bullshit as well.

I needed a lot of distance from the banking industry. Time to regroup, reassess, analyze and relax. That was done during the initial three months of unemployment.

I spent the entire time in bed with a C–rated actor, Reed LeVeine.

Reed was handsome enough to get under nines (industry parlance meaning "a few speaking lines") on the daytime Soaps although dumb enough to make a golden Labrador an intellectual equal. After having sated my sexual drive with the handsome, yet mentally challenged Reedo, I decided to do something more in sync with creating a new me. I dumped the Reed who believed my orgasmic *yes yes yes* meant a committed relationship and got ready to try something new... like a job.

I didn't want to set foot in another bank. Rather, I didn't want to test the waters to see whether my former boss had already seeded the banking community with his radioactive libel. Instead, I decided to try the sample courses on the menu. I interviewed at agencies that specialized in part–time, better known as "temp" jobs. Undeniably, most of them tried to stick me back in finance, to my chagrin. Then came one non–suit–wearing, non–number–crunching opportunity: a temping position in the human resources department at the hallowed Waldorf–Astoria in Manhattan.

The Waldorf. That 47–story landmark of luxury located from Park Avenue to Lexington Avenue in midtown New York City. I was very familiar with the hotel mostly from cutting through the magnificent Lobby during inclement weather. I'd pass outstanding floral arrangements that resembled Flemish still–life oil paintings and peer into the upscale boutiques offering top of the line luxury items. Many of the banking social functions that I had attended over the years were held either at the massive conference rooms off the Lobby or on different floors throughout the block–wide building. Nevertheless, for me, the one facet which distinguished this hotel from others was that it featured world–class restaurants. Ah, the Waldorf.

It was an amazing experience temping at the Waldorf. As my very first action, I befriended the chefs in all the restaurants. That meant I ate well, and of course, free. Although I could've eaten in the employee cafeteria, also known for quality cuisine, for free. In my spare time, I wandered... rather roamed throughout the giant expanse of the Waldorf, exploring all the underground rooms beneath Park Avenue. To my delight, I discovered a furniture factory in one of the basements. I also hoped to uncover the famous underground entry into the hotel from the legendary Grand Central railroad, used by many Presidents including FDR and Harry Truman. Sadly, I could not find the mystery passage. Rumor had it that the homeless found that very same entrance so the area was placed off limits. So off limits that it was struck off the maps.

The most fascinating aspect of my time at the Waldorf was that, unlike the financial arena from whence I came, I had no competition among the staff. This became evident after a few days of work. The personnel people, frantic with requests, were dependent upon the occasional computer–trained temporary worker for assistance. Mind–numbing to take in. To stave off the bedlam, I created a little training program of elementary Lotus 1, 2, and 3. This initiative ignited my interest in the hospitality industry.

The Waldorf had well over fifteen hundred employees and constant turnover, emblematic of the industry. After an hour of my tutelage, most of the staff could access personnel records with alacrity. The turnaround speed in researching data such as insurance coverage, disability, garnishing and unemployment—all this information divided between union and non–union workers—was unprecedented.

My training program eventually came to the attention of the head of human resources, Penelope who now had a more reliable and efficient staff. She gave me additional projects which consisted of writing departmental training and development procedural guides. I had no qualifications nor knowledge with which to do the work. Yet, the more I protested, the more work she gave me, undeterred by my ignorance.

For several months I temped at the Waldorf. A relaxed departure from my former banking career. Although, without a permanent job on the horizon, what I used to find tempting about temping felt more like… well, aimless ambition.

Until a lucky break.

A full–time slot opened up at the Resident Manager's office. They sought someone with extensive analytical abilities. I was definitely qualified. My seasoned finance background and lowly Pace University MBA were superior to that of the hospitality B–school executives at the Waldorf. And… it didn't hurt that Penelope supported me in getting this permanent position which backed up the General Manager.

Once more I was engulfed in financial matters, my lot in life. The position wasn't nearly as much fun as hanging out with Penelope which I could no longer do as frequently as before. However, it was interesting in that number–crunching kind of way to see how a hotel accounted for its expenses on a very tight budget.

It didn't take long before word went out in the hotel community about the new person working in the Resident Manager's office at the Waldorf–Astoria. In short order, other big hotels in New York City contacted me. The recruiters' abundant calls and anxious pitches established that qualified senior level managers in the hotel industry were in demand. Who knew?

At first, I ignored those pesky solicitations. I enjoyed my low stress job and the constant plundering of high–quality bakery products. Nonetheless, my joy was short–lived.

"Linda, I have some amazingly great news," said Penelope while I fed my calculator a long list of numbers. "You're gonna flip!"

"What is it?" Her upbeat attitude was contagious.

"I just got the word. All my hard work here has finally paid off! I'm relocating to Hawaii!" she squealed with joy.

"Hawaii?" Well, she was right because I did flip out. A mega–dose of jealousy hit me. I had to stop tormenting my calculator to recuperate. I took three deep breaths while gazing at my navel. I blew into a small paper bag. Chanted *nam myo ho renge kyo* while completing a full round of beads.

"Congrats girlfriend!" I said with an equal amount of enthusiasm and good vibrations.

She kept on. "Not only that, it's one of the best properties the Waldorf parent company owns in Hawaii. Imagine the warm air, beaches, sunsets, drinks and cabana boys. Ah Hawaii!"

Even though I felt transformationally thrilled for her, on a more selfish basis I couldn't bear the departure of my friend who played a dual role in my life at the Waldorf: protector in her position as head of human resources in those instances when I might've needed her protection as well as my in-house pusher of non-nutrient food stuffs. I felt forlorn. Our days of being cool had come to an end.

Months after Penelope left, I received an interesting call from my former temp agency.

"Darling, would you be interested in a permanent job as Resident Manager at the newly renovated Supreme Superior Hotel?" asked Harriet, the hospitality headhunter. "They're a five-star hotel, you know."

"Well, what exactly are they offering?" I asked.

"About triple what you're making at the Waldorf."

And they hadn't even met me. Easily seduced, I said, "Really now."

"It's quite a different position from what you're doing at the Waldorf. At the Supreme Superior, you'll be the one and only Resident Manager reporting directly to the General Manager."

That sounded interesting. "Is that it? Is there more?"

"Yes. You'll be involved in all facets of hotel management." Then she reeled me in with the lure, "Linda, in other words, no more number-crunching."

That did the trick. I did not hesitate in the least. "Set me up, Harriet!" I said.

During the initial and sole interview, I had a persistent nagging feeling that I made a mistake. A very big one. It could've been the person across the scarred metal desk whose appearance, for lack of better words, was daunting. Hunkered under the swaying glint of a dim light bulb—held by a single filament strung from the water-stained ceiling—was a face that could peel wallpaper. Luckily, a curtain of shoulder-length straight gray hair almost hid Ms. Djorak's visage. I caught brief glimpses of the chiaroscuro of her mashed nose. As well as a jowl-enhanced jaw line poking out from under the gray hair. When the light hit her gray, lifeless fish eyes, I marveled at them, her most humane feature.

The gorgon lifted its head and spoke, "I have to warn you, the General Manager is very intimidating." It might've been a trick of the eye, but I could've sworn she had retractable mandibles.

"That's okay," I replied, "I was once a bond trader." I recalled my yesteryears of bond trading with detached fondness. All that screaming and shouting, yet at the same time, an uncommonly comradely closeness due to the freely shared tubs of Tums and prescription ulcer drugs like Zantac gracing the tops of trading platforms. We had all lived under pressure from moving deals faster than light with the old axiom: you're as good as your last deal. In truth, what came to mind was the memory of my last boss in finance. *Now he was what you could call intimidating.*

Ms. Djorak, the head of human resources, looked down at my resume and paused. It lasted as long as the oft–quoted pregnant silence. The repetitive sound of a nearby drip accentuated the quietness in the concrete room. "He's impressed with your credentials," she stated with the lilt of a South African accent, totally at odds with her physicality. "It's not every day an MBA wants to work an administrative job."

Taken aback, I said, "Administrative job? You gotta be kidding! The agency told me this was the Resident Manager position."

She muttered something resembling an incantation from the Boer Wars under her breath. To me, she uttered, "That'll have to be reviewed at some near point in time."

I was on the verge of a quick retort when the stout woman—reminiscent of Walter Mathieu—stood up and scratched her crotch. Her testosterone–laden action stopped me in my tracks. I mused, *Is it a man? A woman in drag? Or is she Donna the Dominatrix?* With utmost certainty, I had crossed paths with her somewhere before. I racked my brains until I remembered.

A few years earlier, I had found myself on a balmy summer night in the Meatpacking District, when it still was a disreputable sort of Manhattan neighborhood. This was prior to the Disney–like upgrade by celebrity restaurateurs like Robert DeNiro who transmogrified the seedy environment. The street was empty. Cones of intermittent lights enhanced the darkness. Out of the shadows emerged a short and squat woman attired in a red suit topped with a black hat, clutching a red handbag. She approached me with a distinctive lurching gait suggestive of someone unaccustomed to high–heeled patent leather shoes. I stood transfixed like a New York City voyeur sans binoculars. Her proximity allowed me to discern through her thin veil deep, drooping jowls. Poking out from under the heavy crust of pancake powder was a prominent five o'clock shadow.

At that moment, I realized that I played one too many hands of fate and braced myself for the inevitable pistol retrieved out of the handbag. Instead, a deep voice asked for directions.

"Hey, lady, could you tell me where to catch the cross–town bus? I'm kinda lost. This ain't my neighborhood."

I exhaled in relief. "It's two blocks uptown. I'm heading that way now if you wanna follow."

"Thanks." The he/she smiled back at me and extended a masculine hand. "Hi, I'm Donna the Dominatrix. On Cable Saturday nights. Perhaps you've seen my show?"

Soon after, we huddled under the twisted metal skeletal relic of a bus stop awaiting our golden chariot supplied by the MTA. Donna clarified in one simple sentence the question that had puzzled philosophers for centuries. Or rather other innocents waiting at bus stops in equally dangerous neighborhoods—the common misconception of her gender.

"I was once a little boy, you know."

"No, really?" I peered over my shoulder and prayed for a taxi. The gods must've heard me because a bus swung up the avenue and opened its doors. I scrambled up the steps posthaste to a seat. Donna, hot in pursuit and high on estrogen, followed me to the adjoining one. During the interminable ride, he/she described domination not only in terms a layperson could understand but also in decibels for all of Manhattan and its sister boroughs to comprehend as well.

The phrase engraved in my gray cells from that memorable evening was Donna's pronouncement: "It has nothing to do with sex, you know. It's about power."

I sneaked a peek at Ms. Djorak's hands. They appeared more feminine than those of Donna's. Since she didn't show any signs of facial stubble, my suspicions were incorrect. Then again, it was daytime. And fortunately, no indication of a bad moon on the rise.

She rose from her chair and motioned for me to follow. I assumed the interview was over. Instead of being escorted out of the hotel, I found myself walking double time after her through tunnels in subbasement No. 3, up ramps and down narrow corridors. Along the way, I witnessed uniformed staff fleeing in all directions, throwing themselves flat against the concrete walls in their efforts to avoid her. Throbs, hisses and thumps assaulted my ears while sewage, steam and that peculiar odor associated with restaurants assailed my nose. At long last, after mounting three flights of gray concrete steps, Ms. Djorak opened a door and all noise and odors disappeared. Similar to the transition from black and white to color after the tornado passed in the *Wizard of Oz*.

From the back of the house, where the workers scuttled, we entered the front of the hotel, the land of entitlement for the guests. My high–heeled pumps sank in the depth of the plush carpeting. The corridors were wide, artistically lit by wall sconces and adorned in one of those wallpapers used by decorators that had color, yet was so faded by design that no one could determine what color it was supposed to be. I had to change gears again to follow Ms. Djorak who for a heavy woman kept a brisk pace, more than likely from wearing metal studded work boots. She entered an antechamber and beckoned to me.

"Mr. Ganiff, this is Miss Lane." And with that introduction, she swung the mirrored door shut to block escape.

Wedged behind a circular glass conference table sat a robust man somewhere between his late 50's to early 60's. He wore a custom–made Armani suit. The most distinguishing feature of his outfit was a hanky peeking out of the breast pocket. He had a full head of thick, white hair. He was also graced with a patrician nose and an enormous, bushy, black mustache imitating antlers from a Dr. Seuss creature. The singular detraction to his face was his left eye. It rigidly stared at his nose. Other than that, he had a larger than life presence.

He made no gesture of welcome so I plopped down amidst overflowing stacks of paper. With all the delicacy I could muster, I bent over and placed my handbag on the floor. Mr. Ganiff assessed me as I settled in place.

"What do you know about hotels, Miss Lane, or may I call you Linda?"

"Linda's fine, Mr. Ganiff. I spent almost a year working at the Waldorf–Astoria. I was recently appointed as one of the acting Resident Managers."

Mr. Ganiff stared at me. I stared back, transfixed by that left eye held in stasis.

I continued, "Last month. August."

After a few very long, very Zen–like minutes, Mr. Ganiff spoke, accentuating the rich contra tenor of his voice, "I need someone to take care of the day–to–day operations and allow me the freedom to create the overall picture. Unlike other hotels, this one does not have a Resident Manager. I find myself immersed in daily situations. Considering your MBA and background, you'd be doing the job of a Resident Manager for which you will be well compensated. In time, you may eventually receive the title and all the respect it commands." He leaned forward and flashed a low–wattage seductive smile. "So, Linda, what do you think? Can you handle it?"

The prospect of embarking on the next step towards a glamorous new career swayed me. Or, the fact that the description of this position sounded quite different from the one I held at the Waldorf. Or, that I had run through my entire cookie pilfering privileges since Penelope left. Or, the siren song of tripling my salary seduced me... Whatever. I felt that the deal was "done" as they said in the pits of the trading room. I reached down and clutched the straps of my handbag knowing that the interview was concluded. It was shit or get off the pot time.

"Is that an offer, Mr. Ganiff?" I rhetorically asked. "Because if it is, I think you've found yourself the manager you're looking for. Count me in."

Chapter 2

During the second week at the new job, Mr. Ganiff invited me into his office. Before I could say a word, he pulled a bit at the tips of his mustache, then placed his fingers into a steeple in front of his face. Transfixed by his fingernails, he sat quietly for a few minutes. I stood there in anticipation.

"Close the door, Linda," he commanded.

"What about the phones?" I asked.

"BeeBee can take care of them."

I felt uncomfortable as well as acutely aware that we were alone in his office. Normally, it was Grand Central Station in there. The other reason for my discomfort was that he didn't invite me to sit, and I stood there like a fool. I wondered about those manners of his. I had no idea why he wanted me in his office until he pointed at a framed photo of his mother, Rose Marie O'Connell, by the right side of his desk.

"Linda, she was a peach of a woman," he reminisced and added, "you should know this." I shrugged and continued to stand in front of his desk, perplexed. Outside of that one interview and scantly two weeks on the job, I knew nothing about the man and I was okay about that. My shrug and perplexed manner didn't deter him so he kept on.

"She was orphaned at twelve and raised by her middle–class spinster aunt, Charlotte." While he prattled on about his great–aunt Charlotte, I slipped into one of the padded chairs across from his desk. After a minute, I felt my eyes glaze. I bit the inside of my cheek in an effort to stay awake. To no avail. From far away I heard his rambling monotone. No matter how hard I tried, I fell into a deeper stupor.

As if I were at the bottom of a well, I heard a simple melodic tune played by flutes and cowbells. And like a gnat that I couldn't swat away, that annoying, droning narrative and voice which, despite itself, caused me to enter into the initial level of REM sleep.

The voice continued, "She was trained to be the wife of a wealthy doctor in Brooklyn during the beginning of the twentieth century. Not in terms of education, Linda, but in demeanor. Ah, Rose Marie had about her an innate sweetness, grace and natural joy, a lovely compliment to her delicate features and frail body. Oh, did I happen to mention that she possessed a big heart?"

I had a funny idea that percolated to my consciousness: in today's world Rose Marie might've been labeled "mentally challenged."

"Despite her appearance, little Rose Marie was fecund."

"Fecund?" I questioned, perking up for a moment.

"Yes. It means fertile. No trouble getting pregnant." *What a strange disclosure!*

19

He continued, "Had her first child at sixteen. The result of a tryst with the neighborhood Lothario, a young Scotsman. Aunt Charlotte tried to make the kid marry her although his parents wouldn't allow it. Some story about him slipping across the river to a new life. Then followed another child, a second boy at seventeen, the product of a butcher's assistant and better cuts of meat. As I said, she had a big heart."

Why the hell would my boss share all these intimate family details? After lapsing once more into dreamland, I thought that perhaps Rose Marie's heart tended to be a little too big. According to her son's description, she seemed like the type to fall big time for the ploy, the tears, the pain of a young man's tormented anguish at being a recipient of her so many endearing charms.

He continued without taking a breath, "When she was nineteen, she gave birth to a wee treasure of a girl who bore distinct characteristics of an African–American lineage. That's when Aunt Charlotte passed away, leaving my mother a tidy savings account, a well–built three story house and a reputation for possessing a generous heart."

At this point, I had an out–of–body experience and found myself sitting in a darkened amphitheatre before a pair of closed blue curtains. Spotlights flickered on and focused on two adorable doves struggling to lift the curtains with their beaks. Right then, flocks of birds of all sorts—jays, robins, ostriches, falcons, owls, emus and a pterodactyl—swooped out of nowhere and descended upon the curtains. With their beaks, they savagely pecked out pieces of blue fabric. With their talons, they scratched out swatches. All this activity was conducted in silence except for the endless narrative of the life and perils of Rose Marie with guest commentary.

Bit by bit, I began to discern the silver screen underneath the curtain where a movie was already in progress. My narrator intoned his dramatically long saga without cessation, or even a station break.

"Her last and sixth child in 1940 was Rose Marie's favorite. Listen up, Linda, I'm talking about me!" At the mention of my name, I poked my head up and when he resumed talking, I drifted back to my dream. "She fell madly in love with my father, a walrus of a man known for his distinguished long and bushy mustache, waxed into horns. My dad convinced Rose Marie of his aristocratic Russian pedigree although his name had an Ottoman ring to it. People in the neighborhood kept an eye on the goings–on over the years. Provided them with hours of gossip–mongering and other forms of entertainment. At long last, Rose Marie wed her man, and together they raised the six children. A rainbow of races and heritages."

Finally, silence! My prayers were answered.

"Linda?"

His voice penetrated my dream and froze all of the birds in mid–flight. They folded in half, then in quarters and instantly shattered like glass, raining in confetti shards to the ground. I groggily moved my head up, wiping the line of drool with my forearm. Blearily, I looked into an eye that faced a nose.

"Linda!" he yelled.

"Yes, Mr. Ganiff," I said, rapidly retrenching from the land of Nod.

"Did you have a nice nap?" He looked agitated. "I can't believe it! I tell you the story of my life and you sleep? Please, please leave my office. And on your way out, shut the door."

I left his office with bowed head, feeling chastised because in a strange and inverse way he was right. He did open up to me, something that is assuredly difficult to do with a new subordinate. Yes, I did doze. Yet, why did he open up to me? It defied logic. More to the point, why did he have to go on for so long?

The remainder of the afternoon felt like an eternity. I had difficulty concentrating on my work as I thought hard and furious about this wrinkle in my spanking new job. Could it be perceived that I was out of line by falling asleep? All those insecurities, fears and doubts I had for leaving my last position to make this lateral, yet lucrative move came brusquely to the surface. Could this be construed as grounds for termination? Damn, how shameful. Fired not even two full weeks on the job! And for what? Being bored to a state of unconsciousness? Could that be the first step towards being bored to death? Is there such a thing? Then another thought crossed my mind, causing dread to worm its way deeper through my lower intestinal tract. *Could I be subjected to future sessions like this?*

Several portions of Mr. Ganiff's monologue during this lengthy interlude came to mind. I could've misconstrued some of what he said, or incorporated some of the things he said into my subconscious. After all, I was deeply asleep and my perception of reality was distorted. I mean, the whole situation was surreal—I had nothing to compare it to in my years of working in banking. Even more so, considering the topic and its effect upon me.

What it boiled down to was a frank assessment. I had to honestly ask myself this question: *Was this the right job for me?*

Chapter 3

A hotel is a city in microcosm. Similar to New York City, a hotel never sleeps. Although late evenings were quiet, services were performed with the same velocity as during the day.

The "front of the house" services include reservations, concierge, front desk, business center, in–room dining, valet, etc. The "behind–the–scenes" services that the guest takes for granted—air conditioning, heat, water, sewage, garbage, linens and housekeeping—were continuously executed, quietly and seamlessly. As Mr. Ganiff said repeatedly to underscore his intention to impart wisdom, "A hotel room is a room. What distinguishes this room from any other is the quality of service." As my father used to say, "Hotels were invented because Jesus had no place to stay so they stuck him in a manger."

One week after my indiscretion of falling comatose during a foray down memory lane, Mr. Ganiff appeared energized and eager to talk to me again, outside of business matters. He made an executive decision to take me that Tuesday morning on an on–site tour of the hotel. It was time to familiarize myself with the hotel. Unlike the Waldorf, I wasn't free to roam at will when not immersed in work. Trapped behind my desk, I only had a bird's eye view. It would only serve him better to grant me knowledge of the entire hotel. In that way, I wouldn't have to pepper him with any questions pertaining to behind–the–scenes services. Best of all, we wouldn't be rushed on the tour as September fell in an off–peak month and no one would be clamoring for his urgent attention.

After spending a few minutes sprucing himself up which meant a few tugs on his mustache, we stepped into the corridor. Mr. Ganiff explained the hotel's humble origins.

"The Supreme Superior was originally built almost six years before as a studio bedroom condo complex for swinging singles. That's why there are no kitchens. We decided to name the rooms 'ateliers' which means 'studios' in French because in France they have no kitchens." He punctuated this final statement with a simple sweep of his white forelock and twirl at the ends of his mustache.

I was just about to correct him about those kitchen references when he turned to me… the definition of a captive audience. He heralded forth as a seer, albeit with a fixed stare at the bridge of his nose. "This building was launched with fanfare," he loudly confided and with a considerable decrease in decibels to a stage whisper stated, "they spent over $200,000 on public relations and even had a racing car in front of the building to show its upscale nature." His voice rose in pitch and volume to a gut–wrenching crescendo, "But no one wanted to buy in!" Triumphant with his proclamation, he turned around and stomped down the corridor back to the office, curtailing the on–site tour.

That was it? The man abandoned me, leaving me to check out his receding backside. Something I wished never to witness again. Imitating my boss sans sweeping back my forelock and twisting my mustache ends, I spun around and stomped back to the office. I poked my head inside his den and found him reading an article in a religious magazine.

I considered one reason for his behavior: he could've been so caught up in his melodramatic recounting of the hotel's history, he forgot the purpose for leaving his office with me. Another possible explanation was that he had suffered a senior moment, a temporary lapse of memory. Or, he intended to retaliate for what had happened a week ago in an effort to humiliate me. Considering the fourth, fifth or even a sixth possibility, I preferred to keep my choices simple. Like Occam's Razor. He looked up at that moment and caught my eye.

"Hey, Linda. How about an on–site tour of the premises?"

It was déjà vu all over again. "Ahhh, sure." That seemed to validate the first two possibilities (and I gave him the benefit of the doubt for the third one).

"Okay, I'll call Murlise Mutt, our Reservations Manager and arrange for one later this day."

Murlise Mutt appeared average in every respect except she had a narrow face with the longest jaw that I had ever seen outside of the equine race. Her head alone must've weighed twenty–five pounds.

The Supreme Superior—all sixty floors—received a five–star ranking, the epitome of service. Mr. Ganiff was the one who had introduced the highly innovative concept of making three hotels from one with step–ups in amenities, décor and perks. The rooms on the first twenty floors were labeled "Standard." The suites or ateliers on the twenty–first to forty–third were named "Regal." And from the forty–sixth to the fifty–eighth floors were the "Sublime" suites, the acme of the hospitality industry. The final two floors were our convention rooms.

Every suite was equipped with a bedroom, separate living room, mini–bar, bathroom and scores of televisions. The bathroom was a delight, featuring bright lights, oversized counters, twin sinks and a counter–to–ceiling wrap–around mirror. The toilet was in a private alcove, separate from the rest of the room. The basic décor of each atelier was early bland, a mixture of nondescript pastel colors, specially attuned to comfort, and thereby easily forgettable. Standard suites, the bottom of the pyramid, offered these basic hotel amenities plus a copy of *USA Today* for $350 a night, quite high–end even for a five–star hotel.

As a way to ingratiate herself with the General Manager, Murlise took me on this tour. "You have the most important job in the hotel," she gushed. "When I get married and have children, this is the job for me."

I had quite a few theories about that comment.

Using her passkey, we entered an atelier on the 27th floor. Murlise revved up her spiel and fired away. "The Regal ateliers offer for an extra $100 a night a free copy of the *Daily Post*, a fax machine…" She gestured à la Vanna White to a nearby pull–out cabinet and then caressed the shelf with one fingertip. After checking for

23

dust, she wiped her finger on her shirt and then yelled, "Look, a mobile telephone!" And failed to mention the prohibitive cost billed to the room. Exhibiting the panache of a graceless goose, she alluded to "sheets of 325 threads per square inch, thick, fluffy towels, an all–white 100% Egyptian terry cotton bathrobe which can be purchased for $90, slippers and a miniature television in the bathroom." In the middle of the living room, Murlise sighed with contentment. Then we boarded the local elevator to the 50th floor.

"And if you top another $200 per night to the Regal's cost, you've entered hotel heaven," Murlise whispered with reverence while she opened the door. I could almost hear the drumroll. "The Sublime, an experience offered only by the Supreme Superior." Perhaps ateliers were a cultivated science because this one to my uneducated eyes seemed exactly like the one we left a few minutes ago on the 27th floor.

"Sublime clients get picked up at the airport by a chauffeured limousine, handed their mobile phones with their very own pre–printed and embossed business cards on Supreme Superior letterhead with their very own mobile number." She focused straight into my eyes—eyes I painfully attempted to keep wide open. "This is our pride and joy. Sublime guests aren't checked in as our other clientele. Not at all. The moment they enter the hotel, they are personally greeted by senior staff and escorted to their room." She became businesslike. "Note, Linda, that amenities are the same as a Regal atelier except that Sublime guests receive a free copy of the *New York Times*, free usage of a laptop computer," she nodded toward the vicinity of a wall unit crammed to bursting with fax machine, copier, printer, 25–inch television and laptop, "as well as an on–premises secretary and one free massage. Check–out is done in the suite. Most guests would agree that the Sublime experience is definitely worth the money."

Murlise explained that each Sublime floor offered two two–bedroom suites with living room, dining room, mini–kitchen and three bathrooms from combining five studios and a little construction work. In–house these were occasionally called apartments. Each individual apartment was named after its contrived décor. "The top apartment, hands down, is The Principessa, known for its red velvet furnishings. Then we have our notorious Dangerous Liaison done in pink satin whereas the Mae West is decorated in wild–west kitsch. For our homesick and wealthy Japanese guests, we always have our demure Geisha apartment in traditional Japanese style."

I swayed in a stupor while she removed from her purse a portable abacus to count the perks of these particular suites. She also pulled out her 44–page marketing brochure and opened selected pages for me to peruse. The tour wrapped up and I was able to revive a little. Together, we took an express elevator that led us directly to the Lobby.

Later, I returned to my office which I could now identify as a converted living room of an atelier. It was also the sole access to the General Manager's office, formerly a bedroom. I found Mr. Ganiff pacing the floor.

"You're back! I see that Murlise escorted you on a tour. Good, you survived." By the tone of his voice, I knew he hankered for something. "You're a smart girl. Do me a favor and write up what you think would be consistent with my aim for a three–hotels–in–one concept." He turned to enter his office. Before he shut and locked the door, he said over his shoulder, "Put it on your desk before you leave for the evening. Oh, and please don't bother me unless there's an emergency."

I sighed, sat down and called out to BeeBee, my reluctant, inherited secretary in the antechamber across the corridor. "BeeBee, any messages for me?"

"None," replied a voice reminiscent of Selma Diamond, the chain–smoking actress known more for her death due to lung cancer than her role in a popular sitcom, *Night Court*. Remarkably, BeeBee and I were the same age even though she looked at least a decade or two older. BeeBee is what I would call a ravaged beauty. The heart–shaped face, large wide black eyes and pert nose were features of a once beautiful woman. The deep and grooved wrinkles, the tar–stained and cracked teeth confirmed that she had led a very hard life.

BeeBee, at any rate, succeeded in making my first weeks at the Supreme Superior miserable. I dreaded any interaction with this woman. Part of the problem was that Mr. Ganiff's phones did not have voicemail, adhering to his 19th century policy that the phones in the General Manager's office must be answered by living, breathing humans. The remaining part of the problem was that my dear secretary refused to answer the phones, causing me a little anxiety and tons of angst. I found myself tied to the desk for hours while BeeBee took smoking breaks every fifteen minutes.

One day, her fifteen minutes became a two–hour absence. After a few cups of coffee and a historically weak bladder due to years sitting at a trading desk, two hours started to feel like two weeks or maybe longer!

Like the long–awaited prodigal child, she returned, reeking of smoke. Most people sit behind their desks. She, instead, sprawled face–down. I uncrossed my legs and leapt from my chair.

Leaning over her, I shouted, "You know, BeeBee, I'm not an idiot. It sucks that you gotta answer my phones and deliver my mail. I get it. Just do your job and knock off the extraneous bullshit."

BeeBee picked up her head and, in a fluid motion, bolted forward, planting her face inches from mine. She hissed, "Linda, I think you're an asshole." Then she snorted. "That got your nose outta the air awfully fast."

I stood my ground despite her reeking breath. "BeeBee, I don't give a shit what you think. I didn't hire you and you didn't choose to work for me. All I'm saying is for you to suck it up and do your job!"

"You don't get it," she pouted, "your job should've been mine."

"What?" I was at the juncture between laughing hysterically or screaming with appall or perhaps to the john, a destination I needed to explore with a sense of urgency.

"Ms. Djorak promised me your job. I know this hotel inside and out cause I've been here since the opening. I had a special one–year training in the engineering department and Djorak trained me personally on the administrative side."

I could only imagine the personal training BeeBee received from our head of human resources. The way that woman ogled her could be construed as the actions of a possible cannibal or lover. Even though BeeBee was street smart, she was not wise. She had no idea how frightening was her appearance, making children cry and dogs bark. In a nutshell, she did not project the image of an executive of a five–star hotel.

Now, unequivocally, I understood the reason for her resentment. "I don't know what else to say to you. It is what it is."

Turning into the corridor toward the bathrooms, I heard her state with distinct malice and glee, "I still think you're an asshole."

I skidded to a stop. Then I shrugged off that last dig. Otherwise, someone would have to make bail for one or the both of us. As my father often said: "It was simply not worth it."

Five minutes later, I returned from the bathroom. Ms. Djorak trudged in and barreled her way into Mr. Ganiff's office, slamming the door shut. Mr. Ganiff, cowed by Ms. Djorak, intercommed me to join them in his office.

"You must apologize to BeeBee," he stated, avoiding my eyes while Ms. Djorak sat crammed in a chair across from him, a self–satisfied smirk plastered on her face. Still smarting over the last insult from BeeBee, I flared at what Djorak must've told him. Before I could defend myself, Mr. Ganiff spoke again, "This is the Executive Office and we have to put our personal feelings at the door."

I became even more outraged. "Mr. Ganiff, let me explain." It was necessary to clear the slate, or at least put a little equity into the situation.

He put out a hand as if directing traffic to stop. "One moment, Linda." He bellowed for BeeBee to enter. She popped her head in the doorway. "BeeBee, please, in the future, help Linda out with the phones."

"Oh, but I do," cooed BeeBee with her scratchy Harvey Firestone tone, "but you know how busy I am with the invoicing."

"Yes, of course, BeeBee," he intoned and, with a flip of the wrist, indicated he wanted her out of his office. He smiled at me and said, "Problem resolved, Linda." He made the same abrupt wrist gesture at me.

Perhaps he had resolved his problem, but mine became more pronounced. As Ms. Djorak passed by, she stopped to lean over and with all the venom she could summon hissed, "You're on your way to becoming the most hated person in the hotel."

What an accomplishment in such limited time! Guess I couldn't fool around with Ms. Djorak's apparent love interest. A turf war was declared and, of all things, over BeeBee. *That Djorak is one sick bitch*, I thought. She struck terror in my heart.

With strong misgivings, I struggled to focus my attention on work. Also to distance myself from the surrealism surrounding me. Work was always a panacea for me to calm the irregular heartbeats. And in this instance, desire to commit savagery with my teeth. I remember reading somewhere that being bitten to death was one of the most painful ways to go. But I digress. With a heavy heart, I read the paperwork once more, striving to comprehend the content.

"Three–hotels–in–one" was a good concept, I had to admit, even though partially realized. It needed more refining. I learned this aspect at the Waldorf while writing all those procedural departmental manuals without prior knowledge of what the work entailed. Concepts, once created, required continuity of premise, style, quality and design. The other thing I learned in my limited exposure to the hotel industry was that, unlike the financial arena, it didn't matter whether I had the expertise or not. Imagine if that were the case in medicine! Or in transportation! Energy! Government! Ha! Perhaps not that example.

I swiveled in front of the computer and jotted some notes:

From what I could determine during my on–site tour, the three levels of elevated status have inconsistently been implemented. Please refer to my comments as follows:

1) The Corridors:

Should reflect a subtle distinction of the step–ups through different color themes, e.g., Standard floors could have green color embedded in the background colors of wallpaper, Regal done in gold and Sublime in platinum. Just like the American Express credit cards. The idea is to convey sophistication at each level. However, should a client happen to visit the Sublime corridors, he/she would be induced to upgrade, on a subliminal basis.

2) Décor:

Should be distinguishable so that the client would discern the value of paying considerably more money to stay in the same room a few floors higher without impacting the value of the lesser–priced rooms. For example, the furniture in Standard suites could be oak; in Regal, mahogany; and in Sublime, Italian leather and stainless steel. Similarly, desk and flower arrangements in the corridors should also reflect the three steps of upward mobility, taking into account the most important ingredient that the hotel has to offer: the snob factor.

3) Carpet & Lighting:

Installation of detailed carpeting and recessed lighting which would be a vast improvement over the existing one. It is important to maintain subtlety, warmth and sophistication as well as color and quality to represent each of the levels.

Before long, I had written up several more examples of this three–tiered gradation in style including more of my views for consistency's sake. The little hand on my watch approached the eight. Time to head out for dinner. Right after I turned off the overhead lights, I detected in the darkened room a sporadic ray of light flickering from under Mr. Ganiff's door.

Hmmm, I thought with sympathy, *if nothing else, he certainly does put in his share of hours.*

27

Chapter 4
October 1994

Every morning at eight–thirty, the executives met in Mr. Ganiff's office. In order to ensure their promptness, Mr. Ganiff had four plush upholstered chairs available to accommodate eight to ten people; the latecomers had to sit on three ancient, rickety folding chairs stored in the closet next to his office. And the remaining latecomers had to stand, backs against walls encumbered with jutting frames of the usual "poker–playing dogs" artwork. It appeared to me that these tactics constituted a passive–aggressive form of torture.

The purpose of the meetings was to keep these senior managers abreast of current events as well as the prior day's results. Customarily, Murlise Mutt started out with occupancy, the bane of hotels. "So today, Mr. Ganiff, it's that same old story of…" she paused for effect, "one hundred percent occupancy!" She smiled at him. "Yes, not an empty room to be had. Also, no reports last night on any complaints like broken phones."

"Good, good." Mr. Ganiff gave a matter–of–fact nod in Murlise's direction. "That's what I want to hear."

Hans Holook, Director of Marketing, Corporate Bookings and Public Relations followed Murlise. "As all of you know, we're continuing with the same pricing for our winter daily rates. And we're still promoting the last two October weekends as well as the first two weekends in November where occupancy was stuck at around 45%. Now, we're offering our one night at corporate discount supplied with a free Continental breakfast. I must say, at present, occupancy for those time periods is reaching 85%." He nodded to Murlise.

Hans, a dapper man in his thirties, recently returned from an extended illness that he contracted in Dubai while visiting the Sultan, a repeat Supreme Superior guest. Hans claimed that an intestinal virus had caused him to lose over forty pounds, all his hair and reduced his face to a gaunt and haunted look. The scuttlebutt from Han's secretary, Cuneta, contained a story altogether different. She swore that he brought home some kind of deadly sexually transmitted disease.

To Hans' left sat Joe Smith, Director of the hotel's restaurant, *Bliss,* in addition to Food & Beverage which included the in–suite dining and banquets departments as well as the employees' cafeteria. Joe was an unremarkable mild–mannered man and son of a famous chocolatier whose confections were featured throughout the hotel.

"So, Joe, anything of interest?" Mr. Ganiff sarcastically asked. "Like why *Bliss* is constantly empty?" Mr. Ganiff goaded or rather prodded him the way a sadistic child would, armed with a stick, squatting down to do major mayhem to an insect or family pet.

Joe exhaled. "Sir, nothing has changed since our meeting yesterday morning."

K–tunk. Without warning, Mr. Ganiff's hand slapped the conference table while he stared right in Joe's eyes with his right eye. Joe turned white.

"Dammit, Joe. The only time I can light a fire under your ass is when we're doing a special promotion for your father's chocolates. Do me a favor, kindly clarify for me and for your colleagues here who you work for again?" Mr. Ganiff jettisoned another sarcastic potshot.

Joe fidgeted. These morning meetings were perhaps his least favorite part of the daily grind. Mr. Ganiff used every occasion to whittle away at him. Joe no longer defended himself. The poor guy. I guess under similar circumstances I would've developed a thick skin as well.

The real purpose behind these meetings, aside from giving Mr. Ganiff the opportunity to upbraid his staff, was the most important aspect of the executives' roles: to recap the guest lists. It could be said that everyone at the Supreme Superior was what you would call "star–fuckers"—people who would do back handsprings just for the good fortune to wipe a celebrity's behind...

While everyone examined the celebrity list du jour, Murlise announced the VIPs as she was in charge of Reservations and Front Desk as well as Concierge. "We have with us a two–week stay by... oh, my lucky stars... Mr. Engelbert Humperdinck."

All of the executives groaned. Everyone knew that Murlise was an avid, self–professed Engelbert worshiper. Often, I'd overhear her throat singing *Release Me* as she roamed the hotel offices. She boasted that she attended all five Humperdinck concerts performed in the continental U.S. and had dozens of photos taken with the legendary singer. Whenever Mr. Humperdinck visited, Murlise went agog, personally assisting in his check–in. She also carried his luggage on her back and reins in her teeth. This meant countless pictures shown and stories told at every opportunity including the daily staff meetings. She was a true fan, albeit the only one at the Supreme Superior.

Ms. Djorak perked up. "Isn't this the time of year that, ahem," she blushed, a sight to behold, similar to the flush of an eczema attack, "the time when Gillian Anderson should be visiting?"

Gillian Anderson who played Scully in the *X–Files* television series was Djorak's favorite. She swooned at the mention of her name. Rumor among the staff—unfounded because no one had the fortitude to find out—was that Scully pictures were draped all over her bedroom somewhere in Southern Jersey where she lived with her retired female "friend" and a pack of specially bred Rottweilers. This unhealthy fascination became so apparent during one visit that it caught the attention of Big Guy, our head of Security who clandestinely informed his team of this peccadillo and told them "shoot to kill" should Djorak get too close.

Mr. Ganiff piped up and guffawed aloud, "Don't worry, Djorak, you'll get your chance. We'll notify you well in advance." He beckoned to Big Guy who gave him a two–finger salute in return.

Big Guy was an ardent *Star Trek* fan. A few days earlier, the *Voyager* team arrived at the Supreme Superior to promote the launching of its new season.

29

He dragged me to the Lobby so we could gape at the stars who entered the Lounge. "Oh My God, it's Captain Janeway and look, there's the holodeck doctor!" Big Guy kept nudging me in the neck with his elbow, excited to see firsthand the Starship Enterprise crew. Personally, I felt they looked better on the small screen in their Star Fleet uniforms and make–up. Then again, I didn't seem to possess the expertise in the field of celebrity gawking that my colleagues held.

Don Johnson was an all–time favorite amongst the executive staff, as was Liz Taylor, Burt Reynolds and Kelsey Grammer. Big Guy told me that Ganiff had the concierge rent a Yamaha baby grand piano for Mr. Grammer so that he could practice in one of the suites. Gratis, of course.

My first celebrity encounter came when I had drinks with a corporate client in the Lounge during the slow afternoon period. We were in the midst of a discussion when I spotted Jennifer Aniston and Lisa Kudrow from NBC's *Friends* who entered the room. They sat down at the table next to us and flipped their mobile phones on and off until someone recognized them from the Lobby and shouted their character names, "Rachel! Phoebe!" The pair smiled graciously and waved. And their smiles widened when a flock of waiters clamored to assist them with their order.

Teddie, the bartender, raced over with pen and pad, not to take their order but their autographs. "Ms. Aniston. Ms. Cox. What a pleasure to be in the company of such comedic genius! And you're both even more beautiful in person."

No doubt in my mind that the staff would do Olympic caliber calisthenics for any of these a–listers just to get a nod and a wink in return. Nothing at all like the banking industry!

Not every luminary was treated the same, as I soon discovered.

Turning to Murlise I said, "Isaac Stern, the world–renowned violinist, needs a room. His publicist confided that he's getting divorced and has nowhere to stay for the night."

Murlise replied, "Don't know if I can help, Linda. This is a sold–out time, the height of tourist season. Besides, we're seriously overbooked."

"What about one of Mr. Ganiff's comp rooms?" I asked, indirectly addressing Mr. Ganiff. I was recently introduced to this particular aspect of my job.

"Isaac who?" Ganiff snorted. "Who the hell is he?"

"He's one of the world's best violinists. Also known as the person who saved Carnegie Hall from demolition. He was instrumental in making it what it is today."

"Big deal," Ganiff said, waving dismissively. The rest of the staff laughed. "If I haven't heard of him, he's hardly worth pulling favors for. I mean, he's no legendary crooner like Tony Tenneb, or even anything like George Michael. Don't waste my time on b–listers!"

Murlise neglected to mention at other meetings important personages such as

I. M. Pei, a few United Nations delegates, and even the French President, Jacques Chirac.

While spotting Monsieur Chirac's name on the VIP list, I blurted out a question. "Murlise, do we do anything special for Presidents of other countries? I mean, doesn't he require an entire floor for his force of secret service agents?"

Mr. Ganiff scowled. "I'm certain she knows what to do, Linda. Go on, please, Murlise," and aimed his dismissive signal at me. The rest of the executives jumped to the next name on the list and talked with animation about their favorite stars, or one of the other passing non–entity in–vogue musicians that were guests.

The staff meetings were not complete without the interactions from the remaining members of the management team. The head of Finance, José Dorck— a Mr. Magoo prototype—rapidly discussed the budget and reconciliations of past dues. The head of Housekeeping, Ms. Wapiti, the highest paid executive in the Supreme Superior Hotel, having outstripped Mr. Ganiff by over $75,000 per annum, had not much more to add. Cappy, head of Engineering and our beloved Ms. Djorak didn't contribute anything of worth. And then there was Seebok Murray, assistant to the General Manager. Only as per usual, he was absent again from our daily meeting.

From star–worshipping, I soon graduated to serious business. I planned to sit down and finish the final clue to the *New York Times* crossword puzzle, but Mr. Ganiff grabbed me by the elbow and escorted me to the next assembly. "You're here almost a month; it's time to get your feet wet."

Wednesday mornings, right after the eight–thirty meeting, all the department heads met in an unused conference room for the weekly departmental state–of–the–union. Pastries and fresh baked breads were laid out in baskets on a side table next to the beverage station with an assortment of teas, flavored coffees and juices. For the top brass, no expense was spared.

I was unaccustomed to such opulence in an office environment. Even at the Waldorf I was kept within the confines of my cubicle, writing analytical financial reports. It certainly beat the Pizza Fridays that GermBank hosted in order to induce the staff not to leave for lunch and to guilt them into working late.

I followed Mr. Ganiff's cue and queued up for my breakfast. One gentleman I didn't know whooped with joy when he spotted a carafe of fresh–squeezed orange juice. A young woman clapped her hands with glee when she noticed the extra portions of cold cuts. Everyone dished out heaping quantities of food on their plates. Afterwards, they set out to find seats around the table.

Mr. Ganiff hosted these departmental meetings although the true bosses were the expatriates from Japan. They were known around the office as "The Gang of Three."

A top Japanese bank owned The Supreme Superior Hotels, the largest chain of luxury resort hotels throughout Asia. According to the sales brochures, the New

York Supreme Superior was their solitary property outside of Asia. The parent company expatriated a senior–level banker, Mr. Hitsuhana who had lost a fortune on problem loans five years prior to his retirement. They also deployed Miss Suijii, the unmarried thirty–year old daughter of one of the Chief Executives, and her boyfriend, Mr. Shitsu, a married man of fifty who brought his wife and daughter along to the United States.

Our visiting contingent took part regularly in the weekly departmental meetings. Their mission was to write reports back to the Chairman and the President of the Supreme Superior as well as their respective superiors in the Japanese bank. Outside of this responsibility, they didn't have much to do. Well, except to translate financial statements from Mr. Dorck. And to master the *New York Times* crossword puzzles, supplied with the answers from my faxes, copied by Miss Monique, their secretary. They worked very long hours.

Due to the profitability of the hotel, Mr. Ganiff was in charge with full support of his superiors. He still had to report to the Gang of Three, especially when it concerned any and all outgoing checks in large denominations.

Mr. Ganiff took a seat dead center of the rectangular conference table. The table was arranged with a professional set–up complete with stiff, white linen for twenty plus pads of paper and pens for each attendee. Mr. Ganiff wolfed down a plate of hash browns and sausages stacked on sliced bagels. Then, he snapped his fingers and pointed to me indicating the empty seat situated to his right.

"So, today I'd like to formally introduce you to our new addition at the Supreme Superior, Miss Linda Lane. Her position here is to free me to create new concepts for the hotel and to oversee daily operations."

All at once, eighteen pairs of eyes riveted to attention. Out of those eighteen, two pairs imparted fire and brimstone: the ever delightful Ms. Djorak, and a little pale man sitting at the opposite end of the table whose lips possessed a serpentine quality. Seebok Murray had shown up.

Mr. Murray was probably the result of a romantic entanglement gone awry somewhere in the foothills of Pakistan some twenty–eight years earlier between a Muslim woman lost during a jihad and an Irish soldier. Someone at the table stated earlier that he had returned just this morning from his honeymoon with his nubile blond peach bride from Georgia. *So that accounted for his absence during all those executive meetings.* I recognized him as the fresh–squeezed orange juice fan.

"One of Linda's responsibilities will be to keep you away from me," jibbed Mr. Ganiff good–naturedly. A few individuals around the table tittered. I felt uncomfortable under their gaze. "Another is that she's my new right–hand man." At this point, Seebok levitated from his seat and dropped right back down. Mr. Ganiff continued, "Who will attend the daily executive staff meetings as well."

Seebok was a graduate of Cornell University MBA program specializing in hotel management. He embraced all the arrogant qualities associated with Ivy

League dolts. Up until today he worked one–on–one with Mr. Ganiff on special projects that entitled him to many perks.

In fact, all of the individuals around that table, apart from myself, were entitled to many perks that included free and frequent usage of the company limousine fleet. Also, free dry cleaning, free dining with guests at *Bliss*, the hotel restaurant as well as commissions and bonuses on any work they conducted at or recommended to the hotel. Given my temporary status in the organization, the perks that would've customarily been mine were not yet extended to me.

"So," Mr. Ganiff concluded, "if you want to deal with me, you'll have to go through Linda going forward." With a twist of the mustache, he leaned over and whispered to me, "You're also in charge of minutes."

Acting upon the subtle cue, I picked up a pen and wrote the date on the pad of paper in front of me. Mr. Ganiff picked up the baton again.

His success at the Supreme Superior was due, in part, to keeping expenses down. He was quite proud of that fact. At every meeting, he poured forth his perspective. "Most hotels are bound by the union. Since we were built after the last union deal, and we knew the ins and outs of that contract, we've saved much money by not adding staff, thanks to Miss Djorak."

Mr. Ganiff's distaste for the union was matched and checkmated by Ms. Djorak's whose hatred was vitriolic.

"Just remember, here at the Supreme Superior, lower costs make for better profits. When you keep costs down, you pay less taxes as opposed to increasing revenues. In other words, you save more than a dollar for each dollar you save. And that's why we keep the lid on increasing our staff, isn't that right, Miss Djorak?"

While I puzzled over that conundrum, Ms. Djorak ducked her head vigorously in compliance.

Mr. Ganiff tipped his nose in the direction of the head of Food & Beverage, Joe Smith.

"Joe, why don't you tell us what's going on in your department?"

Cookie, the Executive Chef, jumped up and circulated grainy photocopies of upcoming banquets and social functions along with restaurant breakdowns for the past week. Each member of the departmental meeting examined the illegible papers, mostly by holding them upside down.

"This coming Saturday we're having the Blatts' wedding for a hundred people in the Western Banquet Room and the adjoining Marlboro on the 57th floor. We also have the Historical Society's annual meeting for the non–profit fundraiser. That's for fifty. We planned to give them the snapper for the main course because they decided to forgo the appetizers…"

One by one the execs around the table tuned out. Mr. Hitsuhana snored. Ms. Suijii finished an origami squirrel she made from the banquet photocopies to entertain Mr. Shitsu, seated next to her. She moved the squirrel's head by pulling on his tail. This elicited stifled giggles around the table. I gave up writing the details of the arrangements since they were already on the report. After five minutes, or perhaps five years later, Mr. Ganiff interrupted.

"Tell me about *Bliss* revenues."

Joe whimpered, waking Mr. Hitsuhana. Ms. Suijii dropped the origami squirrel onto the table.

The *Bliss* restaurant had a five–star rating from the Staggerts guide although the legitimacy of this rating was in serious doubt. One of the chefs over at the Waldorf complained that you could buy such a wonderful rating for a mere $12,000.

Bliss was plainly out of style with the rest of its competitors, or even worse, the entire food industry. In truth, *Bliss's* menu was devoted to a clientele that hadn't existed since the last cigar–chomping Hollywood mogul passed away fifteen years earlier.

I had the misfortune of lunching with Mr. Ganiff in the restaurant my first day. He wanted to initiate me to the realm of fine cuisine and ordered one of the specials on my behalf. To my horror, an over–sized slab of meat appeared with the excess portion elegantly draped over the sides of the plate. I had no idea what kind of animal let alone species was in front of me. I figured it was either an endangered extraterrestrial or something unearthed after having been frozen in a glacier for a millennium. Perhaps the clue could be derived from the scales and gamy texture. I attempted to drown the meat with ketchup but Mr. Ganiff made the waiter take the bottle away. "Linda, I insist, please eat the food the way Cookie had it prepared."

He sat there happy as a clam with his shrimp cocktail followed by Chilean sea bass and eyeballed me with an indulgent smile.

I put on a good face, chewing on a rubbery piece of rancid fat and gristle, convinced that I was eating the private parts of a yak. My gag reflexes worked overtime. Every time I tried to slip in my mouth the side dish of deep fried potatoes to camouflage the taste, he would ask, "Are you enjoying your meal, Miss Linda?"

"Let's just say, Mr. Ganiff, it's a lifetime experience."

"Would you like for me to order something else?" he kindly inquired.

"Heaven for—!" I stopped myself in time. "Thank you no, I'm trying to enjoy this one which I believe is… ahem, an acquired taste." In actuality, it was a foul, miserable, pitiful excuse of a meal. I suffered not only from bad breath but horrible gas pains for the remainder of the week. I never had gas like that in my life—at one point I could fart Devo's *Whip It* a cappella.

Despite the Staggerts guide rating, people knew better. The restaurant, capable of seating 350, was usually empty. Mr. Ganiff prodded Joe to invent venues to increase patronage… No matter the tactic or strategy, results were abysmal. "How about 'Meet your Favorite Pasta Chef' on alternate Tuesday evenings?

Something different. Anything," implored Mr. Ganiff out of despair.

After my inauspicious first meal at *Bliss*, I came up with a potential solution: shoot the Executive Chef. That was out of the question because Mr. Ganiff and Joe loved the way Cookie prepared these meals. It was the sole opinion they shared in common.

Cookie, a tall redhead weighing ninety–five pounds soaking wet after a six–pack, seemed like a good soul. His culinary path began in the navy where he lost his teeth from scurvy and three fingers (no one knew why and no one asked). After the navy, he saved his money, obtained his GI Bill and studied cuisine where he met Joe (another culinary school grad) and ultimately Mr. Ganiff. Amazingly, Cookie found his niche in gourmet cuisine—none of which was featured in the restaurant—and unremittingly won awards throughout the world in culinary contests.

Mr. Ganiff told Joe to grab Cookie because he felt that Cookie would make his hotel restaurant famous. During Cookie's frequent travel intervals, the restaurant fell into the incapable hands of Joe Smith whose forte was chocolate. Fortunately for the patrons, the cuisine for banquets and functions tasted remarkably better since Cookie's assistant, Billy, a former torch singer, prepared the food.

Bliss was an absolute mess.

Once again, Joe read off another photocopied Excel spreadsheet. Line by line.

"Revenues for yesterday were $1,900 for the restaurant. The breakdown for the three meals was 40% breakfast, 40% lunch and 20% dinner."

"And room service?" Mr. Ganiff's eyebrows shot upward. For the benefit of his lackeys, he exhaled and pontificated as a head master, "That is one of our most profitable centers, right?"

"Yessir. Despite receiving some complaints about the turnaround time."

Mr. Ganiff fixed his right eye at Joe. "And why is that?"

"Well, we were backed up downstairs because we were sold out, and most of the calls took place around eight in the morning. And then the rear elevators were out of commission—today makes it four days—"

Mr. Ganiff barked at Seebok, "Four days? Elevators? What's going on here?"

"I just got back, sir. I have no idea."

Mr. Ganiff's head pivoted to Murlise. "So, what are we doing to remedy this?"

Murlise lifted her humongous jaw and said, "We've placed calls to Uttus Elevators. They haven't come yet."

Mr. Ganiff slammed his fist into the table. He growled at Murlise, "You call those sons of bitches up. You speak to the head guy... what's his name, Seebok?"

"Patterson."

"Yeah, call that cretin up. We just signed a new service agreement with those morons for a quarter mil a year. They're supposed to be here within two hours from the first call. Tell 'em not only are we going to sue them for breach of contract, we want a full refund with interest or we're going to their competitors." He swiveled his head to Seebok. "Set up the appointments with the other two companies who approached us."

Absolutely mind–boggling! My first eyewitness account of the maestro in action. I was impressed with the demonstration of mastery and power he held over his people. He exhibited full–scale take charge in contrast to the mini–meeting this morning where he shot off mini–salvos.

"Now, Joe," Mr. Ganiff said in a very calm tone, "what the hell's wrong with your people? And why didn't you tell me this earlier?"

Joe squirmed in his chair. "Well, we're kinda meeting deadlines except for this morning when we had to use the front of house elevators—"

Murlise started to intervene although Ms. Djorak's voice was louder.

"That's against protocol."

"But they were packed with people leaving—" Joe said in his defense.

Ganiff cut him off. "Enough, Joe. This is hardly the Holiday Inn. Remedy it and I mean right now. When's Ronny coming back?"

Ronny was the Banquets Manager, also in charge of in–room dining, currently in rehab for his alleged percodan habit.

"Hopefully next week."

Mr. Ganiff pointed to Doreen who trembled. "And what junkets have you booked?"

"Tho many, thir!" she replied while waving a handful of papers. Doreen reminded me of one of those little neurotic lap dogs, the way she quivered with excitement, barely containing her composure. She was the young woman at the banquet table who earlier quivered with excitement over the extra cold cuts.

As a relatively new five–star hotel, the Supreme Superior was very dependent upon its celebrity status. Capturing the junket market was the fastest and easiest way of securing celebrities… and building a big–time reputation.

A press junket is usually a two to five day all–around media event whereby the stars meet with reporters from all forms of media to discuss their latest roles, the plumbing of their souls, and to substantiate why they deserve an award or two. Doreen, as Director of Sales/Marketing, was in charge of this area.

She passed to Mr. Ganiff her current Excel spreadsheet with group room bookings made by her and her staff of ten. With her tremulous Minnie Mouse voice and Tweety Bird lisp she said, "For the retht of thith month thtarting Friday we booked with Warner Brotherth to promote their new movie, *Leefal Weapon*

Three and chothe the 55th floor, uthing the Cleopatra room for the junket."

Murlise, the Reservations Manager, perked up. "That's odd, Doreen. You didn't notify me which stars were going to stay here."

At that, everyone at the table perked up, including me, I hated to admit.

"Well, Mel Brookth, I'm sure," Doreen responded. The whole room erupted in laughter.

"No, Doreen, Mel Gibson," Mr. Ganiff corrected with a paternal air.

"Ooh, Mithter Ganiff, I get them miktht up," she cooed while batting her eyelids.

While Mr. Ganiff basked in Doreen's adoration, I stirred my coffee, surveyed the imprinted wallpaper and intently scratched an imaginary itch. Ms. Djorak shredded her cuticles into a mountain of dead skin. And the Chief of Security, Big Guy, focused on Murlise's breasts.

Mr. Ganiff broke out of his reverie. "Hans. Why don't you tell us about the new marketing plans."

Hans straightened up and spoke loud and clear. "Well, we have our great new homepage in development. It outrivals any of the top hotels in the city. And we're in the process of getting the prototype for our new online reservations. I also managed to place a few ads at a relatively low cost for the special weekend promo rate that you asked for."

"Good, good. Let me know when you have something to show me." He tugged on the tips of his mustache for emphasis, then pointed to Murlise. "And what about our perfect occupancy rates? Tell me we're still building on our 100% rate. Three perfect months, even in off–peak season!"

Murlise smiled and nodded. Mr. Ganiff felt the compulsion to put her in her place. "Hey, let's not get too wrapped up in our success. After all, this is New York City. Let's not forget the slump of '89. This industry is feast or famine. So don't get smug with me, you hear?"

"Yes, Mr. Ganiff," Murlise uttered in a low voice, "understood."

"Fine. As long as we share that concern." He shifted in his chair and pointed a pen at Leesa, our head of communications. "And how are your revenues doing today, young lady?"

Leesa, a pallid, middle–aged woman, spoke up. "As you're aware, Mr. Ganiff, telecommunications is the largest growing component of hotel revenues. We're talking about growth exceeding 150% month–to–month from our in–room faxes, computers, modems and Sublime mobile phones." She drew in a deep breath and said, "Up to now we're at the stage where we need a T–1 cable to continue this trend. It'll allow us heavier usage, but it won't be cheap."

"Seebok!" shouted Mr. Ganiff, failing to acknowledge Leesa directly.

"Yes, sir, I'm working on that," he replied. "The NYNEX people should be here for installation next week, we hope."

"We hope?" Ganiff pounded a fist on the table for effect. "We don't do 'we hope' here at this hotel. Let me tell you, 'hope' does not build a five–star hotel. 'Hope' does not pay the bills. 'Hope' is not what distinguishes us from our competitors. No way." He swiveled his head and gave a good, hard glare at every single soul around the conference table. Satisfied with the result, he sat back. "And let that be a lesson for everyone." He waited a few seconds, then muttered to himself, "Where was I? Oh, right." He pivoted and shouted, "Get it done, Seebok. Get the phone people up here ASAP…" he lowered his voice to a growl, "or find yourself begging for work at the Day's Inn down the street!"

A blanket of silence fell over the room. Big Guy, Cappy, Ms. Wapiti, the highest paid executive in the Supreme Superior Hotel, and Mr. Dorck had nothing to add.

Mr. Hitsuhana peered up through his glasses, smiled and shakily whispered, "Rooms are good. Rates are good. Very good. Thank you very much."

"Meeting adjourned," stated Mr. Ganiff and everyone couldn't run out of that conference room fast enough.

Chapter 5

Three days later, I decided to pay my parents a Saturday visit. My mother was keen on making lunch whereas my father wanted to eat out in a restaurant.

"C'mon, Linda. Let's go out for some pasta. My treat."

"Please, Dad, let's stay here at home and eat Mom's cooking. I've had more than my share of restaurant food to last a lifetime."

My mother was in the kitchen chopping, grilling and sautéing. It was a beautiful and surprisingly warm October afternoon. My dad and I decided to sit outside on the deck lounge chairs, drinks in hand.

"How you doing, kiddo?" my father asked, worried about the indecisive look on my face. "Is there something you want to talk about?"

"Well, Dad, I wanted to have this heart–to–heart with you and Mom together. Maybe you should tell her what I have to say. She gets so emotional."

My father bent his head in agreement. "Okay, c'mon out with it." He read me like a book.

"It's about that job at GermBank. Well, before I get into the story, let me just say that I know and appreciate how you and Mom always support me. I don't want to do anything to disappoint you guys."

"My dear, nothing would ever change our opinion of you," Dad said, "except for committing murder."

I ignored his weak attempt at comedy. "You do recall that I just up and quit my job at the bank?"

"How could I forget? Your mother and I discuss it all the time. We thought sooner or later you'd come around to tell us why."

My parents knew how hard I had worked over the years in several different banks, climbing that dastardly corporate ladder rung by rung from lowly trading clerk to bond trader. I parked there for several years before a gastric ulcer wreaked havoc with my social life, incapacitating me. Consequently, I changed direction. It culminated in my crowning glory: the head of Corporate Lending at GermBank with six Germans reporting to me. It was the accomplishment of my career... and my downfall.

"Dad, it all started with a routine due diligence review on a loan portfolio. You have no idea how difficult, almost impossible this was because all the work at GermBank was done strictly in German. And, in order to get anything done, I had to rely upon departmental translators. Still, the work couldn't be done, unless my translation request was sanctioned by my boss!"

While I described the job to my father, it hit me like a ton of bricks. Perhaps that was why they hired me: I was the only person in the bank who did not speak, read or write German. They must've freaked when I made that momentous discovery without their translators or translations!

"Dad, what triggered the whole thing was when I discovered some irregularities orchestrated by my boss."

"What do you mean by 'irregularities?'"

I fidgeted. "I did what was required to do when performing my job despite the language impediment. That's when I found out that my boss set up bogus companies and extended loans to them. Money traveled all over the world, and by the time it came back to the U.S. in the form of loan repayments, it was suitably laundered." I stopped for a moment. "Dad, I'm not even talking about the other stuff he did, like opening up bogus letters of credit for Iraq and setting up loans to South Africa to support apartheid."

My father reacted the same way as I did when initially confronted with these revelations. Stumped.

"What did you do then?" he asked at last.

I didn't want to get into all the gory details. "I did all I could to save my ass and place the onus on him. The bottom line was that I had two options: I could stay to fight a losing battle because I had no support from my senior management, or I could leave the bank with my reputation intact."

I omitted to tell my father that when I approached my boss, with his deep innate sense of paranoia, hostility, anger, vengeance and allegiance to the Ubermensch, he literally laughed in my face. He followed up with a rapid one–two of stripping me first of my authority, then by threatening my career. He promised that I would leave GermBank in ruins if I persevered and declared war on him.

Dad recoiled. "I had no idea, Linda, that you were going through this. Why didn't you tell us?"

I finished my drink and placed the empty glass on the end table next to me. "What could you do? I mean, I always appreciate the emotional support even though this was something that only I could handle."

I left the bank with a sense of shame. My boss, on the other hand, was euphoric because the perverted pillar of banking was off the hook. Deflated, I continued, "I sent a save–your–ass memo to everyone in the bank before leaving. Squirreled several copies in certain files. Still, I don't know what effect they had." I sighed. "I shoulda done more."

My father, his light blue eyes clear and steady, patted my hand. "I'm not going to whitewash it for you, but yeah, maybe you should've done more."

Abruptly, I tried to move away but he grabbed my hands. "Linda, I'm not trying to blame you or judge your actions. Different people handle crisis in different ways. But it's not like you to just walk away. Especially after dedicating all those years to building your career. Now, that's what you did and it's up to you to determine why you allowed this man to continue to do these things."

I felt like a little girl again, insecure and uncomfortable. My father pacified me. "No matter what you do in life, your mother and I will always be proud of you." Out of relief, out of shame, my eyes welled up. He continued, "I'm even more proud that my daughter possesses such a high degree of integrity that she'd walk away from a job that took her years to attain rather than roll in the mud with those pigs." He moved to my lounge chair, making me scooch over so that he could hug me. "All we want for you is to be happy. It doesn't matter what you do; what success you may or may not have. As long as you are true to yourself, you can support yourself and, most important of all, that you find some happiness out of what you're doing." He tenderly kissed my forehead.

"What in the world's going on here?" My mother poked her head out of the sliding doors that gave entrance to the deck.

"Oh, nothing, Mother," my father replied.

"Well, you two! Always keeping secrets from me. I know something's going on." She winked at me, then flashed a knowing smile in my father's direction. "I suppose it can wait till after we eat. Now where's that dang dinner bell so I can ring it to announce that lunch is soived?"

Chapter 6

As usual, I got an earful of BeeBee's grating voice echoing down the hallway, "No, I can not help you." I rushed in front of her desk. She pulled and tugged on the telephone cord line while she adamantly stated, "No, Mr. Ganiff is still in a meeting. Ms. Lane is still in a meeting."

"Who is it?" I pantomimed.

BeeBee closed her eyes, a discreet message for me to buzz off.

For a five–star hotel with a five–star restaurant, the General Manager's office handled a helluva lot of complaints. Stacked at my desk were scads of coffee–stained messages for Mr. Ganiff. Almost all of his calls were from irate guests. Most of the complaints proved valid: A bad attitude from the Front Desk. No air conditioning/heat/hot water. A mouse appearance or two. The typical *Bliss* daily food poisoning. The usual theft and loss. Yet, valid or not, the resolution of the aforementioned types of occurrences should have been nipped in the bud at the lower levels of management. The fact that the General Manager was plagued with this nonsense indicated very poor leadership.

All the same, the executive office had to handle "sensitive" complaints. One that springs to mind was the legendary outbreak of pediculosis aka crabs or lice. We were honored recipients of these guests scarcely a month after I started at the Supreme Superior.

It took almost three weeks of mayhem to locate the source of the infestation. We isolated three floors of Standard suites where a busload of Las Vegas guests had visited straight from the airport. Mr. Ganiff insisted that we kept wraps on this, fearing possible litigation and/or a smear on the hotel's reputation.

We emptied the three floors of all remaining clients. In the middle of the night, we surreptitiously ushered in pest exterminators who wore surgical gowns over the same sort of suits that biohazard laborers don. In order to contain the chemicals from spreading throughout the hotel, they covered all exits, doorways, ducts and air vents with plastic sheets.

"Miss Linda, you have no idea the magnitude of the situation," shouted Mr. Ganiff from his desk. "Let me tell you firsthand that we're not the only five–star hotel with these problems. You'd never stay at another hotel again if you knew that most places host bedbugs along with a few other critters." Mr. Ganiff rolled the tips of his mustache with both hands.

"Wouldn't that put us in a potential legal situation?" I asked out of curiosity, leaning against his doorframe.

"How could that be? We never had crabs at the Supreme Superior to start off with," he said with a wink from his left eye.

Murlise arrived at his doorway wailing in disbelief, "My occupancy runs,

Mr. Ganiff. This damn crabisode absolutely killed me! Three weeks without three floors! What should I do?"

Mr. Ganiff gazed at her with warmth. The munificence of bestowing a papal dispensation overflowed his heart. He declared, "We will not count those three floors in our tallies. Just asterisk the days involved with a footnote."

"Oh, thank you, Mr. Ganiff," she gushed, grateful for his intervention into what might've meant a serious black mark for her.

He cast his eye over at me and excused himself from Murlise. I had to speak to him about a matter that had come to my attention.

"Please come in, Miss Linda." I did. My heart sank when he posed in that position, the one where he formed a steeple out of his fingers and with his good eye stared at his fingernails. A sense of dread overtook me. *No, not again*, I reflected and sure enough, he peered to his right toward the framed picture of his mother.

"Take a seat, Miss Linda."

I sat down with the severest of misgivings. Mr. Ganiff, to the contrary, looked forward to engaging me in his autobiographical lullaby. I could not help myself—that man had the knack of knocking me out. I imagined that if I survived listening to this drek, perhaps one day he would finish and I could go onto bigger and better matters intact and conscious.

I rocked in the chair, desperate to fight off the inevitable slumber during his litany of legacy.

"They called me bright and handsome once upon a time. Well, save for my eye that some said gave me a certain rakish look. To others, malevolent."

And for the rest of us, plain dumb, I considered with a smile.

He continued, "At twenty–four, I was well sought after. I had a Masters in Business from Columbia on scholarship. People considered me good–natured and very open–minded."

He had to be, given such diversity in his own genetic pool and that of his family. Yet, it seemed doubtful that he ever invited people home.

"One evening, at a party in New York City, I met a beautiful young lady who stepped right out of a fairy tale. She was adorable with a bright smile, long jet–black hair and cornflower blue eyes. I was smitten."

Or was it the prominent bosom? I alluded to the wedding picture he had in the credenza unit behind him. *I bet he even wondered how her feet got wet in the shower.*

"I was struck by her very quiet, plain ways. Mabel was a Mayflower descendant quite a few times removed."

A Mayflower descendant! I felt reincarnated into a MAD magazine fill–in–the–blank game as I thought, *with all the shortcomings and religious attachments affiliated with such a pedigree.*

Mr. Ganiff moved onto his courting days. "Her mother stood over us in the parlor with a stick. I resolved to make her mine after her graduation from the FBI."

"The FBI?" I asked with raised eyebrows, temporarily conscious.

Mr. Ganiff chortled. "Oh, not the Feds. I'm talking about the culinary school, Food and Beverage Institute. FBI, get it? Back then they were located here in the city. Anyway, this one day, Mabel and I and another couple went upstate for a picnic, armed with bottles of wine and a basket filled with food, all borrowed from the FBI. We were very taken with the surrounding landscape. Upon our return, we strongly urged the FBI to uproot and relocate there." He winked at me with his right eye and continued, "They did... with my help, of course. I aided them in the procurement of real estate and the financing. They soon made me an honorary member. It's been worth a few accolades over the years... and quite a few free dinners."

He stopped talking.

Whew! Wasn't that bad. Just a small power nap. I stretched my arms and stared at the man whose focus was on his nails.

"Do you have anything to tell me, Miss Linda?" he calmly inquired.

"As a matter of fact..." I ineffectively concealed my yawn, "it has to do with Linda, your former assistant."

As it turns out, the woman I replaced—Mr. Ganiff's former right–hand "man"—was also a Linda... and quite popular among the staff. Linda Luppner was a divorcée in her early twenties with three children. Everyone loved "Linda, the Luppner." Her former co–workers constantly let me know this.

Everyone except Mr. Ganiff.

Luckily for him, Linda Luppner met a Vegas high roller at the *Bliss* bar one evening, flew off somewhere with him, and sent a Western Union telegram to alert the hotel of her new life, thereby creating the job opening that led to my instant career upgrade.

Linda Luppner's sudden departure left me in a peculiar situation at times. One out of every three calls was for "the other Linda" aka "the other white meat." They were friends of friends of friends of Linda Luppner. They all loved Linda Luppner. At first, I had no other choice than to tolerate the transition. Yet, by my second week on the job, I got testy... until a pattern emerged.

"Hey, Linda, it's Barbara from Taylor Travel. How 'bout this Thursday night for my monthly suite comp?"

"Linda, Justin Zane from Lonnie's Limo. How's next Monday lookin' for our little tradeoff?"

Quite a few of these vendors called even now with a sense of entitlement. "Whaddaya mean you're not interested? I thought we had a standing deal," shouted some guy by the moniker of Eli, from 3rd Avenue Flowers. "What the hell happened to the real Linda? What kind of a crazy bitch turns down free flowers?"

As an industry–wide practice, General Managers of hotels were entitled to complimentary guest rooms. At the Supreme Superior, Mr. Ganiff was entitled to at least eight complimentary guest rooms daily. He had the authority to bump out guests on sell–outs for these rooms. Or from any rooms, for that matter. Anyhow, Ms. Luppner also had signing authority for these rooms. Those same privileges that were conferred upon me the first day of my employment although I didn't find out until a few weeks later.

It seemed as if Linda Luppner had some funny business taking place. I found a handwritten tally of her arrangements beneath a stack of memo pads in my bottom desk drawer while I cleaned up. This had been going on for at least five years. No one seemed the wiser, including Mr. Ganiff. After all, no employee questioned the requests from the General Manager's office. That was, if they wanted to remain employed.

When the rooms weren't in use, Linda bartered with her "friends" in service industries: Travel agents. Florists. Manicurists. Masseuses. In return, these friends gave Linda complimentary deals. Deals they lavishly described to me in detail, e.g., monthly massages, bi–monthly hair blow drys and free flower bouquets to adorn the hallway of her apartment. Other deals included deep discounted car rentals anywhere in the continental U.S., free sedan service between Queens and Manhattan and airline vouchers for last second getaway trips to Vegas. Then there were other "friends." The ones who could not afford a five–star hotel, yet for an easy $100 got to sleep in the lap of luxury for one night.

Using information culled by her vendor friends and her little notebook, I easily compiled a short list containing names, products, dollar amounts and phone numbers for Mr. Ganiff's benefit. This was not something I would have ordinarily bothered with, considering that I didn't blow the whistle on a more important matter in my life. However, the sheer arrogance and blatant stupidity of these people offended me, as did the volume of calls in such a short period of time, wreaking havoc to my workday. The milestone 100th call initiated that conversation with Mr. Ganiff.

"Are you aware that your former assistant, Linda Luppner, had a sideline business?"

"Sideline deals? I'm not sure… I don't understand."

I described in great detail the phone calls, messages and information I received since I came onboard. "Do you know how much revenue was lost over five years? Mr. Ganiff, this translates into tens of thousands of dollars."

"Oh really," Ganiff stared at me with his good right eye. He did not appear too concerned. "Hmm, well thanks, Linda. I appreciate your honesty… honestly…" He pursed his lips. "Linda, I mean the former Linda, is not here to defend herself, even if your charges could be proven. So, how about we drop the subject and get back to work, all right?"

I sat there. Baffled. I gave the man some heavy–duty evidence of corporate theft and pretty much let him know that I wouldn't do the same. And all I got was a limp handshake? Not even a T–shirt to say that? What about all that blather about saving money and keeping down expenses to keep up revenues? Something did not compute.

"Um, Linda, you're still in my office. Time you got back to your desk."

He observed that I wouldn't budge, so he stood up and from out of nowhere quoted something biblical. *"For it is written, I will destroy the wisdom of the wise, and will bring to nothing the understanding of the prudent. Where is the wise? Where is the scribe? Where is the disputer of this world? Hath not God made foolish the wisdom of this world?"*

He post–scripted, "Corinthians."

I stared right at him and quoted back, *"A wet bird never flies at night…* Johnny Carson."

"What kind of education did you have?" he shouted in agitation. "Don't you know Scripture?"

"I had a standard academic education. No, sir, I am a practicing Buddhist." *What the fuck was his problem?*

"Stop it, Linda, please. Didn't your parents bring you up correctly?"

Evidently, they did, I thought to myself, *because otherwise I'd be facing ten to twenty–five years for bludgeoning the man in front of me.*

With a sigh, Mr. Ganiff sat back down and twirled the ends of his mustache. "Linda, close the door behind you after you leave and forward the phones to the operators."

That damn attitude of his! Once again, I realized my parents did do a terrific job. I possessed the fortitude to restrain from attacking him. One day, somehow, I intended to give him a piece of my mind about his cavalier treatment. With or without a blunt instrument.

Chapter 7
November 1994

It didn't take me long to find out that working in the hotel industry, or rather, working at the Supreme Superior Hotel meant long hours. Hey, I wasn't always the swiftest bulb in the garden. I expected long workdays in the banking industry. To the contrary, I never anticipated it in hospitality services, and not at the Supreme Superior. It wasn't like this over at the Waldorf.

The word "hospitality" evokes a sense of play, entertainment and friendliness, not work. Not grueling, long, tedious, backbreaking, non–overtime payment due to exemption hours work. Although my scheduled hours were from 8:30 a.m. until 5:30 p.m., I usually left several hours later due to some crisis, like having to find David Copperfield's disappearing bathrobes. Something always cropped up that prohibited me from stepping over the threshold of the exit.

My first two months at the Supreme Superior would be equivalent to ten years of problem–solving if measured by levels of aggravation. I felt thrust into this thankless role due to circumstance. It goes to show: life at the Supreme Superior was a true roller–coaster, seat–of–the–pants management style. It was never dull.

I was the face that most people interacted with as the representative of the General Manager. They had no choice since Mr. Ganiff insisted that the doors to his office be firmly shut. Typically, most situations sucked the marrow out of my bones.

As the de facto Resident Manager, I soothed our guests' egos after confrontations with the Front Desk, held their hands during reports of clothes destroyed by dry cleaning, or patted them on the back when they lost keys or broke lamps. As if I had a choice. Everyone, it seemed, was unwilling to make a stand, let alone to take responsibility. Someone had to stop the buck.

One prime example was the hotel's room service. Every time a complaint came in, Kenin, in charge of room service dining, would magically disappear. And the remaining staff either didn't answer the phones or just as magically lost their ability to converse in English. To our guests, the situation was maddening.

Sometimes the business center would close earlier than their advertised hours, causing complaints among certain Sublime hotel guests who needed access to printers, copiers and fax machines. And didn't want to pay the exorbitant fee for using the same equipment we had provided for them in their suites, once they found out what we were up to. Where was Murlise Mutt? Nowhere to be found.

This is where I came in. "Mighty Mite," the champion of the underdog. More power than a locomotive. Oh well, I grew heady there making final decisions knowing my word became law because nobody, nobody had the balls to challenge my verdicts. Doing so would've required someone to step up to the plate and explain why I made the decision in the first place.

During this probationary period, Mr. Ganiff scrutinized me like a hawk. I got the feeling that he thought I had lied about my former career. Perhaps believed that I was more subordinate than admitted. I was suspicious that Djorak had something to do with this. She was, after all, the master of behind–the–scenes manipulation. A few pejorative comments from those clever lips scattered here and there like poisonous pellets…

Mr. Ganiff wanted to thoroughly understand every decision I made such as why I selected certain mail and/or telephone messages to filter from him. Such elevated tasks for a former executive with an MBA. Oftentimes, he subjected me to a grilling the likes of which I had never experienced, not even under cross–examination from a defense attorney when I sued my landlord for not providing sufficient heat and other amenities. On the positive side, I enjoyed the comedy of watching my boss get inundated with junk.

Every morning, prior to the staff meeting, Mr. Ganiff would lift from his conference table the tower of Pisa composed of papers, envelopes, brochures and lord–knows–what else and drop it on the floor next to his desk. At the conclusion of each daily meeting, he would heave his bulk over the side of his chair to pick up the pile. Then he'd toss the stack back on top of the table to the accompaniment of his chorus of "Damn, sonofabitch, goddamns." Invariably, a paper or two would cause deep cuts—everyone knows how much those suckers bleed and sting—accounting for the bandages in his office that he wore regularly on his fingers.

This daily exercise came to an abrupt conclusion one morning when I heard a distinctive thunk behind closed doors and nothing else. At the time I wasn't too concerned; I was preoccupied with the faxes. Reservations and the Gang of Three clamored for that day's completed *New York Times* crossword puzzle. After a while, though, the unusually lengthened silence bothered me. So I intercommed. He didn't respond. Then I got worried. I tried the doorknob but the door didn't budge.

I raced to my phone and called Big Guy who galloped to the rescue, direct from the Lobby.

He grasped the doorknob in his meaty palm and twisted it a few times. Haplessly, he shrugged. "Oh, I can't open this. It's bolted from the inside!"

I thwacked my forehead with the side of my hand. "Duh, Big Guy. I know that already. Any other ideas?"

He stood there in pause mode and, without warning, turned so that his massive side pressed against the door. He shouted over his shoulder, "At the count of three, I'm going in!"

"Wait a second, Big Guy!" I shouted back, "can't you see that that door is mirrored? You're gonna kill yourself."

BeeBee entered the office. "What are you two doing?" she asked with her gravelly voice, "I can hear you down the hall!"

"Something's happened to Mr. Ganiff. I heard a thud in there and he's not answering the phones. The door is bolted from inside," I explained.

"So?" she responded, "I know a way to get in." She removed the unlit cigarette from behind her right ear, kicked off her shoes and then unlocked the windows behind my desk.

I got very nervous. "BeeBee, are you sure you know what you're doing?"

She opened one of the windows and said, "You can take da girl out of da Bronx but you can't take da Gun Hill Projects outta da girl."

I turned around to Big Guy who leered with an open–mouth at BeeBee, saliva collecting at the corners. "Aren't you going to stop her? We're like forty feet off the ground!"

"I never even thought about that!" he shrugged.

"The height?" I asked.

"No, going out the window!"

Once again I thwacked the side of my head, this time with the palm of my hand. *Just what I need. Two dead colleagues.*

BeeBee hiked her skirt upwards, revealing her thighs. No longer impeded by the tight fabric, her right leg swung effortlessly over the windowsill. Big Guy emitted a strangled yelp. I whipped around to face him and noticed that he was enthralled, enraptured, and when I accidentally looked down, engorged as well. Repulsed, I turned back to BeeBee who balanced her body against the window frame. She sought the two–inch ledge with her big toe. Girding herself with both arms on the sill, she announced, "All right, guys, I'm almost—" and practically jettisoned out the window head–first when the shout came from behind us.

"What the hell is going on here?"

The three of us turned as one to see Mr. Ganiff hunched over, his breast pocket hanky askew. His left eye, formerly staring at his nose, now stared at the upper quadrant of his eyelid. His mustache resembled the peaks and troughs of the stock market. BeeBee regained her equilibrium and withdrew her leg from the ledge. With haste, she slammed the window shut.

"Are you okay, sir?" BeeBee asked in her most concerned voice.

Mr. Ganiff tried hard to conceal a pained expression that flitted across his face. He ignored BeeBee's question. In a low voice he said to me, "Kindly set up an appointment with a chiropractor."

"O–kay. Which one, sir?"

"Does it matter? Anyone! I need someone now. Believe I herniated my disc. Damn junk mail!"

Soon thereafter, Mr. Ganiff made his first baby step toward allowing me to operate without the needless thumbscrews. He let me get rid of the amassed paperwork. At the beginning of this onerous task, I collected all the spilled paper spread on the floor and conference table from Mr. Ganiff's accident. Then I spent two hours retrieving papers and files wedged under his desk, hidden on the bottom of his credenza unit, squirreled away in his bookcase. Despite the bundles of documentation in his office, Mr. Ganiff did not like paper. He dithered when it came to signing his name. He had dog–eared and yellowed proposals. Contracts and correspondence that he had never addressed. I was dumbfounded as to how he managed to stay on top of things.

With this collective mass, I pinched a few dozen manila folders off of BeeBee's desk and divided the topics into a few selected headings reflecting business at hand:

★ Current Projects

★ The Three–Hotels–in–One Concept

★ Upgrades

★ Construction

★ Televisions

★ Employee Reviews

★ Guest Complaints

★ 949A West 53rd Street Legal Documentation (complete with coffee mug stains)

Within hours, I separated all his mail. Out of sheer boredom, I wrote letters replying to some of the older correspondence, relying on native intelligence and judgment. I had peace and quiet to knock this work out because Mr. Ganiff was at the chiropractor when I typed my replies.

One particular letter stood out from the other complaints. The tonal quality was one step short of shrieking hysterics, like a Dominic Dunne novel, though penned by one very irate Donald Silverberg who wanted a full reimbursement for his weekend package.

From time to time, the Supreme Superior hosted special package deals to spur 100% occupancy on those otherwise slow weekends. These packages featured Standard suites at a corporate rate and included one complimentary *Bliss* Brunch. The *Bliss* Brunch was the best deal in town, according to Mr. Ganiff and the Staggerts guide.

Sunday mornings. The Penthouse Floor. For $50 per person, one could eat until one burst. There were three thirty–foot tables shoved against three walls, filled with a cornucopia of breakfast delights. Included in the brunch were free mai–tais, coffee, tea and as many servings a human could consume at one seating of eggs, pancakes, roast beef, salads, chicken and shrimp. Then we have the pastry table.

The pastry chef at the Supreme Superior, a graduate of the FBI, was excellent. So much so that other high–star hotels including the Waldorf–Astoria sent their pastry chefs to him for training. His cream puffs were legendary. His chocolates induced orgasms. At the *Bliss* Brunch, people clawed their way to the pastries, placing mounds of delights on their dishes, tempting the gods of diabetes.

Mr. Silverberg did not complain about his *Bliss* Brunch. In fact, he committed the capital crime of swine–out. He simply felt that he should not pay for his weekend and backed that up with the following excerpt from his letter:

"I went to the Lobby to initially discuss with the front desk clerk that my room service delivery was slow and the clerk in question, Sherwin, put his hands on his hips and physically challenged me. He didn't offer any assistance whatsoever and I felt intimidated by his posturing and forceful nature.

Later that day, my wife and I ventured to the Lobby to discuss one more time with the front desk not only cold food from a late room service delivery but to complain about Sherwin's attitude and guess who was the only clerk there? Sherwin. He also raised his voice to my wife. Then, when we returned to the room, we could not relax because the volume from both television sets was so loud that we couldn't watch our favorite programs and my wife complained about headaches from the sound."

I knew that there weren't any serious transgressions going on. However, a complaint was a complaint. I wanted to explore the validity to what this dissatisfied client wrote. It also gave me an excuse to flex those executive office strings everyone else pulled.

I first called Murlise to investigate Mr. Silverberg's allegations. The Reservations area was set up to track all clients' actions at the hotel through computer logs. Everything was documented at the Supreme Superior. Even guest comments to the staff were routinely diarized into the major computer log, a standard operating procedure. The hotel was state–of–the–art Big Brother.

The keys to each room were computerized. Security had logs of exits/ entrances of every suite and actively monitored the housekeeping staff. Each corridor had trained cameras; live films were stored for three months before reuse. Employees had to go through a rear security station from the same company that manufactured those in London's Heathrow airport. We checked in and out by computerized badges. All staff handbags were emptied every evening before departure. Sadly, in spite of the security measures, most of the staff exited the hotel through the main Lobby, handbags bursting with Supreme Superior memorabilia and products that could easily be removed by portable, battery–operated drills.

"Ah, Silverberg. There he is!" Murlise accessed the files. "Let's see, nothing too unusual. Sherwin did notate in the computer that the man screamed at him a few times because he felt subjected to slow turnaround for room service delivery.

Nothing unusual about that. The screaming, that is." She sighed. "Sherwin is the Front Desk lightening rod for all guest grievances."

"Silverberg claimed that Sherwin put his hands on his hips and physically challenged him."

Incredulous, Murlise burst out into laughter, "Sherwin?"

"Oh, it gets better, Murlise. He wrote that Sherwin has a forceful nature."

Murlise snorted in unbridled mirth, "Is this man on drugs?"

I joined her in merriment. Sherwin was one of the most laid back individuals I ever met. Tall, rail thin and intimidating perhaps to a baby bamboo plant. I knew that on this count the client exaggerated. Yes, Virginia, clients do lie sometimes. I let Murlise know my plan of action. "I'll follow up with the in–suite dining area to make sure our guest isn't stretching the truth about turnaround for a freebee."

Murlise continued to read the computer comments. "Hold on a sec, Linda. Mr. Silverberg did complain about the volume of the televisions in his room." This was a confirmation of sorts since that particular Standard suite was used as a test site (without the guests' knowledge nor consent) whereby the hotel monitored guest reactions toward the new 35–inch screen prototype television sets. The results were measured by the incidence of complaint phone calls to the front desk—a truly viable statistical methodology.

She volunteered to assist. "I'm gonna call Edwing in Concierge to see if he had any dealings with this guest on a one–to–one basis or if anything else occurred."

I next called Joe Smith. "Joe, I have a complaint here about room service from a Donald Silverberg."

"Yes?" Joe responded, "Linda, why are you calling me? I'm the head of the department. I'm not who you should contact. Let me have Kenin, the in–suite dining guy get back to you." Right after he hung up on me, an incredibly handsome man knocked on my office doorframe.

"May I help you?" I asked, stunned to find this Adonis in my doorway.

"Hi, I'm Kenin, head of in–suite dining," he said.

I couldn't stop staring at him. Between his sculpted body and sculpted face, I was in love!

"Hell–o, Miss Linda?" his voice broke through my reveries, "Joe sent me up here?" Of all things, this incredibly gorgeous, macho man performed this strange flick of his wrist! Something told me that we didn't belong to the same church... alas.

"Oh, hi there, Kenin. Yeah, I'm conducting an investigation on a guest. Just need to know what he ate, turnaround time for delivery, if anything happened, you know? Here are the particulars." I wrote down all the details of the Silverberg case and he came over to my desk to take the piece of paper.

"Another angry customer, eh? Shit, it seems like everyone's pissed off around here these days! Okay, I'll get back to you pronto." With the piece of paper held aloft in his hand, he sashayed out.

By 2:00 p.m., I had three separate files on my desk from the various departments. According to the feedback received, the Sherwin episode was easily discounted. The accusation about cold food/late delivery of in–service dining was discounted as well. During that particular weekend, the hotel had lower than normal occupancy and turnaround room service time was unparalleled. There was one valid complaint that stood out—the prototype 35–inch televisions. Front desk reported that Mr. Silverberg stated that there existed two workable volumes: mute and deafening. Armed with this ammunition, I wrote a sample letter for Mr. Ganiff to review:

"Dear Mr. Silverberg:

We thank you for contacting us with your comments during your recent stay at The Supreme Superior Hotel. In that vein, we are conducting an investigation on the volume of the televisions in your suite and apologize for any inconvenience that it may have caused you. Once again, we appreciate your taking the time to inform us of this situation so we may continue to provide quality service."

Mr. Ganiff crowed in delight when he beheld his barren desk. He speedily went through the correspondence in his in–box, signing off on certain letters, changing others to reflect his distinctive and personal style... until he came across Mr. Silverberg's letter and my response. Peering at me, he asked, "What's this all about? What the hell were you thinking?"

I stared right into his right eye. "Mr. Ganiff, I responded to his complaints, thanked him for notifying us of his difficulties and apologized for his inconvenience. Common decency, right?" We locked gazes. Savagely, Mr. Ganiff ripped up my written reply and tossed it on the floor. I stood there, stunned.

"Linda, how long have I been in this business?"

I shrugged, too much in shock to respond even if I had the answer.

"Thirty–five years, okay? I've been dealing with these lunatics way before you were born."

"Mr. Ganiff, with all due respect, I was just—"

"I know what you were doing. Screw 'em!" He pounded his desk to further drive home his point. "The way to deal with 'em is—don't respond. Not worth our time. He'll go away. All of them eventually do if you ignore them."

I couldn't believe what I had just heard. Rather I could believe what I heard although I couldn't fathom why this leader in hospitality was vehement in his non–solicitous outlook. The last time I looked in my Merriam–Webster dictionary, the definition of hospitality meant the cordial and generous treatment of guests. Yet, the word after "hospitality" in the dictionary is "hospitalization."

What inferences can one draw from that?

I remained frozen in place, staring at the shredded letter on the carpet. Mr. Ganiff's condescending attitude and his nonchalance in expressing to me those very same sentiments threw me off balance.

Okay, I considered in retrospect, *that particular letter wasn't exactly egregious. I did manage, though, to clear an avalanche of paper off of his desk. And this is how he thanks me? The same way he expresses his regard for his clientele…*

I had a gut feeling that Mr. Ganiff's thirty–five years should've taught him a thing or two. Nevertheless, I was on the job a little over two months. Unlike my position at the Waldorf, here I interacted with the guests. If a lack of common courtesy was the right way to conduct business in the "hospitality" industry, well, I suppose I had a lot to relearn about this particular field. Now, about trusting that dictionary…

"Oh, Linda, one more thing. Do me a favor and leave my filing system well enough alone. If I want you going through my paperwork, I'll be sure to ask. Don't forget to shut my door on your way out!"

Chapter 8

As the story went, Mr. Ganiff decided around two years earlier that the hotel had to upgrade its 25–inch screen televisions to 35–inch sets for both living rooms and bedrooms. Seebok was put in charge of the project.

It took more than a year of research and product review. Seebok utilized all the skills honed by majoring in Hotel Management at Cornell. According to Mr. Ganiff's innuendos, Seebok had honed quite a few skills not taught at Cornell. From time to time, I would find Mr. Ganiff lurking in my personal office space after having emerged from a protracted tête–à–tête with the subject in question. "Damn Seebok! I guess they were right when they said that imitation is a form of flattery." Standing in front of my desk, he flashed his superficial smile while striking against his pants leg a manila folder containing proposals for lord–knows–what.

Judging from the papers that I unearthed in Mr. Ganiff's office during my initial fumigation, Seebok interviewed five commercial television distributors (commercial televisions proved more durable than the retail ones sold at discount outlets). He came up with their price lists representing the purchase of fifteen–hundred commercial television sets, including all executive offices, the Health Club as well as Mr. Ganiff's personal suite on the 44th floor.

This phase of the project required several months of intense meetings. By perusing the receipts found in an unmarked manila envelope, I deduced that Seebok hosted furtive luncheons at *Bliss*, and umpteen business trips to domestic manufacturing facilities. Piles of petty cash vouchers revealed business expenses for drinks at various trendy bars including Score's, a local strip club. The paper trail indicated that one of the distributors, Deviant Enterprises, had put in a bid far lower than its competitors.

During one of Mr. Ganiff's thankfully short–winded sessions of the "Anal Monologues" (my personal nickname for those repetitive and long–winded homilies), he described the seesawing involved in such a process. "Seebok and I, we held all these meetings interviewing representatives from Deviant. Then we met with Mr. Hitsuhana who had to write a report to the parent company, since this was a huge capital expenditure. We're talking in excess of a million bucks." He held his left index finger aloft in the air for emphasis. "Then finally, after months of wrangling, I signed the contract and the check for the down payment. You know what I always say: An effective manager never makes his mind up immediately."

The details of delivery, installation and removal of the old television sets to the original distributor for some sort of refund were left in Seebok's capable hands.

Six months later, the delivery arrived... much to my chagrin.

The call came from the loading dock. It was Karen from Security.

"Uh, Linda, we have a slight problem down here. Do you happen to know where Seebok is?" yelled Karen over the din of shouting.

"Isn't he in his office?" I asked. Seebok's office was one floor above, located between the Gang of Three and Finance.

"We sent Johnny up there. He reported that Seebok's office was locked and no one answered from inside. We've been phoning him but his voicemail is on and we've had him paged for the past half hour."

Seebok had a history of disappearing. It hadn't affected me personally before now.

"Well, what's the problem down there, Karen? Something I can help with?"

"Linda, it's insane! There's like sixteen trucks down here unloading." Karen quieted for a moment. "I'm looking at the invoice they just gave me. It seems we ordered fifteen–hundred televisions. It can't possibly be that many. No fucking way!"

I thought back to this morning's staff meeting. Seebok was there. He did not specify any scheduled delivery. Instead, his conversation centered on his all–expenses paid honeymoon at the Sands Hotel in San Juan. Come to think of it, that had been his sole topic since I joined the hotel. Guess it never got old.

"Hold on a sec, Karen. Let me get Mr. Ganiff on the line."

With reluctance, I placed the phone on hold and tapped at Mr. Ganiff's office door. The door unbolted and swung inward. I peered in and found him seated behind his desk. He was alone. *How does he do that,* I wondered. *How does he manage to bolt and unbolt that door, let alone open and close it, when he is nowhere physically near it?*

"Mr. Ganiff, we have a situation down at the loading dock. The new televisions are being delivered."

"You mean to tell me that no one can handle it without constantly interrupting me?" Mr. Ganiff glared at me from his piercing right eye. "How am I expected to run this hotel when no one here knows what to do?" He stroked his mustache. "Get Seebok," he commanded.

"Well, sir, Karen from Security already sent people to his office and they've been paging him for half an hour. He's nowhere to be found."

Mr. Ganiff groaned and snatched his phone receiver with disgust. Summoning the utmost decorum, he spoke, "Ganiff here. I understand there's a problem down there. Something about the television delivery. Can you please tell me who scheduled today's delivery?" He listened to Karen, then gaped at me. "Wait, hold on. They can't put anything in the loading dock today. Isn't it Baldwin Laundry Day?"

Baldwin Laundry was the laundry and valet contractor service that picked up and delivered the hotel sheets, towels and linens every Friday. Housekeeping usually hauled its dirty and used ones to the loading dock the day before.

"Miss Karen, wait a sec." Mr. Ganiff pulled the receiver away from his ear and scowled at me. "Get me Big Guy, Wapiti, Cappy and Mutt in here pronto!"

I had the operators page the fearless foursome to urgently report to

Mr. Ganiff's office. Almost instantly, all four converged in front of my desk.

"What gives?" Big Guy asked me amid the group and subsequently murmured, "I was in the middle of oxtail stew. Better be important."

I was about to answer when Mr. Ganiff bellowed from his office, "Get in here now. All of you. Linda, you too."

The five of us stepped inside single file. When everyone stood at attention, Mr. Ganiff, seated, deployed the following tactics: "Listen to me carefully 'cause I do not want to repeat myself. Big Guy, Miss Wapiti, get as many people off their shifts as fast as possible and get those televisions out of that loading dock. Can anyone suggest where we can store them?"

Cappy whined, "Mr. Ganiff, Mr. Ganiff, we don't have many storage rooms."

Murlise looked at Cappy with raised eyebrows. "What about that empty apartment building?"

I should point out that before the construction of what was currently known as the Supreme Superior Hotel, the original developer attempted numerous times to bulldoze a small five story walk–up apartment building. For some unspecified reason, the former landlord of that building could not buy out a little old lady who lived in a studio apartment on the top floor. Her plight of imminent eviction had brought screaming headlines to the three city newspapers for months. As a result, the current hotel building was built around and on top of the apartment building. Therefore, the Supreme Superior became landlord de facto to this little old lady. Since Mr. Ganiff never bothered with any paperwork, she never paid rent. She also had passed away three years earlier.

"Great idea, Murlise. I should've thought of that." He stroked his mustache for emphasis. "Big Guy, coordinate your people to keep tabs on the televisions. Count them. We paid for fifteen hundred and not one less. Oh, and you, Miss Wapiti and Murlise will coordinate the dispersal of the televisions. Start from the top of the building and work your way down."

Ms. Wapiti cleared her throat for effect. "Mr. Ganiff, I'm under the impression that there are no elevators in that building."

Mr. Ganiff stared at her impassively.

"Those televisions aren't exactly light. Could present a problem with my staff since most of the men are... how would you say... small, like me. I don't think they can—"

"Hear me out, Miss Wapiti. I don't have time for this now. If your people want to continue working in this hotel, they will do as we tell them. Capisce?"

Staring down at her shoes, Ms. Wapiti muttered, "Yes, sir."

"Fine. Okay, so what are you waiting for? Go!"

Soon, a flurry of activity similar to a stirred hornet's nest descended around the hotel. Approximately sixty men converged upon the loading dock. The new televisions were encased in oversized, padded cartons. A few were dropped off on the docking bay, vying for space with the soiled linens. Others were spilled pell–mell onto the sidewalk and partly into the street. The majority of cartons were stacked in one lane. Strangely enough, it resembled the Great Wall of China from pictures taken aboard the MIR space station. Cars and trucks crawled at a snail's pace in the densest traffic congestion on one of the most traveled blocks in midtown Manhattan. The bleating and blasting horns echoed in the loading dock. It was deafening. I couldn't hear myself think.

The entrance to the old, abandoned apartment building was some forty feet down the street from the rear access to the hotel where I witnessed Big Guy supervising the logistics.

"Hey you! Yeah you!" Big Guy shouted at one of the housekeeping staff.

The man stopped short like a deer caught in headlights.

"Hey, pick this carton up now. Yeah, you!" Big Guy swung twenty degrees west. "You too!" he shouted at another man who pointed to his chest while mouthing "moi?"

The two small men struggled to pick up the ends of the bulky carton. At last, they succeeded, with sweat streaming down their faces and corded muscles bulging in their forearms.

"Now, I want you two to go there to that door," Big Guy gestured with a massive thumb to the entrance.

Big Guy created a relay line of male workers from the loading dock to the apartment building. It would've been preposterous if it weren't so distressing to watch these people staggering under the weight of the cumbersome cartons. This was labor intensive.

Johnny from Security posed as sentry at the doorway to the former dwelling. He waited for the struggling men to arrive. His pleasant task was to order the men to walk up to the top floor and dispose of the TVs in the first room to the right. Once they filled that room, they could begin the process in the other rooms on that floor. Once all those rooms were filled, they could next proceed with the rooms on the second highest floor. And so on and so on. *How will they ever manage with those huge cartons?* I wondered as I made my way into the foyer.

Inside, the cacophony from the forty–odd male housekeeping staff moving the televisions—each weighing over two hundred pounds—up five flights of rickety steps was ear–splitting. Including the complaints shouted at random in machine–gun Tagalog, Bangla and Spanish. Amazingly, everyone understood each other. Before any time elapsed, the hallways of the vacant building echoed with voices, shouts and whistles to alert those coming down the narrow steps to pay attention to the ones coming up.

Without warning, a chilling scream reverberated in the fifth floor hallway.

It came from a tall Caucasian man in his early forties. He had stepped out of an unoccupied apartment on that floor and bolted into the stairwell. For a moment, he studied the peculiar scene surrounding him, and then shrieked this time in verbiage, "What the hell? What's with all the noise? What are you people doing in my home?" His voice ricocheted all the way down to the foyer entrance.

What the fuck? I thought to myself when I realized what was going on. *A resident in this abandoned building? Wasn't this place uninhabited?*

Several of the frightened housekeepers scattered onto the fifth floor hallway. The unexpected resident chased after them, halting the television relay race.

Out of curiosity, I pushed my way onto the crowded stairwell. I tried to shove past the flustered staff and their heavy cartons. It was of no use.

Between the fourth and fifth floor landings, one of the housekeepers—straining to hold a television set—yelled back at the man in Tagalog. Another hurled invectives in his native language. In a matter of moments, workers on the top two flights joined in the verbal fracas. The surprised man persisted in confronting the staff on the landing. I got a glimpse. The buffoon stood in a pair of overalls and had slung over his shoulder a white canvas bag with a yoga mat rolled inside. He bore a slight resemblance to the oft–referenced great white hunter pacifying the tribes at Subic Bay, or was that at Nouakchott?

Behind the front line of screaming housekeepers, twenty others pulled out wads of singles to bet on the outcome. Several of the more adventurous Supreme Superior staff put the cartons down where they stood on the stairwells. Time for their smoke break. It was also time to shove my way back outside... if only I could.

While maneuvering around the narrow maze of bodies and boxes, I pictured Big Guy and his security team outside, scratching their heads in puzzlement. With anyone else, it would've registered by now that people entered but no one came out. Reminding me of that slogan from the old roach motel television commercials, "they check in but they don't check out." *So, what were they waiting for?*

Back upstairs, the great and mighty, albeit dim–witted hunter must've become cognizant that he was one versus many. That, and the fact that none of the box–carrying invaders seemed to speak or comprehend a word of English. At least in his presence. His voice upped an octave or three when he yelled, "Get the hell out of here, all of you! Get out now or I'm calling the cops!" He beat a hasty and cowardly retreat into his apartment and promptly slammed the door.

A shoving match of another kind soon erupted in the corridor. It initially began between two colleagues fighting over the interpretation of the outcome of their bets. Given the tight space, it was only a matter of time before their surrounding co-workers got involved through an accidental cuff or two to the head. Fists flailed and money flew, as did some of the carefully packed televisions.

I dropped to my knees to avoid the barrage of punches and mayhem and crawled between legs to descend the stairwell. The foyer wasn't much better. It took me several frantic minutes, squeezing between the crowds and cartons until I reached the front door. Once outside, I drew in a deep breath of fresh air. I felt lucky to have escaped with my life, or at least without losing my earrings. Miraculously, there were no runs in my pantyhose.

Big Guy stood on the sidewalk, hands on hips, facing the traffic in front of the hotel loading dock. The big dolt was bragging to the frustrated motorists stuck in the traffic jam about how well he was handling the situation. I ran up to him and tapped him on the back. He whirled around. "Linda, where are all my little helpers? What's happening in there?"

"Shit! It's total chaos. You gotta do something or someone's gonna get killed! I nearly got trampled."

Big Guy sensed my urgency because he took off running. He reached the apartment building and opened the door. The din inside was louder than the honking traffic. He entered, swinging the door closed behind him, not before freeing quite a few chicken feathers in a puff of air.

I waited for several minutes at the curb. No one came out. Then, I took a few mincing steps toward the apartment building. Suddenly, Big Guy toppled out with a loud thud. He had two flailing housekeeping staff under his right arm, three under his left and one snapping at the five of them while holding onto Big Guy's uniform shirt. Without a break, they shouted, grasped and punched each other. Big Guy sought to pry them off of his body. Each time one man ducked a punch, Big Guy got walloped. The door popped open again and several split and dented cartons tumbled out, styrofoam pellets pouring and floating from the boxes.

Fisticuffs were not my forte. Therefore, helping Big Guy was out of the question. Instead, I stood at the corner yelling "Yoo–hoo" like a damsel in distress, signaling with a yellow paper hanky. It didn't take long to summon the attention of the neighborhood police car parked down the street. Three of New York's finest jumped out of the sedan and raced over to the scrum. The police peeled the men from under Big Guy's arms and back and placed handcuffs on their wrists.

Within minutes, a whole squadron of flashing lights arrived. Four backup officers entered the apartment house with their pistols drawn. Moments later, a cascade of Supreme Superior workers ran into the arms of the law stationed on the sidewalk. They didn't stand a chance.

So much for our housekeeping staff! I thought.

Upstairs, in the executive office, I took a few minutes to catch my breath and examine the scrapes on the palms of my hands. Luckily, no nail breakage. Clearly, Mr. Ganiff had been advised about the incident outside. My suspicions were confirmed when he burst out of his office, gnashing his teeth in a pique of rage.

"Linda. Call Seebok. Page that imbecile! This isn't naptime. We need to figure out what the hell he's up to!"

Over the past two hours, I hadn't been able to find BeeBee either. The jutting alcove wall across the hall sliced off a corner view of BeeBee's desk. Situated behind her desk was the entrance to the telephone department where she oftentimes snuck in, hiding amongst the operators. This time she didn't hole up in there. I sniffed a whiff of stale cigarette smoke signaling her arrival. She then waltzed in.

"BeeBee, there you are," I ran up to her. "Where've you been all afternoon? Do you have any clue what's been going on downstairs?"

BeeBee shrugged and flashed me an oblivious tar–stained smile. She stepped past me. "Cigarette break," she murmured in a low, scratchy voice. "Ms. Djorak and I, we had a few things to go over and…" Her voice trailed off.

Once again, BeeBee would be no help at all. At least she was back in the office, enabling me to scamper back down to deal with the ongoing crisis.

"Watch the phones," I shouted as I raced out of the room, "and page Seebok until he answers."

Every floor in the Supreme Superior had passages for staff elevators and employee stairwells. I headed down to subbasement No. 2 where the employee cafeteria was located. Cookie's best friend, Fred, had recently been hired as chef for the employees. Even on a large budget, for some reason the food served was either two–day old banquet leftovers or oxtail stew. In the confusion of today's television delivery, the cafeteria's menu was the least of my concerns.

I entered the glass–enclosed room for smokers, behind the cafeteria. Within moments, I spotted a heavy–set woman with shorn steel gray hair wearing a blue uniform. She sat at one of the pre–fab tables surrounded by several walkie-talkies blaring and droning. The volume was turned way down.

"Oh, hi, you must be Karen from Security. I'm Linda."

She motioned for me to sit across from her.

"Whew, Linda, you have no idea of the madness going on down there." Karen pointed to a pack of Marlboros and lit one up. "There's this mountain of TV sets blocking the loading dock. Been there for hours."

"Still?" I asked, though I wasn't surprised that the situation remained unresolved.

"Yeah." Karen took a drag of her cigarette, then tossed one in my direction. I readily snatched it, eager to smoke my first one since I graduated from university. She continued, "The Baldwin Laundry folks are really pissed about it. Their people are dropping off this week's linens through the Lobby which is pissing off the check–in clerks and bellhops not to mention the doormen! Everything's screwed up today. Now a riot team of cops are outside trying to sort out the mess."

I reached for a lighter and with expertise lit the cigarette. "The whole thing sucks," I said before inhaling. After a brief puff, I continued, "It's hardly surprising, given what I've seen so far. This place can make anyone crazy. Sheer insanity is what goes on here." I enjoyed the taste and flavor and wondered why I had given up this particular vice.

Karen leaned forward and whispered, "You know what you need?"

I looked up.

"A good woman." She winked at me.

I didn't foresee that one. I emitted a nervous laugh. "Karen, I'm straight."

She recoiled with embarrassment. "I know, Linda, you're cool. You're also pretty when you're stressed out like this. Figured I'd at least ask."

The emergency meeting took place at four o'clock in the afternoon. We all huddled in Mr. Ganiff's office. He was in rare form, pacing his office, shrieking at a black and blued Big Guy while tugging at the ends of his mustache. Subdued, Big Guy folded his hands in his lap and hunched over, trying to suppress his trembling.

"Are you a moron?" Mr. Ganiff thundered at him, "twenty–seven of our housekeeping staff are in jail. Twenty–seven! Lord knows how many of them are illegal aliens!" He whirled around to Ms. Djorak, planted like a gargoyle.

"Get them out. Do whatever you can. How the hell are we supposed to make the beds with a third of our daytime housekeeping arrested?"

Murlise Mutt poked her head into the office. "Mr. Ganiff, I thought I'd let you know, we still have around 800 televisions to go. For now, they're off the sidewalk. Oh, and Baldwin Laundry, they're now unloading the hotel's linens and towels on the sidewalk. We're gonna need some help getting them inside."

Right behind her, Seebok sheepishly walked in, a smug look spread over his reptilian face. "Hi boss."

"Seebok, where the fuck were you?"

"You didn't get the message?"

"What message?"

"That my wife fainted on Lexington Avenue. They took her to the hospital."

Everyone stared at Mr. Ganiff for a signal as to how to proceed. Mr. Ganiff lost control of his facial muscles. We followed the progression of the slight twitch of his left eye develop into a full–blown spasm. It rolled vertically while staring at his proboscis. I even detected a puff of smoke escape from his ears.

"Don't worry, she'll be all right." Impervious to the exchange of looks around him, Seebok continued, "Some pedestrian called EMT by mobile phone. She's home now, resting quietly."

Mr. Ganiff sat down. "All right. Could everybody leave the room except for Seebok and Miss Djorak? Now? Out!"

The crowd piled into my adjacent office. Ms. Djorak closed and bolted the door behind us. While everyone queued up to leave the General Manager's office, a nondescript, slender, balding man slipped in. He took a seat on my corner chair and propped open the *Daily Post*. Before I could open my mouth, Doreen came rushing in.

"Ith Mithter Ganiff in there?" she indicated with a toss of her head at the closed doors.

"Yes, Doreen, but he's in conference."

"With who?"

"Well, that's private, Doreen."

"I have to thee him. Now!"

"Is there something I can do for you? He's quite busy at the moment."

Doreen narrowed her eyes into slits and considered her plight. She calculated her access to Mr. Ganiff and decided right there to have me as an ally.

"Here," she thrust a batch of papers at me. "We're hafing problemth with rethervationth. One of my corporateth couldn't book any Thublime thuiteth becauth of Murlithe'th people."

I glanced at the papers. "Okay, let me review it and give it to Mr. Ganiff when he gets out."

"How long do you think he'll be in there?"

"Oh, I don't know. Could be a while. He's got a mess on his hands."

Rather than waiting, she spun on her heels and marched out.

I placed the batch of papers on the edge of my desk. The nondescript man was still there reading the newspaper. "May I help you?"

He gazed up at me and smiled, displaying incisors a Doberman would envy. "No thanks, I'm perfectly all right."

"Do you know where you are?"

He nodded and flipped another page.

"Excuse me, sir, may I have your name?"

"Certainly," he responded without looking up, "it's Keith Robenstine."

"Um, okay. Mr. Robenstine, do you have any business here?"

"Yes I do, sweetie. I'm an old pal of Mr. Ganiff's. You don't have to announce me. When he's through with Seebok and Djorak, I'll just poke my head in."

The thought flashed across my mind: *How did he know who was in that room?* Well, he certainly acted like a Ganiff friend. I proceeded to wade my way through

the three–foot stack of mail that BeeBee had dumped on my desk earlier.
Could this be intentional or was this slack office etiquette? Or even a combination
of the two? I couldn't determine because of the very thin line of distinction.

While I separated junk from correspondence, the door to Mr. Ganiff's office
unbolted and Ms. Djorak strutted out with all the ease and flair of a urinating rhino.
She spotted Keith and greeted him cordially. A few seconds later Seebok emerged
with a slight smile spread across his meandrous lips. Once again, he absconded
from another predicament unscathed. "How" was the operative question.

Keith Robenstine, in a twinkling of an eye, stood up and bolted toward
Mr. Ganiff's door. Before I could get up and body–block him, Keith dashed inside.

"Well, hello, Mr. Robenstine," said Mr. Ganiff with a big grin while he stood up
and shook the man's hand. Then he yelled, "Linda, please shut the door. Hold all
my calls for now."

Funny time for a social visit in the middle of a major crisis. At least with the door
closed, I could sneak out to take in the chaos unfolding downstairs. Whether
I could help restore order was another matter altogether. It was worth a shot.
Ganiff wasn't going to get his hands dirty.

Surprisingly, BeeBee was at her desk.

"You're in charge of the phones," I said.

Down in the Lobby, bedlam prevailed.

The Lobby was an impressive work of marble. It featured dark green marble
walls surrounding equally dark marble counters for the Front Desk and Concierge.
The small rectangular shape of the Lobby combined with the fifty–foot high
ceiling contributed to the claustrophobic impression of standing at the bottom of a
sacrificial well in Chichenitza.

Keeping the tradition of a small–staffed hotel—in Mr. Ganiff's low overhead
mentality—the Lobby had on hand one doorman, one bellhop and three clerks.
The place was a madhouse.

In the center of the Lobby, ready to topple, were piles of luggage stacked on
the trolleys. Standard guests waited impatiently on a conga line that meandered its
way toward the rear elevators, looping around the trolleys. The din, reverberating
in the marble interior, produced migraines. People in queue muttered in discontent.
Battles were waged at the counter. Pacing the Lobby were two security guards who
shouted into their walkie–talkies. Rory, the teatime pianist, struck a chord on the
Steinway in the adjoining bar, signaling the onset of his twenty–minute Broadway
medley. That chord ricocheted into the Lobby, adding to the commotion.

The moment I stepped foot into the Lobby, hotel–savvy guests attacked me.
Though I didn't wear a badge nor uniform, they could tell I was "one of them"
because the staff showed immediate deference. Complete strangers tugged on
my jacket and tapped me on the shoulder to garner my attention. One man in an

Armani pinstriped suit pushed his face into mine. "Hey, lady, I've been waiting two hours. Wot's it gonna take to check into this damn place?" A woman with her crying preschool daughter in tow almost yanked my left arm out of its socket. "Please," she begged, "ma petite cherie just wants to get upstairs and unpack her poupée. We've been here three hours and can't find the bellman who took our luggage." She flagged a $100 bill in my face.

Where the hell was Murlise? People were getting desperate. Something had to be done.

I recalled we kept one of those newfangled microphones for wild late night corporate karaoke parties. I considered using my two–fingered whistle or a bullhorn, but remembered something my father told me when I was a trader in a deafening trading room: "If you want people to hear you in a noisy place, talk softer and pitch your voice lower and you'll get the attention of everyone around you."

I scrambled through the crowd, hiking on top of and over scattered suitcases, right up to the piano. "Hey, Rory, quick question. Is that wireless mike here?"

He continued playing with his left hand and with his right extracted the mike from a hidden panel under the piano.

"Do you know the *Rocky Horror Show*?" I asked him.

Rory executed a perfect glissando. "Who doesn't?"

"Okay—can you play that sad Dr. Frankenfurter song?"

Rory stopped the upbeat, loud tempo of *Gotta Wash that Man Right Outta My Hair.* He opened my request with simple, quiet chords. I stood next to the piano and sang softly into the mike, "On the day I went away." I pointed the mike in Rory's direction so he could join in with the chorus, "Goooooodd byyyyye."

"Was all I had to say," I warbled, noting the continued confusion in the Lobby.

Rory chimed in, "Now–ow I." I continued with, "Want to come again and stay."

"Oh oh oh my, my," Rory hit the beat.

"Smile and that means some day." Memories of that song and my innocent childhood bared my emotions. Deep from within my soul, I poured forth, my eyes shut. I opened my suit jacket and unfastened the top two buttons of my blouse. And, in that moment, my mind blanked. Damn, I forgot the lyrics. In the seconds allotted, I had to improvise and quickly!

"I've seen blue flies

Through, ah, fire disguised

And I smell lice

I'm growing gnomes

I'm growing gnomes." Rory gave me a shot to the thigh which knocked me out of my trance. The first thing I noticed was the silence. You could hear a pin drop!

65

As usual, Dad was right. Whatever it took, I had to re–establish some order.

Rory stopped playing and I tapped the microphone. Addressing the stunned patrons in the Lobby, I spoke in a deep and sultry voice, "Ladies and Gentleman, on behalf of the Supreme Superior Hotel I wish to apologize for the delays we're experiencing this afternoon. Due to a police investigation outside, our services are running a bit behind. I promise that once everyone calms down, we will get everyone checked in and out comfortably, and without further delay. Thank you for your patience." I handed the mike over to Rory who clicked it off and closed the lid to the piano keyboard.

There was no applause. Nor cheering. Nor thanks. Glancing at the expressions on our guests' faces, I could see that my brave little speech had an impact.

I stepped back into the Lobby to assist the clerks and facilitate the checkouts. The majority of complaints were easy enough to remedy. As a consequence, the clerks moved faster. I gave the authority to the front desk to amend bills within reason. By the simple deduction of a $2.00 telephone call and approving requests for a bigger suite, I helped to restore ambiance as well as partial order.

Almost as important, I instructed the bellhops to sort out the luggage towers in the center of the room. The result was a shortened conga line and a whole lot less yelling. Within an hour the Lobby was back to normal, or whatever normal was on your typical afternoon at the Supreme Superior.

Before I could bask in my sense of accomplishment, Big Guy approached me with a playful grin on his face. Ogling down at me, he said, "Hey, Linda, good work with the microphone. By the way, nice set of pipes, never noticed before."

"Thanks," I replied with a bit of a laugh and a nervous twitch till I followed his line of vision. Bad Boy peeked down my shirt which prompted me to refasten the top two buttons. I felt compelled to defend my actions. "I don't know what came over me. At any rate, if it worked…"

"Sorry to ruin your shining moment, but the other reason I came by was to tell you that the gorgon wants to see you."

I groaned.

"She's in her office and none too friendly, I'm afraid."

"I'm afraid as well. What's it about this time?" I asked although Big Guy had already headed in the other direction en route to the main entrance.

I had to go to the back of house that led to the employee staircase. I walked down three flights and from there followed a circuitous and shadowy cement passage to Ms. Djorak's office. Well, I found BeeBee. Standing beside the monster from the deep sea.

"Aren't you supposed to be upstairs covering the phones?" I inquired with hands on my hips.

BeeBee did not respond. Instead, she snickered in my face as she strolled past me to exit the office.

"Please sit down, Linda," said Djorak without the slightest trace of sincerity.

I slid into a seat opposite her desk and crossed my legs, awaiting some criticism of my job. She never disappointed me.

"Linda, just who do you think you are? Running this place like it's your very own fiefdom!"

I did not respond to the malice emanating from this troll except for uncontrolled blinking, an attempt to withhold my fury.

Spittle formed in the corners of her liver–shaped lips while Ms. Djorak continued, "How dare you try to take over Murlise's job!"

This absurd accusation stung me. "What in the world are you talking about? I was down in the Lobby trying to help quiet things down. Do you have any idea what was going on there? Murlise was nowhere to be found. Otherwise, the Lobby wouldn't have been in such disarray." I couldn't hide my annoyance any longer.

"Listen, Missy. Let me make this clear. I don't like you. I don't appreciate your smart–ass attitude. So I'm warning you now—don't stick your nose into other people's business. I know your kind."

"My kind?" I repeated, incredulous.

"Yeah. Not too many Jews around here 'cause that's what you Jews do. You like to worm your way around, get involved in everything and before anyone can stop you, you'll run the place. I won't stand for it. The Supreme Superior won't stand for it. We're not one of those organizations that hire people like you. We don't even hire Negroes, as I'm sure you've noticed!" Through a prideful smile she added, "Out of over a thousand employees, there are only nine Negroes, and almost all are phone operators!"

Ms. Djorak's dead eyes shone with a luminous gleam that reflected insanity and a touch of dementia. She was a racist, no question about that. Perhaps even a misogynist. Either way, this was yet another troubling development in a day I couldn't wait to put behind me.

Djorak enjoyed her harangue and continued in a singsong voice, "Negroes and Jews; nothing but trouble." Then she sat up straight and said, "Since we hire other minorities, we get away without hiring you lazy, shiftless throwbacks." Ms. Djorak smirked, confident of her power. "Let me warn you, Linda. Don't play innocent with me. I know everything you say, everything you do. You happen to be lucky that Mr. Ganiff likes you so far. I'm telling you, you'd better watch your step and keep on looking out to protect his reputation, or you'll lose the only ally you've got around here. Understood?"

Oh, I understood all right. As they say or rather my mother said: "With an ally like that, who needs enemies?"

67

Chapter 9

"To top it off, that bitch is also an anti–Semite!" I laughed ruefully.

Monica, a good friend, laughed as well. We had met eons earlier when Monica was in charge of the undergraduate women's dorm where I resided as a freshman at university. She performed this harrowing task in exchange for free lodging while she wrote her doctorate thesis in music theory. But it paid off. At long last she achieved notoriety as a composer. Our relationship continued on, although she still perceived me, in spite of the intervening years, as a disciple to her mentoring.

"Well, Linda, you got yourself into some fine mess. You're surrounded by TVs all over the place, laundry piled in the streets, and targeted by a hostile warrior of the Sapphic persuasion. Or was she a neo–Nazi racist? Along with all those celebrities... what more can a woman ask for?" We giggled over a heavy–handed salad at *Bliss*, a true gourmet delight, featuring glistening gelid peas and carrots topped with orange slices.

Out of the corner of my eye, I spotted Mr. Ganiff. Leaning forward, I whispered, "Don't look up, that's Mr. Ganiff. The guy in the blue suit, heading this direction."

We both hid our faces behind a pair of tall menus, staring down at our dismal food while he strolled by. Thankfully, he didn't see me. At least he didn't come over and interrupt our meal.

Ganiff took a seat at a far table joined by Keith Robenstine and another gentleman, a short, handsome man with long, thick, black curly hair. The trio gesticulated wildly and I could overhear snatches of their discussion.

Robenstine said something to the effect of, "At least I'm not a momma's boy," to which the short man said, "at least I'm not a thief and a schmuck," while Ganiff screamed at the two of them to "shut up and act civil for once in your youthful, dysfunctional lives." Then, the short man jumped to his feet and ran out of the restaurant, cursing a blue streak. This intrusion caused a stir amongst the thirteen luncheon diners, a packed house by *Bliss* standards.

"Linda, do you really want to work here? Seems very toxic," said Monica, her face reflecting her concern.

I fidgeted with an orange slice on my salad plate. "Toxicity aside, I do find it interesting here. In a certain way, I'm learning more about people as well as about myself."

"Are you certain you don't want to go back to banking? I mean, you did pretty well there for a long time. And don't forget, you were compensated very well for those long hours with large bonuses."

"Interesting question!" I arched my eyebrows. "I don't know, I feel that it's best not to go back for the time being. At least in hospitality, the sky's the limit... I think. Right now, all I'm doing is administrative work for a killer salary. Mind you, I have very little support..." I hesitated. "You know what's weird here?"

"What isn't?" Monica asked.

"That everyone on the executive staff questioned my background. They simply can't accept that I'd leave a lucrative career in finance to work in a hotel, especially here at the Supreme Superior."

"Come now, that isn't what occurred. You didn't leave banking for hospitality!"

"Well, not really..." I said, "but close to it." I tried to ignore Monica's snicker. "Anyhow, one of the executives here, one I don't even like who's the head of this ill–conceived restaurant told me in confidence that that bitch, Djorak, circulated my resume to all senior staff."

"What the—? Cut the shit, Linda and stop changing the topic with nonsense. Why are you really here?" asked Monica.

"What do you mean?" I tossed the half–frozen peas on my plate into her butter dish with the tines of my fork. There was no avoiding the truth or holding back. This was Monica, the quintessential Geiger counter of bullshit. "I have no fucking idea. Right now, all I know is that I'm so sucked into what's going on around me that I'm losing my perspective. Dammit, right now I don't know where to go or what to do." Imploringly, I begged her for support.

She responded with a wise expression on her face, transforming into my very own personal Master Po, a Kung Fu guru on a widely acclaimed television series in the 1970's. "I get the feeling that there was more to your leaving that last job in banking than what you've been telling me."

I cleared my throat to speak. Monica interrupted me with her indicative pointing finger. "It's perfectly okay not to let me know what happened. But I know you, Linda. One thing's for sure: until you resolve whatever issues you have that made you leave GermBank, it will only come back to haunt you. In this job at the hotel or even another job in banking." Monica took a sip of water. "It's that karmic thing, where you're doomed to repeat stuff. And I suggest, my dear, that you take heed of my advice. Ignore it at your own peril."

★ ★ ★ ★ ★

Mr. Ganiff returned to his office an hour later. He waltzed by me with his usual friendliness. "Linda, I'm not to be disturbed for the rest of the day. Hold all my calls." He closed the door behind him and locked it.

Moments later, the short man from *Bliss* restaurant burst into my office, looking in all directions. "Is that piece of slime here?"

"Which piece of slime are you referring to?" I asked.

That comment stopped the man in his tracks. He smiled, showing off nice dimples and perfect white teeth. "I've been rude. My name's Calvin. Calvin Nikrovetch. That piece of slime is my brother–in–law, Keith."

Calvin took a seat in a nearby chair. "Did you ever notice him picking his nose? He has this nasty habit of picking it at the dinner table while we're eating. Then he just

69

has to touch us or our food." Calvin shuddered. "He's repulsive. A shit. Slime. Bottom feeder. I don't know why my wonderful sister married that loser." Calvin pressed on without coming up for air. "He's a liar. Can't trust a word he says. He'll steal money right out of your pocket. I know, I had to bail him out." He let out an ululating wail that no grieving North African tribesperson could emulate. "My poor sister!"

I had an idea that the Keith he was referring to might've been the Keith who was here not too long ago, the same one in the restaurant. Yet, I didn't want to interrupt him for fear that he might turn violent, or that he might let loose with another gut–wrenching wail. My ears were still ringing.

Calvin rocked back and forth in the chair. Still seated, he grabbed the armrests. Taking small and dainty steps, he and the chair plopped in front of my desk. He was now close enough to confide in me. "He borrowed Ganiff's son–in–law's Amex card." Picking up on the blank look on my face, he explained, "His oldest daughter's second husband, Clod. That's what we call him. He's a nice guy, boring as all hell and no spine at all. His real name is Clyde. So Keith stole Clod's Amex, ran down to Florida, spent a week charging up a storm. Then a month later, Wham! Clod got zonked with the bill—twenty–five grand! They're trying to get it back from Keith."

I wasn't sure I followed the bouncing ball here although the story became fascinating in its own way.

"So why don't they call the police?"

Calvin let out a bitter laugh. "Can't—they're in business together." He picked up on my forehead creasing in puzzlement. *What in the world was this crazy man talking about?* I thought.

"Hey how long have you been here?" It must've finally registered that he was talking to a total stranger as opposed to talking to a known stranger.

"Almost three months now. My name's Linda."

"Ah, another Linda. Good, I don't have to learn a new name. Sorry to bombard you with all this crap. I'm sure you'll learn quick enough. Hey, I gotta run. Is he back?" he gestured with his head at the closed doors.

"Returned about two seconds before you got here."

"Ah, he's probably reading Scripture in the toilet."

"What?"

"The guy's a Born Again. He and his wife. They're hooked on Billy Graham. Watch out—he'll try to indoctrinate you. Anyhow, he's always in the can. If you put food in front of the bathroom door, he'll last for days."

"There's a bathroom in there?"

"You haven't been in that office?"

"I try to avoid it at all costs. Not for more than ten minutes at a time."

"It's across from the closet. Most people think it's another coat closet."

"Oh, that's what I thought. Never got brave enough to open it. What's he doing in there for so long?"

"That's the $64,000 question. Maybe you'll solve that mystery and let me know someday." He stood up to leave. "Hey, nice meeting you, Linda." As he reached the doorway, he turned around to get in one last word. "Oh yeah, tell him I was here—Mr. Ganiff, not that slimy piece of shit, and let him know that I'm still working on the estimates."

He got me yet again. My facial expression must've indicated that I had no idea what he meant.

"Nikrovetch Contractors. Get with the program, Linda. We're gonna do the three million dollar job for renovation. If he gets it approved, of course. Which he will!"

With a wink, Calvin was gone.

The phones rang off the hook. Doreen kept calling to speak to Mr. Ganiff and wouldn't leave a message. After the thirteenth call in less than ten minutes, I lost patience.

"Doreen, what is it?"

"I don't want to dithcuth it with you. You moron, I jutht got a call from Copperth and they want to canthel the contract with uth."

"What did you call me?"

"Moron!"

"Why the hell are you calling me a moron?"

"Becauth you fakthed my memo to them."

Facts? Fasts? Memo? I was angry and befuddled. "What in the world are you talking about, Doreen?"

"Remember, the memo I gave you? The one I wanted to dithcuth with Mithter Ganiff?"

I dropped the phone and searched the top of my desk. Someone else had already been there. They left paw marks. I dug deep in my in–box and found the clipped papers she had handed to me earlier.

"Doreen, everything is here for Mr. Ganiff. I didn't fax anything. I never even used the fax machine today." I looked at the fax machine behind me—it still had a two–inch layer of dust that didn't appear displaced. I also read the Post–It note Doreen wrote: "*Mr. Ganiff, that woman is a bitch. Let's just pacify her and move on.*"

"Doreen, let me talk to Mr. Ganiff for you and we'll remedy this."

She unceremoniously hung up.

I debated for a moment, then decided that Mr. Ganiff needed to be disturbed. I hit the intercom button. He picked up after the tenth ring.

"What!"

"Mr. Ganiff, we have a situation here."

He sighed. "What's so important that you needed to disturb me after I told you not to?"

"Mr. Ganiff, someone faxed to Doreen's client a private and troubling message. Now they're threatening to pull the account."

"Who is this someone?"

"Doreen accused me. But it wasn't me."

"Who do you think it was?"

Who would have motive and accessibility? I wondered. The drama unfolded right in front of me. Like a movie. Earlier that day, the moment I left the desk, BeeBee, under direct orders from Ms. Djorak, crept to my office and rifled through the papers on my desk. She had to find evidence to discredit me. She knew from past experience that Mr. Ganiff would be busy with Keith for a few hours; both of them locked behind the door doing lord–knows–what.

The camera zoomed in. She spotted papers concerning the hotel's largest corporate client, Coppers & Libel. Its corporate travel agency had several arguments with the underpaid clerks in our reservations department about rates and availability. Like a thunderbolt, BeeBee was struck with divine inspiration. An aura from heaven surrounded her. Music swelled. She smiled. Birds fell from trees. She took Doreen's comments on the top page and carefully, in order not to displace even a mote of dust, faxed them to the corporate client. Then she skipped back to her desk.

"BeeBee," I concluded. "She's the only one who would've had access." I failed to mention cause and opportunity.

Without question, he accepted what I had surmised. He didn't have to rely on intuition and gut instinct as he was quite abreast of internal office politics.

"Fine, then let's get BeeBee and Doreen into my office, pronto," he barked.

As usual, BeeBee wasn't at her workstation so Security had to hunt her down which they enjoyed because Big Guy and his lads were able to use all their toys: battery powered flashlights, walkie–talkies, earpiece inserts, emergency K–rations, Swiss Army knives and manacles. They found her hanging out in Ms. Djorak's office.

When BeeBee entered my office, I went right up to her. "So, up to some new tricks, huh?"

"Fuck off," she eloquently told me.

"BeeBee, how many times do I have to catch you? Don't you get it by now? I'm two steps ahead of you." I thought I'd fuck with her mind a bit.

BeeBee emitted a hacking sound which I interpreted as laughter. "Linda, you know nothing. Nothing. You know what? I'll leave you alone, all right. You'll fuck things up in no time." She slid by me to enter Mr. Ganiff's office.

Oh, she disliked me. Lord knows, she made it quite evident, with that deep voice repeating her rhetorical complaints to whatever daemon to whom she prayed. Yet, I felt that deep deep down, very deep if you can dig deep enough, she had a heart of gold. I truly wanted to like her… at least until she stabbed me in the back. Well, now after our little exchange, the gloves came off.

BeeBee joked around with Mr. Ganiff while I waited in my office, feeling rather peeved until Doreen arrived. I followed her into his chamber. The three of us sat crammed next to each other around the conference table. BeeBee put on a sour puss, advertising her displeasure to be seated so close to Doreen and me. Doreen sneered first at me, then at BeeBee and then back–and–forth in succession. Under the conference table, I flipped the bird to both of them, too intent on malice to notice the glass top.

"Hey, Linda, what the hell? I saw that!" Mr. Ganiff grumbled.

I shrugged. Quickly, I crossed my arms and legs.

Mr. Ganiff sat forward and scowled. "I'll make this short and sweet for all involved. I don't want to hear any more about sabotage. If I even feel anything is being done, I will fire all three of you without hesitation. Do you understand me?"

Numbly, the other women nodded their heads.

"Doreen, you stay here, and you two are excused." He pointed in my general direction. BeeBee and I stood up and walked straight out. Doreen shoved the door closed behind us, almost catching the heel of BeeBee's right shoe.

While Mr. Ganiff and Doreen had their tête–à–tête, BeeBee returned to deliver the mail. This time, staring right into my eyes, she hoisted the fifty–pound mailbag over her shoulder and energetically poured the contents over my keyboard and coffee cup—no doubt her form of retaliation. Come to think of it, all of BeeBee's actions were forms of retaliation. I wanted to reach out and backhand her although I rationalized that if I wanted to keep this job or continue to stay out of jail, violence was out of the question. I bit down hard and exhaled.

Doreen and Mr. Ganiff were behind closed doors for quite some time. My curiosity almost drove me mad. Since I couldn't easily snoop through the bolted door, I sorted the mail. One envelope in particular contained an invitation to a free one–hour reflexology treatment at a new health spa around the block.

General Managers of major New York City hotels receive a lot of freebees such as gift certificates and movie passes. The purpose of these promotional items was crystal clear: to succor favor and receive new business.

As a matter of fact, gifts and favors of all types flowed into the General Manager's office at the Supreme Superior, one of the hottest hotels in New York City. Rarely was the staff or I the recipient. Sure, I hungered to receive perhaps one or two of the bountiful booty that came in daily. Regardless, Mr. Ganiff had plenty of extended family with whom to share the loot.

All of a sudden, the door to Mr. Ganiff's office swung open. Doreen deeply inhaled and escaped. Mr. Ganiff stepped out of his burrow, stretched his arms over his head and then proceeded to stare at me like a rabid hawk while I opened and sorted his mail. I chose to ignore him. Nothing too exciting about separating junk mail and collating complaint letters, correspondence and vendor solicitations.

Without a word, I stood up and handed him the pile. Included was the spa invitation, along with bills and subscriptions to religious magazines. I took a seat once again at my desk.

Mr. Ganiff stood by his door, thumbing through the opened mail. His face lit up as he came across the health spa invitation. He dumped the rest of the stack on top of a reception chair and yelled from over his shoulder, "Hey Linda, I'll be back!" It was a threat. Like a bat from hell, he ran from the vestibule, spa invitation clutched in his hands, creating a vacuum that produced suction, almost pulling me after him.

Ninety minutes passed. He returned, physically relaxed from a massage with his fingernails perfectly manicured.

"How was it?" I asked, knowing full well the destination of his marathon run.

He harrumphed. "It was a Hungarian woman. She did that reflexology stuff on my feet. Would you believe she had the nerve to say that I'm impotent?" he stomped around in his office. "Me, impotent? Me? I have six kids. What does that bitch know?"

Hmmm, I thought, *somebody struck a nerve.* I used considerable restraint not to burst into laughter at this awkward topic of conversation. I had to say something; I couldn't help myself. "You said she's Hungarian? Perhaps she doesn't do too well in pronouncing the letter 'r.' Maybe she meant 'important.'"

Mr. Ganiff chuckled, then broke into a hearty laugh. "Now that's funny, Linda. Maybe you're right. She did have difficulty saying a lot of things. I could barely understand anything she said."

Mollified, Mr. Ganiff returned to his desk. "Oh, for the record, Linda, you were thoroughly right in disturbing me today. I don't like getting involved in these office spats. Be that as it may, sometimes, especially where it may potentially cause irreparable damage to the hotel, I do have to intervene." He flashed a warm smile. "Linda, give me some credit for knowing what's going on outside of my office. I know these people far longer than you. In their own special way, they're doing what they feel is best for the hotel." He turned back and slammed the door shut.

I couldn't figure out if he paid me a compliment, or put me in my place. Nothing new about that. For some reason it seemed the same to me.

74

Chapter 10
January 1995

Murlise and Ms. Wapiti conducted a joint operation under Seebok's supervision. Their staff incrementally moved the TVs from the almost abandoned building and had them installed in every suite of the hotel, including the Health Club, the executive offices and the Ganiff's residential apartment. The new TVs replaced the old ones which were returned to the former distributor for partial refunds. It took a record month and a half to finish the installation thereby concluding the episode of the TV debacle. Or so we thought.

It started off as a trickle. Then a slight gush. And, after all the TVs were in place, a hemorrhage. An overwhelming number of guests filed complaints with Murlise's office. Daily. Many of the new televisions were incompatible with Time Warner City cable, so most of the channels could not be accessed. Others simply malfunctioned. The majority of complaints centered on the volume. Blood literally flowed from our guests' ears. Murlise was inundated by the calls, so much so that she couldn't do anything but respond to them. And she knew who was to blame.

In an effort to express her sarcastic tribute to Mr. Ganiff, Murlise employed the same tactics as our clientele: a merciless and relentless barrage of phone calls. All headed my way. She also wanted to murder Seebok, the man who ordered these defective TVs... As usual, he disappeared.

When Murlise finally caught up to Mr. Ganiff, she was livid. "So what the hell do we do about our frequent guests? Even some celebrities are canceling future stays solely because their TVs don't work! I mean, you try explaining to Ted Turner why he can't get CNN in his hotel suite! It's absurd!"

"Tell them to get a life," he stated, "it's a television for Chrissake."

"They might not return," wailed Murlise, "that'll just kill my occupancy runs. The whole thing could've been avoided if we hadn't bought these pieces of crap from Paraguay, or whatever third–world country we got them from!"

"Then good riddance. Let 'em go somewhere else. They won't be satisfied. Mark my words, they'll come back. Because we're the hottest hotel in town. No one in their right mind judges a hotel stay based upon the volume of their television." Mr. Ganiff suppressed a yawn and picked up a Sharper Image catalogue.

That was the truth. The Supreme Superior became overnight the "in" hotel after months of plugs on Page Six in the *Daily Post*, planted by our very own public relations maven, Barby Mandy. The plugs were so successful that even housewives in Idaho wanted to spend a night in the hottest hotel in Manhattan. Businessmen came because of steep corporate discounts and state–of–the–art in–room technology. Celebrities justified their stay because we were situated in the bosom of the corporate arm of Hollywood, across the street and down the road from Creative Agency Associates' Michael Ovitz, the William Morris Agency, Time Warner and

MTV, to name a few companies.

Alternatively, attaining status as a hot hotel in Manhattan was easily achieved when some of your competition were out of commission and tourism was at a historic high. The Essex House on Central Park South had recently shut down for massive renovations. The Plaza had closed 50% of its rooms due to a fire. All this while tourism continued its sixth consecutive boom year following a drought of an equal number of years. In view of these circumstances, I could understand how easy it was for Mr. Ganiff to succumb to his cavalier attitude. Damn, he tooted from the roofs!

And then we have the Seebok. Good for nothing other than knowing how to placate Mr. Ganiff, no matter the circumstance.

According to Doreen—the lisping fly on the wall—Seebok had a vested interest in Deviant Enterprises, the company that won the television commitment. She obtained this info from a recent chummy night out under the guise of "Executive Staff Bonding." Being seated next to Seebok's intoxicated loose–lipped wife was all it took. The wife bragged that they had received for their home two 35–inch color stereo televisions during negotiations. For the office, Seebok accepted a camcorder, a VCR and a new hard drive for his computer. It turned out that Deviant's competitors weren't as forthcoming, so Seebok fudged their estimates north.

Part of Deviant's competitive advantage was that their televisions, particularly the ones purchased for the hotel, were manufactured in Nairobi. Suffice it to say, not exactly the finest circuitry, hence the volume burnout problem that upset our patrons.

Sure, Mr. Ganiff was enraged at Seebok. Yet, the recent gifts Deviant forwarded to Ganiff's children and grandchildren mollified his anger. The list included:

★ Ten color Sony TVs;

★ Five camcorders;

★ Three computer systems with Nintendo attachments; and

★ Five two–year subscriptions to Omaha Meats.

These perks didn't include the automatic 25% rebate for the total contract. Mrs. Murray, in her drunken stupor, also divulged to Doreen that representatives of Deviant met with Mr. Ganiff personally after work on the Lower East Side. They handed over brown bags filled with soiled dollars. Doreen laughingly dismissed those allegations. "Mithter Ganiff, a pillar of the community going clandethtinely to a theedy bar? A thelebrated hotelier acthepting money in brown paper bagth? What bullshit!"

I wasn't too sure about that. I certainly had a soupçon of suspicion.

Seebok carried several manila folders when he came down to speak to Mr. Ganiff. He flung them onto the conference table, knocking the telephone onto the floor and tipping a cup of tea into Mr. Ganiff's lap.

A high–pitched yelp emanated from Mr. Ganiff. "Seebok, you moron! You scorched my thighs! You idiot, you ruined my suit! Get me some paper towel from the bathroom."

I was minding my business, reviewing the recent batch of guest complaint letters. Up till the Marx Brothers and their antics cut into my concentration. Listening was not enough; I had to see this to experience it. So, I dropped what I was doing, and stood up halfway to lean and peer over my desk. Right in time, too. Seebok ran over to Mr. Ganiff to blot his crotch with the paper towels.

"Seebok, get your hands offa me!" This time, he roughly pushed Seebok away. Then, Mr. Ganiff twisted around and over his chair to pick the telephone up from the floor. He winced and then bleated, "Damn, my herniated disc!" and flung the telephone in the air. It came crashing down on the glass top of the conference table. Moments later he said, "Geez, Seebok, sometimes I wonder about you."

Didn't we all?

Seebok gestured in my direction. "Just close the door," said Ganiff.

Disappointed, I returned to my work. I was typing an internal memo when the speaker of my intercom crackled to life. Either Ganiff or Seebok mistakenly hit one of the buttons. Or the wiring became unhinged due to the violent way at which the telephone was tossed.

Seebok complained to Mr. Ganiff in a whiney voice, "Those rats at Deviant won't return any of my calls. I think they're avoiding me since we got that last batch of guest complaints."

"Oh, Seebok, I wouldn't be too concerned about that right now."

They had no idea that I could hear them. And, I had no intention of informing them that the intercom speaker was broken; it even emitted a barely audible peep of a beep, an alert that it was in operation. Luckily, neither of them heard this peep of a beep. Anyhow, when it came to Seebok's idiocy, I couldn't resist the chance to spy. This qualified as great entertainment value. I picked up the receiver and held my breath to make sure they, in turn, couldn't hear me although the odds were definitely in my favor.

"Aren't you a little bit upset, sir, that we may lose clients?"

"Did it ever occur to you, Seebok my man, that perhaps our clientele are a little too pampered?" chuckled Mr. Ganiff. "We're talking televisions, not bedbugs." He emitted a self–satisfied sigh. "Forget the faulty TVs. Right now I have $250,000 sitting in a checking account at my bank in Cape Cod. Not to mention those steak subscriptions! Deviant sure knows how to deliver. This was the best Christmas ever!" He chortled with glee for a few more minutes.

I couldn't believe what I had heard! So, it was twue, after all!

Then came a rustling of what sounded like papers. "Oh, by the way, did you procure my reading material?"

Unexpectedly, Mr. Ganiff's door swung open. I looked up and saw Seebok lurking in the doorway. Quickly, I put the intercom on hold and replaced the phone in its cradle. Seebok, without missing a beat, turned around and entered Mr. Ganiff's office once again. Quietly, he shut the door behind him. Once more, I picked up the phone. A gasp and a choked scream came through loud and clear.

"I thought you left, Seebok. Don't startle me like that."

"Sorry, Mr. Ganiff. There was something I forgot to tell you. I was able to bargain a small contract with another vendor for a new projector unit, a real state–of–the–art device. He had both the projector and its screen mounted on the ceiling in the main conference room. At no charge. This one's totally remote controlled, screen and all. We scheduled a little demo this afternoon. I'll have Linda invite all staff."

"Hmm, sounds interesting." Ganiff's voice oozed warmth. "Just make sure this thing was manufactured in a more industrialized country this time. Maybe someplace like Iraq."

Some two hundred employees, mostly housekeeping, waitstaff and busboys were available for the projector demonstration. Present among them were the Gang of Three and Mr. Ganiff. People were crowded four abreast in a room that ordinarily accommodated fifty people tops.

The presentation began with the vendor, Mr. Kutner who introduced the new product and all its high–tech features. Seebok turned out the lights rendering the room pitch black due to the heavy window treatments. At that instant, there was a whir. A very loud whir which grew louder with each passing second. We heard a familiar shout: "Turn on the lights, dammit!" That was Mr. Ganiff's contribution to the demonstration.

The lights came on. The projector screen continued to smoothly unfurl. Until the damn thing stopped halfway. Seebok, at the other side of the room, frantically pressed buttons on the remote control. A handful of the crowd cackled. The screen didn't budge although Seebok's actions did produce an audible buzz across the room, followed by a plume of smoke from the console.

Mr. Kutner was flustered. He went to apologize to Mr. Ganiff, but Ganiff would have none of it.

"Get this show on the road. Time is money!"

"This has never occurred before, sir. Never. I'm not certain what to do. Mr. Murray, please stop pressing all the buttons! You're killing it!"

With the screen locked halfway in place, the projector launched its short demo film, ironically a step–by–step tutorial regarding those particular projector units and how they were supposed to work.

"Hallelujah," said the vendor and Mr. Ganiff simultaneously.

The movie might've been informative except that the projector trembled, blurring the image. Moreover, only the top part of the film played on the screen. The bottom half of the indecipherable footage played on the intricately patterned wallpaper. It reminded me of independent guerrilla film–making and I expected any moment to see hysterical people running amok in woods at night. All of a sudden, the screen flapped up and slammed against the ceiling. A huge thud exploded across the room. The force of the blow caused the projector to fall right out of its fixture. It came crashing down to the floor below in the center of the room, missing Mr. Ganiff by inches. Everyone in the audience clapped, impressed with the demonstration.

"Hey Theebok," shouted Doreen, "you really know how to put on a show."

That was the signal for everyone in the room to depart. Unfettered laughter followed. Everyone, that is except for two.

"Seebok, in my office, now," thundered Mr. Ganiff, "I'll have your ass for this!"

Chapter 11

Live from Mr. Ganiff in the General Manager's office—the rhetoric and dialogue of the ongoing Anal Monologues, Selection #12!

"I've been in this field for over thirty–five years. Since my early thirties, I have been a General Manager for the best five–star hotels throughout the United States. I was brought out of my retirement because this hotel needed me. They wanted me to lead them as *the* Five–Star Hotel of New York City."

Mr. Ganiff puffed his chest in front of the mirrored door while readjusting his cravat and peered over at me with his one good eye. "I've been thinking."

Those three words usually signaled that Ganiff was up to something. Usually something negative and/or pejorative.

"You're going to have to clean up that New Yawk accent a bit. It's a little too… how would you say, ethnic? If you're planning a career in hospitality, you should consider an elocution coach."

Talk about striking between the eyes with an iron poker—I took great pride in this accent. It took me many years to cultivate including those all–important ones used to produce that superb Long Island nasal twang. I was raised or rather buried in the cultural desert of suburban New York City and grew up in a neighborhood consisting predominantly of working–class first generation Italian–American families.

What I most enjoyed in the hood was the overwhelming amount of kids. Each family, observant Roman Catholic, had between nine and eleven kids. Of course, every family had a Tony. There were so many, in fact, that each mother devised a special whistle or caw to call her very own "Tony" home. Five o'clock at night was a frightening time if you weren't from the neighborhood—the echoing hoots, shrieks and ca–caws resembled the sounds emanating from Dr. Moreau's island.

Before I could react to Ganiff's passive–aggressive intentional dig, "Mr. Class Act" continued accent–less, "In case you didn't know, I grew up in Brooklyn."

Oh, yes, this dig took hold and I took heed to my womanly intuition. Everyone knows, or rather the New York tri–borough snobs know that in the pecking order of accents, Long Island rates significantly better than Brooklyn although worse than Queens. In other words, the man insulted my accent, implying that I came from a lesser caliber background, socio–economic or otherwise. Evidently, he didn't recall his own familial disclosures during those horrid discourses that I had suffered through. It occurred to me that even if that was not his intent, he couldn't refrain from hurting, maiming and wounding. Like the tale of the scorpion and the frog. He was the scorpion and I was the frog. As the tale went, it was his nature.

And then it hit me, wham, right between the eyes! Not the iron poker. The thought. The recognition. The awareness. This man was an unmitigated bastard! The true person was tucked far away from his holier–than–thou public persona.

Mr. Ganiff specialized in internecine warfare amongst his executives. His game plan consisted of manipulating his subordinates. It was relatively easy because they all despised each other, yet had to work together for long hours including occasional weekends. Ganiff enjoyed their cutthroat revenge. Right up his alley. Sometimes, out of sheer spite, he would pit Murlise against Doreen or Seebok against Wapiti to ensure that his Machiavellian schemes would unfold. For he found that the more involved the bickering amongst his handpicked executive staff, the less attention was focused on him.

To combat this viciousness, some counterpunched with their own defense mechanisms.

Seebok sharpened his claws and sabotaged his opponent using his expertise in computers such as uploading a virus to the targeted executive's departmental records. Murlise and "highest paid" Wapiti were straight shooters in their schemes whereas Doreen became a coquettish vamp, flirting outrageously with Mr. Ganiff, openly vaunting her supposed sexuality in exchange of his support. For the past five years, Doreen constantly plotted against Ms. Djorak without success. Djorak sidestepped every maneuver. Naturally, Ms. Djorak detested most of humankind, though Doreen was her favorite enemy. All Doreen's juvenile performances fraught with insecurity…

During a recent executive meeting Ms. Djorak exclaimed, "In all my time as Director of Human Resources, I've never known anyone who is as good to their staff as Murlise."

Water shot out of my nose. She must've calculated that comment to coincide precisely when I took a large swig from my bottled water. In essence, she succeeded in achieving a two–for–one. With one remark, she gave me the whammy in addition to her primary intended target, Doreen. And the game began.

Everyone knew that Murlise was in fact a closet bitch, no matter how she hid it. Tales abounded of her ruthlessness conducted strictly behind closed doors. Yet, upon hearing the lavish praise from Djorak, Doreen once again succumbed to jealousy as demonstrated by the sudden arch of her back. Her eyebrows shot up far into her forehead and resembled caterpillar–thick inverted "V's." A black cloud literally formed over her head. Mr. Ganiff quickly donned a yellow rain hat and opened an umbrella in her direction in order to protect himself from the spew of venom, spittle and ectoplasm. The scorecard now read: Djorak—1, Doreen—0.

Djorak's underlying objective was to inflame the recent clash over bookings between Murlise and Doreen, and their respective departments. Murlise prevailed whereas Doreen was in the midst of shoring up her career. Business schools presented case studies on the classic confrontation between two departments selling the same product from two different angles. In this particular situation, Doreen's clients obtained preferential corporate rates on block bookings. These rates were an inducement for the client to contractually agree to book rooms in bulk. Occupancy improved, and at Christmas, Doreen received a nice bonus.

Behind the scenes, Murlise and her staff had been quoting to individuals from the same companies in Doreen's portfolio even better rates on rooms than those from the block bookings. However, when the clients tried to reserve rooms at these preferential rates, they were promptly informed that the only rooms available were those under the block bookings. At the higher contractual rates. Thus undermining Doreen's efforts at every conceivable level.

That was the conflict, short and sweet.

Doreen's clients went ballistic, in particular Coppers & Libel, the hotel's and Doreen's largest client. It had been the source of many scuffles all around. That afternoon, Doreen entered Mr. Ganiff's office and dropped down to her knees. My jaw dropped down to my knees. With superwoman strength, she pushed aside the heavy chairs that flanked his desk. This was much better than late–night cable television! She then clasped her hands together in prayer. "Mithter Ganiff, pleathe thir," she begged. "I need your help. If we don't renegotiate thith, they will leafe uth!" Disappointed that no x–rated acts would be performed, I snuck back to my desk.

"No, Doreen, I told you no! No. No. No. This is a binding contract. We'll give them better rates when the arrangement nears renewal. That should be in July, right? It's around the corner, only seven months away," he shouted back at her, thoroughly enjoying the spectacle.

She beseeched him with tears streaming down her face, "Right now, thir, they do not want to renew. They're looking at the Kitano. The Markth Hotel. They're pithed." She swallowed hard and continued, "Remember, thith ith the company that retheieved that fakth from your offithe, the one in Nofember with my Potht–It thtatement?"

Mr. Ganiff's face remained impassive.

"Thir, thith client wanted to leafe uth a few monthth ago. Remember?"

He groaned as his memory resurfaced. "Oh, that damned fax came back to haunt us?"

His statement was punctuated by an even louder, "Yeth, thir, that'th the client!" from Doreen. "What should we do?" she wailed.

Ganiff sniffed and paused a few moments before responding. Almost paternally he said, "Let's wait and see what happens the closer we get to the renewal date."

The wailing and breast–beating cut too deeply into my train of thought, causing the fillings in my teeth to twinge. I had no other recourse but to close the door to Mr. Ganiff's office.

So, in case I wasn't clear, let me rephrase the original premise. Ganiff took pleasure in torturing his staff. It was his hobby, second to lord–knows–what occupied his interest in the bathroom. He was bored. Even his six children bored him.

He had five daughters, four of whom were married twice; three right here at the Supreme Superior. Around the hotel, the buzz was that those marriages cost big money. We're talking about what would've been charged for food, beverage, flowers, entertainment, limo service and hotel rooms. All was provided free for the General Manager. All costs were absorbed, swallowed by the hotel.

At this point, I formed some sense of Mr. Ganiff's corruption. Furthermore, of all of the people to verify this for me... The source of this information threw me off–guard: the prodigal son. Mr. Ganiff's pride and joy. The last child who still lived at home. Ignatius Elmer Ganiff II.

One day, he wandered down from his aerie to see his father. Of course, père Ganiff did not respond to the intercom, nor to the repeated knocking on the portals to his office where the door was bolted shut. Frustrated, Iggy Two settled down on one of the guest chairs, crossed his legs and talked about his favorite topic. Himself. No introduction, no presentation. *Like father like son*, I reflected.

"What do you think of my shirt?" he asked me. Before I could respond, he straightened out the sleeves and snickered, "Designer. Ralph Lauren."

I made a production of rotating my eyes heavenwards.

"You have to understand, uh... uh..." he said while looking mildly ferklempt at me.

"The name is Linda." In a codependent fashion I helped him with his inept social skills.

"Right, uh... uh... uh..." he said to me, imploringly. *Damn, he forgot my name already!* I coached him with "Linnnnnnnnnnnnnnn" until he remembered. "Uh, Linda, you have to understand, I lead a very different life than you."

"Trust me, Iggy Two, I don't need much convincing."

"Oh, but you do," he sniffed, "I grew up in the best hotels with the best food and the coolest life."

"Good for you. I'm not impressed," I said, knowing that that remark would agitate him.

"You wanna hear something good?"

"Try me, Iggy Two." I got bored of this game. Unlike his father, he was way too easy.

"One of my sisters was married here last year and my father had Tony Tenneb sing at her wedding." He waited for a reaction.

"This is what you call something good?" I taunted him, "Iggy Two, I have work to do."

"Okay, how about this," he cleared his throat. Then he cracked his knuckles followed by his neck which he moved from side to side. He got up and did side bends from left to right to snap his back. When he finished popping his entire spine, he sat back down. He whispered, "My sister's wedding was free. We had over two hundred guests who stayed here. For free. We ate here. For free. We used the limos. For free. Best of all, my dad gave away Nintendo games to all of us. That was free too!" I didn't react. He continued, "My dad said it cost over $600,000!"

So the rumors were true, I thought. For Iggy Two's benefit, I yawned.

Mr. Ganiff perpetually complained about the prodigal son to me. "He has an IQ of 70 but wears Ralph Lauren down to his underwear. We sent him to Italy for his birthday, yet he couldn't tolerate the pensiones after a lifetime living in five–star hotels. He gave us an ultimatum, five–stars or home. So we brought him home."

The funny thing was that I liked Iggy Two. I could tell he liked me. There was an instant recognition as we were both victims, victimized by the same person, his father. In that regard, we bonded.

General Managers of five–star hotels tend to inherit celebrity status due to their access and ability to mingle with the stars. They're often privy to insider information. One memorable staff meeting took place when Mr. Ganiff brought in three oversized photo albums depicting the three decades of his career. There were pictures of him and his wife cavorting with Frank Sinatra, Liza Minnelli, Barry Manilow and the former President Jimmy Carter.

"See this picture? That's Tony Tenneb! I was his biggest supporter for all those years before MTV discovered him!" bragged Mr. Ganiff. "He would've starved if it weren't for me."

I had already met Tony Tenneb en route to the Health Club. The hotel's gym was a small exercise room filled with the latest equipment, private steam rooms and saunas. The bathrooms inside were impeccably clean. Inexplicably, few guests used the premises. In terms of emptiness, the Health Club was a major contender to *Bliss*. As a countermeasure, the executive staff were allowed, even encouraged to use the Health Club. Yet, no one did. Which explained their perpetual flabby appearance. I wasn't allowed to work out in the gym since I was merely the de facto Resident Manager on probation. Even so, no one said anything about using the bathroom!

Tony Tenneb lived down the street from the hotel. When he was in New York and had some free time, he took advantage of the facilities that Mr. Ganiff generously offered him. One particular afternoon, Tony popped in to see Mr. Ganiff. I jumped out from behind my desk when I recognized that unmistakable tenor.

"Oh, hi, sweetheart. No need to get up for me. I wanted to see if Mr. Ganiff was around."

"Oh, Mr. Tenneb. I'm Linda. What an honor to meet you," I stammered, "well, we met in front of the Health Club once before, but not formally." I extended a hand and received a warm shake from the gray–haired legend. "About Mr. Ganiff, he locked his door an hour ago. I'll try reaching him for you."

For ten minutes I pressed the intercom button on my desk inviting carpal tunnel to visit and reside in my index finger. Tony, seated on the reception chair, flipped through the pages of *Cigar Aficionado*. Occasionally, we'd exchange a smile. After a while, Mr. Ganiff emerged. At first, he had a huge scowl on his face… until he realized the reason for the interruption.

"Oh, hi, Tony. So nice of you to drop by like this. What can I do for you this afternoon?" He put on his most disarming politician's smile.

"Sorry to disturb you and your new assistant like this. I just wanted to say a quick hello while I'm in town."

For a moment, it appeared as though Mr. Ganiff might formally introduce me to his famous acquaintance. Mr. Tenneb beat him to the punch.

"Yeah. The new Linda. We already met." He flashed a smile in my direction.

Mr. Ganiff placed his beefy arm around the icon's shoulder and turned to me dragging Tony along. "Linda, I made this man who he is today."

Tony Tenneb grimaced and struggled in this unwarranted embrace. "Sure has been a few years. I knew your boss when he was half the size that he is today… both in stature and waist size."

I bit down on my tongue to hold back from embarrassing my boss.
I was confident that he could do the job quite competently without my assistance.

"Yeah, my wife and I are getting older and fatter." Mr. Ganiff patted his more than ample stomach.

"So, Mr. Ganiff, I wanted to let you know that I'm moving a few blocks uptown next month. Wanted to say thanks for all your hospitality while I've been in the neighborhood. You've been great."

"Oh, I see," replied Mr. Ganiff, staring down at the floor, "that's too bad." Looking up with a twinkle in his good eye, he added, "I'm guessing that while you're in transition, you'll need a place to stay. Why not live here for a month? You can have the top floor penthouse, the Principessa. I'm offering it to you for… how about four hundred a night? It's a steal!"

The Principessa rented at over $2,000 a night. Hands down, this suite was one of the best in all of Manhattan. I visited up there once and the sweeping, unobstructed panoramic views of Manhattan, Queens, Brooklyn and New Jersey from the living room and both bedrooms awed me. The mammoth Jacuzzi in a separate room connected to the master bathroom awed me even more.
Also included in the deluxe suite was a mini–kitchen and a formal dining room for sixteen. The Principessa was a piece of heaven with plush, velvety furniture and exquisite décor.

"Mr. Ganiff, that's kind but I think I got it covered."

Ganiff begged him, not taking no for an answer. "C'mon Tony, you need a getaway. Why not? You make more money than God. Moreover, the price is right. We promise to spoil you rotten."

85

Tony mulled over the offer. Then he begged off. Softly, I warned him, "You better go for it otherwise you'll never get out of here alive."

Reluctantly, Mr. Tenneb reconsidered. "Well, maybe, I guess. I'll give you a call tomorrow morning to let you know the dates involved. Really, this is a very kind offer. You really shouldn't."

Later on, Mr. Ganiff explained to me his philosophy in dealing with celebrities. "The only way to get something from people like Tony Tenneb is to give 'em something for free... or in this case, for dirt cheap." In fact, Mr. Ganiff made certain that he received twenty–five guest passes to each of Tony's upcoming performances at Radio City Music Hall. Backstage passes too! "The way I see it, Tony will feel indebted enough to me that he'll have to sing at my daughter's wedding... again."

Mr. Ganiff's recently divorced fourth daughter, Reba, had become engaged to another man the past weekend. *Condolences to Tony*, ran through my mind. Ganiff must've used his telepathic abilities. "Well, at least it's worth a try," he said.

I'll say this for Mr. Ganiff: he certainly attracted a few hangers–on through the years. The most prominent of all was Steven Koneman, the quintessential stereotype of a successful executive—short, middle–aged and loud. Steven was the little emperor, complete with customized white hair, manicured nails, tailored suits, diamond stud cufflinks and oversized dental caps clamping down on the omnipresent cigar when it wasn't brandished as a substitute penis.

Steven Koneman was also a big–mouthed abrasive braggart who earned over six figures in Hollywood, representing corporate clients in a public relations firm. His claim–to–fame around the hotel involved a bunch of female escorts while sticking us with the bill. He reveled in all sorts of scams according to Edwing the Concierge, saddled with arranging Steven's shady requests.

Mr. Ganiff had recently told me that Steven and he had met scarcely two years earlier. "I think he contacted me just to mooch off us. Free meals, rooms, limos and whatever else he and his coterie of pals can get. The guy's a big number but he's bad news."

I had the misfortune of receiving a Steven Koneman phone call direct, live from Los Angeles.

"Linda, how the hell are ya?" boomed an unfamiliar, yet cocky voice.

"This is Linda, but Linda Lane, not Luppner."

"Where the hell's my babe, *the* Linda?" Koneman shrieked.

"She no longer works here."

"Oh, no way! You gotta be kidding me." He seemed genuinely disappointed. "When did she leave? Where did she go? Ganiff didn't do her in, did he?"

"Sir, I honestly don't know the specifics. With all due respect, I'm handling her responsibilities now. Is there something I can help you with?"

I wished I never asked.

"Well, Linda, just wanna let Iggy know I'm arriving next week and we gotta spend some quality time together. I'll fax you my flight plans. So arrange my suite, limo, etc. Gratis. Do ya need to write this down?"

During my first face–to–face confrontation—which I persistently re–live like a bad LSD flashback—Koneman barked out orders and demanded services that didn't exist at the Supreme Superior or at any other five–star hotel in the tri–state area.

Pointing a bejeweled and manicured index finger at me, the little emperor stamped his little foot like Rumplestiltskin. "Whaddya mean, you can't get me free entry to Winged Turtle for eighteen holes? I got my clubs here and everything." Mr. Koneman referred to one of the most exclusive golf country clubs in the nation.

"It's a no go, sir. I spent the better part of the morning talking to their management. You have to know members there. In order to play golf, you have to be invited by a group. You just can't pop in."

"Linda, not to insult you but you're doing a real bad job. The other Linda always came through. Perhaps you're incompetent. Maybe I should talk to Ganiff baby about your position because you don't know what you're doing." He poised his knuckles in front of Ganiff's closed door.

I ground my teeth while my blood pressure soared. "Listen, Steven," I said with clenched mouth, "why don't you go to the Lounge and mooch, I mean, schmooze. Have a complimentary drink for twenty and I'll get back to you after I meet with Mr. Ganiff."

"Capital idea," he said and jauntily strutted out of the office.

I stood up and pounded on Ganiff's closed, mirrored door. I succeeded in startling him because he actually got to his feet to open the door.

"You have to do something about Koneman. That troglodyte monopolized my entire morning with ridiculous requests. On top of it, he threatens my job! Not even Arnold Palmer has unlimited access to the Winged Turtle! What planet is he on?"

He was shocked to see me lose my composure. After expelling a deep sigh, he said, "Listen, Linda. Much of a shmuck that he is, the guy is a friend of mine. Let me take care of this with him, okay? In the future, there are no excuses. You must find a way to accommodate him. Now, get him on the line."

"He's not in his room. He's downstairs in the Lounge. I gave him carte blanche at the bar to shut him up."

Mr. Ganiff raised his hands towards heaven, gesticulating wildly. Without decorum, he lowered them to smooth out his mustache and shuffled out of the office with hunched shoulders.

I wasn't the sole staff member who despised Koneman; you could hear a collective groan during the daily sessions when Murlise read his name on the VIP list.

Ms. Wapiti, usually silent during these meetings, got up her gumption to complain about his monthly visits. "Every time this Koneman shows up, it causes a serious surge in sick days with my staff. This occurs in a place where we operate with chronic shortages even during the busiest season. He's a menace!"

Big Guy was next to speak up. "This Steven, he's a vindictive nasty schmuck. That's his positive attribute." Everyone in the room said "Amen."

Though we all shared the same opinion of Koneman, I must admit, his constant goading of Mr. Ganiff amused me. His penultimate trip was vintage Koneman. From the Lobby, he called Mr. Ganiff who put him on speakerphone.

"C'mon Iggy baby. Join us down here at the Lounge." Voices were yelling in the background.

"Who are you with?" asked the bemused Ganiff.

"Oh, I have some very important clients. Executives from the NFL." Steven didn't even attempt to muffle the phone when he shouted to someone on his side of the line, "Teddie knows what I like to drink. Get me a double. Get yourself a double. Put it all on my tab."

Ganiff groaned. "Steven, please don't drink the bar dry. I'm gonna end up paying for it."

"Dontcha worry about it, Iggy. These are the big boys who'll bring in the big bucks. Come, join us."

"Steven, it's only three o'clock. I do have to put in a few hours."

One hour later, Steven called again.

"Linda, babe, I need your help."

This time, I groaned. "Yes, Steven, what can I help you with?" I dreaded this interaction as I did all my interactions with this twisted tiny tyrant.

"I need a limo. For tonight. Gotta get it comped. I wanna take a tour of Italian restaurants on Arthur Avenue in the Bronx with a bunch of potential new clients. Wait. I want the big boy to join us. Let me talk to Ganiff baby."

I switched the call to Mr. Ganiff who sighed in resignation.

"Hello again, Steven. Is it possible to get some work done today without interruption?"

"C'mon, Iggy baby, join us. It's just for a few hours. Let me reassure ya, it won't hurt schmoozing with these guys. They're the ones who'll bring in the big bucks."

"Steven, please, I had a very long week and want to stay in tonight."

"What's wrong, wifeypoo gonna punish you? Have you had any fresh air lately? Or do you want to stay home and watch the Missus knit?"

"Fine, I'll join you," Ganiff capitulated. "Only if you're paying for it. I'm not getting stuck with this bill."

Wishful thinking.

The following day Ganiff bellyached about Steven and his pals. I asked him point blank, "Why didn't you tell them to pay up?"

Mr. Ganiff threw his hands up in the air and said, "He'll make my life a misery. Too powerful a guy to fuck with."

He then spent the entire morning frantically trying to reconcile spending over a thousand dollars for one meal with people he didn't know for business he would never get. Moreover, he exceeded his entertainment budget for the month. No way could he expense it with the accounting department. Or at least not legitimately.

It must've been bad for him because he docilely approached me, receipts in hand and asked, "Hey, Linda, how are your creative bookkeeping skills? I have this problem with Koneman and I could use your input."

Suffice it to say, I couldn't help him. The prevailing bottom line: Steven Koneman was a cheap, lying shithead to be avoided at all costs. Yet, for as much grief as he caused me on the job, nothing could compare to what he did in destroying the life of one of our younger employees during this last trip to New York.

It happened on Monday afternoon after a wild weekend of partying. Koneman burst into Mr. Ganiff's office shouting, "One of your staffers is a dead man. Or woman."

"Steven, what's wrong?" Mr. Ganiff replied, mildly concerned.

"Someone stole my antique leather cigar holder. It's the one I inherited from my great–grandfather. Damn thing is priceless."

Mr. Ganiff personally launched a major investigation. This included three-dozen staff members and more than four hundred manpower hours. "Search the dumpsters! Check the security tapes! Tear this place apart till it turns up!" he shouted into his phone. Thankfully enough, he didn't ask me to perform this one task.

All week, Steven Koneman plagued me via fax and phone demanding an update, utilizing his staff at the outrageously named KKK (otherwise known as Koneman & Kindred Klients Public Relations, LLP)—not to be mixed up with the other KKK. Needless to say, I did my best to avoid him.

Finally... a verdict.

Fortunately, or not, Alletti Sanitation had failed to pick–up for the week. This enabled our staff to unearth from that unholy and retch–inducing mound on the loading dock a five–day–old trash bag that originated from the hotel bar. Inside was a plastic, resealable bag containing the item in question.

The housekeeping staff member who made the find was ready to pitch it back when one of his colleagues stopped him.

"Why in the world would there be a dried piece of shit soaked in beer in the hotel bar garbage?" This solitary question led to many other questions which led to some philosophical discussions. These discussions ultimately involved Ms. Wapiti and Big Guy who realized that no, this was not a desiccated turd but the object of our massive investigation.

A check of the employee time sheets from that night showed one busboy on duty at the hour when Koneman was served. By process of elimination, Gary Yong, a twenty–six year old, was fingered as the culprit.

Through the grueling Q and A conducted by way of Gary's faulty English, we reconstructed the events that led up to and followed the theft of the much–revered family heirloom. In truth, a drunken Koneman had left the item in question lying on a table in the bar lounge the night before barging into Ganiff's office. Gary Yong threw it out, thinking that the cracked plastic container was garbage. How was he to know otherwise? Actually, it looked like a desiccated turd. Gary used ice tongs to dispose of it, placing it in a sealable plastic bag in the event that it might contain a disease or two. You never know what people do when they're under the influence. Gary carried out his job very conscientiously.

Koneman demanded retribution.

When Ganiff interceded on Gary's behalf, Steven went ballistic. "Even if this guy's no thief, he's a moron for chucking out an antique like that. Iggy baby, either he gets the ax or I'm taking my business to the Four Seasons."

Mr. Ganiff knew that this threat was not entirely negative. Koneman's departure would surely boost morale at the Supreme Superior. It also meant the imminent destruction of the hotel's five–star designation.

Koneman had Ganiff by the balls. KKK was the leader in the esteemed and coveted public relations market. Without lifting one manicured fingernail or displacing one hair on his coiffed head, Steven could make or break the hotel. A few well–placed articles and quotes from celebrities could undermine years of effort. That was the subtext with which Mr. Ganiff dealt.

The final outcome of this scandal was the immediate termination of Gary Yong's employment. Poor guy. The innocent busboy cried when Mr. Ganiff delivered the news in Koneman's presence. The office door was intentionally left open, so anyone passing by could hear the merciless execution.

"Sir, I do nothing wrong. I very sorry. Just doing my job. Please, no," he sobbed, "I working to help my parents. They from Thailand. Very old. My wife, she have breast cancer. I need insurance for chemotherapy."

"Well, you shoulda thought of all that when you so callously discarded Mr. Koneman's precious antique. You should be thankful that he doesn't sue you for damages. Now go on, get the hell outta here. Your services are no longer needed."

All this to salvage the Koneman frail ego—a lukewarm at best friendship.

What an utter disgrace, I couldn't help thinking. I also felt saddened, powerless and disgusted by this display.

From time to time, Kenin popped up to my office with that beautiful face and body of his. "Hi girlfriend," he said as an introduction, followed by some gossipy tidbits to ingratiate himself with me. He assumed that I had the good ear of the General Manager. I did nothing to dispel that image.

Still saddened by the recent firing of the busboy, I had to get a handle on the banquets area and Ganiff's "off with the head" attitude. Insofar as the actual inner political workings of the company, I was clueless despite having worked at the hotel for approximately four months. This was directly attributable to the fact that I was tucked away in the executive office. Being situated atop the corporate pinnacle does culminate in a sketchy picture as to what goes on in the trenches.

Therefore, I relied upon Kenin to describe in–depth the criteria required to obtain a position in banquets. I was taken aback by what he disclosed. He, on the other hand, reveled in my sense of outrage by saying, "This is how it's done, Mary." (For those closeted people, not necessarily gay, "Mary" was an affected appellation applied to any woman or any man, for that matter.)

The Banquets Department of the Supreme Superior was, in fact, a lucrative opportunity. Not to mention labor intensive. Most of the staff (busboys, waiters, dishwashers, set–ups, clean–ups) earned over $90,000 a year on tips alone. We're talking the 1990's! This was the American dream, especially for the staff who came from impoverished countries. It also accounted for the endless stream of applicants.

Kenin stood in front of my desk. "There's a reason why things are the way they are. There are a finite amount of positions available in banquets. Once you add the ability to earn oodles of money, you got yourself a tithing system of sorts."

"What do you mean by a tithing system?"

Kenin sighed. "Mary, in order to even get a job here, all applicants must forfeit their first year salary and tips to Ronny. In turn, he gives cuts to the Director of Marketing as well as the Director of Food and Beverage, your pal, Joe."

I didn't know whether this was an industry–wide practice or one only in place at the Supreme Superior, but nothing would've surprised me.

"Another thing, Linda." He took his role as schoolmarm seriously, and pulled out of his vest a handy twelve–inch ruler. With a little too much glee for my comfort, he thwacked that thing against a nearby pile of stacked papers. "This is Banquet Life 101. Tipping is an integral part of the Supreme Superior system. Rest assured, upon the conclusion of the contracts with the clients which are mostly corporate, sometimes social like weddings, an unobtrusive white envelope will find itself into the banquet manager's grubby fingers as he shakes hands with the client." Once again he hit the papers for emphasis.

"How does that work? Who gets what?" I eyed the ruler and hoped he wouldn't use it on me.

Kenin shook his adorable head, "C'mon, girlfriend. You know the players." I shrugged. He sighed in disbelief. "Okay, this is remedial Banquet Life." Whack went the ruler. "You said you were a banker?"

"Kenin!" To avoid that ruler, I pushed my chair backwards, hitting the credenza unit behind me. Dust sprinkled down from the fax machine.

From his back pocket, Kenin pulled out a chart rolled like a papyrus. With a flick of his wrist, he unfurled it on top of my desk. Then, with his ruler, he pointed to the large rectangle box on the chart. "We start with the top chain of command." Tap. Tap. "Ronny receives his customary 30%." Around the rectangle box were dollar signs. Inside the box was a stick figure holding a pharmaceutical bottle with an oversized label containing one word: Percodan. The ruler moved down to a row of several boxes where little stick figures sat behind desks. "Then he distributes 40% evenly amongst his corporate staff which includes me, and the remaining 30% goes to the busboys, waiters, dishwashers, etc." The ruler traveled down to a tier of hunched over stick figures carrying trays with stick figure blood, sweat and tears. Kenin rolled the chart up prior to shoving it back into his vest.

My head spun from Kenin's revelatory dissertation. I had no idea that the Banquets Department was rife with tithes, forfeitures and downstreamed monies. In a way, what I discovered was that the Supreme Superior could be a viable competitor to GermBank in terms of questionable transactions.

★ ★ ★ ★ ★

One week later, I selected, out of all the scattered mail dumped on my desk, an envelope addressed to Mr. Ganiff. Both the envelope and the letter inside were scribbled in perhaps the worst handwriting and grammar I'd ever seen, however, the content was gut–wrenching.

"Dear Mr. Ganiff,

I write to say sorry you and to hotel customer for mistake I make to throw out cigar case. Please let me come back and working more at Supreme Superior. I beg you to take my forgivness. I dont know any idea I throw something important. I need to working to help my wife who is very very not well without working she cant get cancer treatment to get better I take care my old parents they dont working. You must please let me come back for my working. I say thank you hearing me.

Gary Yong"

After wiping away the tears from my cheeks, I placed the letter on Mr. Ganiff's desk, hoping the man had a speck of compassion buried somewhere within his heart. As I entered the boss's office after lunch that afternoon, I found that he had crumpled the page and tossed it in the garbage.

"Mr. Ganiff," I pleaded in my most sincere voice, "the man is desperate. He's really done nothing wrong. Why not give him a warning and let him come back to work? C'mon, we know it's an honest mistake. I mean, he could've called the Board of Health on us. The damn thing looked like a desiccated turd!"

Ganiff drew in a deep breath, stretched his arms above his head and let out a sizable yawn. "Ah, Saint Linda, if only you would devote this much energy toward doing the more important things around here, you might someday be a successful hotel manager."

"With all due respect, I—"

"Give it up, Linda. My decision is final. I've already had Ronny hire a replacement; a very nice man from Indonesia. Met him in my bible study group. They don't come any more clean–cut than that."

He dismissed me in the usual, cold way. I couldn't let go of the predicament of a young man whose wife may have been dying without proper medical care. I just knew I had to do something to help... with or without Ganiff's approval.

Good to his word, Ganiff presented Steven Koneman during his stay with a new hand–made leather cigar case featuring his initials engraved in 24–carat gold. The very next day, I found on top of my desk the invoice from a boutique for submission to Mr. Dorck in Finance. It set the hotel back a few grand. That, at least, could be expensed.

It was also a substantial gift, given that Steven consistently freeloaded (or in his vernacular "getting it comped") at the hotel bar and at *Bliss*, alone or with clients, potential or otherwise. After each expensive endeavor, he cited his favorite line, "these are the guys who'll bring in the business" to Ganiff who swallowed it hook, line and sinker. To those of us who knew better, it was an effective defense mechanism to avoid criticism or accountability. As a prolific leech, Steven was unparalleled.

Curious, I contacted Murlise. "What is it with that Koneman? Why exactly do we allow him to do what he does?"

"Oh, that runt," she said. "Don't get me started about him! Do you know that over the past two years he did not generate a cent's worth of business for this hotel?" she continued with sarcasm, "to the contrary, he reaped millions of dollars of promotional revenues from the new clientele he pampered on our tab."

"Meaning the big boys who'll bring in the big bucks, right?" I laughed sardonically and she joined in. "Come to think of it," I mused aloud, "he never did tell us who would be the recipient of those big bucks. I mean, he makes us think it's the hotel that's gonna benefit from all the freebees when actually it's for him and his company. Well, we can't say he's a liar... in this regard!"

Chapter 12

Half of what I learned on the job at the Supreme Superior came from eavesdropping. A necessary tactic to undertake when working for a highly secretive boss who lived behind locked doors. Most positions provide some sort of orientation or on–the–job training. At the Supreme Superior, training for the most part fell within the range of sink–or–swim. Or ingratiation with dubious people possessing equally dubious agendas. What I discovered late one Thursday afternoon was that eavesdropping could also be a two–way street.

It was four–thirty in the afternoon and things were quiet for a brief moment. Ganiff was locked in his office. I decided to phone my father to finalize plans for our upcoming Saturday outing.

"If Mom wants to go to that place on Second Avenue, I'll do it. I'm telling you, it's not the best Italian food in Manhattan."

My father said, "Your mother likes the food there. She went with her girlfriends several times. Afterwards, I want to browse some of the new books at Barnes and Nobles, if that's okay with you."

"It's okay, whatever makes both of you happy." I was indifferent about the plans because they were just an excuse for me to hang with my parents. "So, I'll meet you guys there at noon. Love ya, Dad. See you Saturday."

After I hung up the phone, Mr. Ganiff sauntered into my office, hands jammed into his suit jacket pockets, whistling nonchalantly as he casually strolled up to my desk. With the utmost kindness he could muster he asked, "What plans do you have for the weekend, young lady?" The sincere tone of his voice—an occurrence rare as a blue moon rising—startled me.

I responded in kind, "Uh, if you must know, I'll be seeing my parents here in the city. My father and I, we're gonna do lunch, then hang out in Barnes and Noble. He's into books. We'll have to plant my mother in Starbucks."

"Interesting," Mr. Ganiff murmured, "so you really want to be with your father? Spend time with him?"

"Sure, of course." I shrugged and stared at him the way a mongoose stares at a snake. "We're very close. We talk almost every day."

Ganiff looked at the floor for a moment of silent reflection. The subject matter had struck a nerve. "The only time my daughters call me is when they need something. Especially money. It's like I hardly know them since they left home," he griped as he ambled back to his office, his head bent down and shoulders hunched.

"Wait a second, Mr. Ganiff. Since you asked, I should explain myself better."

Ganiff spun around and took a few steps back in my direction.

"Mr. Ganiff, what you don't understand is that it's taken a lot of time and effort for my dad and me to build a close relationship. We weren't always this way, you know?" I took a breath and continued, "for most of my life, my father and I had a stormy relationship. We couldn't see eye–to–eye. As my mother often said: 'If he'd say black, you'd say white. You two could never agree on anything.'"

"What turned it around, if you don't mind me asking?" Ganiff stared intently at me with his good eye.

"Well, I guess over the last five years or so, I changed. I valued having a terrific relationship with my father more than being right."

"You mean that both of you just stopped arguing? Just like that? I don't understand."

"Mr. Ganiff, it was hard. You have no idea. Now we're enjoying the results of that hard work. We're able to converse, even argue and still show each other love and respect."

"You're telling me that you're a grown woman who continues to enjoy spending time with your old man? I didn't know such a thing existed." Ganiff seemed genuinely surprised.

"It's true. I like spending time with him. He's smart, funny and a candid observer of events. More importantly, he's my biggest supporter even though he doesn't always agree with the choices I made in life."

"Such as?" Ganiff took another step in my direction.

"Oh, like the university I attended. The jobs I've taken."

The latter comment flew over his head.

"Very interesting," Ganiff answered, his eyebrows arched high, "here I thought that being a Daddy's girl lasted just until they hit puberty. Who knew?"

Who knew indeed? I gave up a little info on myself and Ganiff, in turn, became a little more… human. To call it a breakthrough might be stretching the truth a little. Yet, I do believe that our father/daughter conversation helped to change Ganiff's viewpoint of me.

At least temporarily.

After that day, he included me in many of his open–door one–on–one meetings. He also endorsed my involvement as a true representative with decision–making powers, much to Ms. Djorak's dismay.

I didn't have to be a rocket scientist to see that he lived vicariously through my relationship with my father. The man brought the topic up daily, grilling me as to what we did, what we talked about, where we went. His invasive probing notwithstanding, I basked in the newfound amity with my boss. It sure as hell beat what had been the alternative.

The question remained: How long would the harmony last?

Barely five months after I had joined the Supreme Superior Hotel, Ganiff greeted me with a bold proclamation, "Linda, I'm off to Japan for my annual meeting with senior management. Time to present our annual budget and marketing ideas. Most importantly, to secure funds to start construction!"

In addition to his three–hotels–in–one concept, Ganiff's latest master plan centered on the renovation of the convention rooms on the 59th and 60th floors. He explained that we could make more money with larger receptions rather than the smaller parties we had been hosting. Each reception floor held three rooms that separately contained no more than 50–seated people or 150 in total. After the construction, each floor would seat up to 280 people, an increase of over 130. Multiply that by an average of $60/person and multiply that by multiple daily and evening events. The end result of this scenario meant that all expenses related to the construction portion of this project would be recouped in less than a year.

Fabric, wallpaper and furnishings, selected by Maurizio, the hotel's original decorator, would add another million dollars to the budget to an aggregate $3 million giving a leeway of $200,000 for over–runs. The budget was very tight.

He lugged a bulging briefcase with a piece of paper sticking out of the side.

"Wait a sec. You're leaving just like that?" His spur–of–the–moment travel plans blindsided me for a second before it sunk in. With barely contained glee, I asked, "How long will you be there for?"

"Two weeks. Maybe three. Depends on how quickly I can get that money from them. You know how much this expansion means to me."

Indeed, I did. Ganiff had received bids from different contractors and narrowed down the search to three competing companies: Nikrovetch Contractors, Mountainside Builders and Sensai Construction Co. The figures were widely disparate with Nikrovetch hitting the $1.8 million target benchmark whereas Sensai's proposal hovered around $3 million and Mountainside fell between the two extremes.

Mr. Ganiff's desire to handle these delicate negotiations in person was another matter. In New York, Mr. Hitsuhana represented our head office's desire for Sensai to perform the work. Sensai was an affiliate of the Japanese parent company through related ownership. Mr. Ganiff was just as adamant not to award the contract to them. He had sewn up the deal with Nikrovetch, the least expensive vendor.

The covert negotiations had taken place for weeks. Mr. Ganiff and the Gang of Three locked antlers every morning, followed by countless hours of wrangling with Calvin Nikrovetch, honing and fine–tuning the pricing. Mr. Dorck from Finance became a fixture in Mr. Ganiff's office, devising projected figures based on cost assumptions and projected income. This was undeniably the most passionate I had seen Ganiff get about anything.

"Linda, listen up. While I'm gone, I need you to be my eyes and ears around here. I'll be checking in with you several times a day. Be sure to stay on top of everything going on, you hear?"

"No problem," I said, surprised that he entrusted me with this kind of authority.

"Oh, and keep an eye on Seebok, will you? That guy has a penchant for biting off way more than he can chew. Think of yourself as his babysitter in my absence." He turned to enter his office. "Now, I must get organized for the trip. In the interim, set up all the folders and the executive proposals. Please do not disturb me."

Doreen came to my office while I was in the midst of frantic last minute Ganiff packing. The first thing she did was check to see whether the boss's door was closed. It was. The second thing she did was to inquire, "So, when ith he leafing?"

"Soon. He has to pack and get to JFK airport for an early evening flight. He'll be back in two weeks give or take a few days."

"What'll you do while he'th gone?"

"Oh, I'll continue to be a secretary with an executive salary." I flashed her a sarcastic smile. "Another way of putting it, an executive treated as a secretary."

"Why do you thay that? You're doing an ekthellent job. Eferyone notitheth the change in Mithter Ganiff." Doreen sat down on the chair nearest my desk.

Perhaps Doreen came here to sympathize or to make friends. If nothing else, her compliment enabled me to lower my guard for a moment. "Sorry to sound so negative. It's just… well, I do have a secretary, that BeeBee, who's never here and no help at all." I sighed. "So many other things occurring here… Otherwise, everything's okay."

Doreen nodded. "I have one quethtion. Why are you here, I mean at the Thupreme Thuperior?"

"Well, other than the money, I came here because it is a new hotel. It's not like the Waldorf where I was physically removed from the core operations like interacting with the clientele. I do enjoy the excitement around here. A crisis–oriented place for sure!"

Doreen laughed. "Tho, I gueth you're thettling in. You plan to thtick around, make a career out of it?"

I smiled and shrugged. "Well, it's hard to tell. Hopefully, Mr. Ganiff will no longer be preoccupied when he returns from Japan and will recognize that my probation has been over for a while. Then I guess we'll see what's in store."

When Seebok joined the Supreme Superior, he followed Mr. Ganiff's pontificated edict to reduce costs throughout the hotel. To the letter. He put his Ivy League education to use and analyzed every department, searching for generic alternatives to replace the existing infrastructure, no matter how well the present system worked. Which explained why things were the way they were.

A few hours after Ganiff's departure for Japan, Seebok decided to take on a project that would impress his boss upon his return, and save the hotel a fortune in the process. That very same day, I found him in the file room, a former broom closet located next to his office. He sat cross–legged on the floor, covered head to toe with legal documents.

"Whatchya doin there, Seebok?" I asked, wondering anew about this lunatic.

"Oh, hey Linda. Reviewing all our contracts." He held a sheath of papers in his hands. "Here's one I can renegotiate now because the automatic renewal is up and we have ninety days!" He fluttered the contract in my face and said with gusto, "Take a look, it's the most expensive contractual expenditure we have! Mr. Ganiff'll be so proud of me."

What a juggernaut! I could tell right away the insanity of the situation because the name on the papers flashed beneath my nose was Alletti Sanitation. I could imagine the efficacy of this renegotiation.

Alletti Sanitation was the unionized company responsible for trash removal, not only at the Supreme Superior but at every hotel across Manhattan. All New York City hotels used them, for good reason. Simply put, they were the only game in town. There was no alternative, a fact challenged by no one, hence the automatic renewal in place on this evergreen contract…

When I snooped by Seebok's office later that afternoon, I caught him on the phone with a potential competitor who could offer lower rates than what we were paying.

"Hi, this is Mr. Murray from the Supreme Superior Hotel… I'm returning the call I missed with the head of Flushing Waste Management… Oh, good. Well, the reason why I called in the first place was to find out if your company would consider making an offer to handle our sanitation services… Yes, we're currently with Alletti… Yeah, I know all about them. That doesn't mean we can't talk to you guys about it."

For a moment, I felt like walking in and educating Seebok about the birds and the bees. Even with my limited exposure, I knew that no one dared mess with Alletti. Try mentioning someone else for work and dire consequences would ensue. Seebok then switched the call to his speakerphone so I decided to hang around for the floorshow. I observed him from the sliver of his semi–opened office door.

"We'd be flattered to make you a competitive proposal if you're serious about breaking rank with Alletti," said a detached voice on the other end of the line. "Flushing Waste doesn't handle any hotels, as I'm sure you know. We cleaned up many large areas like the Tennis Center here in Queens after last year's U.S. Open. Lemme point out though, we do have many big clients in Manhattan."

"That's great!" Seebok shouted, pumping a fist in triumph. "Well, I'll get you all the particulars of our sanitation requirements and a detailed breakdown of all the services we purchase from Alletti. If your proposal comes in better than theirs—"

"Mr. Murray, I'm certain that we could come in with a much lower bid. Hell, I'll even throw in a little something for you as a token of our appreciation to land a gig like this."

"That's so nice of you. Um, it took you long enough."

Ka–chank! At that moment, my little man grew from an innocent and an ingénue to a cosmopolitan acting like an innocent and an ingénue in the wonderful wide world of extortion. Beyond any doubt, he was his mentor's acolyte. Now that my suspicions had been confirmed, I wondered all the more about Seebok's underlying intentions for these cost–savings programs. Especially, whether he had Ganiff's knowledge and/or endorsement.

"Hey, you like music?" asked the man at Flushing Waste.

"Music?" Seebok shrugged his shoulders. "Yeah, sure. Who doesn't?"

"Great. For giving us this break, let me give you one of those portable Sony disc players. Straight from the factory."

Seebok could not contain his enthusiasm; he squirmed with joy in his chair. A Cheshire cat grin spread across his youthful face, distorting his features into a semblance of a human. "Man! That's awesome. I've been wanting one of those for a couple of years."

"Great, well why don't I come up to scout out the hotel and deliver the gift in person? It's the least I can do."

As I crept away from Seebok's door, I thought about what Ganiff had told me earlier about keeping an eye on him. Out of nowhere I recalled a line my father often repeated to me: "Hit him with a stick with a nail in it. Once his eyes stop rolling, he'll understand." Another way of putting it, "Until you've gotten burnt a few times you'll never learn." Justification enough for me. Dad's words of wisdom held more credence than the Anal Monologues from Mr. Ganiff.

Time to watch Seebok stick his hand in the fire.

On the second day of Ganiff's field trip, I looked up and saw the silhouette of my father outlined in my office doorway. "Hey, Dad, what a nice surprise! What brings you here on a weekday afternoon?"

"Well, I was in the neighborhood. Your mother went to see some afternoon reading thing with her girlfriends right by that David Letterman building, across the street on Seventh Avenue. Some new playwright, I don't know what she was talking about. Anyhow, I figured, I have this free time while she's busy. Then I thought, why not take out my best girl for some lunch?"

"Why not here? I insist, lunch is on me. Actually, it's on the Supreme Superior, since meals are the one perk I get around here." I picked up my handbag and joined my father. We walked down the corridor and took the main elevators to the Lobby, a rare treat for me, fraught with risk should Djorak get wind of it. Corporate policy dictated that employees use the back of the house elevators except for those instances when we accompanied clients for hotel–related business.

I decided to take my father to *Bliss* to show off a bit. The maitre d' nodded at us and opened his arms wide to indicate that we could choose any table we wanted in the monstrously empty room.

My father selected a table near the exit. "Linda, you look happy today."

"That's because my boss is out of town. I feel relaxed for the first time in months."

"Good! I'm glad you're doing better since our last heart–to–heart." My father pulled a chair out for me.

"Oh, about GermBank?" I sat down and whipped the napkin across my lap.

Seated, my father unfolded his napkin, placed it on his lap and picked up the menu. "Yeah, it was a bit difficult for me to absorb at first. I could not imagine how you felt in that situation. Isolated, alone. You did what you could. I can see now that trying something new would help you gain some perspective. Oh, I'm sorry, Linda, I couldn't tell your mother. It would've upset her needlessly."

"I understand, Dad." I placed my hand on top of his.

The waiter came over and we placed our orders. In moments, our soup du jour arrived: a magnificent Lobster Bisque, guaranteed to clog an aorta in twenty minutes flat due to the copious amount of fresh cream.

My father peered at me. "So, things're getting better for you here?"

I hesitated, "Well, in some ways." I savored the soup and appreciated the sneak preview of the white light. "Mr. Ganiff's trusting me a bit more these days which is progress of sorts. With him gone for a while, I'm feeling like… well, the term 'human' comes to mind."

"Yeah, you sure looked harried when Mom and I were with you that Saturday." He handed over his unfinished soup to the waiter who served us our entrees. "I kept wondering whether it was still too soon for you to make a leap into a different industry. I know you haven't gotten over what happened to you at the bank and—"

"Dad, c'mon, it's been well over a year. I trust I'm over it."

My father gestured with the knife in his left hand, the European way of eating. "My dear, kindly let me finish my thought before it flies out of my head. Where was I?" he chuckled and said, "okay, I remember. Perhaps you made a poor choice by leaving the Waldorf too soon even though it seems like you're weathering the storm in this godforsaken place."

I took a sip of my iced tea, one of the few things *Bliss* was incapable of screwing up. "How do you define weathering, Dad?"

100

My father leaned closer to me, "It means, basically—"

"Sorry, Dad. I meant that as a rhetorical question." I took a deep breath. "I'm gonna let you in on why I'm upset." It all came forth like a verbal vomiting of vileness. "First off, I have this miserable excuse of a secretary who's never here, won't help me when she is, and hangs out all day smoking. Then there's this Ms. Djorak I've been telling you about. She's that psycho who made the anti–Semitic comments to me. Also the racist comments. Not to mention her daily threats! Most of the staff are lazy and can never be found when needed." I took another sip of tea. "Plus, I don't have my official title yet. I'm hoping that part'll change when Ganiff returns and sees that the place is still in one piece."

Dad took the first bite of his undercooked veal. He frowned, dropped his fork and knife and raised the linen napkin from his lap to his lips so that he could politely remove the morsel. He wiped his mouth, then smiled at me. "Sweetheart, it'll never be perfect. Never. No matter where you work, or what you do, or anything." He looked down at his plate and continued, "Perfection doesn't exist. If you can manage to tough out the bad times…" He reached for some overdone fries. "Hey, ask your mother. You know I'm hardly perfect though I'm up there on the scale from one to ten. She still hasn't followed through with her threat to have me dismembered." He laughed. "We're even happy most of the time which is saying a lot."

Dad made a fair point. Maybe I had outlasted the indoctrination period. I knew from past experience that the start at a new job could be a little rough going. Although I felt that my time at the hotel was over the top in that regard. Yet, I had a few achievements: Ganiff demonstrated a scintilla of respect for me and Doreen seemed to come around slowly. Could the others be far behind? Okay, well everyone except for BeeBee who hadn't cracked a smile since 1983 for which I was certain many people were thankful. What about Ms. Djorak, Wapiti, Seebok, Murlise? They couldn't all be such miserable wretches… or could they?

Chapter 13

[This Page Intentionally Left Blank] ★

★ *In homage to the Supreme Superior Hotel which does not have a 13th Floor.*

Chapter 14

After lunch, I kissed Dad good–by and then returned to my office. No Ganiff around meant I had time to breathe and reflect upon my status at the Supreme Superior. Even the hotel seemed quiet during his absence.

My reflections turned to Gary Yong, the poor busboy with a cancer–stricken wife who'd been brutally fired for the crime of throwing out a desiccated turd that belonged to Steven Koneman. I figured that as long as Ganiff wasn't around, I could do my best to help.

Since Ganiff had coldheartedly disposed of the busboy's pleading letter of apology, I didn't have the man's contact information at my disposal. I could've called human resources, though that would have opened a Pandora's box should Djorak have gotten wind of it. Then I remembered my resourceful man, Kenin. I phoned him and, within minutes, he sent me a fax with Gary's home address and phone number.

At first, I hesitated phoning Gary at home, not knowing whether I'd be disturbing his ailing wife. After all, it was three o'clock in the afternoon… "But no time like the present," I always say.

Gary answered the call.

"Hello, Gary. You probably don't remember me, but my name is Linda and I work in the executive office for Mr. Ganiff at the Supreme Superior Hotel."

"Oh, hello Miss Linda. Mr. Ganiff, he got the letter I write?"

"Well…" I realized much too late that he might misconstrue the purpose of the call and think that we were going to rehire him. "Gary, the reason I'm calling is to let you know how bad I feel about you losing your job. Of course, I'm not in charge around here, but I wanted to see if there was anything I could do to help you."

The line went silent for a half–minute. The former busboy then spoke up, "I'm not understand you. Do you call me to get back my job at hotel or not?"

"Gary, even though I work in Mr. Ganiff's office, I don't have the ability to get you your job back at the Supreme Superior. I was hoping—"

"So why you call and say to help me if you can't give me back job?" his voice strained, "you understand my wife is very very sick. Needs help. I need job. My parents, they need me to make money too so I help them."

"Yes, I understand. That is why I'm phoning you. I have a few contacts at other hotels. Until I get through to them, let me write you a letter of recommendation from the General Manager's office. That should help you start in getting a new job."

The line went silent again. Then he took a deep breath. "Why you be nice to me? You never meet me before. Why do you say to help me get new job, Miss Linda?"

I felt sympathy for him. Gary Yong did absolutely nothing wrong to lose his livelihood. Mr. Ganiff and his buddy, that asshole Steven Koneman, were responsible for ruining Gary's life, warranting my pure, unadulterated disgust. The poor fellow desperately needed work and needed an ally. I might be the only one who could assist in getting him back on his feet. Gary had no idea that I, too, had undergone a similar predicament at GermBank. If I had someone like me to help me out back then, I wouldn't have been where I was.

"Gary, you need to hear where I'm coming from. Mr. Ganiff is not a very nice man. He had no right to take away your job like that. He should've given it back to you after he got your letter. I'm sorry that he has no compassion, but I do think I can help you if you'll let me."

"How can you, Miss Linda? Please say."

I reached for a sheet of letterhead from the middle drawer in my desk. "Well, to begin with, I have your address. I'm going to type up a letter of reference and mail it to you at home. If nothing else, the letter should let other hotels know that you come highly recommended. Secondly, I'm gonna make a few calls for you, see what I can do. I used to work at the Waldorf for a little while. Maybe one of their restaurants needs a busboy or a waiter."

Another swift intake of air. "You do this for me? This is nicest thing. You a very nice lady, Miss Linda. I don't know what to say."

I didn't either. I hung up and typed away.

After slipping the letter into the mail slot down in the Lobby, I decided to head back upstairs. I wanted to check up on my dear friend, Seebok. I wondered, *what new kind of scheme was he concocting?* I peered into his office. He wasn't there. When I returned to my desk, a pair of voices emanated from behind the closed door of Mr. Ganiff's room. I picked up my phone and hit the intercom button. Sure enough, Seebok was inside with another gentleman.

At that moment, BeeBee strolled by with a cigarette tucked behind her right ear. I placed the phone against my chest, disconnected the call, and asked her if she knew who was inside.

"What's it to you?" she replied in her razorblade voice.

"BeeBee, give me a fucking break. Just tell me who's in Mr. Ganiff's office or," I lifted the phone receiver for a moment before I burrowed it back into my chest and shot out, "I'll have no choice but to call Security."

BeeBee scoffed, "It's that idiot, Seebok. He needed a quiet place to meet with Nick Alletti, the garbage guy. He asked if he could use Ganiff's room. I told him it was okay. Not like Ganiff'll ever know."

"Nick Alletti? The President of Alletti Sanitation? He's here meeting with

Seebok?" My heart leapt into my throat. Lucky day for me! This oughta be fun.

I again hit the intercom button that connected to its counterpart situated on the conference table in Ganiff's office and resumed my snooping. Once more, kudos to Seebok who caused that intercom unit malfunction in the first place. Directly or indirectly. Besides the ability to listen in at my discretion, it no longer made a tiny peep of a beep on the phone to alert the recipient of the connection. Peep or beep regardless, I listened closely to the conversation on the other side of the line.

"Look, Mr. Alletti, I have here an estimate from an outside vendor for a thirty percent reduction in sanitation costs. Thirty percent!" Seebok rattled a piece of paper, more than likely in the man's face.

Nick Alletti laughed aloud, in all probability back in Seebok's face. "You kiddin me, right? Do you know who the fuck you're dealin with?"

"I do," Seebok answered in a confident voice. "I also know that this is our window of time to stop the automatic renewal of our service contract if we're dissatisfied. I believe it is as per the contract..." He faltered for a moment. "I think it is as per the terms of the deal. Anyhow, we've been having some problems with you guys."

"Problems? Just what kinda problems we talkin about?" Alletti's voice bumped up a few notes.

"I have a list here. Let's see... late night garbage pick–ups aren't always made. We have days when you guys do partial pick–ups, skipped pick–ups and sometimes no pick–ups at all. We also got the Board of Health on our case about overflowing garbage bins stacked up on the loading dock."

"This is why you called me up here?" Alletti's voice reached Pavarotti's famous High–C, "to gripe about our service?"

"Hey, do you blame me? With service like this, I have no alternative but to shop around, find a way to improve efficiency, especially with what we pay you. What's wrong with a little comparative shopping? That is, you can work on your current pricing and..." Seebok's voice dropped, "you can provide me with a little sweetener. An inducement..." His voice trailed off.

Nick Alletti laughed through the walls and through the intercom, a sound not associated with humor. "What makes you think you have the clout to cancel our automatic renewal?" He laughed some more, the sound of which grated my nerves and caused the intercom to stutter. "Just who the fuck are you anyway? Some little pissant, that's who you are! Think you can break my chops, you piece of shit? I'm tellin you, I know you ain't the honcho who handles all the shit here. Just where is that man, the fat fuck, Ganiff? Is this some sort of sick joke he's playin?" A momentary silence before he spoke again, "Nah, he don't have a sense of humor."

"Well, I, um..." Seebok's voice didn't sound too confident. "Mr. Ganiff put me in charge of this negotiation. He's away on business and requested that I deal with it before he got back."

"Hmmm, I see," said Nick Alletti. "Ganiff asked you to get outside pricing," his voice increased up a notch or two, "to maybe try and replace us?"

"Well, um... no, not exactly." Seebok recaptured a bit of his moxie, a little more secure now that the ball landed in his court. "The fact is, sir, that I have a better offer on the table. You can't blame me for checking out the competition. It's good business."

"We have no competitors in this business, you lamebrain," Alletti snarled, pounding a beefy fist more than likely on Mr. Ganiff's desk. "In hotel sanitation, we're the only game in town. Go ahead and try bringin in an outside company and see what happens." He chuckled again.

Seebok sputtered a bit. It sounded as though he tried to catch his breath. Talk about a guy in over his head.

"Lissen up, asshole. You say it's gifts you're lookin for. Somethin to shut you up?"

"Uh, well, that would be great if you could. It would wipe the slate clean with us," Seebok replied in a shaky voice. "I don't want anything major. My other vendor promised to throw in a gift or two. Already brought something by this morning."

"You have no other sanitation vendors!" Alletti thundered, "like I tole you... nah, never mind. You just don't get it. Quite frankly, you're wastin my precious time."

The squeak of the chair meant that the city's hotel sanitation boss stood up. The door to Mr. Ganiff's office unbolted. "Gifts," he grumbled on the way out, "this moron's lookin for a handout. Oh, we're gonna give him somethin to be happy about!"

★ ★ ★ ★ ★

The following day, ahead of the appointed time, I took a seat at my desk. Mr. Ganiff had been calling in for his morning update at eight–fifteen on the dot. His punctuality was refreshing. Perhaps he checked in to make sure that, God forbid, I wasn't slacking off in his absence. This time I arrived at five to eight to be safe. I hadn't even touched my coffee when the phone rang.

"Linda, what's the latest?"

"Oh, good morning, Mr. Ganiff. Everything's fine. No major crisis, unless you count Steven Koneman. He's asking for a comped room for a client next week."

"Oh, great! Fine, give it to him. I'm glad that I'm not around so I don't have to cater to his every need."

We spoke civilly for several minutes about general office matters. Sure enough, he couldn't refrain from educating me with a little tidbit.

"Linda, you have no idea the kind of sushi they have here. There are things I didn't even know existed! Absolutely amazing. Far better than what you can get in New York."

I refrained from responding, hoping he'd stop talking. *Wishful thinking!*

"Let me tell you one thing," he continued with enthusiasm, eager to dispense a little Ganiff wisdom to ensure that the Anal Monologues would continue despite his physical absence, "in certain restaurants, they have pictures on the menus of the food for each meal. When they serve you the food, it looks exactly like the picture!"

"What about the taste?" I asked to appease him.

"That's another story. I don't think it matters to them as long as the pictures match. It also depends where you eat."

I paused because of a violent sneezing sound coming from the corridor. A set of hurried footsteps approached my office. Trish poked in her head. In an attempt to give semblance to a promotion without actually doing the nasty deed, Mr. Ganiff had recently hired her as Seebok's Executive Assistant. It placated the man, for the time being.

"Holy shit! Do you smell that?" She fanned and pinched her nose.

"Smell what?" I asked, looking up from my desk.

"Excuse me," Ganiff said from his end of the line, "what's going on?"

"Oh, Mr. Ganiff. It's, well, someone came in here to report a foul odor."

"Odor? From where? *Bliss?*"

"Trish, what smell are you talking about?" Repeatedly, I pointed to the phone receiver with my free hand. She didn't get the subtle hint. Frowning, I hissed at her, "I'm on the line with Mr. Ganiff and I didn't notice a thing."

"How could you not?" she replied, indifferent to my frantic gestures. "I think it's coming from my office. You know, Seebok's office upstairs. Can't get in and don't wanna 'cause it smells like someone died in there! You can smell it in the hallway and even down here."

Great, I thought. *Seebok is dead in his office, and as usual, Ganiff isn't around to deal with it.* "Mr. Ganiff, sorry to do this to you. Let me call you back."

He yelled, "Wait! Wait! Wait!" before I hung up. Quickly, I dialed Big Guy down in the Lobby.

"Linda, the Front Desk was telling me about some recent complaints. Something about a stench by the fourth floor executive offices. Shouldn't we call Housekeeping?"

"Maybe we should meet up by Seebok's office. Don't forget to bring your keys. The door is locked from the inside."

Trish and I met Big Guy by the rear elevator bank. The smell from Seebok's office was overpowering. Trish had grabbed some bath towels from a housekeeping cart which we used to cover our noses.

"You don't think he's in there, do you?" Trish asked through the white towel.

"I hope not," I answered, grateful that the towel not only muffled the odor, but my facial expression which ranged from hysteria to horror. My mother always told me I couldn't play poker. I did, though, worry about Seebok, especially after his contentious meeting with Nick Alletti the day before.

Big Guy fumbled for the key on his ring. Most of the building used the latest in security cards except for the executive offices. Big Guy's key ring held twenty or more of the old fashioned types. It should've been an easy go except that Big Guy couldn't juggle the towel and the key ring at the same time. I couldn't tell if he were naturally clumsy, or he feared what awaited him on the other side of the malodorous door. Trish and I stood there, our arms wrapped around each other, ready for the worst.

Just when the tumbler of the key cylinder clicked, someone behind us cleared his throat. Trish screeched like an eagle.

"Morning," said Seebok to the three of us. "Hey, what's that smell?" he asked as the horrible odor wound its way into his nasal receptors. "Wow, reminds me of home cooking. Are we hosting some sort of food expo here?"

"Seebok, we thought you were… well never mind," said Big Guy.

He turned the latch.

Like a tsunami, the stench flowed through the doorway and hit us with a force so powerful that it burnt the hairs off my eyebrows and upper lip, saving me countless hours from dyeing and plucking. The stench also reminded me of a butcher shop on a scorching August day with no air conditioning.

Then he flicked on the light switch. While we were still reeling from the odor, the brutal sight before us almost rendered us blind. Spread out across Seebok's desk were dead animal carcasses in various forms of rigor mortis. Big Guy's eyes widened. A few more were wedged in the desk drawers. Tongues dangled out of the side of their mouths, eyes wide open. Splayed on its back, legs stiffly up in the air, one critter had the markings of a partial autopsy as evidenced by the classic Y formation. Gagging, I turned to leave, not before spotting a hoof jutting out of the credenza unit. Trish, with one hand hovering by her chest near her heart, pointed with the other to a rabbit haunch. It stood straight up from the fax machine. We avoided at all costs the tail sticking out from under the overhead bookshelves because it was apparent that a horse's head was stuffed inside.

From these remains, we identified a few of them: Cats. Dogs. Monkeys. Rabbits. Gerbils. Parakeets. Perch. Camels. In all likelihood, stolen from some sort of petting zoo or pet store. A dismembered cougar served as the centerpiece. We were mystified about the significance of that. The rest were mutilated, eviscerated and unidentifiable rat–like things. Someone sighed next to me. The petite Trish staggered and fainted into my arms. I had to drag her out into the corridor where she wouldn't be trampled, or worse, splattered by the puddles of blood.

When I returned, Big Guy shouted repeatedly, "What the fuck?" He took two steps toward Seebok with his arms raised in fighting mode. An antler and a river of blood flowing from the carnage impeded his progress. "Seebok, you deviant, what the hell have you been doing in here with all these animals?"

"I… I swear, it wasn't me!" Seebok's eyes bulged from their sockets. "These aren't mine. I had nothing to do with this. I promise you, it wasn't like this when I left here yesterday."

Big Guy stepped over the mess on the floor to walk further into the office. "Look at all this blood. Who the hell would do something this vile?"

I had my suspicions, but kept them to myself.

Seebok refused to go much further than the doorway. He shook like a leaf. "Call housekeeping or 911, or something. I'm not going back in there till someone cleans this up."

Some ten minutes later, four unlucky members of the housekeeping staff were assigned to mop–up duties. When the women arrived and witnessed the ritualistic slain bodies of those poor animals, each one of them cried hysterically. "No, no no touch this," shouted one of the women. "Santeria! Santeria!" she shrieked over and again, before fleeing the office. The others followed suit.

"What the hell're they talking about?" Big Guy had his hands on his hips and a clothespin on his nose. "Get Ms. Wapiti here! Get this shit cleaned up!"

The chaos prevailed for several minutes. Crowds of Supreme Superior personnel and hotel guests gathered in the hallway near Seebok's office. I could have made a fortune if I had had the foresight to charge admission.

Johnny, Big Guy's second in command, set up cordons around the offensive room, kindly taking into account Trish who hadn't yet risen from the floor. Initially, this effort kept people at bay. Nevertheless, their morbid curiosity overcame their senses. They pushed forward as one collective mass. Big Guy tried in vain to keep the curiosity seekers away. He grabbed his walkie–talkie shouting, "May Day! May Day! Send in reinforcements." Johnny pushed back, no doubt reminiscent of his younger days when he had worked as a bouncer at Studio 54.

On the plus side, the reek of decomposing animal flesh acted as an effective barrier. People gagged as they moved closer to the source of the smell. Doreen stepped over the cordon and declared, "Thath the motht dithguthting thing I've efer theen in my life." To prove this statement, she added her very own personal vomit to the mess on the floor, missing the antlers by inches.

Two more cleaning women arrived with mops, trashcans and plastic medical waste bags. Looking around the room, one of them shouted "Santeria" to the other.

Both women covered their eyes and ran off crying.

"What the fuck?" Big Guy asked again, and I gathered this time it was a rhetorical question. He was at the end of his rope. "Why won't anyone clean up this damn office? What the hell are they screaming about?"

"Santeria," explained Ms. Wapiti, who arrived in the nick of time, "is an ancient sacrificial rite, or so I'm told. Anyhow, these women think that Seebok is a practitioner of these rituals where animals are slaughtered in strange and devious ways. For all these years, he never allowed Housekeeping in here, so now they know what he's been up to. It scares them. It scares me!"

"And it scares the shit outta me too, Wapiti. Sacrificial rite or not, we gotta get someone up here to take care of this. The front desk is swamped with complaints about the stench."

"Plus," I piped up, "the blood may seep into the floor below and more than likely end up dripping in Mr. Ganiff's office!"

That sentence alone propelled the entire room into action. It took nine people almost an entire workday to clean up. Even then the smell of rotting animals still lingered, despite the vat of bathroom odor eaters pumped into the air vents.

Seebok remained shaken, but not sufficiently so. He had the audacity to inform me later on that day that he wouldn't go back into his office until certain conditions were met.

"First, I want the locks to my office changed. Whoever did this must have the key." He was oblivious as to the responsible party. "Secondly, I want security cameras and motion sensors installed. I wanna catch the bastard who did this to me."

The change of locks was done easily enough. Security resolved this matter within minutes of the clean–up. Housekeeping delivered a new desk from one of the storage rooms in the subbasement after the sodden blood–stained carpeting was stripped from the floor and replaced with old linoleum tiles. Still, we had to justify the expense of installing motion sensors and security cameras. This meant that the Gang of Three had to approve the expenditure in Mr. Ganiff's absence. We all knew that that definitely was not going to happen. Seebok had no other choice than to return to his office later that afternoon.

I headed back upstairs after five o'clock, curious to see if things had returned to some degree of normalcy. It appeared as if Seebok was once again on his speakerphone. Trish caught a glimpse of me outside the office and came running over to the doorway.

"Shhh." She put an index finger over her lips. "He's on the phone with that Alletti guy. Clueless as ever."

The two of us stood on either side of the open door, trying hard not to laugh.

"No, I never got a message from you earlier today. What time did you call?"

asked Seebok.

Nick Alletti gave out a loud chuckle that reverberated through the speakerphone. "Knucklehead, I didn't say I called. I wanna know if you got my message."

"Oh, um, did you send a fax? I haven't been at my desk much today so I might've missed it. It's been a bit crazy here."

Alletti laughed again. "Yeah, I can only imagine."

"What were you calling about, Nick? Are you ready to make me a counteroffer? You don't have to match the other guy's price," Seebok spoke in a conciliatory voice, "you just have to be in the ballpark and I'm sure we'll re–up with you guys."

"Oh, right, the other guys. Must've forgotten about them." He ceased to speak for a moment. Then he exploded, "You halfwit, there's a reason why your renewal is automatic. Automatic, you fuckin bonehead. Don't they teach you how to read a contract at school, you fuckin nimrod? Did you even bother to read it, huh? Ain't no exit clause in there!" Nick paused to catch his breath. "Lemme spell it out for you so you don't get lost in the translation. It's us or no one. Got it? Is there any part of this that I need to make clearer?"

"Ah, no sir," Seebok sounded shaken like he lost ground again. "I... I didn't say we weren't renewing with you. I'm trying to get the best price."

"The best price, Mr. Seebok, is whatever fuckin price I tell you our services cost, and not a penny less. So you tell your friend Ganiff to lay off and stop testin me and sendin his birdbrain associate to torment me. Repeat after me, jerk, it's auto–renewal," Nick coached him.

Seebok didn't say a word.

"You fuckin moron, I told you to repeat after me, okay?" Nick shrieked at him.

"Okay," Seebok repeated.

"Not, 'Okay,'" Nick shrieked at even a higher pitch, "repeat after me, the words, you fuckin asshole."

"You fuckin asshole."

"Are you tryin to goad me?" A moment of silence. I gathered that Nick was trying to get control of himself.

"Let's try it again, God help me. Repeat the words, it's auto–renewal!"

"It's auto–renewal."

"Good," said Nick. He expelled a loud sigh.

"What about my gift?" whined Seebok.

Whack whack whack went the receiver against a solid piece of furniture. When the noise died down, Nick calmly replied, "Your gift? Ah... right.

For auto–renewing our existing agreement." Another moment of silence. "You just love gifts, huh? What kinda gift are you lookin for? You want a kickback? Maybe a commission on the deal?"

Trish and I exchanged concerned glances. She whispered, "You think we should butt in now and save the nincompoop?" She took a half step inside the office but I grabbed her back. This was primo entertainment.

"Oh, no," Seebok replied, "I couldn't accept... I was thinking... electronics. Maybe a new stereo, a computer, or something."

"Electronics, huh? Guess you don't like pets." A brief silence. Then, there was a noise representing the wheels turning in Nick Alletti's head followed by his subdued voice, "Tell you what. Why don't you make me a list of the kinda things you're lookin for and fax it over to me before you leave today. I think I could probably do a little somethin for ya."

After he hung up, Seebok, from his new desk, scrawled a list of all the gadgets he always desired and could never seem to afford. A laptop computer. A projection TV. A multi–disc CD carousel. A cordless shaver. Trish was anxious to slip away.

"I gotta go," she whispered, "more than likely he'll have me type up the list so that Nick Alletti won't have to read his illegible handwriting." She slipped back in.

I returned to my desk downstairs and discovered that I had missed a call from Hank Sandstone, Manager of Human Resources at the Waldorf. The hotel operators left a scribbled message on my desk to call him back at my convenience. Hank, formerly a department head at the hotel, had replaced my old friend, Penelope.

I gave him a buzz back. He answered on one ring.

"Hey Hank, thanks for getting back in touch with me."

"Linda dear, how's the job going at the Supreme Superior, you turncoat?" We both laughed. Hank added, "Funny thing, I heard from Penelope as well today. She's doing great. Told me that she no longer wears suits like the old days."

"No suits?" I asked, surprised. "Isn't she still corporate?"

"She is. Rumor has it that it's a little more relaxed on the islands. Says she wears some sort of Hawaiian dress with a bare midriff. Even puts a honeysuckle behind her ear!"

I asked, "Has my friend gone native?"

Hank responded, "Think she was already there before she left. From the stories that circulated around here, it's a good thing you two were separated. Crazy chicks!" Hank cleared his throat. "Never mind that. Let's move on to business. You have great timing!"

"Do I? I'm not used to too many compliments these days in my new career."

Hank chuckled. "Well, it just so happens we could use a few good busboys over here at the moment. Specially those who worked at a five–star hotel and trained to give five–star service. Why don't you have your guy come over first thing tomorrow? I'll make it a point to meet with him. Set him up. Thanks for thinking of us."

"Hank, you're wonderful."

"Of course I am, Linda. Feel free to contact me, any time, to place any highly qualified people from your hotel. Takes the pressure off of our training and development as well as the cost!"

After he hung up, I couldn't dial fast enough.

"Hello, Gary answering."

"Gary, it's Linda over at the Supreme Superior. You got a minute?"

"Miss Linda, oh, hello. Thank you for the letter you send me. It's very, very nice. Just came here."

Letter? Suddenly, I recalled the letter of recommendation. In the thrill of the moment I forgot all about it. "Do you remember that I told you I might be able to help get you a job at another hotel?"

"Yes, Miss Linda. This means so important to me, to my family."

"Well, I got great news. I got off the phone with the Waldorf. My guy wants you to see him first thing tomorrow morning. They might have something for you right now."

It took a moment for the information to sink in. He must've been holding back his tears because his voice turned thick.

"Miss Linda, this is real? Waldorf Park Avenue, yes? Famous hotel from movies?"

I giggled. "Yes, yes, the Waldorf–Astoria! I used to work there and the manager knows me. He's a terrific guy. Anyway, go see him first thing tomorrow. Please don't let me down."

Gary Yong took down the contact information which I had him read back to me twice to make sure that nothing was lost in translation.

"Okay, so I go there in the morning, Miss Linda. Even if I don't get job, I say so much thank you for helping." His voice became wobbly again as though he were overcome by emotion. "This means so much everything. My wife, she is so... she needs me to be at job with insurance. What you do, Miss Linda, you are a good woman. I really mean it."

At last, I thought, *someone around here who appreciates my efforts*. If helping Gary and his ailing wife was a way for me to stick it to Ganiff, all the more meaningful.

"Holy shit, Linda! You gotta come up here and see this. It happened again," Trish yelled from the corridor in front of my office early the following morning.

Phone receiver glued to my ear, I was already tuned into the Ganiff show. This episode had him boasting about his flawless presentation to the Board of Directors, the one that I put together in record time. He was in the midst of recapping the Board's reaction to his brilliant plan for the hotel expansion when Trish interrupted me once again from another important conversation.

Now, in front of my desk she ploughed on, impervious to the fact that I was on the phone with Ganiff. "Linda, you are not gonna believe this! They did it again last night. Someone broke in and set fire to the place. Everything's... I don't know... melted."

I covered the phone and glanced over at Trish whose face shifted between horror and amusement—de rigueur when confronted with a Seebok situation. "Um, fine, gimme a minute to finish up with You–Know–Who," I whispered, "he still doesn't know about yesterday. I'm hoping to keep it that way."

"Linda, you there?" Ganiff sounded impatient. "Is there a problem I should know about?"

"Um, well nothing I can't handle," I lied. "Seems there's an issue with the locks on Seebok's office. I'm gonna go and check it out."

This time I didn't call Big Guy. The doorknob had been drilled out and left on the floor.

The scene inside was not unbearable, as had been the case twenty–four hours earlier. At least not unbearable to Trish and me. There was no blood. No animal gizzards strewn about. No hacked off animal limbs flung helter–skelter. No buckets of guts similar to a George Romero movie.

Nevertheless, the Alletti family had sent another message.

Seebok walked in behind us. His high–pitched scream alerted us both that he had arrived.

"Ohmigod, what have they done to... What happened to my computer? My printer? My radio?" He slid to his knees and sobbed, tears streaming down his face. "The horror of it all!" He banged his head on the newly installed linoleum. "How... how'd they get in here? I thought we changed the locks yesterday." Once again, Seebok carried on further, "Oh, the inhumanity of it all!"

Every electronic item in Seebok's office had been methodically melted down and left on display. Every precious gift the man had groveled for: a CD player, an RCA TV, a VCR, a talking alarm clock from the Sharper Image.

On Seebok's new desk lay the smoldering ruins of what had once been his computer and monitor, now a heap of melted plastic and wires. Even the cheap laptop he'd stolen from his alma mater was unrecognizable.

Trish and I looked at each other and shrugged. Seebok scraped himself off the floor and made his way to his desk, a shell of the man he once was. "Who the hell would do this to me?" He threw his hands up in the air. "Why me of all people?" He dropped down into his swivel chair, the sole plastic item not melted down. Atop his desk sat a single piece of paper. Examining it, his face turned ash white.

"What is it?" asked Trish. "Did someone leave a note?"

Seebok was deep in thought. After a while, he looked up at us, puzzlement written on his face. "It's not a note, it's a list. Something I had you type yesterday."

Trish stepped over to Seebok's desk and snatched the page from his hands. "Yeah, that's the list I faxed to Alletti." She studied it. "There's something scribbled down here at the bottom."

"What does it say?" I asked, my mouth hanging wide open from the suspense.

She squinted, trying to decipher the handwriting. "I think it says: 'Happy Birthday you dumb piece of shit. Hope you got everything on your wish list. Cordially yours.'"

"It's not my birthday!" Seebok leaped from his chair. "That's not until March." He pouted and shook his head in disgust. Until it dawned on him. Dawning recognition is an amazing thing. You read about it in books, nonetheless to experience it is akin to watching the sun turn green right before it sets.

"Holy shit! That piece of paper must be from Alletti. He's gonna kill me!" He ran over to me and grabbed my shoulders, "Do you think he will, Linda?"

"I don't know, Seebok." I attempted to remove his grimy hands from my suit jacket, finger by finger, but he caught me with a Vulcan death grip. "He did write 'Cordially yours' at the end. I mean, that's not necessarily a death threat, is it?"

He withdrew his hands and grabbed his hair, moaning, "I'm so dead, so dead. He's gonna kill me, isn't he?"

"Hard to know." I shrugged. "He did write that you're 'a piece of shit.'"

"No, Linda, he wrote, and I quote, a 'dumb piece of shit,'" Trish corrected.

"Thanks for the clarification, Trish," I responded, at which she shot me a one–finger salute.

Seebok once more fell to his knees, slobbering. My tone sounded pretty callous when I replied, "Don't know, kiddo. Don't know if you're a dead man. It does seem fifty–fifty." I turned to leave for my office but couldn't refrain from shooting off one more volley. "A fine mess you put me in, my friend."

It was a fine mess indeed. I had no choice other than to tell Ganiff about Seebok's misadventures with the hotel sanitation boss. Within a half–hour, Seebok and I were seated at the conference table in Ganiff's office on a video teleconference.

"Linda, didn't I tell you to keep an eye on this fuck–up?" Ganiff railed from the Supreme Superior Hotel's main videoconference room in Tokyo. Though his face appeared somewhat calm, I could see his chest heaving. I shot Seebok a baleful glance while Ganiff continued his harangue. "Do you see now why I asked you to do that? I asked you to do one thing and one thing only, Linda and you couldn't do it. I'm sorely disappointed in you." He was so enraged that I could smell burning from the newly laid transoceanic fiber optic cable system. Then he turned his attention to my companion. "Seebok, what the fuck were you thinking? Who told you to take this on?"

"I thought—" Seebok stammered.

"You thought what? That you'd save us a few bucks? Become a hero? Seebok, you just don't fuck with these people!" Ganiff pushed his nose to the side, a New York gesture for made men. "Didn't they teach you anything at Cornell?"

"I… I was only trying to—"

"Well, you failed miserably," Ganiff retorted. He reached down for a piece of paper in front of him. "I got off the phone with Alletti. Here are the new terms and conditions for our contract renewal. Which, incidentally, is a matter of course because it is an evergreen contract. There's no end date! That's what evergreen means, forever!" He picked up the paper. "Alletti just faxed it over. A thirty percent increase! Thirty percent, Seebok. After every *aut–o–ma–tic re–new–al*, there is a step up in pricing, something we never had before. Trust me, we got off easy." Ganiff sighed resignedly and pushed his nose to the side again. "We're all lucky to still be here to talk about it."

I stared at the video image of Ganiff and pretty much thought, *Who me, Kemosabe?* I wasn't responsible for this madness. Nevertheless, for once I admitted that Ganiff was right about something. Seebok was lucky to have escaped with his life.

How is he getting away with all this idiocy? I kept asking myself. *It couldn't merely be for comic relief. What did Seebok have on Ganiff that kept him employed through all this turmoil? What was the relationship between these two men that kept Ganiff supporting him time and time again?*

I was determined to find out. That would be the integral key to the lunacy surrounding me.

Speaking of lunacy, Doreen sauntered into my office.

"Hey Dor–een. Mr. Ganiff's away. In Japan." After that videoconference meeting, let's say that my mood did not warrant a Doreen–style investigative interview.

She looked at me. "I know that. Jutht wanted to know if you heard from him." Her eyes narrowed. "Or rather, if he hath heard whath been happening here."

I sighed with impatience. "Doreen, not only does he know what went on, he didn't even have to use the phone. You could've heard his shrieks all the way from Tokyo."

116

Doreen flopped down on one of my guest chairs. She commiserated with me. "Oh, that'th not right. You did your betht and it wathn't your fault. It wath that damn Theebok!"

She peered behind her and then turned to face me. In a conspiratorial manner she whispered, "He'th a menathe all right, that Theebok."

"You think I don't know?" I said. "Doreen, since I've been here, I feel like I take the hits for him and I don't even like him!"

"You're not the only one!" she said and gently patted my hand. She rose to her feet and said before she left, "If it giveth you any contholation!"

Perhaps no consolation yet. Although misery at the Supreme Superior makes the day go faster.

Chapter 15

All the department heads were summoned to a conference room on the second floor upon their arrival on Monday morning. The boss—who had gotten home bright and early Sunday—sat at the head of the conference table with a wide grin spread across his face.

"Ladies and gentleman, I'm pleased to announce the acceptance by our head office of my proposal for the three million dollar allowance to upgrade our banquet floors upstairs." He stopped and waited for our polite applause which eventually came. "So, capital improvements should be commencing shortly. Within a year's time, our top floor convention rooms should be on par with every major hotel in this city." Tepid applause followed. Ganiff beamed.

After the meeting, Ganiff trotted back to his office at double pace. I followed in his wake. He pointed at one of his upholstered chairs. "Take a seat for some notes, Linda." Prior to his trip, he had had me draft the three proposals from Nikrovetch, Mountainside and Sensai. "I need you to alter them a bit to make certain that Nikrovetch wins this deal. You hear me?"

Without any warning, his mood swung from joyousness to insane rage in less than a nanosecond. He rose from his desk and slammed his door shut. In fury, he paced the room.

"Linda, so here I figured I was the conquering hero coming home from battle victoriously. Instead, I'm confronted by Mabel who thrusts a pile of papers into my arms, asking me what in the world is going on. Before I could even put down my attaché case, all hell's already breaking loose."

What was that man talking about? I reflected, puzzled. "Mr. Ganiff, I thought I had everything under control while you were away," I said, sidestepping the Seebok incidents. "What're you talking about?"

He tossed a wad of papers at me. "This fucking maniac has the nerve to put his fucking letters under my door! Linda, did you know about this?"

"Know about what? Mr. Ganiff, which maniac are you referring to?" I prayed it wasn't another surprise gift from Nick Alletti. I scanned the loose pages to determine the source of his ire.

Scrawled in block letters were threatening messages from Mr. Donald Silverberg. He was the griping client to whom I had drafted a response several weeks earlier, only to have it discarded by Mr. Ganiff.

Mr. Silverberg had evidently paid off one of our bellhops to slip these missives under the door of the Ganiffs' private suite on the 44th floor. Silverberg was furious that Ganiff had never responded to his letter. Nor to the messages he had left over the previous two weeks with Mr. Ganiff's assistant (namely me), nor to the faxes he had directed to Mr. Ganiff's attention. So he had gone one step further and had his letters delivered directly. This was a man on a mission. He wanted his money back.

"Mr. Ganiff, I had no idea. I mean, sure, the guy called here a handful of times asking for you while you were gone. I ignored him like you told me to. How was I to know that he'd go this far with his complaints?"

Ganiff's face turned scarlet. "Fine, whatever. Get Harry Landsman on the line."

"Who?"

"Harry, our attorney. This Silverberg claims he'll sue us for a refund. Let's see what we can do. Oh, and please close the door behind you."

The customary screaming pierced the closed door. This time, however, the timbre was slightly different. Through my trusty friend the intercom, I heard Harry lay down the law. He said he would handle the Silverberg case within the realm of quid pro quo, as the old saying goes. Handling Silverberg was the quid part. The pro quo was that Mr. Ganiff had to stop dithering about signing the eviction order for the illegal tenant in the West 53rd Street apartment, something he neglected to do over the past four years. At this point, I had to escape far away from the shrill wails that reverberated through the intercom and phone wires, resulting in a stereo effect akin to microphone feedback. Luckily, BeeBee returned from her two–hour cigarette break, just in time.

Before I could get too far, Ganiff caught up to me in the hallway. He tapped me on the shoulder.

"Um, Linda, since we got the money for our construction project, we're probably gonna get started on this very soon. So, I was hoping to take you on a behind–the–scenes tour of the hotel. See some areas that you haven't been to before."

"What areas are those?" I asked, unsure of the mood swing as well as his intentions. I couldn't figure out why he was being so nice to me. I knew he still hadn't gotten over the Alletti situation. It was a fresh bone of contention. And, for some reason, he blamed me. Not Seebok, me! Despite Ganiff's comical gestures of compressed noses and nostrils, it was evident that the man was scared for his life. Unbidden, a thought appeared that I couldn't shake. *Was he out to murder me in retaliation?*

"Linda, if you're going to become a full fledged manager around here, you need to see the nuts and bolts of this building. I'm talking the ventilation system, the generators, the electrical system and so on. The heart and guts of this place. Do you want to join me?" He walked in step with me down the corridor.

I was intrigued, weirded out, even frightened out of my wits. Outside of my orientation tour, Ganiff had never bothered offering any other instruction. Now this. I figured that if he wanted to give me a crash course in running the hotel's infrastructure, I might as well take full advantage. On the other hand, since a visit to the bowels of the building was rare indeed, he could kill me and bury my body, and no one would be the wiser.

"Okay, let's go!" I said.

We rode the elevator down to the Lobby, then took a stairwell down to a basement level to which I'd never previously ventured.

"When they decided to acquire this particular building, management approached me and asked me for feedback." Ganiff's voice rebounded off the concrete walls, floors and ceilings. Navigating another round of steps in the maze of corridors, I paid attention to the uneven flooring rather than his discourse. And even more attention to dropping shredded pieces of gum to mark my trail, a precautionary and preemptive move for leaving evidence in case of my untimely death.

He continued, "There are in existence three subbasements. Management wanted to add another for an in–house laundry. After extensive study, I determined that the depreciation would be too rapid to justify such an expense. They heeded what I had to say." That explained why, unlike other major hotels in New York City, the Supreme Superior did not have their own in–house laundry facility.

"According to my figures, it was cheaper having a laundry service and a good contract than having the equipment and doing it here. Depreciation, wear and tear, extra personnel." I knew what he meant although I did not agree. I wisely kept my remarks to myself.

Lastly, we entered a vestibule filled with security ramps and cameras. Cappy, the building's chief engineer, released the lock that opened to a room resplendent with groans and arrhythmic vibrations from immense metallic engines suspended from the ceiling like stalactites. Ganiff stepped in like he owned the place. Like the curious fool I was, I followed him inside. At the very least, Cappy would be a witness, credibility notwithstanding.

"This here's the air–conditioning generator. We have three units for the hotel. One of 'em is the back–up. Nevertheless, we barely use them to capacity." Ganiff stood at attention in front of a huge engine that dominated the room. "When I entered this industry," he shouted above the noise, "I spent my first year with the engineering crew, crawling in and around the machinery. Other General Managers wouldn't bother to step foot in here." With a succinct duck of his head, he nodded in the direction of another room where even more ominous noises and smells originated.

The smells were quite distinct—they were back of the throat–catching types of odors: those of a witches' cauldron equipped with mandatory long wooden spoons to stir the customary inclusion of animal by–products like eye of newt. Ingredients included a twist of metal scrapings, several gallons of burnt oil, a filled flacon of propane, quite a few pinches of sodden rubber topped off with copious quantities of lead–injected commercial paint. Each individually distinguishable but a noxious stench combined together. This smell meant serious machinery business. Nothing

I was too interested in and definitely not a place I wanted to explore. Might find a series of bodies buried back there. Perhaps former hotel union representatives.

Unflappable, Ganiff pointed out various oversized pistons, clamps, engines, rotisseries and other assorted mechanical objects. For my edification, he identified them by their technical names and explained their functions over the din, losing for a few minutes all the oily charm he naturally exuded. The racket gave me a headache, especially in that hot, stuffy and putrid environment. Even so, the crash course seemed well intended and my fear of being dismembered ebbed away.

"Should you ever consider the position of General Manager, Linda, it is necessary for you to familiarize yourself with this equipment. Your ignorance alone could cost the hotel millions. Never rely on anyone. Especially Cappy. He's about as dumb as they come."

Sure enough, Cappy stood right there at the doorway; short, bandy–legged, with a quick grin, eager to please though nervous. Ganiff tightly grabbed my elbow and shoved me out of the room. He released me to slap Cappy on the back. "Hey there, tight ship."

"Mr. Ganiff, Mr. Ganiff," Cappy pulled on Mr. Ganiff's tailored suit jacket to get his attention.

"What is it, Cappy?" Ganiff rapidly lost his bonhomie.

"I don't understand this light bulb project," he complained. "Do you want me to get quotes on those new long–lasting bulbs, the ones that Con Ed wants us to use? Is that what you want me to do?"

"Dammit, how long does a simple project like that take?" Ganiff whooped, "I mean, how long does it take our chief engineer to screw in some light bulbs?"

Cappy yammered on, "But Mr. Ganiff, sir, please listen," growing nervous until his speech jack–hammered into a rapid stutter resembling the putter of a motor boat, "but but but but but but."

"I don't want to deal with this, Cappy. Give Linda the figures. She'll submit them to me."

He turned his back and stomped out en route to the employee cafeteria. "Hey Linda, care to grab some lunch with me?"

First the grand tour, then lunch with the boss… And, no vivisection in–between. Had I hit the jackpot? What happened to this man in Japan? Complacently, I followed.

The moment Mr. Ganiff entered the concrete structure on the far side of subbasement No. 2, all conversation stopped. Housekeepers, bellhops, maintenance, security, kitchen help—all the 135 different languages spoken at the Supreme Superior ceased mid–sentence. Eyeballs protruded. This definitely counted as an event. At the counter, we ordered the specialty of the house—oxtail stew, left–over banquet salad and Sara Lee angel food cake. Under ordinary circumstances, the portions would've been significantly smaller, rendering the meal much more palatable. Well, it goes to show the advantages of consorting with the General Manager. We hoisted the trays and hauled them to the middle of the room where we slid onto seats attached to a pre–fabricated Formica laminated table.

The congealed clumps of the oxtail stew glistened under the reflection of the overhead flickering fluorescent lights. Mr. Ganiff loudly extolled the quality of his meal. "How utterly delectable." He hoisted a steaming pile on his fork to shovel into his mouth, whereas I plucked at the bone splinters that had gotten trapped between my teeth and stuck in my gums. With gusto, he polished off the stew. I made a production of wiping my lips to avoid eating the glop heaped on my plate. The chunks and copious quantity of gristle turned my stomach, yet I had to eat the slop because we were performing for the benefit of the hotel. Yea, rah, rah Supreme Superior Hotel.

BeeBee was in the adjacent smoking room separated from the rest of the cafeteria by a glass wall. Her tablemates included Ms. Djorak, Big Guy and Murlise. Plumes of cigarette smoke curled around her head. I must've had a hallucination because I could've sworn that she made the gesture of slitting her throat. The one similar to the gesture that the Poles made to the Jews interred in the cattle cars en route to Auschwitz. I shook my head in disbelief.

"I always make it my policy to be with my people, to keep my fingers on the pulse of the hotel," Mr. Ganiff expressed as we made our way through the tunnels back to the front of the house for coffee at the hotel lounge. "Plus, I like the food every time I go there. It's always excellent."

★ ★ ★ ★ ★

That afternoon, I was swamped with a flurry of telephone calls. Clearly, BeeBee wasn't at her desk to help me. The lack of support was daunting. It ran counter to my work load which consisted of comparing construction quotes, writing Ganiff's speech to the Chairman of the hotel chain, and putting together press releases for the upcoming holiday season.

For the past week, I had focused on meeting deadlines for press/public relations releases and articles, since the extremely well–paid hotel public relations executive, Barby Mandy, was functionally illiterate. Instead of confronting her, Mr. Ganiff passed her work onto me and I found another hidden talent: Copywriter.

Doreen strode in with a huge grin on her face. "Hi, Linda. Did you enjoy your lunch with Mithter Ganiff?"

From behind the mound on my desk I said, "Oh, hey Doreen. Yeah."

"That wath the firtht time he efer went to the cafeteria," Doreen confided. "I can't beliefe he ate that shit! I gueth he wanted to impreth you."

"Or kill me," I answered. "He already had his opportunity in the sub–

basement." Doreen looked at me strangely as I continued, "Well, I guess he didn't want to get his hands dirty so he decided to poison me instead." I failed to mention that he had already had a shot at poisoning me, recalling the first meal at *Bliss*. Then, out of the blue, my synapses connected. "What, Doreen? He told me he eats there all the time!"

Doreen giggled. "Trutht me, if Mithter Ganiff had efer eaten there before, eferyone would be talking about it... jutht like they are right now."

First time. How interesting, I thought to myself, *the guy isn't even back half a day and he's already up to old tricks.*

Then Doreen confessed her real reason for stopping by.

"Linda, I'm tho pithed off today. That bitch. I can't beliefe that fucking bitch."

"Who? Which bitch are you talking about?"

"My athithtant. Thelena. She jutht pulled another no–show and now I have to thpend my time and energy to court her clienth."

Selena was one of the original plus–size cable TV talk show hostesses who married very well. Her latest career was selling block rooms to corporate clients. She was effective in her job. Very effective, as a matter of fact. Several of those clients became her lovers, if one listened to Cuneta, the marketing department's secretary and all–around gossip. Cuneta told me that Selena spent more time in the bedroom showrooms than anywhere else in the hotel.

"With Thelena, when she thayth court, it meanth court. The kind where I have to play with ballth in sheeth." She sighed. "Lately, I've been thleeping more with her clienth than with my huthband." She shook her head. "What'th worthe ith she thtill geth her commissionth."

Well, that was illuminating. Since I had nothing to add, I turned away, though Doreen pressed on.

"Who'th in the offith with Mithter Ganiff?"

"No one now."

"Wath Robenthtine there?"

"No."

"Nikrofetch?"

"No."

"Murlithe?"

"C'mon, Doreen. No one stayed with him after the meeting."

"What'th he doing?"

"When I left him, he was on the phone."

"With who?"

"Please, Doreen, not again."

The interrogation dragged on in this manner for another ten minutes.

Drained, I headed down to the subbasement No. 2 via the rear elevators to cage a smoke—a recently re-acquired habit since the television delivery incident. I stepped into the glassed room on the smoker's side of the cafeteria. Two housekeeping staff were dissing the hotel at full volume.

"Ili Babycakes," said the woman with the most volume. She was Carole Carlson, a gorgeous middle-aged black woman attired in a full-length seal fur over her uniform which she wore with elegance. "Whatchya doin' down here? Don't you eat at *Bliss* all the time?"

"If you want to know, I do alternate."

"Whaddya know," she said, "look at her, Wilma. You'd think they'd put a sistah up in the executive office? Ha!"

Wilma, an attractive middle-aged Filipino woman, nodded along with Carole and then said, "You missed out on the discussion, Linda."

"What about this time?" I addressed Wilma, avoiding Carole.

Carole cut in, "Oh, the upcoming strike."

Wilma and I exchanged exasperated, yet tolerant glances. We understood Carole's passion.

"All the hotels in the hood are joining in 'cept the Supreme Superior. Wonder of wonders," she laughed. "Have you seen my girlfriend, Ms. Djorak?"

"C'mon, Carole, stop goading me. Give me a minute to relax. It's no secret that woman despises me."

"Lemme tell ya something about her. They know down at the union that I'm the only African-American housekeeper in the entire hotel. The eight other sistahs are telephone operators. They know she purposely doesn't have many of us here. So they appointed me as their union rep."

I laughed. "That should make her cringe!"

Carole laughed right back. She pointed at her fur. "Lissen up, I don't need this job no more now that my son is on MTV and sold a million CDs. I watch him every day in the Health Club where they have those special wide-screens. My son, he keeps sayin' to me, 'Momma, leave that hole' but I tole him not until I get back at that Djorak. That bitch made my life miserable the past few years, always insulting me and putting me on notice for nothing." Carole loudly said, "I got her good to go with the fact that there are no African-American men in the entire hotel. Can you believe that? In New York City? What kind of bullshit can she dish out to the President of the hotel association to justify that?"

I blew out a mouthful of smoke and inhaled without coughing. Before I could get a word out, Carole spoke up once more.

"I mean, she makes sure that we don't get paid overtime. Since she's the one who hammered out the union contract, she knows how to slip between the cracks. And, girl, you don't wanna get me talking about us being understaffed!" She gave me a mischievous grin. "You know what drives that sick woman crazy?" she paused for effect, "I wear these furs while I scrub toilets!"

I grinned along with her. "Gotta hand it to you, Carole. Our bigoted Djorak has certainly met her match. Perhaps you'll be the one who'll teach her to practice one of the long–forgotten Christian concepts, like turning the other cheek." Carole and Wilma nodded their heads in agreement.

Carole possessed the clout and the power to bring Djorak down. And she was right about so much that was so wrong at the hotel. She had nothing to lose, especially since her heart was in the right place. In other words, we all need a hobby and Carole had found hers.

On my right were four individuals huddled around the standard pre–fabricated table. They were crammed into the attached plastic chairs poring over four sheets of photocopied *New York Times* crossword puzzles. A quartet of middle–managers for Food & Beverage, Front Desk, Reservations and Sales/Marketing. They recently discovered the delights of these puzzles. As a group effort, they were intellectually immersed in uncovering the clues during their break.

Over Carole's voice that distinctly extolled the virtues of the hotel union's solidarity, I called out to the crossword puzzlers, "Need any help?"

"Yeah. We're having some difficulty. Do you do crosswords?"

"Every morning. I try to complete them before I go to work."

That utterance produced a plethora of questions.

"Hey, Linda, what's another word for bookings that starts with an 'r'? This is a biggie, 11 letters," yelled the Front Desk manager with a big smirk on his face.

The Sales/Marketing guy tittered, "Here's a clue. What is it that an Upper East Side woman does for dinner?"

To indulge both managers, everyone in the room shouted "Reservations!" including Carole who halted mid–tirade about drumming up support for the upcoming hotel strike. But no one laughed.

I ended up correcting certain clues and dispensing advice on how to handle the hints given by the *New York Times* crossword puzzle editor, Eugene T. Maleska who two years earlier had succeeded the legendary Will Weng, most known for his sense of humor. We joked around for a few minutes before my colleagues fell silent. I turned around to face what killed the lighthearted bantering.

There loomed the silhouette of a hulking form. Ms. Djorak. Behind her lurked BeeBee who magically materialized in a puff of nicotine.

125

My smile evaporated. "Uh, BeeBee, if both of us are down here, who's watching the phones?"

"Oh, I switched them to the operators," she flippantly responded. Ms. Djorak leered.

"Ohmigod, not again," I wailed. Under my breath, audible only to Terriers, I muttered, "Fucking BeeBee!" She purposely went against a new Ganiff mandate.

He recently approached me. "I understand, Linda, that it's boring to stay at your desk all the time. I know it's not what you were hired to do."

What is he getting at? I wondered. I didn't have that long to wait.

"I appreciate that you have to walk away from time to time. But from now on, Linda, you're gonna have to limit your forays."

"Why?"

"Because I need you here to answer my phone. No one else knows how to filter calls. Definitely not BeeBee, nor our operators. They don't even know the difference between emergencies and regular calls. When you're not here, those imbeciles phone me constantly because they're too stupid to determine whether a call is important. As a result, I end up taking every call. And, most of the time it's from our guests with a complaint to make!"

I felt that all too familiar drop in the pit of my stomach. A panic–stricken look spread over my face. "What about when I have to get away?"

"BeeBee can cover for you but only for those very limited times when you must get away." He took one look at my face and said, "Yes, I mean it. There's no compromising."

Damn, I thought, *BeeBee gets to frolic whereas I'm trapped. There's no justice.*

I rose from the table with an elegance that I hadn't heretofore possessed and approached Carole. I shook her hand while patting the fur draped over her shoulder. Then I turned and waved goodbye to my fellow crossword puzzlers. Within seconds, I found myself in the adjoining hallway behind the cafeteria. Once out of sight, I sprinted down the concrete corridor, skidded on one heel past the locker rooms and made a sharp left toward the rear elevators. Housekeeping's central office was adjacent to the elevator banks and very steamy due to the spot dry cleaning performed on premises. While waiting for an elevator cab to appear, I pressed the up button several times. Ms. Wapiti materialized in a burst of steam.

"Oh, Linda, I'd suggest you head up to the Lobby to pick up the elevator there."

"What happened?" I asked, trying to catch my breath from my sprint and subsequent on–set of a panic attack.

"For some reason, they don't come all the way down here. Makes it the third consecutive day."

"Thanks for the tip."

I ran to the concrete stairwell and decided to race up the six flights of stairs using the toes of my high–heeled shoes. I ended up limping the final five and a half flights. And hoped it would be quiet at my office because all I wanted to do was collapse in my chair… except for one obstacle: the enormous backside belonging to the beautiful Selena that jutted into my office, blocking all entry. She was flirting with Ganiff from his doorway.

Doreen ran past me. In an attempt to slip past Selena in the doorway, she nudged into her so forcefully that they both burst into Ganiff's office at the same time. That provided me with the perfect opportunity to return to my desk. From there, I could spy on the two women vying for his attention. For some strange reason, they decided to dance. Doreen's version of dancing consisted of twitching her butt which induced her protruding belly to bounce in unison. Selena merengued around chairs, desk and conference table in delicate and dainty steps. Ganiff appeared quite bemused; his left eye jostled up and down while focusing on his proboscis. He repeatedly pulled on his mustache tips.

I would've laughed aloud if I hadn't still been out of breath from the jaunt upstairs. Conserving my energy, I fell back in my chair, yanked off my shoes and vigorously massaged my aching toes and calves. On a positive note, Ganiff didn't notice that both BeeBee and I had been absent; the ladies provided an invaluable distraction. The ringing phone disrupted the dancing competition.

"Linda, it's Marie. You wouldn't believe what's happening on twenty–three."

Marie was the assistant to the President of the William Morris Agency, situated across the street from the Supreme Superior on the 20th floor. The agency sent us several of their clients due to proximity. Marie occasionally reported in with the more interesting spectacles as many of our guests failed to shut their curtains in spite of their prolific and creative sexual habits. They provided our neighbors with comic relief and an education, not to mention free advertising for binocular manufacturers. Sales surged from this one building.

"Linda, who is it?" Ganiff shouted.

"It's Marie. Sighting on the twenty–third floor—two men, one woman and a whip," I yelled back while peering into his office from afar.

"Send her my best," Ganiff said good–naturedly, then turned his attention to the two women prancing around his desk. "Ladies, please permit me to do some work."

"Oh, Mithter Ganiff, do we have to go?" Doreen coquettishly asked while batting her eyelashes like the wings of a hummingbird.

He guffawed. "Sorry, ladies. I do have a hotel to run."

The two women stopped dancing and turned to leave the office. As they did, Mr. Ganiff added, "Don't forget to close the door behind you."

The moment Selena closed the door, the lock turned, as did Doreen who hissed at Selena, "Before you run off to Mithter Ganiff, you should dithcuth the matter with me. I'm the one who writeth your refiewth. I'm altho the one whoth been thleeping with your clienth ath well!"

Doreen's candid display of venom surprised me. It also surprised Selena. In return, Selena shot a look to kill. Doreen reciprocated with a scowl bred from pure maliciousness. Captivated by this interchange, I failed to notice the intercom buzzing and buzzing. As enjoyable as these scenes were, they should've been conducted behind closed doors, not in front of me. It was corporate policy not to leave witnesses. I had no option but to shoo the two of them out. I also had to answer the intercom.

Ganiff voiced the oft–repeated question, "Linda, has Nikrovetch given you the revised estimates?"

"Uh… not as of yet," I said, "he's been telling me 'tomorrow' every day."

"Then page him. Do it now! I need his breakdown pronto."

All at once, Ms. "highest paid" Wapiti entered my office with Mr. Dorck. Wapiti proceeded to lean her tiny frame onto and over my desk. In the process, she managed to block access to my phone. "I need Mr. Ganiff now!" she demanded, her face inches from mine.

"I'm sorry. Do you have an appointment?"

"It's rather important," Wapiti insisted which I sensed, given her odd invasion of my personal space.

I reached around Wapiti's silk blouse and buzzed Ganiff at his desk. He must've heard Ms. Wapiti's voice as he didn't bother to pick up the intercom; he unlocked and opened the doors to his office almost at once. "C'mon in guys," he said and left the doors open thus affording me total license to eavesdrop without any intercom trickery.

"Mr. Ganiff," Mr. Dorck asserted himself, "we have a problem with Baldwin Laundry."

In my mind's eye, I imagined Ganiff's reaction. In all probability, he cast the Ganiff glare, a concentrated blast of ill–will from the right eye.

Ms. Wapiti spoke up in a concerned tone. "Mr. Ganiff, my people just completed their annual linen inventory. Some of the sheets, towels, pillowcases and blankets have been disappearing at an alarming rate. We've probably lost over 60% of our stock. Our cost to replace these items has forced us to overrun our budget by over 30%."

Agitated, Ganiff tapped the glass conference table with his fingers. The rhythm quickened into a fast–paced mazurka that might've been written by Chopin. I tiptoed to the doorframe and sneaked a peek into the office. Ganiff's head was bowed towards his chest.

"Recently, we performed several inventories of the weekly laundry and noticed that often we get back half of what we send out," added Mr. Dorck.

Like a gopher, I poked out my head again. This time, Ganiff's mustache tips dug into his chest.

"We believe that Baldwin Laundry's been losing our stock. We want them to reimburse us for our expenditures."

Ganiff's head yanked up, as did his mustache in a perfect "V" formation. He spluttered, "You will do no such thing! Maybe your counts are off. Or maybe your staff is misplacing the laundry here at the hotel. Surely that could occur."

At that moment, Calvin, the owner of Nikrovetch Contractors, bounced into my office. He wore his customary outfit—tight jeans, sweatshirt and leather jacket.

"You called?"

I straightened my posture and scooted back to my desk. "Uh… yeah, Mr. Ganiff needs your quotes. He keeps asking for them."

"I'll have 'em tomorrow," he said, taking my former position at the doorway. He peeked inside.

"Oh, Calvin, is that you? Get in here," beckoned Ganiff from the conference table. He then refocused on Mr. Dorck and Ms. Wapiti. "Here's the bottom line, guys. Redo the inventory and get back to me. I'm sure everything's fine. Now, please, I've got more important business to deal with, as you can see."

The less than dynamic duo were summarily dismissed. Calvin slid by them and slammed the door shut behind him, impeding my further education.

In front of me, Mr. Dorck peered through his glasses at Ms. Wapiti. "Did you get what went on in there?"

"No, José. The things that happen here defy my comprehension. On the plus side, at least he wasn't furious," said Ms. Wapiti dejectedly. "In order for us to conduct the inventory, we have to pull people from your department as well."

"Fine with me. The sooner we get this done, the sooner we can resolve the issue," said Mr. Dorck, ducking halfway out of my office area. He stopped for a moment to allow Ms. Wapiti to pass him. "After you," he gentlemanly said. As one, the pair left.

My fragile loyalty towards Mr. Ganiff unraveled soon thereafter with the revelations cast by his timid son–in–law. Clyde Hammergesundschmidt sat in front of my desk, awaiting his weekly berating by his father–in–law who was, as usual, doing lord–knows–what behind closed doors. Clyde adjusted his coke–bottle glasses more than once while he frenetically clunked his heels against the legs of his chair. I truly felt for the young man.

"Hey Linda, do you know how long he'll be?"

"Your guess is as good as mine, Clyde." I glanced up from typing an internal memo.

I guess Clyde wanted to ingratiate himself with me as a possible ally, or to allay his conscience. Whatever his reason, his next words rocked my world.

"So, you know that Mr. Ganiff is the ultimate owner of Baldwin Laundry?"

That stopped me from typing. I swiveled my head to face him. He now had my undivided attention. "You know this as fact?"

Clyde bobbed his head. "Oh yeah, he and Robenstine are partners. I think my father–in–law is the silent partner, if you know what I mean."

I was stunned. *No wonder they call Clyde "Clod"!* What he disclosed… could be a major conflict of interest, if not something outright criminal.

He continued, "You know that check the hotel issues every Friday for Baldwin Laundry? My new responsibility is to deposit it at Marine Midland Bank in Mr. Ganiff's personal account. It used to be Robenstine who collected the checks and placed them in the commercial account. With what he did to me, my father–in–law will never let him near our money again."

"Why, what did Keith do?" I said, bursting with curiosity.

Clyde turned beet–red and blinked in Morse code. He shook his head with dejection. "He asked to borrow my American Express card to pay bills at the laundry. So I lent it to him. Then I didn't see him, and out of nowhere I started getting calls from Amex, asking me about all these charges in Miami, of all places—to hotels, florists, limo services, restaurants, stores. I accepted them all because it was Keith charging them." He sighed. "Little did I know then that Keith had no intention of repaying me."

It took all my strength, internal resources and a little tantric breathing to maintain my composure. I had many follow–up questions, however, when I opened my mouth… another ill–timed interruption. This time from Cappy, the building engineer. He approached my desk, meek and trembling.

Mr. Ganiff's short temper unnerved Cappy. He coped by spending his days hiding in the subbasement, rarely venturing outside. *If only I could get away with that,* I often wished.

I had recently met one of Cappy's friends who insisted that Cappy was a maven in the stock market and made millions over the years. It seemed damn near inconceivable to reconcile that fact with the man quaking in front of me. The guy was scared of his shadow after Mr. Ganiff tormented him for five years.

"Linda, Mr. Ganiff wants the light bulb estimates." He reached into his pocket and handed me a crumpled piece of paper.

"Ah, c'mon, Cappy. Couldn't you have put this on a neat piece of paper?" I inquired because I, as well, was subjected to Ganiff's railings against the little man. And I anticipated a barrel full of shit for submitting that crumpled wad to my boss. Moreover, Cappy had walked right in front of Clyde, impeding full disclosure of Ganiff's dubious dealings. I wanted to throttle him.

"Better this than nothing, right?" He raised his shoulders. "Oh, and no need to tell him I was here. Now back to whatever it is I was doing." He scooted out.

Similar to a turtle, Clyde withdrew into himself. At precisely that moment, Ganiff bolted out of his office. Clyde rose halfway out of the chair until Ganiff gave him the stop signal. He sank right back down.

"We're gonna talk later so come back in a few days," Ganiff whispered.

"Like when?" asked Clyde timorously.

"In three days, okay?" Ganiff's voice became more forceful.

During their exchange, I acted as if I could decipher Cappy's handwriting by holding the wad up in the air towards various light sources. I even ventured to type up his sloppy estimate.

Ganiff adjusted his cravat by the reflection of the mirrored panels on the front of his door. Then, en route out to the hallway, he shouted, "Oh hey, Linda, follow me" and motioned with one hand toward the elevator, blatantly ignoring his son–in–law.

"What's the rush?" I asked, catching up to him.

"Want to meet a real living legend? Liz Taylor is checking in."

How in the world did he know? I thought while on the move. The phones hadn't rung and Ganiff didn't have a computer or fax machine in his office. Considering his antiquated ways, I knew there was no way that he had a mobile phone.

In the Lobby, most of the senior managers lined up near the elevator banks to witness this historic event. An assistant wheeled Ms. Taylor in through the main entrance. Instead of a glamorous academy award–winning actress waltzing in at the top of her game, we beheld a frail and tired woman with hair cropped short and grandmotherly white. If not for those violet eyes, you could hardly tell it was Elizabeth Taylor.

"Miss Taylor, welcome." Ganiff ran over to greet her. "How was your flight into JFK airport?"

No reply. She wanly lifted a hand mid–way which drifted back into her lap. She was clearly in no mood for a welcoming committee.

Nevertheless, Ganiff kept on, insensitive to her needs. "As the General Manager of this Five–Star Hotel, it is an honor and pleasure to welcome you once again to the Supreme Superior. We appreciate your continued patronage."

131

Ms. Taylor grimaced. "Excuse me, sir, but I'm in a lot of pain. Do you mind if I go to my room now?"

Ganiff bowed. His moustache tips swept the marble floor. He pointed to the elevator banks and bellowed with good cheer, "Enjoy your stay. Good luck with your hip replacement surgery. We wish you a speedy recovery."

Liz Taylor's face turned fire engine red. She rocked in her wheelchair from side to side, pushing down on the armrests with all her strength to dislodge herself. She desperately wanted to stand. "Excuse me!" she shouted as her aide pushed the wheelchair into the elevator.

My last view of Ms. Taylor was that of a face contorted by anguish, similar to the painting, *The Scream*. The doors closed and the numbers ascended on the elevator console. I imagined that, could she have freed herself from the wheelchair, I might've witnessed one of the world's most beloved actresses strangling my boss.

Mr. Ganiff was oblivious to the upset he had caused. He continued to shout in the direction of the closed elevator doors, "Might I suggest that you avail yourself of our magnificent sauna in our Health Club—it'll make you feel better!"

In the elevator well, there were muffled retorts of a hysterical caliber, or perhaps that was my imagination.

I read in the tabloids the next day that Ms. Taylor's forthcoming operation had been kept an airtight secret from the media, family and friends. In fact, the sole purpose of her visit to the Supreme Superior was to stay there in privacy until the scheduled surgery. One paper reported that Ms. Taylor's press secretary confided in Mr. Ganiff because that was the only way in which she could have gotten a room in the sold out hotel—the hottest place in New York City. To think that this insensitive fool blurted her secret in front of a room full of people, including scores of paparazzi hidden amongst the potted plants in the hotel entrance, was mind–boggling.

Whether or not Mr. Ganiff knew it, he had displayed a twist on an old adage: killing 'em with kindness.

Chapter 16
February 1995

"It was real cool, I mean, way cool."

With my eyes at half–mast, I spaced out while the teen–age boy droned on about a party he recently attended. Tall, lean, this time bald with earrings, Iggy Two was a handsome boy. He impatiently waited for his father to free himself from a phone call so they could discuss his grades.

"Yo, Linda, thanks for letting me hide that Howard Stern book in your desk. Every time I try to read anything outside of Scripture, my mother finds it and throws it out. She even looks under my mattress!"

I smiled. "No problem, Iggy Two. If you tell anyone and it gets back to your parents... Well, let's just keep it between us."

Iggy Two nodded. "You're the only one who treats me well. My folks, they always act like something's wrong with me."

"As far as I'm concerned, you're a typical teenager. A regular pain in the ass." We both laughed. "Hey, what did your parents think of your shaven head and the new jewelry?"

Iggy Two grimaced. "Dad went ballistic. Mom cried. They're gonna punish me, maybe send me to some special school this summer."

Mr. Ganiff's door flew open and he entered my office.

"Son, please come in. Linda, don't you have work to do?"

Another epiphany came to me. At the Supreme Superior, hard work did not pay off. I relented a little, slacked off a bit more and no longer hunted the pervasively absent BeeBee around the hotel. When I had to flee from that office, despite my boss's directive, I forwarded the phones to the operators with instructions to place any important calls through to Mr. Ganiff.

As if he would notice that I wasn't there. The man locked himself up in that office for hours. If it weren't for meetings or emergency interruptions, he might stay locked in there for days.

The walls trembled while Ganiff reamed out his son behind closed doors. I opened my desk drawer and retrieved a portable make–up mirror to distract myself from the yelps. A Fu Manchu sprouted on my chin. *Not too pretty!* Although I avidly plucked the rascals, they always managed to grow back—thicker, fuller, little white wires that were increasingly harder to yank. Kenin, the in–suite dining manager, advised me to undergo electrolysis. He proceeded to show me his hirsute neck with a wide, empty swath in the center.

"Before you go to the electrologist, you must let all the hair grow out," the in–suite dining manager warned, "that means, no plucking, no shaving, no nairing.

You gotta cut the ends with a fine scissor."

"How long does it take?" I asked.

"Two months. Maybe three."

I heeded his advice and found that although the hairs were not visible, my chin felt as rough as the bottom of my feet. *One or two more months,* I reflected.

"Admiring your image, Narcissus?"

Snapping the mirror compact shut, I looked up and saw Keith Robenstine. Seated in one of the guest chairs with a copy of the *Daily Post* in his lap. My *Daily Post.* The little bastard must've snuck up on me. A mere two seconds before, the paper had lain folded on my desk.

"How'd you do that? I didn't even hear you."

Keith stared at me silently with a vapid look on his face.

"Mr. Ganiff is busy with his son," I volunteered.

"Ah, the boy prodigy. That's okay, I'll wait."

Exasperated, I threw the mirror back in my desk drawer, and reached for my overflowing in–box. I kept myself busy rearranging the incoming faxes. The top one came from Harry, the hotel's lawyer. Our kvetching friend, Mr. Silverberg, was now suing the Supreme Superior for damages to the tune of $5,000.

Beneath the Silverberg papers were some assorted legal briefs. The first contained a motion to evict the anonymous tenant at the otherwise abandoned West 53rd Street building on our property. According to information unearthed on Harry's side, the anonymous tenant had moved into the little old lady's apartment while she was still alive and continued to live there after her death with full squatters' rights.

While I reviewed the pages, a new fax came in off the machine behind me dispersing the remaining layer of dust. I grabbed it off the tray. The cover sheet displayed the logo from the NYC Hotel Association. One word alone was visible beneath the masthead: URGENT. My curiosity piqued, I read the second page that shot out from the machine:

TO: **All NYC Hotel General Managers**

FROM: **The NYC Hotel Association**

RE: **Imminent Citywide Hotel Strike**

From what I could see, the hotel strike was going forward. That would surely pepper things up around here. I pored over the details of this strained labor situation when another fax followed. This was as well from the NYC Hotel Association:

Please circulate immediately to all staff!

This is an NYPD criminal advisory. A male perpetrator is suspected of multiple criminal trespassing violations and has staged armed robberies at five (5) Manhattan hotels over the past 30 days. The alleged perpetrator has been known to hide in isolated areas of the hotel premises for up to a week before conducting a robbery. We strongly urge that you notify your Reservations and Front Desk areas to stay alert.

A final faxed sheet came out of the machine. It featured a photo shot of the perpetrator, taken from the footage of one of the victimized hotels' security cameras.

I phoned Big Guy. Since he didn't answer at his post down in the Lobby, I faxed the hotel advisory to his office. I repeated the process for Murlise and Sherwin and stopped the moment Ganiff's door swung open with a quick "swoosh." Out he walked, firmly escorting his son with a death–like grip on the shoulder.

"You got to work harder, son, not only for your mother and me, but mainly for yourself."

Iggy Two dipped his head. He winked at me when our eyes met.

"Go, and be well, son. I'll see you at dinner." Ganiff's right eye espied Keith cringing in the guest chair. "Ah, Mr. Robenstine. Let's talk."

Keith got up, tossed the *Daily Post* on my desk and followed Ganiff into the office.

What I wouldn't do to be a fly on the wall for that conversation. I tried employing my intercom trick, only this time it didn't work. Ganiff had more than likely knocked the phone off the hook. Luckily, he didn't disconnect my line.

One of the Food & Beverage managers rang. He was sweating over his daily crossword puzzle. "Linda, quick, 24–down! What's another word for thesaurus?"

Ganiff intercommed me before I could respond. "Linda, did Calvin give you the estimates of his final proposal yet?" his voice sounded gruff.

"Sorry, Mr. Ganiff. I called him earlier. As usual, he told me 'tomorrow.'"

"What a load of shit! Does this guy want the job, or what? Get him for me now. Tell him to move his ass."

Criminal minds must think alike because I had hardly finished dialing Calvin's digits when he appeared in my office.

"Someone looking for me?"

"Hey, how'd you get here so fast?"

He grinned at me, dimples flaring. "I was downstairs in the Lobby when your number came up."

"In our Lobby? Doing what?"

"Finished eating at that piece of crap you call a restaurant."

We both laughed.

"Hey, Linda, do me a favor while I'm here. Get me a comped room for tomorrow night."

"For you?" I asked, looking up from my desk.

"No, a friend."

I smiled back at him and said playfully, "What am I gonna get in return?"

Calvin fumbled in his jacket pocket searching for something. Finally, he pulled out a rumpled white envelope. "Well, let's see here. I got free tickets to the opening of the new 007 movie."

"How many?"

"Two."

"You're giving me both your movie tickets for a comped room?"

A brief moue of disappointment passed over his face.

I said, "I'm just messing with you."

His eyes flashed. "I was gonna give you one ticket. It's for tomorrow night. Wanna go with me?"

Oh yes. I felt strangely and perversely attracted to him. I found his quixotic nature refreshing, albeit a little off–center. Calvin was very charismatic in his own, unique individual way. A masculine build. That rugged jaw line. The man was hot.

"Listen, the reason I called was because Mr. Ganiff wants to speak to you. Oh, and be warned—your brother–in–law's in there."

Calvin's face turned beet–red. "That scum–sucking swine! You can't let me in there. I'll kill him. I swear I'll rip his face off!"

I looked at him and wondered about his mood swings. Then again, I wondered about the mood swings among many people I met at the Supreme Superior Hotel. I shook my head clear and said, "Calvin, let me announce you."

Seconds later, the door swung open and Keith appeared in the doorway.

"You shithead!" bellowed Calvin.

Keith sneered. "What are you gonna do? Belt me?"

"Linda, call Security. I swear I'm gonna kill this bastard!"

He almost grabbed Keith as he walked by, but Keith feinted and darted in such a fashion that all we saw was a blur.

"Did you see that rat bastard run?" he asked me with raised eyebrows.

"Calvin, quit screwing around! Where the hell're those figures you promised me last week?" yelled Ganiff from behind his desk.

"Tomorrow, Mr. Ganiff." Calvin immediately calmed down and flashed us a confident smile.

"I've been hearing 'tomorrow' for a week. Just get 'em for me, damn it!"

"Well, I'm still trying to get the breakdown from the subcontractor."

"How the hell can I award you the deal if you don't give me the figures?"

"You'll get them tomorrow." Calvin wheeled around and faced me. "Hello Linda, what about my room?"

"It's done. I just have to fax Reservations for the confirmation. It's Suite 2303."

"Okay, great! See you tomorrow."

"With the estimates?"

"No, the movie. I'll call you later with the details." He winked at me and departed.

Ah, I daydreamed. *A night out with Calvin. It couldn't hurt to have a little fun, I supposed, no matter how volatile the guy was, could it?*

Moments later, I came back to reality. Another security alert caused the fax machine to chug and whir. This fax was a repeat of the earlier hotel bandit situation including a new photo of the perpetrator. Since I hadn't received a call back from Big Guy on the matter, I decided to go to him, papers in hand.

Big Guy was neither at his post in the Lobby, nor was he at the security center on the second floor in–between other administrative offices. In his place sat Johnny, hovering in a somnambulist state behind the security counter. From a reclining position, he stared blankly at scores of camera banks.

"Johnny, where's Big Guy? I've been trying to reach him for a while now."

"I don't know. The guy doesn't exactly report to me."

I didn't anticipate that sort of response. On the face of it, he didn't sound uncooperative, simply zoned out. Upon further inspection, he was sleeping with his eyes open!

Savagely, I kicked the desk. He didn't change position. Nor did he blink. "Um, okay. Well, did you guys receive my fax?"

"What fax, Linda?" Johnny was still entranced in front of the monitors, deep in dreamland. I wondered whether Ganiff might've paid him a visit to dispel a little family folklore.

I tried to jar him a bit. I did a little dance routine called "The Soupy Shuffle" from a 1960's children's show and topped it off with a little fang action. No reaction. I then segued into some jazz dance movements where I moved my head from side to side like an Egyptian wall painting. Still no reaction. I picked up a bullhorn from

137

his desk and yelled not even a foot away from him, "Johnny! It's a security alert! There's some nut out there who's been checking into hotels around the city just to rob them!"

The hair on Johnny's head stood up at attention. Still, I couldn't snap him out of it. Nothing. Nul. Nyet. Nada. Rien.

Slow as molasses, he unexpectedly leaned over, one vertebrae at a time in what would've constituted a perfectly executed Pilates move and examined the tray to his fax machine. "Nope, nothing there," he said in slow-mo.

Something didn't seem right, besides Johnny. When I looked at the fax machine, I noticed a little red button on the top flashing away. "You have no paper inside!"

Of all things, that comment triggered something in his brain. His head whipped up and his eyelids flapped open like a paper shade. "Ah, damn." He stretched and, at long last, glanced at me. "That explains why we haven't been getting any faxes for a while!" He slowly bent down and picked up some loose paper from an open cabinet beneath the machine. "Hey, can you help me? I'm not very good with these things."

I grabbed the blank pages from him and placed them in the cartridge of the fax machine. Instantly, it produced printouts.

"Johnny, what's going on with you?"

"Sorry, Linda. I've been in front of these screens for like twenty-four hours straight. I'm hypnotized." His eyes were bloodshot and he did have a certain hangdog look about him. "Was I in a trance?"

"Practically comatose." I chuckled. "I think you were sleeping with your eyes open."

"Again? Damn," he said without explanation. I wanted to know how he did it just in case Ganiff intended to serenade me again about his lineage.

I had a hunch. Since Johnny hadn't yet seen the alert, he had no idea as to what our random hotel madman looked like. Which meant, if this criminal happened to wander into the Supreme Superior, our hotel security would've done nothing to stop or question him.

"Here's the picture of the bandit," I handed over the faxed copy. "Please circulate it among the Front Desk and bellhops, okay? Also, do me a favor and rewind the Front Desk cameras for check-ins for the past few days, all right?"

"Why should I do that?" he asked.

I did my utmost to exhibit patience. "Well, we have to make sure that the guy in the picture did not already check into the hotel. If he did, we have to take appropriate steps."

"Oh," he responded. "Wait a minute, Linda. That means I have to pay attention to what I'm scanning on the screens."

Admittedly, I wanted to bitch–slap him. Instead, I hit myself on the forehead. "Duh! That's the point. Wait a minute—isn't that what you're supposed to do here?"

"Uh, yeah… sure… C'mon Linda, it's way too much for one person. I may go blind, you know." He attempted to guilt me into letting him weasel out of this onerous task.

"You may be fired, you know, if the guy is already here and you didn't do this," I volleyed back.

"Touché."

"Yes, touché," repeated Big Guy as he trudged to his security station. "Wazzup my friends?" A Duane Reade shopping bag was tucked under his arm. He followed my line of vision and apologetically said, "Had to pick up some personal provisions."

I recapped the latest episode in a few sentences. Johnny pushed buttons on his keyboard to manipulate the cameras and the tapes.

"Good going, Linda. Would you like to join us in Security?" he deadpanned and then gave me a wink. "You can't unless you pass the CPR test!"

The Supreme Superior provided one training program, First Aid. I aced the bandages and tourniquet sections. Nevertheless, I could never remember the sequence for mouth–to–mouth resuscitation, the basis for the written exam.

He softened the blow by saying, "Look, you're doing a terrific job and I'm grateful you are, especially since Johnny didn't refill the fax machine with paper. Otherwise, how in the world would we know what's going on here?"

Well, at least he didn't find my actions threatening. Prior to leaving the security station, I was stopped by Big Guy's entreaty. Cupping his meaty hands in a pleading gesture, he asked, "Would you do us a favor, Linda, and get in–suite dining to send up some vittles?" Big Guy added, "something tells me it's gonna be a long haul. A very long haul."

"Are you trying to convince me?" Johnny shouted back, "I bet you a fiver that yours truly will be pulling this long haul all by my lonesome."

I left my two knights squabbling as I made my way back to the office. *Hmmm, now I take orders from Security. Apt reward for hard work… A dog's day is never done*, I mused.

Chapter 17

"Linda, call for you on line one," shouted BeeBee in her thick raspy voice above the chaos of another Supreme Superior morning. Hey, at least she bothered to answer the phones for once.

"Who is it?" I asked, looking up from a pile of folders.

"I dunno. The guy claims he's your broker," she scoffed and headed towards the operators' office.

Back when I worked at financial institutions, I was legally prohibited from trading stocks on my own account due to my access to confidential documentation. This insider information and the usage of it were strictly regulated under laws enforced by the Securities and Exchange Commission. As investments went, I could only hold mutual funds which meant that I was a passive investor. I had no other alternative but to take a back seat to the actions of the managers who administered the mutual funds.

After I switched over to the hospitality industry, I was no longer restricted, so I resuscitated this little hobby of mine to survive the workday. Not that I had a great deal to invest or a lot of time to devote. From past experience, I learned that trading certain preferential stocks would give me a return on my investments that exceeded overall market performance.

I intended to purchase shares of Philip Morris common stock because of a recent sharp price drop. I'd done deals like this several times before. Either the stock was likely to rebound or to split. Either way, in a matter of a few months I stood to make a nice profit. Some things were predictable. At least in the short–term.

"Hey there, Jack. Yes, please let me know where Philip Morris is trading at? Okay, I'll hold for a sec." Out of the corner of my eye, I espied Mr. Ganiff sidling up to me. "Yes, it's that low? Okay, put me in for four hundred shares of Class C common. Thanks!"

"What're you doing, Miss Linda?" he said in an attempt to emulate sincerity.

"Talking stocks with my broker," I responded as I hung up.

"You dabble in the markets?"

"Oh, from time to time." I tried to sound cagy.

Ganiff puffed out his chest and proclaimed, "The stock market is the best casino of the world."

"I guess," I shrugged as I answered. I wasn't sure if he was cynical or critical.

"Do you have any tips?" His tone switched from accusatory to that of supplication.

"Yeah, don't bet on horses," I quipped. He guffawed in return, quite over–the–top.

"Well, what do you know about stocks?" he exclaimed. For my benefit, he rolled his good eye and turned to enter his office.

"For your information, Mr. Ganiff, trading was my background. Bond trading, that is. Or have you forgotten?" Like a schmuck, I had swallowed the bait, and now hooked, followed him into his office. I explained, "I know how to trade. My portfolio is kicking ass. Last year I had a 68% return or almost $10,000! So far this year it's 30%. Furthermore, I never invest in trendy stocks."

"Oh, must be true then," he said. Stifling a theatrical yawn, he tugged at the tips of his horned mustache. "Makes you wonder why you'd ever need a day job with success like that."

"Believe what you want," I muttered as I crossed the threshold back out of his office. I made it halfway to my desk when he called for me again.

"Linda. Got a second?"

"Yes, sir." I turned around.

"Perhaps one day I'll show you my portfolio."

"Um, sure. That would be nice. Thank you." He did not pick up on my sarcasm.

"Linda," Ganiff again called out, seated behind his desk.

"Yes, sir," I yelled from my desk.

"Could you please close the door to my office? Kindly place all calls on hold. I've got some private business to deal with."

"Sure. No problem." I stepped out and swung the door shut. Instantaneously, he locked it. *How does he move so fast,* I wondered for the umpteenth time.

The phone rang at my desk. Johnny from Security. "Linda, I think we got a hit on the videotapes. I followed the suspect on each camera and isolated him on the tapes right up to when he entered his suite."

"Damn! He's here in the building? That's terrific!" I said, feeling the onset of an adrenaline rush. The surge dissipated whatever crippling fear I might've had knowing that an armed lunatic was loose in the hotel as opposed to an unarmed one. Or several unarmed ones like my colleagues.

"Yeah, yet I'm not too sure it's this guy. The truth is, I'm going blind from all this non–stop surveying. Not to mention the spot checks I have to do throughout the day! Big Guy is off premises for the time being. So, can you come down to review the footage with me?"

I was on the verge of responding when I noticed a shadow gathering momentum on my desk like a solar eclipse. Gulping, I almost dropped the receiver except I somehow managed to pin it close to my chest with my free hand. "Let me get back to you," I mumbled as I awkwardly stretched out my arm to drop the phone onto its console. I looked up to see a giant protruding girth rapidly approaching. To get out of its way, I slid back on my chair. And witnessed through tightly stretched fabric the outline of a pair of morphed pendulous breasts flopping asymmetrically over a distended belly. It kept on coming so I continued to slide down the seat until my butt almost touched the carpet. The back of my head now rested on the edge of the chair cushion. In the nick of time it halted. Peering down from above stood a bloated face framed by an American Bandstand equivalent of a flip hairdo.

"Hello, Linda. I am Mrs. Ganiff," she imperiously said.

Ohmigod! I thought. *What a nightmare!*

As was customary among most General Managers, Mr. Ganiff and his wife lived rent–free with Iggy Two at the hotel. Their apartment, a specially built suite, consisted of two bedrooms, an oversized living room, kitchen, dining room and two full baths. Iggy Two told me that before coming to the Supreme Superior the parental Ganiffs had retired, living in their home on Cape Cod. Mrs. Ganiff had preferred that home with the family nearby. Now, according to Mr. Ganiff, she occupied most of her time organizing her Scriptures group and, he sheepishly admitted, spying on her son.

From Day One, Mr. Ganiff made it clear that he had banned his wife from the executive offices. Doreen had once mentioned that the Missus used to come down periodically to check up on her husband until he put a stop to it. Way before my time. Up till now, Mrs. Ganiff was nothing more to me than a mythical figure perpetrated by her husband and a very resentful Iggy Two. Yet here, before me, she stood in all her bulk and splendor.

I smiled, and at the same time, hastily scrambled up the chair to shake her hand. "It's a pleasure to finally meet you. I've heard so much about you."

The hotel matron stared at my outstretched hand and gave me a once–over, head–to–toe appraisal. "Is my husband available?"

"Let me buzz him for you," I coolly said, and reached for the receiver with my unshaken hand.

The door unlocked and swung open. Mr. Ganiff stood behind it. "Dear, what brings you down here?"

"Oh, Iggy darling. The church group needs a room for our bible class this Thursday night. It's getting so large and living rooms just aren't big enough."

Mr. Ganiff turned to me and squinted. "Linda, do we have any comp rooms available?"

I glanced over at a clipboard hanging on my wall. "No, unfortunately not, Mr. Ganiff. As usual, we're overbooked."

Mr. Ganiff looked over to his wife and shrugged. She glared back at him with raised eyebrows that suggested she wouldn't be taking no for an answer.

"Whatever it takes, Linda, bump someone out. Preferably from one of the top Sublime suites. Also, call Cookie and get a set-up for twenty, no, thirty—pastries, tea, coffee, juices, mineral water. Have Housekeeping remove the sofas in the suite and put in nice chairs with twenty fold-ups. Also, a large bouquet of this month's flowers." He then turned to his wife and smiled. "Anything else I've forgotten, dear?"

"Bibles," added Mrs. Ganiff.

"Oh yes, tell Concierge to get them through our church. You have the number. Have them pick up forty bibles, pronto."

The Ganiffs continued speaking to each other in the loudest voices imaginable in front of my desk. I did my best to block them out while dialing Murlise in Reservations.

"Yes, Linda. What is it? I'm a little swamped right now."

"Sorry to bother you, Murlise. Mr. Ganiff needs a special favor, a Sublime suite for his bible study people for Thursday. I know we're booked solid but—"

"Linda, we're packed like 110%. There's no way. What am I gonna do, throw out a celebrity?" Murlise was furious.

"I hear you, Murlise. I'm sorry to inconvenience you. I do sympathize." What I wanted to say could not be spoken aloud with the Ganiffs standing within earshot. Our bitchfest would have to wait. At least on this end.

"Him and his fucking bible group. The man is out of his mind," she said in frustration. "Hey, did I ever tell you about Ganiff's Born Again festival? The one right before you came here?"

"Ah, no," I said.

Mr. Ganiff picked up on the change of my voice and stopped conversing with Mrs. Ganiff. "Linda, what's going on?"

I lied through my teeth. "Murlise put me on hold; she's going through her reservations to determine who to bump."

"Oh, okay," he said, mollified and then resumed conversing with the Missus.

"Are they right there?" asked Murlise. "Don't bother answering, I can hear them. So good, let me tell you what happened the last time with these people." She spoke very fast while she thumbed through her reservations tickets. "As usual, it was peak time and Ganiff made me throw out over one hundred paying guests last second for one freebee night. It was his Born Again annual reunion. You can imagine how it absolutely flattened my occupancy runs!"

"Well?" Mr. Ganiff leant over my desk.

"I'm still on hold, sir," I responded. He turned back to his wife.

"They used up our fleet of limos. *Bliss* was actually full but they didn't pay and you shoulda seen them, they ate like locusts! I mean, I don't give a damn; I don't own the hotel. Except he burnt me the following day. He had the audacity to malign me for the poor occupancy stats he caused!"

The bible group incident wasn't the only story circulating and reaching legendary proportions.

Mr. Ganiff had a very large family of his own—six children and their three current spouses, seven grandchildren, his wife's family, his nieces and nephews. At a minimum, there were thirty–five family members, and when a few dozen more from bible class were added, every holiday became a festival at the Supreme Superior. From offhand comments and asides, especially from an array of managers, I pieced together the innuendos: Mr. Ganiff had the hotel sponsor smorgasbords, suites, limos and entertainment. Iggy Two confessed that they always had a quart of caviar present, although no one ate it except Mr. Ganiff, and only a teaspoon at that. Ganiff always insisted that the clean–up staff throw out the leftovers, "or else!"

Not too long ago, I eavesdropped through the intercom to hear a disgruntled Mr. Dorck. He was discussing Mr. Ganiff's personal expenditures, in particular, the restaurant tab he ran up from treating Steven Koneman and guests to dinner and drinks and whatnot.

"No, disrespect, sir, over the past five years I have used the most creative accounting imaginable so that our head office reps here in New York would not notice that we've lost over a million dollars in revenue. Not including over half a million in food and beverage."

Mr. Ganiff wheezed. "So, what are you telling me, Dorck? After doing all that, you can't manage to squeeze out another ten grand or so?"

Mr. Dorck emitted a loud sigh, "Sir, all I'm asking for is a little breathing room here. How do I explain it? I need more valid expenses to justify the invalid ones." Dorck did not even touch upon the three weddings for Mr. Ganiff's daughters, for which the hotel had footed the bill. I came across the receipts and assumed that Ganiff made the payments. Until Murlise stripped the wool from my eyes.

There were other "hidden expenses" such as $200,000 to redecorate the Ganiff's suite at the hotel, plus his nightly wine cellar raids. The latter was the topic of concern for all the busboys and busybodies at the hotel. Say what you want about the food at *Bliss*, but they had a widely acknowledged wine cellar. What remained of it, after having been extensively pilfered by Mr. Ganiff who also demonstrated an amazing aptitude for imbibing vast quantities. This seemingly accounted for the network of veins that had recently sprouted on the man's proboscis.

All the pieces fell into place. *Ganiff was intent on paring the staff to the absolute minimum to make up for the shortfall in Supreme Superior earnings.*

"If he wants to bring the Supreme Superior down to its knees, he's doing a great job," grumbled Murlise on the line, interrupting my inner reflections.

Three eyes peered down at me. "Okay, thanks, Murlise. I'll tell him it's done."

"That took long enough," griped Mr. Ganiff in lieu of thanking me. "Now, onto the next item on the list, the church. Oh, and don't forget room service! Chop chop," he said, at which Mrs. Ganiff giggled.

Ms. "highest paid" Wapiti and Mr. Dorck entered while the Ganiffs stood over me, waiting for me to complete all the calls.

"Hello, Mrs. Ganiff," they said in unison.

"Dear, it's back to business for me. See you later." Mr. Ganiff dismissed his wife with a wave of his hand as if she were his employee. He then led the way to his office, leaving the door open.

Mrs. Ganiff did not depart. "Linda, I want you to phone me the moment you've made all the arrangements. This way I'll know you did the work and did it right." Now I understood all the more why she and Ganiff deserved each other.

In exchange for her condescending behavior, I leant forward, grabbed her by the wattle and bitch–slapped her. Hah, that only happens in movies! Or in my dreams! Instead, I shot her with my version of the Ganiff glare.

Impervious or inured, she continued, "So, will you phone me?"

"Yes, Mrs. Ganiff." I took her lead. I repeated what she said in a parody of a robot. "I'll call you after I make all the arrangements so that you will know I did the work and did it right." Strangely enough, she appeared content with my words. *Go figure.*

Soon, the giant dark shadow lifted. I ignored Ganiff's instructions to contact Cookie. He was probably out of town anyhow for another culinary competition. Instead, I got on the line with Ronny, our Banquets Manager, and requested a set–up for the bible group.

"Damn, another one of those church events?" Ronny asked.

"Well, it's not an event, it's a bible study," I informed him.

"Oh, same thing in my book! Let's see, they want a set–up, right?"

"Yes. For forty."

"I see," his voice became gruff, "I take it all the delectables from the bins?" Ronny referred to the room by the loading dock with the floor–to–ceiling bakery bins, one of my favorite spots in the hotel.

"Pretty much so, yes. Don't forget the juices, mineral water, coffee, tea, etc."

His voice dropped lower and thicker. "This is for Thursday night around eight–ish. And, the bill will be forwarded to Mr. Ganiff's expense account?"

"You got it, Ronny."

145

The line was quiet.

"Hey, Ronny, are you there?"

"Damn, Linda. I don't know how we're gonna to do this."

"What do you mean?"

"Well, Thursday night we have quite a few bookings for clients who *pay* for our services. You know, the ones who *tip* us which keeps my staff living the American dream instead of being hammered into the ground by these parasites who eat and drink for free!" He snapped, "Did you know that after every one of these Ganiff functions, I lose my best trained people? My banquet friends at The Four Seasons and The Peninsula love these Ganiff events. They want to phone him personally to thank him! Do you have any idea how many months it takes me to train people who don't speak English, come from a different culture and are expected to know the nuances of a high quality banquets area? After two hours of a Ganiff sponsored event…" Ronny spluttered, at a loss for words.

"Hey, I hear you. I do. I also have him practically standing over me. So I'll assume that it'll all be set up on Thursday night?"

"Yes, ma'am," he sighed in resignation.

When I hung up, I realized that Mr. Ganiff had not closed his office door—an inducement to pry. I was pulled in two directions: assist security in apprehending a dangerous thug, or eavesdrop on the laundry situation. *Well*, I rationalized, *this time the choice was simple. Why rush, what with Big Guy off premises.* I simulated phoning another department and placed the dial tone on hold to hear them better.

Dorck spoke first, "Mr. Ganiff, we had over a dozen Housekeeping staff as well as my five from accounting and finance to review the inventory. They worked all night and did it without overtime."

"Ah, I see. What did you find out?" asked Ganiff.

"That our figures are correct."

Ganiff exhaled heavily. "Do it again."

"Excuse me, Mr. Ganiff, what did you say?"

"Do it again. Obviously, your people made a mistake."

"Mr. Ganiff," Mr. Dorck explained, "inventory takes a lot of time. Especially when the staff has to account for all the linens in the hotel. These people did it voluntarily."

"Well, perhaps these amateurs don't know how to do inventory."

"Mr. Ganiff, that inventory caused my people to be late with their housekeeping duties." Ms. Wapiti spoke calmly, "We're already majorly understaffed."

A chair squeaked from the brusque movement of Ganiff's bulk. Furious, he yelled, "Well, if your people want their jobs, they'll have to do the inventory again.

146

Do you hear me?"

"Yes, sir," said Ms. Wapiti and Mr. Dorck simultaneously; they sounded peeved.

"Have them do the inventory next Friday for both incoming laundry as well as outgoing. Next Friday, okay? Now leave me to my duties. Dismissed. Both of you."

They stumbled past me, cursing beneath their breath. While they exited into the hallway, Mr. Ganiff yelled out, "Linda, shut my door! No, wait, get me Clyde. Then shut my door. I've got... some serious business to attend to."

Funny business seemed more like it. In the meantime, I had real business to attend to.

"Johnny, I'm sorry to be," I consulted my watch, "forty minutes late." I panted from the sprint to the security outpost and managed to gasp out the remainder of my apology, "You know how it goes here. Ganiff takes precedence."

"Not a problem, Linda. I've been reversing and fast forwarding footage since yesterday afternoon and need another pair of eyes here. Rather be safer than sorrier." His eyes were reddened from strain. He gestured to the seat next to him. I sat down. He had taped the faxed picture of the felon that I had given him the day before to the side of the monitors.

"Here's the clip I found from two days ago." He had already set up the video for my review. With a click of the button on the panel, I observed on the monitor a man who resembled the fax.

"You're right. That could be him!" I studied the picture and turned back again to the monitor. "Okay, partner... yeah, that could be the guy."

In the videotape, our alleged felon carried two heavy duffle bags. Stopping in front of the Front Desk counter, he set the bags down at his feet, making sure they wouldn't leave his presence. After he checked in, he shooed one of our bellmen away. The man lowered his head, grabbed the bags and headed for the elevator banks. That moment was time stamped 14:53:32.

"I finally finished reviewing the elevator and corridor tapes starting at 14:53:33. I got the hit when he exited on the eighth floor. I followed him on the corridor cameras and located him entering Suite 802." Johnny puffed his chest with pride. He fumbled for the elevator tape and then popped in the cartridge. "Need your eyes once more 'cause I don't want to fuck this up, okay? All we need is for the cops to mistakenly arrest the wrong person." A few thoughts entered my head right then. This time, Johnny fumbled with the monitor buttons and continued, "Could you imagine? Djorak would throw me outta here on my rear!"

I was more involved in watching the screen than listening to Johnny. "Oh, that's him again!" We zeroed in on the elevator tape. Our unnamed crook stowed his luggage in the corner of the elevator cab, pressed a floor button and turned to face the doors that slowly came to a close. Suddenly, a pair of hands inserted themselves where the doors almost met. With superhuman strength, they were pried open. Our friend Seebok jumped in. In one move, he swept by our culprit to press a floor button.

"That's Mr. Murray, right, from the executive office? I thought I recognized him." Johnny pointed at the screen.

"Yeah, what's he doing on that elevator?" Hotel staff either rode the back of the house elevators or the express ones that stop on the Sublime and top conference floors. Usage of the other front of the house elevators outside of accompanying clients for hotel–related business was strictly prohibited, leading to disciplinary actions and ultimately termination of employment. Unless the staff member was fortunate enough to procure permission from Ms. Djorak. A Herculean effort at best. Watching Seebok on that elevator was most disconcerting, the typical reaction I experienced when dealing with him.

The tape ran on. Oblivious to the other occupant in the elevator, Seebok proceeded to place his finger up his nose and industriously dug around inside his nostril. Johnny and I groaned.

"Yeah, Linda. This is the part I shoulda warned you about. It gets better." Johnny stared at me with a barely contained grin.

Indeed it did. Seebok extracted a nugget, examined it in the dim elevator cabin lights and casually flicked it. It landed on the alleged criminal.

"Whoa," I said, "look at that!" This time, I pointed at the screen.

Our felonious guest examined the sleeve of his jacket. Then looked up at Seebok. Like watching a silent film, we observed the sudden baring of teeth and movement of lips and guessed as to what was being said. My bets were on "hey, you asshole" whereas Johnny whipped out a fiver to put on "you stupid mothafucka." The enraged fellow took two steps right into Seebok's face. Before any further action could ensue, the elevator stopped and the doors opened. Dramatically, the criminal shoved Seebok into the cabin wall and then ran out, bags in hand. Seebok's knees buckled. We watched him slide to the floor.

"Did you see that, Linda?" crowed Johnny with delight.

"Yeah! Seebok could've been killed by that guy!"

"No, no, not Seebok," Johnny was disappointed. "The guy, you know, our alleged criminal guest, got off on the eighth floor. Okay, you verified him so I can turn off the tape." He reached for the control panel.

"Wait a minute," I said while pulling at his arm, "it took us this long…" Not much more to witness except that Seebok straightened up from the floor of the elevator cab, fixed his jacket lapel and with composure exited on the 15th floor. Granted, the situation appeared strange although not as incriminating as our visiting suspect—at least from what I could gauge from snippets of security tape.

"Um, Johnny, one wee favor? Can you follow Seebok on the 15th floor corridor tapes? To find out which suite he entered? Pretty please?"

"Okay, I'll get you the number. Later. Let me call Big Guy on his mobile so he can tell us what to do next." He picked up his greenback and repocketed it.

"In the interval, I'm gonna phone Murlise for that guy's name." I rapidly dialed the other phone. She responded immediately. "Hey, Murlise, need a quick favor. You know that guy who checks into hotels only to rob them?"

"No. What're you talking about?"

"Uh, I thought I sent you a fax about it. Didn't you read it?"

Murlise was dumbfounded. "No. This is all news to me."

"Well, anyway, now that you know... Guess what? He's here! Checked in two days ago. Johnny and I verified it. He's in Suite 802."

"Let me look into this," Murlise hummed, "I'll get back to you in an hour or so."

"Murlise!" I shouted with a degree of urgency, "this isn't a joke. We need that name now... for the police!"

"Holy shit, Linda! This is for real? The cops? Wow, how exciting! I mean, we have a criminal here?" she laughed. "We have many criminals here but finally, one who's actually pursued by the authorities?" She typed forcefully on the buttons of her keyboard. "Okay, got it. Suite 802. He signed in under the name of Mortimer Wilbur. That's W–I–L–B–U–R. His AMEX card went through without a problem."

"Thank you very much, Murlise! I guess Big Guy'll keep you posted on the next step whatever that might be." I hung up and turned to Johnny, "Mortimer Wilbur is the name he used to check in."

Johnny grabbed a pen and jotted down the name on a piece of hotel stationary. I could barely contain my excitement at this turn of events. I thought about hanging around to witness the big hullabaloo, assuming this was the right guy, and that he was still in his room. However, I already had another appointment that would induce an additional jolt to that part of my brain where the pleasure center resides.

"Listen, I gotta go someplace; shouldn't be gone for long. Phone me when you know, okay?"

"No problem. Trying to summon Big Guy but he's not answering. When I do, you'll hear from me, all right."

Ah, I thought, *Linda Lane, crisis–seeking junkie.* Another line added to my ongoing job description at the Supreme Superior.

I ran across the street and rode an elevator up to the 20th floor. The doors opened onto the reception room of the William Morris Agency. I craned my neck to view the 25–foot ceiling and the long metal stairway against one side of the wall.

Striking architecture notwithstanding, the décor was bland beyond description. I figured they hired the same decorator as the Supreme Superior.

Marie greeted me in the middle of the room.

"Linda, surprised to see that I'm Black?" she said with a smile as she shook my hand. She was a physically imposing woman: model tall and thin with a gracefully long neck. Also dressed in a chic, tailor–made corporate suit with the requisite four–inch spiked shoes.

"Surprised to see I'm not?" I responded.

She laughed. "C'mon, let me introduce you to Andrew, head of our New York office. He's been a big fan of the hotel for many years." She escorted me down a long corridor to a large corner office. "Andrew, this is Linda from across the street."

The first thing I noticed upon entering the office was not the small, nebbish–like man rising with an outstretched arm, but the binocular collection on the window sill. Absent–mindedly, I shook his hand. He followed my gaze and burst out in laughter at my distraction.

"A little hobby of ours, I'm afraid. Let's just say that we've had more entertainment from the windows of the Supreme Superior than we've had from any of our clients' Emmy award–winning sitcoms." We broke into a communal chuckle. Andrew continued, "I always wanted to meet someone who works in that place. Especially in the management area. You must have tons of stories!"

"Oh, I do," I nodded and smiled. "I could keep you laughing for days."

"Too bad we can't make a TV show just from what we see." The telephone rang and Andrew instinctively retreated to his desk. "Okay, Linda, I'm sorry. Work calls forth. A President's job is never done."

"A pleasure to meet you," I said as Marie led me out of the office.

"C'mon, we're going spelunking," said Marie as she grabbed a key out of her pocket.

"You don't know how much I appreciate this," I said.

"Hey, it should be fun. I have been here for almost twenty years and I don't even remember this schmuck."

The schmuck to whom Marie referred was Steven Koneman. Let me amend that: the repugnant Steven Koneman. Every time he arrived from L.A., he would boast about his years at the William Morris Agency in an effort to impress anyone who would listen. They were the same recycled and stale tales, all centered on his very intimate relationship with his idol, Frank Sinatra whom he always referred to as Mr. Sinatra, placing emphasis on "Mister."

Marie and I walked down another long corridor until we reached a locked door. She inserted the key, turned the knob and flicked on the overhead fluorescent lights. The room was filled with floor–to–ceiling file cabinets.

150

"Oh my God!" I said, thrilled and surprised to see over fifty years of the company's history. "Where do we start?"

"We?" she asked, taken aback, "no, it's me. It shouldn't take too long to locate him as everything is labeled by year and filed by last name."

Flabbergasted, I asked, "Marie, how in the world do I repay you for this? It's going to take you forever!"

She chuckled. "Not forever, Linda. Have no fear! I just gotta search for a ten–year period from maybe thirty years ago. Trust me, it's not as bad as you think." She turned off the lights and shooed me out of the room.

"I don't get it. Is there anything I can do for you?"

She smiled and tucked some folders under her arm. "No. Let me explain. Andrew and I have been here for over twenty years. We don't cotton to people who claim they worked here, or did things here they never did." She locked the door. "We're family here, Linda. We're protective of the agency. William Morris has been good to us, to me. In turn, I'm good to this company."

I was floored. What a difference of mentality from across the street. I grabbed her sleeve.

"Say, not to push my luck, but do you guys have any jobs in finance?"

She looked at me with a sadness that I identified as pity. "I'll check but," she hesitated, "we have such low turnover in those positions. Most here are lifers."

I must've had a rueful look on my face when I said, "It's worth the wait," because Marie patted me on the back.

"It may take years, Linda. Though we'll keep you in mind if we're not retired by then."

At the precise moment I entered my office, I caught sight of the back of Mr. Ganiff's head right before he slammed the door to his office, cutting off further access.

There were no messages on my desk from the operators. So I phoned Johnny. "Well?" All this adrenaline running through my veins made me jittery. Criminals, liars and thieves, oh my!

Johnny said, "Suite 1515."

"Huh?" I then remembered my request. "Oh, thank you. I'm asking about the guy. The criminal. The other one, you know?"

"Oh wait a sec, Big Guy just got back. Drumroll, please. Let me put him on the line." The receiver dropped on a desk with a resolute thunk followed by a muffled exchange of voices. Eventually, Big Guy retrieved the receiver.

"Linda, my girl. What's going on?" he said in a jovial mood.

Huh? How can he be so casual? "What's going on?!" I repeated. "How about that criminal guy Johnny and I identified?"

"Him?" Big Guy said. "Everything's handled. Don't worry."

"What do you mean by handled?" I asked.

"As I said, don't worry. NYPD's directly involved. They conducted a mass sweep of all our floors including those scary ones in the basement. He's not here on premises. Right now, the cops are hanging out all over the hotel and in his suite, waiting."

"So, it is him? The guy from the alert is staying here?"

"He is, Linda. Or he might still be. If he comes back for his stuff. We can't do much yet..." Big Guy's voice trailed off.

"So, what're you going to do then?"

"Me? Not much. I'm debating whether to go downstairs for a bite to eat. Heard they have oxtail stew today—"

I yelped, "No, that's not what I meant. What are we going to do with a potentially dangerous felon lurking about?"

"Oh, we have Johnny here monitoring the camera screens—"

"I'm going blind in the process," wailed Johnny at top volume in the background.

"Yo, kiddo, it's just for a few hours more!" Big Guy shouted back in my ear. "What is your problem?"

"What is my problem?" Johnny and I bellowed at the same time. His voice won. "Big Guy, check out my eyes! Pretty soon, you'll be special ordering Braille screens!"

"Hey, knock it off! I can't take the shouting!" I screamed back, "my ears are bleeding!"

Johnny continued his harangue in the background. "Better get me a seeing–eye dog. One who's computer savvy and flexible with his dewclaws!"

"Sorry, Linda," said Big Guy. He must've pulled the receiver away from his mouth because what I heard next was muffled. "Quiet, Johnny. Don't you worry because the union has good vision benefits." He shifted his focus back to me. "Here's the plan, Linda: Johnny's gonna monitor the security screens, and I have a guard hanging around downstairs. NYPD has a bunch of their undercover guys hanging about as well. The minute they see this mope, they'll pounce on him." His voice hardened and got serious. "Do me a favor. Don't say a word about this to anyone. I mean, if someone at the Front Desk finds out, they might tip this guy off by their reaction, and he might go postal, or run away. The fewer the people who know about this, the better."

I groaned. "I told Murlise. I faxed her and Sherwin. I asked Johnny to circulate the fax."

"Oh, okay," said Big Guy, "I'll give her a buzz. Knowing Murlise, she only informed Sherwin. Whatever that's worth. Don't you worry about the faxes. No one reads them anyhow unless they're related to crossword puzzles."

"What about Mr. Ganiff?"

"This is a need–to–know basis." Big Guy breathed hard. "The only reason why I'm telling you this much, Linda, is because you're the one who tipped us off. Otherwise, you would only have known about what happened through reading the *Daily Post.*"

"Well, besides the newspapers, how will I know in the meantime when this'll be resolved?"

"Oh, I'll let you know. Don't you worry your pretty little head."

I couldn't wait! All of a sudden, I remembered that I had another rendezvous tonight. Ah, another zap to my pleasure center.

Chapter 18

"Hey, Linda, gimme a five letter word for filth that starts with the letter 'g.'"

I sat at the lounge bar, almost empty at seven o'clock, peak after–work hours. The bartender, Teddie, served me a large iced tea, then went back to his crossword puzzle. From time to time he would glance up at me, expectantly, for a hint or a reply.

"Um, let's see. Starting with a 'g.' Well I would say Ganiff but that's one letter too many. How about grime?"

He laughed loudly. "Grime. That's what I needed. Though I agree, Ganiff would've been perfect. If we dropped an 'f.'"

While we filled in the rest of the puzzle, one of Big Guy's security staff repeatedly performed a reconnaissance of the bar. It appeared as though he conducted surveillance every two minutes. Could this be related to the pending apprehension of the thug on the eighth floor? If so, why did he keep coming back to the Lounge and only the Lounge? This bore the distinction of something highly unusual and very unsettling. I also feared that the friction from his repeated rounds eroded a deep groove into the carpet as well as the marble floor underneath. Which might prove disastrous should a client fall in and break an ankle.

Teddie had completed the final horizontal clue when Calvin came sliding in next to me.

"Hey, pretty lady. Your coach awaits."

"Oh, hi Calvin." I found myself inexplicably excited and fought to suppress a sudden overwhelming compulsion to lick his face. I was infatuated with Calvin. He was hot.

"Where's your jacket?" he asked.

"You think I might need one?" I felt warm and comfortable in the Lounge. Even warmer, due to the onset of a hot flash emanating from my nether regions.

"Um, Linda, it's winter outside and a bit chilly," he said.

"It is?" I tittered in embarrassment. "You know I live in a womb. I always cab it to and from the hotel and then rarely leave the premises. The relatively few times I have the opportunity to venture out is close by…" I realized I was babbling, and embarrassed, petered to a halt. "Guess I'll be a little cold tonight."

"Worst case scenario, my dear, I'll lend you my leather jacket." He grabbed my hand and escorted me to his chariot, an '87 Jeep Liberty, parked right in front of the Supreme Superior. I felt a little nervous; I could almost taste his pheromones. Was this a real date, or a thank you for the complimentary room?

En route to the movie theatre, Calvin made an oratory disclosure while driving on the streets of New York. "I'm afraid that I messed up my life."

"How so?"

"Well, I was going out with this girl for a few years, and then felt that I had to marry her or lose her. So I took the plunge."

What a way to find out he's married!

He forged ahead. "Major mistake!"

"Oh, I see," I said, showing empathy that I didn't feel. "A mistake? How so?" *Talk about a mistake, helluva way to kick off a date,* I thought. *Typical Calvin!*

He nervously laughed. "There's no romance between us at all. We're more like friends. Or maybe roommates. No sparks. I do admit she's a terrific mother and we both just adore our daughter."

Great, I thought with a drop of sarcasm. *First I find out that he's married, now he has a kid! What else does he have in store for me? An addiction to controlled substances? International arms smuggling?* I combed my imagination for other possibilities. *Prison record?*

He looked over at me. "She isn't the love of my life. Or if she was… well, we've fallen out of love."

Hmmm, perhaps a prison record, I speculated.

I also wondered whether his wife shared the same views about their marriage and relationship. No matter how he justified himself, it chafed me. I was pissed. Why did he have to wait until now to advise me of his marital status? He should've told me beforehand. Furthermore, why should I get involved with a married man? Puh–leeze. Relationships are difficult enough to handle when there are two people involved. Who needs a third? My sour expression must've given me away.

Calvin must've known that he blew it. We were never truly alone before and our respective jobs had kept us at a distance. Now, those boundaries were gone and yet even more in place. I tried to loosen things up with light conversation to make the best of an uncomfortable situation. Since Calvin was an inveterate fan of Howard Stern, the radio shock–jock, I said, "Calvin, I have a confession to make."

Calvin handed a twenty to the clerk behind the snack bar counter inside the massive multiplex cinema. I picked up my box of malted milk balls and he gathered his jumbo popcorn and soda. We stood behind the cordons for the opening night of the new James Bond movie, *GoldenEye*. He turned to me, wide–eyed. "Ah, can't wait to hear this one, Linda."

My eyes met his. "Down boy, it's not that juicy. Just thought I'd let you know I met Fred Norris a few years ago. We hung out a few times at some functions." Fred Norris was one of Howard Stern's on–air radio crew.

"Really?" asked Calvin.

"Really," I repeated. He didn't react the way I thought he would.

"This is what you call a confession? Damn, Linda, after all the shit that I've been telling you, and this is how you reciprocate?" All indications pointed to a tempest in the making.

155

The door to the theatre swung open and we followed the line inside. I couldn't calm him down or even divert him. Irritated, I asked, "What do you want from me, huh, Calvin? Hey, I don't get out much. For me, this is a big confession." He glanced over at me, and shrugged in defeated acquiescence.

We found two spots dead center in the large theatre. Calvin put his popcorn bag between us and we sat apart like friends. I wondered if this mirrored his relationship with his wife. The beginning of the film turned out okay though the junk food tasted better—I love those malted milk balls. Right when the action hit high–gear, my bladder sent a message loud and clear.

I nudged Calvin with my elbow and pantomimed for him to move his legs in. "Sorry, I gotta pee," I whispered in his ear while I positioned myself to stand up. I felt desperate, convinced that my kidneys would explode. *Damn, I shouldn't have finished that big iced tea back at the hotel.* I disturbed half the aisle so that I could go to the bathroom, and couldn't have timed it better upon my return—everyone had to stand up again mere seconds before James Bond performed his last incredible heroic deed. I killed it for half of the spectators.

Calvin shrank in his seat. When the lights came on, he bolted out of the room. "Can't believe you did that, Linda." He laughed at my expense.

Oh, no, I thought. *It's bad enough getting abused all day long. Now Calvin, of all people, is gonna pick on me for having to pee during the movie.*

He went in a whole different direction. "Hey, I admire you. I had to take a whiz the minute we sat down. I didn't have the guts to make half the row stand. In fact, wait here a sec while I go pee now," he said prior to dashing off to the men's room.

On the way back to my mid–town apartment, we didn't say a word. He pulled up to my building entrance and we continued to sit there in silence.

I moved forward to give him a kiss on the cheek, but he moved to do likewise and wham! We clunked heads.

"Ow, sorry," he said.

"My head!" I moaned. I rolled my eyes with undisguised disgust, then moved forward again to give him the obligatory peck on the cheek. That's when the dolt bolted forward as well, yet again, and thunk! "What the fuck is wrong with you? Haven't you ever kissed a woman goodnight before?"

"Oh, Linda, I'm sorry."

I extended my hand. "Night, Calvin. Thanks for the flick. See ya tomorrow."

Laughing, he shook my hand before I left the car. Then he called after me, "Hey, Linda. I'll have the estimates for Ganiff tomorrow."

I laughed back. I couldn't help myself. Even on a night out from the office, he had gotten the final word and it was all about business.

156

Chapter 19

"I told you, Linda, I know everything you do here at the Supreme Superior. I have spies everywhere," snarled Ms. Djorak. She pointed at her eyes for emphasis. "Do you know that you looked like a whore? A hooker?" Ms. Djorak's jowls shook like a rabid English bulldog. She was in her element, all aglow with evil and misdoings.

"What in the world are you talking about?"

"Supreme Superior employees do not loiter at the bar. Not during work hours, or after!"

"How did you know about that?" It came to me in a flash—the security guard walking in circles around the bar. Despite our bare bones security staff, a certain someone assigned one security staff member to spy on me. How remarkable that I was just as important as a dangerous, armed criminal hunted on premises! I gave a rueful laugh. "One of your minions, I take it. Well, excuse me. I was waiting for someone. A friend."

"I don't care who you were whoring for! You are representing the General Manager of this hotel. People look to you as an authority figure, not a call girl!"

I wanted to reach across the desk and strangle the woman. How dare she hurl insults and complain about where I hung out after hours! Who the hell was she to question me? I got up and stomped out of Ms. Djorak's office, passing several people milling around in the human resources' waiting room, barren of all furniture and décor. They parted to either side so that I could pass.

I walked down the dark concrete corridor, through the women's locker room and scrambled up two flights via the back stairs to the rear entrance of the kitchen. I needed a place of refuge. That, and someone to commiserate with.

At the cold counter, Lydia, a recent graduate of the FBI, greeted me. She avidly chopped assorted melons on a glass cutting board. "Hey Linda, what brings you back here? Love? Romance? Hunger?" she asked while adding the sliced pieces to the colorful mound on the counter.

"No, I just got reamed out by Djorak… again. All because I waited at the bar to meet a friend last night. Hell, I didn't even have a drink."

"Yeah, this place is pretty fucked up. I don't know what's worse—that bitch Djorak, or the insatiable Mrs. Ganiff."

"Mrs. Ganiff? What do you mean, Lydia? Does she come round here often?"

She rolled her eyes. "That witch, she's driving all of us chefs crazy. You can't just make a *Bliss* salad for her. You have to make sure that all the vegetables are absolutely top notch. She inspects each leaf! Then, they have to be cut just so." She wielded her paring knife and demonstrated with a slice of cantaloupe.

"Who ever heard of rose radishes in a Waldorf salad?"

I shrugged while Lydia continued chopping and venting. "My all–time favorite Mrs. Ganiff slick psycho–rich–bitch move is how she places an order for a few roasts, then while we're cooking 'em, she changes her mind and insists on organic chickens."

"That is messed up. Though hardly surprising," I said with a smirk.

"She comes here mostly during peak hours. Never seen anything like it— she must have radar. Like when we had to cater four major affairs for the top Penthouses, all at the same time. What lunacy! She ran around here like an enraged hippo, barking orders, demanding that we drop everything for her. I felt like dropping my pants and mooning the old bag."

BeeBee strolled by, an unlit cigarette dangling from her lips. *What the hell is she doing here in the kitchen?* Lydia spotted her and pointed her knife in BeeBee's direction. We quieted until after she passed us.

"That's another one—Djorak's lipstick bitch," Lydia whispered, "she comes in here, acting all puffed up and important looking. Then she yells at us junior chefs, telling us that Mr. Ganiff wants special lobster lunches. The last time she pulled that stunt, we had a special order all right—a genuine special order from Ganiff for his venison lunch at *Bliss*."

I chuckled and accepted the piece of cantaloupe harpooned at the end of the knife. "Damn, I had no idea. I thought I knew everything. So how long's this been going on?"

"For the last few months."

"Really now?" I reflected fast and furious while chewing on the juicy and tasty piece of fruit. "You know what? Next time she asks for anything, tell her you'll have room service deliver it to Mr. Ganiff's office. You know, so that there'll be a record of it and she'll know the jig is up. Tell her it's my orders."

Lydia tipped her head so that her chef's cap pointed in my direction. "Willing to oblige ya, ma'am. Oh, and thanks for listening."

I nodded back at her, then left the kitchen through the exit behind the elevator banks and strolled into the Lobby. A few guests were lined up at check–in, others sitting in the plush chairs. The bellhops didn't appear to be too busy. The two doormen, though, were outside whistling up a storm for a taxi.

Sherwin, a Front Desk clerk, signaled me over and pulled out a crossword puzzle. "Linda, need a little help here."

"Sure, let's take a look."

He read, "Another word for rotten. Starts with a 'd.'"

"Djorak?" I responded without thinking.

Sherwin laughed. "No, Djorak has six letters whereas the clue has ten."

"Decomposed?" I blurted out.

He wrote it down and looked up. "Okay, now, for the down column, what's a five letter word for evil–doer?"

"What the hell?" The clues didn't sound like a standard newspaper crossword. I lunged over the counter and tried to grab the folded paper out of his hands. But Sherwin was stronger. I glimpsed an article entitled, *My Dark, Satanic Lover.*

"What the—Sherwin, where did you get this crossword puzzle?" Before he could respond, I pulled on the paper and saw on top, in lieu of a name, a picture of a devil. "Sherwin, is this a satanic magazine?"

"Oh, that's what it is? I found it here. Thought it was the *Daily Post.* Although I did wonder about some of the clues."

I looked askance. "By the way, did you happen to see the fax I sent out the other day?"

"You send out faxes?" he asked, wide–eyed and perplexed.

"Yeah, sometimes. I do it when I'm bored of making phone calls."

"What was this one about? Don't think I saw it."

"Well, you didn't miss much. Just some crazed, armed lunatic, robbing hotels around the city. Nothing too exciting." I looked at him with consternation, thinking, *Get with the program, Sherwin!* It must be nice to live in his part of the universe.

"Sounds like fun," said Sherwin with a smile. "Well, great, add me to your mailing list."

I spotted Big Guy at the far side of the front desk whispering into the walkie-talkie. He noticed me and signaled in my direction. "Hey Linda, hats off to you yesterday! Great work."

"Ah, shucks, it wasn't nuttin'!" I smiled sheepishly.

"If you didn't go to my office with that photo and follow up the way you did, we woulda been victims. I don't know what else to say!" He walked up to me and patted my back. "Oh, last night before that guy was arrested, New York's finest searched his room. You wouldn't believe what he had in there: Uzis, ammo, you name it." Big Guy whistled for emphasis.

"Thanks, Big Guy. Never knew about that last part. Does Ganiff know?"

"Of course! Spoke to Mr. G and Djorak about the whole deal. Even wrote a memo just so you would be commended for saving our ass."

"No, punished would be more like it."

Big Guy gulped. "Huh?"

"This is a very funny place, isn't it? You almost gotta wonder whether the real criminals were hauled off."

"Hey Linda, you're my new hero," shouted Edwing from behind the Concierge desk. He had spotted me talking to Big Guy. I walked a few steps over and flashed a lopsided smile.

"Seriously, Linda, Big Guy's right. A commendation here is a pretty big deal. I got one and other commended employees got up to twenty grand!"

"For real?" I stopped for a moment. "Twenty grand from the hotel?"

"Oh yeah," he went on, "and a grainy photograph published in the Japanese Supreme Superior newsletter with Mr. Ganiff presenting the check. It's not uncommon. Besides, it's good internal PR. Keeps employee turnover down a percent or two."

I contemplated approaching Ganiff about this special recognition as I trudged back to the executive floor. For twenty thousand bucks, I'd happily raise the subject. Although not if he were in one of his fickle moods. I was in no frame of mind for another temper tantrum.

With the scent of a bloodhound, Mr. Ganiff emerged from his office and tapped me on the shoulder as he approached my desk.

"Yes, sir?"

"Linda, I want you to know, you're doing a good job," he said, throwing the dog a bone. That ingrate knew damn well that I had exceeded his expectations. "Oh, and sorry for the delay in notifying you… You're off probation! Have been for a while. So… Welcome to the Supreme Superior Hotel. You're a full timer now!"

He couldn't fool me. As if taking me off probation—several months later than prescribed no less—wasn't already inevitable before my earlier heroics. I was the best manager he had. I made his life easier; kept the disruptions to a minimum because of my willingness to assume authority. In my excessively paid administrative role, I fielded almost all the calls, handled the correspondence, wrote the public relations material, settled disputes and remedied in–house problems. My shouldering the workload gave Ganiff the freedom to pursue his interests that revolved around spending the day in the bathroom and concocting new and intricate ways to fleece the hotel.

I watched him watch me and imagined the thoughts running through his head. Too bad I didn't have puppets. I would've placed one on his left shoulder representing the Devil who'd be whispering in his ear with a deep voice, "C'mon, Ganiff, keep the bitch off–center, as you do with the rest of the staff, before she gets wind of your side projects."

And then I would've placed an angel puppet on his right shoulder whispering in falsetto, "What the hell does she know? She claimed she was a banker, yeah, sure, must've screwed her way up, or something 'cause what's she doing here?"

Deep in thought, his head swiveled left and right. Almost like the RCA dog listening for his master's voice. His countenance kept changing like a *Star Trek* shape shifter, vacillating from congenial heart–rending acknowledgement back to his typical callous demeanor. *I'll talk to him when his good mood lasts a bit longer,* I promised myself.

Right at that instant, Ms. Wapiti apprehensively poked her head into my office, followed by Mr. Dorck. Ganiff waved them into his berth, "C'mon in, c'mon in. Let's see what you have." Their appearance did not further perturb him. He shut the door behind them.

On a hunch, I lifted the receiver. Sure enough, the intercom picked up their comments.

"So, what do you have for me?" asked Ganiff in a jovial tone.

Both Mr. Dorck and Ms. Wapiti responded together, then argued.

"Go ahead."

"No, you can speak for both of us."

"You have all the results in that folder, there."

"Goddammit!" Ganiff shouted, "will someone, anyone tell me the results?"

Ms. "highest paid" Wapiti stepped up to the plate. "Sir, once again, we had the staff conduct an extensive inventory and the results," she shuffled papers, "correlate within a ninety–nine percentile of what they performed prior to that. Do you want to see the charts?"

Mr. Ganiff let out a theatrical sigh. "No thank you, Miss Wapiti, I'll take your word on that. Now here's what I want you to do. Starting next week, you're gonna do a daily inventory off–premises."

"Mr. Ganiff, the trip out to Baldwin Laundry, it takes at least ninety minutes each way!" Ms. Wapiti's voice broke.

"Don't worry, Miss Wapiti, it's for one week. Only five workdays."

After a while, Ganiff spoke again. "The cost of this commute will be taken out of your department's bonus fund. And you, Dorck, I want you to do the adjustments. You got that, Dorck?"

"Yessir," muttered Dorck.

"It is my contention that after this inventory, we'll get to the bottom of it. Meeting concluded," he said.

And the plot sickens, I reflected as I hung up the receiver.

Chapter 20

Calvin submitted his estimates, albeit quite a few days later. My shirtsleeves were rolled up to my neck, trying to massage or massacre his figures to fit within the broad–based categories of those submitted by the other two competitors. To make matters worse, Sensai and Mountainside appended to their estimates separate Excel spreadsheets that provided in extensive detail itemized cost breakdowns and analysis. I felt a lot of pressure to get this work done: Ganiff had a meeting later that day with the Gang of Three to present the numbers for submission to headquarters in Japan.

There was no doubt in my mind that Nikrovetch would win the award. A lot rode on the contract. I suspected a lot more went on behind–the–scenes than what I was told.

I also read the legal papers from our favorite disgruntled guest, Mr. Silverberg who, indeed, was litigating against the Supreme Superior. An exchange of correspondence between Ganiff and Landsman, our corporate attorney, revealed that Ganiff wanted to go to trial. On the flip side, Harry Landsman wanted to pay the man off.

Harry arrived to make his argument in person. Once again, the door was closed. Once again, I picked up my intercom, eager not to miss out on this conversation. *Should be too good to be true!*

"It's not good business to give this schmuck five grand," complained Mr. Ganiff. "It'll start a bad precedent. We can't have it."

"Believe me, Iggy, you don't want this to escalate further."

"What do you mean by escalate? It's already escalated. He wanted a free weekend. At this rate, he can come here for a month!"

"If we go to court, given the fact that this guy's also an attorney, you'll end up paying way more than five grand in court fees, my fees, you name it."

Ganiff exhaled in frustration. "Is there any other way to extricate ourselves out of this?"

"Well, I'm certain there are many, Iggy. Given the tenaciousness of this man, just pay him off. End the case. Then go on to bigger issues."

"Like what?"

"Iggy," Harry said, "you have a bigger problem with that unnamed tenant at West Fifty–Third. You should've signed those papers years ago. Now, you're gonna have even more problems evicting this guy."

"Honestly, Harry, I didn't know anyone lived there."

"Ignorance does not absolve you from following the law. The Supreme Superior is legally the landlord."

Mr. Ganiff huffed. "Well, what do we do? Buy the guy out?"

Harry spoke in a conciliatory manner, "I'm not suggesting that now, Iggy. You just can't start an action four years later."

"Let's say that the building is not used for residential purposes."

"You can't say that! You had the Supreme Superior renovate the second floor of that building for your daughters' use when they were between husbands. Please, Iggy, before that, you allowed Walter Cronkite to use one of the small studios as an adjunct office when he wrote his memoirs. Surely, you haven't forgotten."

"Well, they can't prove that the Supreme Superior was a landlord 'cause all the rent they paid went directly to me. It was my deal, separate from the hotel."

I almost fell from my chair. *Ganiff had a hand in that too! This guy's like a child in a candy factory, gimme gimme gimme.*

"That's part of the problem, Iggy."

"What problem!" shrieked Mr. Ganiff.

Harry sighed. "I'm trying to do my job in spite of your side deals and meddling. I'll start cracking on this eviction case right now."

He heaved his bulk out of the padded chair and waddled up to the door. I hung up the phone when the door opened from Ganiff's office.

"Iggy, I'll have my girl contact yours for those documents. They must be signed." He suddenly turned around and caught me jockeying for a better position to overhear the last fragments of this senior level exchange of business. I jolted back in my seat, whipped out an emery board from my desk drawer and began filing my nails.

"Uh, do me a favor, Linda," Harry pretended to ignore my indiscretion.

"Yes, sir," I answered, nodding, eyes downcast.

"Please get him to sign these papers ASAP. If left to his own devices, Mr. Ganiff will allow Mr. Silverberg to own the Supreme Superior. Now we can't have that, can we?"

"Hey, Harry, I heard that," bellowed Mr. Ganiff from behind his desk.

Harry handed the file over to me, partly eclipsing Seebok who endeavored to sneak past.

"Hi Linda."

"Seebok, long time no see," I said with a big smile, "how're things going since the big meltdown?" Other than the morning meetings, Seebok had been almost invisible of late. Except for that one unidentified flung object or "ufo" sighting Johnny and I had viewed on videotape. Over his shoulder, Harry gave me a salute before heading out of the office.

"Oh, things're great. Working on a few projects with some outside vendors."

163

Seebok craned his neck to see if Ganiff was inside. "Is the big man free?"

"Yeah, go ahead." I waved him along.

He knocked on the doorframe.

"Yes, Seebok," Mr. Ganiff wearily responded.

Standing in the doorway, he said, "Sir, I've been meeting with some vendors for a more competitive and up–to–date phone system. Ours is pretty antiquated."

"Not right now, Seebok. No time for this. Later."

"Mr. G, I need—"

"Seebok, I said not now! I've more pressing matters to deal with."

A few minutes after Seebok left, he telephoned me, "Hey Linda, got a sec?"

"Um, sure. Didn't I just see you down here like not even five minutes ago?"

"Yeah. I see you're not too busy right now, so come upstairs and check out my new computer. It's very cool."

"You mean the one we ordered you after the Alletti disaster? I've the same one on my desk."

"No, this one's different. I got it from one of the vendors."

"Oh, I see." Back to his old tricks again. "Is this a gift for your hard work in mediating the new phone system deal?"

"Oh no, Linda, you don't understand. They want to show how cutting edge their company is. It's not a gift. It's more like a demonstration."

I shook my head. "Seebok, what do phone systems have to do with personal computers?" A valid question given the technology for that period.

He laughed at me. "Linda, see how little you know? Come on up and I'll show you."

I pictured Seebok's tiny office, one floor above mine and perpetually locked… now more than ever, even when he was in there. A result of his constant paranoia since the Alletti gift–giving incidents. Seebok rarely invited his colleagues into his bunker. Trish, his assistant, would often joke that the room was equipped with more technology than NASA from all the vendors' gifts.

I had to admit my curiosity was piqued. Not due to some sudden fascination with computer telephony. After the last Seebok escapade, namely the sanitation contract renewal, my internal antennae screamed "warning, warning, Bill Robinson," a line from *Lost in Space*, a 1960's sci–fi TV program. This guy was a one–man disaster unit.

As I strolled to the stairwell, I ruminated about how my position had usurped Seebok's prior role. The Supreme Superior resisted putting into place a formalized Resident Manager who would have all the power and perks of the General Manager.

Instead, they hired qualified people with no superlative executive titles, a slightly lower salary, lesser to non–existent perks and no power to potentially threaten Mr. Ganiff's position. Hence, the oversupply of candidates both in and out of house. In the insular world of the hotel industry, the right–hand to the General Manager was an esteemed position. One which provided that person with unlimited power to abuse hotel privileges to their heart's content.

The way I looked at it, Seebok remained my sole in–house competitor. Trish told me that he unrelentingly pestered Ganiff to name him Resident Manager. Why Ganiff would ever give this screw–up of a man a promotion was beyond anyone's comprehension. Yet, the guy still had a job in spite of himself. *Gotta be a reason for it,* I surmised. *I need to get to the source!*

From my earlier encounters with Seebok, I knew that a price would be exacted should I accept an invitation to visit his office. Certainly, Seebok never did anything for free. The guy would demand blood from a stone. He had learned from working at the Supreme Superior that he could extract most anything from mostly anybody—with one exception, Alletti.

After holding intensive internal debates, I decided to go upstairs. Trish spotted me from her desk. She ran out and pushed me flat against the corridor wall while placing her finger against my lips.

I pulled her finger away and whispered, "What's happening? More dead animals?"

She shook her head. "No, Doreen and Seebok are going at it again."

"What are they fighting about?"

"I've no idea. Neither do they anymore. They've been at it on and off for hours. She ran up here again for another go at him. We had to let her in because she made some racket when she kicked the shit out of our closed office door. I think Seebok spread some rumor and it must've gotten back to her," replied Trish in a hush.

The two of us fell to our knees and crept to the doorway of Seebok's office. One of the housekeepers lumbering by noticed us. She made the sign of the cross, then pushed her cart faster. I peered in. Doreen shouted at Seebok.

"You're a mean man, Theebok.'"

Seebok imitated Doreen in a nasal voice—perfect pitch, I hated to admit, "You're a mean man, Theebok."

"Thtop it!" she shrieked.

"Thtop it!" he mimicked again in perfect pitch.

Trish and I reined in our laughter. I spoke in a hushed voice to her, "This is just too good. Can't get any better than this. They're like second graders."

"Don't think your little game will thtop me from going to Mithter Ganiff," Doreen threatened.

"What game? Doreen, whatever is plaguing you, come clean, tell me and… I'll thtop it!"

Doreen stamped her foot in rage. Seebok laughed harder. He sat back in his chair with his arms folded behind his head, legs propped up on his desk, ankles crossed. She ran towards him, hand in a fist, arm upraised as if to slug him. Seebok recoiled and with a panicky look crossing his features, retracted his legs and bolted up.

Doreen hissed at him, "I don't like you. I never liked you. Furthermore, I know what you're up to. If you continue to bother me, I'll, I'll fuck you up real good!"

Seebok snarled at first. Then, he flashed the smarmiest smile he could conjure and said, "That was the first time in five years I heard you say an entire sentence without your lisp."

The earsplitting shriek from Seebok's office made Trish and I shrink further into the hallway.

Next door, Mr. Dorck poked his head out of his office. He spotted us and shook his head in our direction. "Psst. Over here, you two. What in the world is that terrible noise?"

"It's nothing," I deadpanned, "just Doreen arguing with Seebok."

"Oh, good to hear it. I mean, it's good to know, I mean…" he stammered, "I mean, at least I know I can leave my office without fear of bloodshed."

Right at that moment, Doreen left Seebok's lair. She spotted the three of us and headed in our direction, both hands clenched into fists while muttering, "That fucker. That fucking bathtard fucker."

"Perhaps I spoke too soon," said Mr. Dorck. With that statement, he ducked back into his office and sealed the door closed. Slid the bolt shut. From the hall, we heard him push a chair under the knob.

"Hey, Dor–een," I greeted her.

She stopped and glared at me. "If I even thee you go in hith offithe, I thwear, Linda, I'll rip you a new athhole, you hear me?"

"Loud and clear." Even though in the corporate pecking order I had a slightly higher status, I allowed her the indiscretion to dictate an order to me. You never know when payback, blackmail or an apology might follow. I kinda hoped that this would be a trick card up my proverbial sleeve.

She grabbed me by the elbow and accompanied me down the hallway. Right before we left the floor, I turned to wave a forlorn good–bye to Trish.

"Babycakes, before you say my name, don't! I have to speak to you," said the disembodied voice whispering at the other end of the line.

166

I had just returned to my desk when the phone rang. On the other end was the sole person who had ever considered calling me "Babycakes" and still lived to tell the story. That was Carole Carlson, the only African–American housekeeper at the hotel.

"Okay, you got my attention," I said.

"Good, I need to see you now, but we gotta go where they won't suspect us of talking. Some place no one goes to," suggested Carole.

"Let me think," I responded. The major drawback was that security cameras covered almost every square inch of the hotel. Out of nowhere, I had an idea. "Where do you watch television? The Health Club, right?" The perfect spot. Carole once told me that she liked going down there to watch her son on MTV. I liked going there to use the immaculate toilets in total uninterrupted privacy. There were no cameras inside, and none of the executives would ever be caught dead in there!

"That's it," she replied, "see you in five."

I forwarded my phones to the operators and left. For once, Mr. Ganiff wasn't ensconced behind closed doors. He had gone upstairs to visit the Missus to do lord–knows–what.

Carole grabbed me the moment I stepped into the Health Club. She swung me over to the women's cedar–lined locker room and shoved me inside. For the first time since I met her, she looked upset.

"I got wind of some serious stuff going on here. There's been talk in Housekeeping. We've been working very long shifts and no paid overtime, so I know this upfront," she said, and then blurted out, "Mr. Ganiff has something to do with the theft of our linens!"

"What? Are you sure?" I peered into the three toilet stalls to ensure that they were empty. Then I sank down onto the bench in the center of the room.

"Linda, we're not all stupid. Most of us are poor but we ain't stupid. Like we can't figure out what's behind all those inventories, and how he's defending that Baldwin Laundry? It ain't right, I'm telling you. Something's not right with it at all." Seated next to me, she folded her hands in her lap on top of her fox fur.

"What else do you know?"

I could tell the stress had aged her in just a few days. "Well, we've always had a little theft, okay? It comes with the territory. Over the past year or so, we all noticed that what goes out to Baldwin Laundry, half of it comes back, or not even that much. Ain't no secret. Ms. Wapiti, she's been trying to be okay about it, you know, trying to work with it. It's just too much now. I mean, sometimes we don't have no linens to make the beds at all! Instead, we've just been changing sheets for those rooms that change guests. Oh, and with towels, now that's worse."

My head almost imploded. This is a five–star hotel, right? Disgust registered on my face.

"Yep, Babycakes. Remember that—what you guys called it—the 'Crabisode'? There's a lot more going on than what you guys're told... I mean you guys like Ganiff and you."

"Excuse my ignorance, but are you telling me that people like Murlise and Doreen and Joe and all of the rest of the executive staff know what's going on?" I was incredulous that this scandal had not reached my ears.

"Babycakes, puh–leeze. I'm not talking about those people. They wouldn't know if a crab or even a lobster bit them on their ass. I'm talking about the little people here. People like me. People who know that a five–star hotel should be a five–star hotel not a flea–bag motel with... ahem, five–star pretense."

I had no idea about this at all. I didn't know what to say and I did not want her to know what I knew about Ganiff and Baldwin Laundry. I stared at my hands.

"Lissen up, Linda. This discussion is not why I phoned you."

My head snapped to attention. "You gotta be kidding."

She sighed. "I think I did something that may jeopardize me—not my job but me personally."

"Oh, shit, Carole! What is it?" My eyeballs protruded and I felt a slight flutter in my chest.

"I submitted a complaint to the hotel association. I said that the Supreme Superior had abused the union's contract. I wrote that—wait a sec..." She pulled a paper from the pocket of her fur coat and read, "There were housekeeping personnel who were required to conduct frequent and extensive inventory, even off–property, without receiving any compensation. This unlawful situation placed undue pressure on the remaining staff who had to compensate for extensive shortages. Moreover, staff has been ordered to disregard the hygienic standards that are advertised by our hotel. This constitutes a breach of contract with the hotel association and probable grounds for condemnation by the Board of Health." She stuffed the document right back into her pocket and looked up at me.

"I had no idea you could write like that! I'm impressed! You a lawyer in a past life, or something?"

She removed the paper, rolled it up and smacked me several times in succession. "Stop clowning around. Don't you get the significance of what I did?"

"C'mon, Carole. Stop hitting me! You're gonna give me paper cuts. Everyone knows those suckers hurt like a sonofabitch!"

She shot me a look to kill even though she did put the paper back in her pocket. "The minute they notify Djorak, I'm a dead woman. She's wack. But, if I quit my job, she'll win. So here's the thing I need from you. A promise, Babycakes. I know you have a good heart. I've heard stuff about you helping people out.

I know you care, and I need that commitment. Can you do it?"

I thought for a moment. Carole who didn't need the job, had imperiled herself, probably her physical well–being, for others. For integrity. I was touched.

"Yes, of course I'll help you. You're a friend. Just say the word."

She inched closer to me and spoke in a tone above a whisper, "Linda, the moment you hear anything about me, or the hotel strike, or anything, please give me the heads up, okay?"

"Why do you need to know?" I felt uncomfortable relaying quasi–confidential information that could easily be traced back to me.

"I need to know what Djorak and senior management are up to. I need to be one step ahead of them." She was nervous. "I don't trust these people, especially Djorak." With hesitation she added, "Listen… I just don't want to end up on the front page of the *Daily Post*, if you get my drift." Regaining her confidence, she pulled out another piece of paper and a pen, this time from her apron pocket, and scribbled a bit. "I'm giving you my private mobile phone number. Just call me, okay? If I don't answer, then," she cast her eyes around, "put a pen in the middle stall. I'm here a lot during the day anyhow."

She gazed into my eyes. "Linda, can you do this? I'm relying on you!"
She handed me the slip of paper.

I weighed what she had said. *To whom do I owe allegiance? To Ganiff and Djorak? Ha! Or perhaps to people who care about the quality of their work performance, maintain high standards and aim for a better workplace.* I stared back into her eyes and extended my hand with only a slight hesitation. "Carole, I hate making commitments, especially those that bite back. Given the circumstances and what little you are asking from me, I will honor this. Let's shake on it."

We shook hands and separately left the Health Club.

Chapter 21

Mr. Shitsu was the second in command of the Gang of Three. He was also my very first call early the next day. He wanted to set up an appointment instead of Mr. Hitsuhana, the head man, to review the banquet hall construction proposals. It was known that Mr. Hitsuhana did not understand English very well. However, the true reason for the substitution in the power structure was that Japanese management never did trust Mr. Hitsuhana, given his background.

During his last years as an executive in banking, Hitsuhana–san had demonstrated very poor decision–making skills. He had almost toppled the bank from a portfolio filled with bad loans. His punishment was relocation to New York rather than ritual seppuku, the traditional and honorable form of suicide. I had the feeling that after spending the first week in that tiny office with the other members of the Gang of Three and their secretary, Miss Monique, Mr. Hitsuhana often contemplated the latter option.

Under direct orders from Japan, Mr. Shitsu was compelled to exhibit his partiality toward Sensai. Furthermore, he had to demonstrate to the head office that he had sufficiently petitioned Mr. Ganiff regarding that sentiment, to the effect that it would behoove Mr. Ganiff as well to show partiality towards Sensai. It all made sense, considering that one of the Board of Directors at the Japanese bank owned Sensai; Mr. Ganiff swore up and down that he knew this as fact. "I'll be damned if I give the work to them," he groused.

Because Ganiff intended to use Nikrovetch, he attempted to convey an impartiality that he didn't have. To appear aboveboard with a glimmer of respectability, he made it mandatory for me, the insider/outsider, to attend the meetings and take notes. I did not care for this role and endeavored to weasel out of it, but Mr. Shitsu agreed that it would be a wise move to include me as well. Both men required a witness.

The three of us sat in a small conference room on the executive floor. I distributed my Excel spreadsheet containing the breakdown of each major facet of the construction project and associated cost as per the three contractors. Mr. Shitsu studied the figures, then pushed the paper aside. He adjusted his glasses and sighed. Mr. Ganiff imitated him.

Bored and exhausted as well as unsure as to how my presence would add value to this process, I stayed mute.

"Mr. Ganiff," said Mr. Shitsu after a period of time, "it appears Sensai's proposal is very high. I am greatly surprised. How about you?"

Ganiff nodded. He said nothing and fought back a smile.

"Okay, then. We will talk to Sensai. We'll make sure their figures match those of Mountainside. I'm certain that they will comply."

Mr. Ganiff peered at Mr. Shitsu. "You do realize, Shitsu–san, that Mountainside is still over the budget. Nikrovetch is the one company that can match the amount we've been approved to spend."

Mr. Shitsu's face grew strained. "This isn't only about price. This is about quality construction. About reputation. Mr. Ganiff, we will have Sensai's figures to match Mountainside. I strongly suggest that you choose them for this project. Thank you very much."

Mr. Ganiff was incensed. He leaped from his seat and trotted out of the room, leaving Shitsu and me behind. From the hallway, he motioned for me to follow. When we returned to my office, he stood facing the wall, blowing off steam, or struggling for composure.

"Get me Calvin on the line."

"Yes, sir." I reached for the phone and dialed.

Ms. Djorak trotted into the room, panting. She stopped for a second to catch her breath, then blocked the entrance to Mr. Ganiff's office.

"Mr. Ganiff."

"Not now, Djorak. I've an urgent matter to deal with."

"Mr. Ganiff, it's imperative that I speak to you now."

He tried to nudge past Djorak to enter his office but she wasn't moving. Next, he tried to push her away with his butt. Like the Rock of Gibraltar, Djorak didn't budge.

"Miss Djorak, I must get in there. Please move!" He was very polite considering he was exerting all his strength to shove her away with both his arms.

Djorak stayed in place. Arms akimbo. Legs, laddered with multi–colored varicose veins, planted like tree trunks. Jowls clenched firmly. No way in hell could she be ousted.

"Mr. Ganiff, we have a situation."

"No, Miss Djorak, we will have a situation if you don't move your ass now!" he roared.

With that threat, she stepped forward. Ganiff's momentum carried him crashing into the doorframe en route to his chair. "Ow, my herniated disc! Why the hell didn't you move, damn it?"

Ms. Djorak spat out the two most hated words she could ever summon, "Hotel strike."

Mid–step, he froze. "What the hell did you just say?"

"Hotel strike," she repeated again, this time with greater urgency.

Ganiff pressed the intercom button and shouted, "Forget Calvin for now. Cancel all calls. I have a situation here with Miss Djorak."

When the Supreme Superior was first purchased, Ms. Djorak negotiated the original contract with the hotel association. This was the union for almost all employees, e.g., housekeeping, front desk, bellhops, waiters, cooks, doormen, busboys, dishwashers, engineering, operators—the backbone of the hotel's operations. Security was in another union, not as contentious as the hotel association.

Carole in Housekeeping had often repeated what the good people at the NYC Hotel Association told her—that Ms. Djorak's negotiation tactics were legendary. Djorak used brain, brawn, and it is conjectured, the directory of her former colleagues from the black ops branch of the South African Army. These people had transitioned after the abolition of apartheid to the more lucrative mercenary field, specializing in terrorism. As a result, Djorak had been able to establish a union contract independent of the other major New York City hotels. She also ensured that the ratio of union workers to rooms remained at a significantly lower proportion than at the Supreme Superior's competitors.

Although the impending union strike would affect nearly all the major New York City hotels, the Supreme Superior was almost immune. Almost, in that three major hotels were on the same street. Despite the fact that the union workers at the Supreme Superior were not on strike, they were compelled to attend the strike rallies conducted in front of these other hotels.

I picked up the intercom. Clear as a bell sang the dulcet voice of our Ms. Djorak.

"Mr. Ganiff, I believe we should focus on Carole Carlson. You know her."

"I do?" he asked, puzzled.

"Mr. Ganiff, she is our only Black housekeeper who is, incidentally, the head of our hotel's union chapter," she paused, evidently seeking his reaction. None was forthcoming. "Sir, you know Carole! She's been around here a long time and she absolutely knows where the bodies were buried." Seemingly, nothing registered because he remained silent. Frustrated, she continued, "The one who wears the furs!"

"Oh her! Yes, that Carole. Why didn't you tell me before?" He belched in an explosive burst of air. "What do you suggest that I do about her?"

"Sir, with all due respect, I would prefer for you to do nothing. My job is to protect you and the hotel, in that order."

Oh really, I thought.

She continued, "This Carole poses a considerable threat. One that needs to be remedied. I have to muzzle her, and quickly. It's because of her past complaints that the head of the hotel union wants to meet with you for mediation. Or possibly a renegotiation of our contract with the union. We don't even know what she's up to now. She's an absolute menace!"

I felt my pulse soar. They had no idea that Carole had recently submitted another batch of complaints to the hotel association. This was gonna get ugly, and soon!

"I'll have none of that," roared Ganiff at Ms. Djorak, "I refuse to meet with them."

"Sir, I don't think we have much of a choice." Her tone grew ominous. "I have to stop her so that she doesn't spill any of her union poison around here to make the natives hostile. It's mandatory that I make sure that no one, and I mean no one, from this hotel attends the demonstrations, even in sympathetic support."

"Djorak, do whatever it takes. Use your magic and know–how, like you did when you got us the first labor deal."

"Thank you, sir, thank you." I imagined her bowing to Mr. Ganiff, and kissing his ring. As I hung up the receiver, I envisioned that psychopath pirouetting on her way out of his room.

She passed me by without hissing, spitting or growling. Her face held a look of self–contentment.

"What got into her?" I asked Ganiff when he emerged from his office.

"Oh, I gave her the go ahead to resolve a potential labor dispute. Carte blanche. I hope I can live with that stain on my soul."

As he returned to his den of inequity, I pondered, *how can a soulless man assume he has a soul?* Enough contemplation. I had a promise to keep. I had to wait until he walked out of earshot. Except he never closed his door when he reentered his office.

Time for me to use a little creativity. BeeBee was at her desk, a miracle in and of itself. I bellowed in her direction, "Gotta go for a pit stop. Be right back." I pantomimed answering the phones and staged left to walk down the hall to the Health Club. The middle toilet stall was open, so I availed myself of the facilities and afterwards left a pen on top of the toilet paper rack. Given the fact that there was no privacy at my workstation, I felt that this was much safer than calling Carole's mobile phone. Anyhow, she would check the Health Club, at least three to five times daily. Should she find a pen in the middle stall during one of her forays, she knew to contact me.

When I returned to my desk, I found Seebok knocking at Mr. Ganiff's door, briefcase clutched in hand.

"Ah, Seebok, my good man, c'mon in. Oh yes, please close the door behind you." Mr. Ganiff's mood had lightened in the brief time I was out.

The door shut. I took that as my signal to pick up the intercom.

"So, Seebok. What do you have for me in that attaché?"

"Sir, here's your weekly selection of reading material." There was the sound of a zipper unzipped, followed by a thunk from bound paper hitting a desk. "You know, Mr. G, the kind that always has a happy ending?"

Mr. Ganiff chortled in delight. "Did you dispose of last week's selection? Because here's some more." This time, I heard magazines tossed from afar. "I do want to thank you for picking this stuff up for me. You know, in my position, it's kinda difficult." He laughed for a second. "Can you imagine what would happen if someone in my church catches me with this stuff? Or someone in the hotel? You're a goddamned lifesaver, Seebok."

I perched at the edge of my chair, biting my nails. *What in the world was he talking about? Pro–choice leaflets?*

"Hey, no problem, sir."

There was a noise like pages fanned and then a sudden change in the timbre of Mr. Ganiff's voice. "Wait a second. Did you go through these magazines? The corners of these pages are crinkled, like someone folded the ends while they were leafing through them!"

"Um, well, sir."

"Seebok! That's disgusting! How can you go through another man's stash? These here are my ladies. My fantasy dreamgirls!"

Pornography? I almost dropped the phone. *This is the purpose for their cloak and dagger routine? What lowlifes!*

"Well, sir, well… don't forget, tomorrow is video night! A nice selection."

Videos, too? I thought. *What the hell is it with these guys? At work no less?*

"Oh, I have to thank you again for that great tape, *Three's a Crowd and Tigger Too*. It never gets old!" Happily, he continued, "I took it upstairs the other night, popped it into my bedroom VCR and laid down. Next thing I know, my darling Mabel unzipped my pants. She wanted to know what was on the tape but I told her, 'Mabel, don't you worry your little head. I'll mute it. Anyhow, you won't be watching it.' I repositioned her head so I could get a better view of the screen and… What's wrong Seebok? You look a little green there."

I also tried my utmost not to gag. And was grateful this time that my phone rang. I immediately switched off the intercom and picked up the call.

"Babycakes, please, Health Club in five," said Carole.

I waited several minutes, then ran past BeeBee while gesturing to my belly, "Something I ate downstairs. Maybe the oxtail stew," and made headway to the Health Club again.

Carole grabbed me and propelled me towards the women's locker room in an arm lock. She said, "Don't worry, I already checked the stalls."

After she released me, I said, "Okay, here's the deal," and recapped the conversation between Ganiff and Ms. Djorak.

For a few minutes she sat, pensive.

174

I took her hands and asked, "Is it worth it, this union stuff? I believe you're risking your life. You know how insane Djorak is. She won't stop at nothing! She has no idea that you just wrote the union again. Can you imagine what she'll do when she finds out what you wrote?"

"Oh stop it, Linda, you're being melodramatic," she said unconvincingly as she slipped her hands out of mine. "To answer your question, yes it's worth it. It's worth every drop of my blood."

After that remark, I reflected on what she intended to do. I understood, at last, the concept of greatness and living according to one's commitment. My train of thought evaporated when Carole jabbed me in the waist with her elbow.

"Stop staring at me like that. It's like I'm sitting with Karen from Security."

175

Chapter 22
March 1995

Mr. Ganiff played a perfect game of ping–pong with the Gang of Three over the re–re–re–revised estimates for the construction project. Initially, Sensai reduced its price by $500,000. Realizing that they still were significantly higher than the targeted figure, the company then whittled its price dollar–by–dollar. It took a little time but Sensai matched Mountainside's estimates, much to Mr. Ganiff's dismay. Management's push was still on for Sensai, yet Nikrovetch had underbid them by almost a million.

This price jockeying became a daily ritual for a whole month, much to my amusement.

Bundles of faxes were forwarded from the Gang of Three to my office. I'd then update my spreadsheet with the new numbers. I spent hours conducting creative accounting, reliving number–crunching hell on earth. Mr. Shitsu followed up with impromptu meetings with Mr. Ganiff. It grew tiresome. Neither man relented. The meetings devolved to one pair of eyes locked onto one eye facing a proboscis.

The two men became quite adept at staring each other down. I guess it beat alternate kinds of masculine contests such as the one that involves fly unzipping and long distance urination, also known as the "pissing contest." Preferable to the other type of contest that involves fly unzipping and... let's just say, where they use tape measures—or perhaps not with these two individuals.

Their concentration became so intense that I stopped attending the meetings altogether and returned to my desk for more pertinent matters... such as... examining my growing facial hair. Invisible to the human eye—unless my overhead desk light hit the bottom part of my face at a certain angle—I could feel the prickly stubble. The hairs started from under my bottom lip, bisected in two, almost down to my jawbone and reunited over the chin. If I were a man, it would've been a perfect Van Dyke.

Needless to say, the amount of stubble sprouting on my chin had me spellbound. This led to some very deep philosophical questions like, where else is hair growing? I pulled up the sleeve of my sweater to examine my forearms. On a hunch, I hiked up my skirt to peer at my lower legs. While my head was under the desk, someone knocked.

I peered up. Just my luck. Steven Koneman.

Stored in my desk drawer was the fax that Marie at the William Morris Agency had sent the previous week. What a find! Contrary to all those stories that I had politely listened to, Steven Koneman was not, nor had he ever been an agent. He was a peon in the promotions department where he sold dolls of television stars. He never represented Frank Sinatra. Moreover, Frank Sinatra was no longer at the agency when Steven Koneman worked there. The best part of the discovery was his performance review. He didn't even last a year as he was let go for incompetence.

"Interrupt something?" Steven smirked down at me.

"Uh, hello. How long have you been here?" I felt more confident in my interaction with him. I had the goods on him. I felt armed with knowledge.

"Long enough to see." His smirk grew wider.

"See what?"

"Whatever kept you busy under the desk."

I rolled my eyes. "How may I help you, Steven?"

He adjusted his diamond cufflinks, his designer tie and ran his manicured nails through his tailored haircut. He peered into Mr. Ganiff's office to see him sitting across from another man; both immobile. Then he swiveled back to me and said, "What the hell is that all about? Looks serious."

"Don't ask," I whispered, "they'll be a while."

"Oh." Koneman appeared disappointed that someone was more important than him. "Well, okay then. Hey Linda, do me a favor. I have a few potential clients coming here for a drink and dinner at *Bliss* tonight. Can you ask Mr. Ganiff to join us?"

"Tonight? Nothing like short notice."

"Yeah, it's tonight. By the way, they might be potential clients for the Supreme Superior and its facilities." Steven winked.

"Well, can he get back to you? I don't know how long he'll be."

Koneman was annoyed that I couldn't give him a definitive yes. "Fine, but please mention to the G–man that I introduced a new client, a top–notch honcho from MGM to you guys."

I spun in my chair to face my computer. "Great. What's his name?"

"Jay Krieger," replied Koneman.

I found the name on the Reservations database. "Oh, here it is. Standard suite, corporate discount rate, coming in five o'clock tonight."

"Yeah, that sounds right. Linda, give him the full Supreme experience—limo, mobile phone, no check–in, blah, blah, blah."

I glanced up at him, unable to contain my annoyance. "Steven, this guy is paying the cheapest rate. Why should I upgrade him?"

"Feggedaboudit. Don't sweat it. I'll speak to Ganiff baby tonight."

"What exactly does that mean, Steven?" I asked.

"Ah, Linda, my little corporate Pollyanna. You just don't get it, do you?" He rocked on his heels. "You think by doing your little job and adhering to the little rules that you're gonna strike it big, dontcha?" He laughed.

I scowled at this idiot. He moved closer to me which made me recoil.

"Steven, move away now!" I said, wishing I had a strand of garlic cloves to brandish. "Enough with the threats and innuendos. I'm warning you!"

"Ok, Linda, let me spell it out fer you. Ya wanna move up here, ya gotta play like the big boys. Like your predecessor. Take a page from her. That doll really knew how to play!" Before he left, he turned around and said, "So, you either bump up my man, Jay, or I'll go to Ganiff, ya hear?"

I groused under my breath. Let him. "Go for it, Steven!" I shouted at his receding back.

An hour later, Mr. Ganiff was still in his office with Shitsu. Neither of them noticed me in the doorway. They were holding a massive stare down, waiting to see who would blink first. I had to break the deadlock because the silence had become too eerie. I walked into the office to interrupt these dolts.

Mr. Shitsu got up and bowed in my direction. He had the demeanor of someone who wanted to say something, yet couldn't. A few precious moments of indecision passed. The man left. Mr. Ganiff thanked me profusely by exclaiming, "What took you so long?"

"The two of you are getting better at this." In all honesty, I enjoyed the proliferation and duration of their staring contests. It bought me hours of peace and quiet. I endorsed it highly, and would push this endeavor of theirs for as long as I possibly could.

"My God, it felt like an eternity." He rested his head on his hands. Muffled, I heard him ask, "Was that Koneman who popped in before?"

"Yes, sir."

"Shit! What does he want now? It's bad enough that he's getting the Sublime experience paying discounted rates."

"Well, he came here to hit you up for one of his cronies for the same Sublime deal that he has. And because I was reticent to do his bidding, he threatened my job. Oh, he invited you to join him and a bunch of his pals tonight for drinks and dinner at *Bliss*. Evidently, you're treating."

"Oh, no, Linda. I can't. Not tonight. The Missus will kill me. It's bible study night." He stamped his foot in disgust. "That means Steven'll have to pay. Oh, he'll nag me till I'm in my grave but I'm not giving in this time." Ganiff reached across his desk and picked up the phone. "Now, would you mind leaving? Close the door behind you. I'd better call Mrs. Ganiff before she murders me."

I shrugged. It wasn't my problem. As I turned to leave his office, Mr. Ganiff propelled himself across his desk and grabbed my arm, his left eye full of urgency.

"How about you joining us tonight?"

"Why me?" I was taken aback at this spontaneous invitation as well as the manner of conveyance.

"Well, I think it would appease Mrs. Ganiff. Mabel will think it's business so I can sleep with both eyes closed tonight."

I shook his hand off my arm. "No way. Not Koneman. Thanks, but no way."

"How about this, then, Miss Linda: If Steven sees you with me, he'll think that you're in my good graces—which you are, incidentally—and he'll leave you alone." His right eye twinkled with merriment. "How 'bout that?"

Hmmm, now that got my attention. A chance to show Steven that I, too, can play with the big boys. Time for a little payback. I should make Ganiff sweat it out a little because I didn't want him to harbor any ideas about making this a regular request.

I said, "Oh, I don't know, Mr. Ganiff. I've plans tonight after work. A hot date with a hedge fund manager. Maybe tomorrow."

Ganiff's face reddened. "Please, Linda. I'll make it worth your while, okay? You come tonight and I'll see to it that Koneman leaves you alone for the foreseeable future." He squeezed my hand. "Besides, I'm desperate. Please."

The sound of him begging was music to my ears. "Okay. I'll cancel my plans for you just this once. Count me in for tonight." I yanked my hand away from his and wiped it against the side of my skirt. "To reiterate, it's just for tonight. Then tell your buddy boy Koneman to leave me the hell alone!"

179

Chapter 23

When I arrived at the Lounge, Mr. Ganiff, Steven Koneman and Jay Krieger were already on their way to a momentous bar tab. Mr. Ganiff downed copious quantities of white wine. Steven matched him drink by drink, except his poison was Scotch on the rocks. Jay, a very distinguished–looking upper–echelon businessman wearing the quintessential designer power suit, nursed a bourbon. I ordered an iced tea.

Steven, as usual, recounted the same ol' Sinatra story to Mr. Ganiff in a state of inebriation. "So I said to Mis–ter Sinatra, aren't you glad you have someone around like me to look after you? To bail you out of these messes? And Mis–ter Sinatra says to me, 'Steven, if I ever have another son, I'm gonna name him after you.'" Steven took another gulp of his Scotch. "Ah, little Stevie Sinatra. That was my dream, . y'know?"

Drunk to the gills, Mr. Ganiff smiled benevolently. I laughed, knowing that the man was full of shit.

"Who's up for a cigar?" asked Koneman, breaking out a case of expensive Cubans and slipping one into his new cigar holder—the one purchased by the Supreme Superior.

Ganiff reached out, took one from Koneman's hand and then whiffed its aroma. "Mmmm, these are the real ones." He smiled.

"How 'bout you guys? Jay, Linda you up for a little smoke?" Koneman pressed on.

Jay and I exchanged glances and shook our heads in unison. "Not a smoker," he answered. He smiled at me. "Thanks anyway."

"Suit yourselves," Koneman replied. He proceeded to bite off the tip of his cigar. He then pulled a silver lighter from his pocket, lit up and inhaled.

Mr. Ganiff was a social smoker at best. In his drunken state, he bit off the tip of the cigar, spat it out into his drink, and snatched the lighter from Koneman. With jittery hands, he lowered his head to ignite his Cuban. Instead, he lit his left mustache tip. A flame of orange and pink shot upwards. "Motherfucker!" he shrieked. He reached for a linen napkin, dunked it in Steven's Scotch and attempted to douse the enkindled moustache. The flame shot even higher.

Jay and I couldn't hold back. We doubled over in laughter. I hadn't laughed so hard in months, maybe longer. I couldn't stop.

Ganiff jettisoned from his chair and stumbled towards the men's room, more than likely seeking a mirror to survey the damage. Koneman, perhaps feeling a twinge of guilt for the mishap, followed Ganiff, giggling all the way.

Jay and I were alone.

"Hey Linda, you're off the clock now!"

I reigned in my laughter and coyly gave him a subdued grin.

Jay continued to speak softly which was difficult to make out over the piano cranking out a Broadway medley full volume. Nevertheless, I discerned the gist of his plan. Something about blowing this sorry joint and grabbing some dinner.

Moments later, Mr. Ganiff emerged from the men's room, no worse for wear. Koneman followed him back to our table like a stray puppy. They both sat down.

"Sorry about that," Ganiff said to Jay in a low voice. "Anyway, Steven and I plan to head over to *Bliss* for dinner. You're both welcome to join us."

Jay stood up and faced me. He winked, then turned back to Ganiff and Koneman. "Thanks. I think I'm gonna go up to my room, relax for a while. But you guys go, have a good time."

Mr. Ganiff and Steven Koneman staggered up, knocking their chairs into other guests and toppling tables in the Lounge. It took two waiters, a busboy and the Security force of two to lead the intoxicated pair to their seats in *Bliss*.

I picked up my handbag and, from the back of my chair, my coat. Leisurely, I walked into the Lobby. Jay sidled up to me.

"Looking for someone?"

"Yeah, a man who knows a good restaurant."

"How about *Bliss*?"

I smiled. "No, I said a good restaurant."

Jay helped me with my coat, took my arm and escorted me outside. Even though we were strangers, I felt a level of comfort with him due to the way he had reacted to Ganiff and Koneman. It gave him credibility.

I noticed he only wore a suit jacket.

"Where's your coat?" I said, "you do realize that even though it's early spring in New York, it's still damn cold!" I began noticing the weather outside of the shifting vagaries of hotel politics, taking a page from Calvin's reaction on our sole date.

Jay smiled. "I enjoy the cold. Can't get enough of it!"

What a bullshit artist, I thought, *and a show–off too!*

We walked up West 54th Street. Jay was quite familiar with the neighborhood. "Linda, we have a pick of several fine restaurants around here. You got *La Côte Basque* there," he pointed eastward across the street. Then he turned westward, pulling me along with him and pointed, "*Le Cirque* is there and up a few blocks, towards the northeast side, the *21 Club*."

Jay Krieger exuded charm and masculinity. He possessed a rugged handsomeness, a quietness that accentuated his confidence, reminding me of a short version of Harrison Ford. Earlier that day, Steven confided that Jay recently separated from his second wife. Steven, in order to prove he was part of the

181

Hollywood in–crowd, took great pride in disseminating gossip before anyone else got wind of it.

Since Jay wasn't wearing a coat, I selected a restaurant closest in proximity. We entered *La Dolce Vita,* a very well known neighborhood Italian restaurant. The smell of toasted garlic bread assaulted my senses. The place was packed. Paul Newman and his wife, Joanne Woodward, dined in the corner. The blue–eyed acting legend spotted Jay and flashed that timeless smile. Moments later, Ms. Woodward waved. I was impressed. "Jay, how do you know them?"

Jay smiled. "I work for MGM Studios. It's a small world in L.A., trust me." The maitre d' also noticed the interaction and led us to a reserved table. That wowed me even more—no one–hour wait.

I ordered the specialty of the day, veal ravioli. Jay asked for manicotti and a bottle of chardonnay. While we nursed our wine, Jay asked me what I wanted to do in life.

"Well, I've always wanted to write," I admitted.

"What kind of writing?" Jay sipped his white wine.

"Pornographic science fiction."

He almost spat the wine out. "Come again! Did I hear you correctly?"

I laughed. "Oh yes, I've written quite a few short stories already. About extraterrestrial species mating, you know, that kind of thing?"

Jay burst out laughing. "You're kidding me, right?"

"No. I'm quite serious." His visage appeared bemused. "Not!" I thought it necessary to add.

After that exchange, the ice broke. Our conversation flowed fast and furious, full of laughter until I asked him the question behind the chatter.

"How did you and Steven meet?"

Jay picked up his glass and ruminated while gently swirling the wine inside, examining the way the light reflected off the fluid. He took a sip and put the wineglass down. "You must mean, how did Steven ambush me?" He gazed deeply into my eyes. "I'm not a complete idiot. I know he's a piece of shit. After all, Steven does have a rep. He is, however, an effective PR guy, amazingly one of the best in town." He took another sip of his wine. "Now, back to your question. I was innocently minding my business at a local celebrity golf outing in Palm Springs when out of nowhere two thugs came over to me, grabbed me from behind, shoved a pistol in my ribs and said, 'Buddy, you have to meet this man'—"

"You gotta be kidding!" I laughed.

"Quid pro quo, Linda! Gotchya." He chuckled. "One of my guys at work was either strong–armed or blackmailed into presenting him to me at this celebrity golf

182

thing. The rest is history." The waiter was at his elbow, ready to serve our entrées.

After one bite, I looked at Jay. "If I didn't know any better, I'd say this tastes just like Chef Boyardee."

"Really? Let me taste." He leaned across the table and opened his mouth, waiting for me to feed him.

I speared a plump ravioli and plopped it in his mouth. He chewed and his eyebrows shot up. "You're right. Imagine paying thirty–five bucks for a plate of canned ravioli. You want something else instead?" He patted my hand.

"No, that's quite all right." I let his hand stay on top of mine.

I regaled Jay with the story of Chef Boyardee. "Ganiff told me that Chef Boyardee wasn't a chef although he did work in a hotel. He came up with the idea of canning ravioli. I'm sure there was much more to the story even though I can't remember it. Ganiff tends to knock me out cold with his tales."

"Fascinating story," said Jay and roared in laughter.

The Newmans stopped by our table on their way out. "Hey, Jay, what are you doing in my town?" asked Paul Newman, his blue eyes as beautiful as in the movies.

"C'mon, Paul, isn't every town your town?" Jay responded and they laughed.

After the Newmans left, we ordered cappuccino that tasted like dishwater. And then we shared a very soggy tiramisu with a sunken center. Jay signaled for the check.

We walked cross–town to my apartment building. Jay had his arm around my waist for the majority of the stroll. Surprisingly, the man did not shiver once from the cold! I wanted to invite him up to my apartment, however, we had just met. After all, he was an acquaintance of Steven Koneman, no matter how hard he soft–pedaled it. Still, I was attracted. I could feel moisture seeping through my underpants. Hormones blazing, I leaned forward to kiss him and Jay cupped my chin.

Well that stopped me. I recoiled in horror—my hairy chin! He must have felt the bristles 'cause his hand dropped to his side.

I told him, "I would love to invite you upstairs but…"

Jay smiled. "There'll be other times. Good night and thank you for such a wonderful evening."

He sauntered away. At my apartment, I undressed and went to bed, masturbating to the fantasy of Jay humping me wildly. Suitable outlet for all my mounting frustrations.

Chapter 24

The phone on my desk rang promptly at eight–thirty the following morning.

"Morning, pretty lady. Thanks for last night."

"Oh hi there." I checked in all directions to see who might be listening in. The executives lined up in front of my desk for first dibs at the regular chairs for the meeting. No need to advertise my social life… presuming I could even call it that.

"Catch you at a bad time?" inquired Jay.

"Kind of," I whispered.

"Sorry, Linda. Just had to touch base before I check out. I've meetings all day. Then I fly out to L.A. I'm too overbooked to see you today."

"Oh," I moaned, disappointed.

"Hey, don't despair. I should be back in New York in two weeks. Give me your home number so we can stay in touch."

I obliged him, then joined the rest of the latecomers, standing against the wall in Ganiff's office.

Seebok discussed his latest projects. "So, we'll be testing the new automated voicemail system. It's a major upgrade to the old system. We're about to implement the T–1 cable for increased computer and cable usage. At the same time, we have the installation of new security cameras for all floors. These new ones, they have great new features, like infrared, zoom and auto–identity checks with a hook–in directly to the federal agencies." He coughed and then added, "It'll save wear and tear on Security's eyesight and reduce the recent upsurge in vision medical benefits."

Mr. Ganiff nodded and then proceeded to harangue Joe Smith on *Bliss* results. "Joe, I ate there last night and have to admit that the food was abysmal."

"Abysmal! Why do you say this? We're one of the highest rated eateries in the whole city."

"Joe, there were half–frozen peas with my braised boar. Even the meat was pink. I couldn't have been the only one served raw meat and frozen veggies."

Miserable, Joe searched for a clever defense. None came. "Okay. Isolated incident. I'll talk to Cookie. We'll figure out what went wrong last night."

Ganiff leaned forward in his chair. "Joe, you have to do something about attendance. There were three couples last night. Maybe you should have *Bliss* join those discounted food clubs. Have special chef nights or wine tastings. You must improve on results. Otherwise we'll need to revamp the place top–to–bottom."

"Mr. Ganiff," Joe pleaded, "for all the hits we're taking at *Bliss*, we are doing exceptionally well with in–room dining and catering functions," and with an anxious nod to Doreen, perhaps for intervention he added, "with all due thanks to Doreen and her team."

What Joe neglected to mention was that Cookie's assistant chef, Billy, a former torch singer, was a marvelous and creative chef. Kenin met Billy years before at a gay cabaret. He'd tasted his food and raved to everyone at the hotel. The corporate clientele adored Billy's salads and sandwiches. They kept returning with their functions due to his menus. Billy was also put in charge of the menu and food preparation for in–room dining which accounted for the high quality and volume of meals in that area as well.

Doreen puffed out her chest, too late to intervene on Joe's behalf. But that didn't prohibit her from inhaling the compliment.

"I'll expect a report on my desk first thing tomorrow morning on how you intend to improve table counts by 100%," demanded Mr. Ganiff.

Ms. Djorak was next. She cleared her throat. Her tone was ominous. "As some of you may be aware," she tipped her head towards Murlise and Ms. Wapiti, "any day now will be the impending hotel strike. We're not sure of the exact day, since our hotel is exempt from this labor contract. Therefore, my information is limited. Irregardless, we must inform our staff that participation in the other hotels' strikes such as joining picket lines or distributing literature will result in instant termination." She tilted forward. "I know for a fact that we have a few union rats under our roof. One of them is that Carole Carlson in Housekeeping. She's the ringleader."

Big Guy piped up, "I plan to beef up my staff during the day to prevent our housekeepers, busboys and any other union members from sneaking into the picket lines next door."

"Well, it sounds like you guys know how to handle the strike situation," Mr. Ganiff acknowledged. "Now, I want to let all of you know that our Japanese management and I have not settled our differences on who to retain for the construction work. Sooner or later, I shall prevail. Once that's done we can move onward and upward!"

Neither Ms. "highest paid" Wapiti, nor Mr. Dorck made mention of the missing linens although Ms. Wapiti left a bill on Mr. Ganiff's desk for replacement towels on her way out. My eyebrows shot up when I realized what she'd done. This was the first time the woman had exhibited any moxie. Standing behind Ganiff, I angled for a better view of the bill and could only discern that there were quite a few digits. Six of them.

"Ahem!" Mr. Ganiff cleared his throat aloud to startle me. "So, Linda, what's next on my schedule?"

I stepped around to face him. "Well, let's see… you've another meeting with

Mr. Shitsu."

"Oh, great!" Mr. Ganiff couldn't have been more displeased.

The clash between the two men had escalated. Sensai refused to reduce their costs. Logistically, Nikrovetch had to receive the contract, but Mr. Shitsu continued to balk. Sooner or later Japanese management would be compelled to make the rational choice because maintaining the budget was more important than retaining an expensive Japanese contracting firm, no matter how close the ties that bind. Mr. Ganiff knew that the gods smiled down on him.

Mr. Shitsu was due to arrive at the executive office any minute now. I figured that this was the time to step away. My first stop was the Health Club down the hall. I placed a pen in the middle stall of the women's toilets. The room was quiet and, as usual, empty. *Good*, I thought, *no prying eyes.*

On my way back, I decided to make a detour downstairs as well as a little side trip that would enable me to filch a croissant from the bakery bins. I entered the Lobby midst a dozen extremely tall men. I stretched my head upwards. These men were taller than trees. Some of them were devilishly handsome.

They argued over which elevator bank to use.

The Supreme Superior believed in discretion. The uniforms were discreet. The décor was discreet as was the signage. So much so that it blended into the fabric of the Lobby walls. Out of the six elevator banks, two were designated as express elevators connecting to the upper level Sublime suites and the convention floors. What difference did it make to our guests? They couldn't see the signs! As a result, most ended up on incorrect floors. Our guests had no idea where they were, a common hotel occurrence.

"Guys, it gotta be this one here. That's what the check–in lady told me. The flat–chested blonde."

"Shawn, that's not a girl, that's a guy! Damn! 'Her' badge read 'Sherwin.'"

"Like you can read the signs any better, man? It's this one right here... I think?"

"May I help you?" I asked, looking up at two of them.

"Yes, ma'am. How do we get to the thirty–fourth floor?" One of the gentle giants flashed me a wink. "We got in from Seattle; just wanna settle in."

"Oh, thirty–four is this way," I pointed out the correct elevator banks. "Hey, do you guys play basketball? 'Cause if not, I'm sure you'd be pretty good at it."

"How could you tell?" quipped another seven–foot two–inch tall gentleman.

"Lucky guess," I joked.

One of the men bent down and brushed my cheek. "Well, we're quite good at a lot of things on and off the court. 'Cept my man, Shawn here."

Shawn shrugged.

186

The man continued, "Yo, Shawn, only the courts for you! Hey little lady, you're welcome to head up with us and show us around our rooms."

The whole group laughed. I laughed along with them.

"Sorry, guys. I'm a still a bit worn out since the Lakers left on Friday. Thanks for the offer. Maybe next time."

The Supreme Superior had cornered one of the most significant travel markets, according to Mr. Ganiff: the tall people market. Or in the politically correct vernacular, the "overly–vertical–challenged population." The Supreme Superior, in order to cater to this niche segment, had to purchase specialty beds over seven feet long. And custom–made bed linens, blankets and duvets. All this contributed to the inflated cost of inventory. As a result of Mr. Ganiff's vision, our hotel had no competition in this particular niche, resulting in a cornered market of NBA guests.

"Oh, Linda, do you have a moment?" Edwing from Concierge interrupted my flirtation with the Seattle Supersonics.

"Hi Edwing. What's doing?"

"Linda." His hands trembled. "I have a problem. You know Ganiff's pal, Steven Koneman? He's totally outrageous."

"Lemme guess—a catered affair? With hookers?"

"Oh, c'mon, that was his last trip." My ears perked right up. Edwing sighed. "This is even worse. One of our new guests, Mr. Krieger, is flying out tonight on American Airlines. Steven's on United. He wants me to not only book him on the same flight but have him seated next to Mr. Krieger. It may not sound like a big deal, but the energy necessary to circumvent all those layers of privacy… it's very costly and time–consuming!"

Oh, I understood what Steven was up to. It was no secret that he badly needed MGM on his roster, especially at this nth hour. Unfortunately, Jay was immune to the traditional Koneman process. It was an intricate process whereby the victim (in this case, Jay) sampled the Supreme Superior and all the freebies associated with having Steven in his midst. Then the victim would be reeled into Koneman's intricate web of indebtedness. Since conventional methods failed, Steven had to rely on his highly cultivated stalker skill set. More than likely, he decided to forego subtlety and trap his prey during the six–hour return flight. Which would give him ample time to do his Steven thing, whatever that might entail, until the contract from MGM was signed, sealed and safely stored in his back pocket.

Edwing got angrier by the second. "You know, I resent calling in my markers from several people through my network. For naught."

"For naught? Whaddya talking about, Edwing? No FPM for this?" Concierges, especially those in the top hotels, operated by the credo: a few pennies more. Or for the initiated: FPM. Those FPMs can purchase in nanoseconds orchestra tickets to sold out plays and concerts without advance notice. For FPM, the concierge can make a reservation at any "hot" restaurant, or go out of their way for special Koneman requests.

"You have to understand my position, Linda," Edwing explained, "Koneman is one of those guys that I can not afford saying no to."

A sense of foreboding overtook me. "Well then, guess I'd better warn Mr. Krieger."

Edwing cringed. "You can't. I promised it would be confidential."

"He extracted this favor and in confidence? Ah! I'm astonished! As they say, 'heart be still!' So, how're you going to do this?"

The concierge looked down his nose, haughtily. "Honey, you don't get to where I am without a few contacts."

"Well, what do you want from me? Where do I come in?"

"Please, you gotta let Mr. Ganiff know about it. Just…" his voice trailed off.

"Just what? I can't help you if you aren't clear with me." I found it difficult to wade through his attitude and innuendos to understand precisely what it was he wanted from me.

A loud "ding" reverberated from the elevator banks signaling the availability of a cab. The basketball players stepped inside. The Lobby quieted when the doors closed. Edwing lowered his tone and bent forward to get closer to me.

"Let me remind you, you never heard it from my lips, okay? You must tell Mr. Ganiff," he said, and then lowered his head to whisper, "that the miser never gave me a single penny for this!"

Upon that admission, I gasped. This was a big deal. I nodded my head in agreement. The color returned to his face.

"Thanks, Linda. Maybe this way I might get some cash indirectly, though never enough to recoup from this escapade. At the very least, it'll be something for the wallet in case Ganiff might need something from me later on. Like something to hide from Mrs. Ganiff."

★ ★ ★ ★ ★

I returned to my office to find Ganiff pacing.

"That little Jap bastard," he muttered.

"What's wrong?" I asked.

"The sonofabitch cancelled our meeting. Says his girlfriend fell off a horse. Broke a few ribs."

"You mean Shitsu's girlfriend? Miss Suijii? Where is she? Where is he?"

"In the hospital consoling her."

I was nonplussed.

"Linda, let me tell you the story about their relationship because I think you're getting everything mixed up. If you do, you may pull a Seebok and screw everything up."

Pull a Seebok? How dare he compare me to that fuck–up!

Ganiff sat down at his desk to prepare for Anal Monologue mode. He seemed to reconsider, and decided to give me the full lowdown. His hands clasped in place while his right eye swiveled to the picture of his mother, now propped on the far left corner of his desk. Out of fear for my health and mental well–being, I interrupted him before he could begin.

"Mr. Ganiff, please, sir, I already know the story. Should I recap it for you? Miss Suijii and Mr. Shitsu have a long–term romance." He appeared crestfallen. I decided to placate him as well as myself. "I'm gonna head down to the cafeteria for a bite." The cafeteria was my last attempt to find Carole because she had never responded to my pens or calls. I asked him, "Do you want me to bring anything back?"

"No thanks, Linda. Just not in the mood for oxtail stew. Bon appetit."

En route to subbasement No. 2 through the rear stairwell, I bumped into Seebok. He was on his way up from the mailroom carrying a thick envelope.

"Oh, hi, Linda. Wanna see pictures of my family?" An odd invitation for sure.

"Um, here? Why not upstairs?"

"Why not here? It's well–lit."

We moved to the closest landing. Under a fluorescent light bulb, suspended from the concrete ceiling by a slender wire, Seebok passed to me color photos of an apparently starved extended family. Many of them were seated toothless and barefoot in front of a mud hovel. To my shock, he proudly pointed out each individual.

"Who is this?" I asked, pointing to a gaunt man who displayed his toes. I peered closer. Something did not seem right about the picture.

"Oh, that's my uncle, Finster. He taught me how to read and write. Did you notice he has twelve toes? The last two at the end are prehensile. He was known throughout our village for his feats. He's a terrific climber of shrubbery."

Did I hear correctly? Did he make a joke of 'feats'? What could I possibly say? To move onto safer ground, I picked out a normal–looking person who, upon closer inspection, was remarkably beautiful, garbed in a colorful sari. "What about her?"

"That's my younger sister, Anneal. She's a minor actress in Bollywood, and we believe she's destined for greater things."

"Where were these pictures taken?"

"The foothills of Pakistan." He looked at me, waiting for a positive reaction.

I went the high road. "You definitely are your mother's son."

He beamed with joy, thinking that he had made a new friend. "Hey, when you're free, come visit me in my office. I still want to show you the new computer."

This impulsive demonstration of kindness blindsided me. Seebok had that effect on me where I found myself perpetually torn between hysteria and remorse. He possessed admirable attributes: intelligence, determination (as exhibited by his success in overcoming a background of dire poverty) and very good taste in clothing. Part of me felt sorry that he was such a fish out of the water, vying to fit in somewhere. Anywhere.

Seebok was also an opportunist. I couldn't reconcile his good qualities with his compulsive nature, his acute avarice and selfishness that resembled bipolar syndrome. Not to mention his inane wheeling–dealing. Let's not even discuss his recent status as a porno pimp. He looked down at me, tapping his foot with anticipation. I smiled. "Hey, sure! Love to come upstairs. Once I have some free downtime, that is!" *Okay, I can be a kiss–ass as well.*

I didn't see Carole in the cafeteria. Instead, I ended up grabbing some oxtail stew and Sara Lee cake, and dragged those items on a tray into the cafeteria's smoking lounge. I took the seat across from Karen in Security. She leaned forward, excited to see me. "Linda, I gotta tell you what happened this morning. Shhh, it's confidential."

"What?" I mumbled while slurping oxtail stew, an acquired taste for staff members at the hotel. Especially those of us who had no free time for lunch, staggered 24–hour shifts and limited accessibility to food outside of the hotel. Most of the restaurants nearby were expensive because they were targeted for the tourist/business class. To top it off, they were not open during those hours when the majority of us had mealtime. In summation, the cafeteria at the Supreme Superior Hotel was our sole access to food. I resorted to eating this all–time Supreme Superior classic mostly out of desperation because the food at *Bliss* was often inedible.

"Had to saw handcuffs off one of the guests," she revealed in a whisper.

"Huh?" I shrugged and wiped the slop from my chin.

"We got a call at daybreak. One of our executive regulars. He goes for the transvestites. Anyhow..." Karen exhaled smoke from her cigarette, "his wife called all night into this morning. She was worried because he never answered the phone. So, Big Guy and I used the passkey and entered. We found him butt naked, arms and legs handcuffed together. He told us he screamed for hours."

"Ah, that's why the Front Desk had so many complaints about noise. I thought it was because of Seebok's defective TVs," I interjected.

"Yeah, I heard about that, too. It's a pity 'cause he sometimes brings his wife. Nice lady. Lord–knows–what diseases he brings home."

I asked, "Karen, does this happen a lot?"

Karen snorted. "Girl, you have no idea what happens here at night. Let's just say it gets nasty. In spite of it all, the overnight shift is always the most interesting."

"How so? Any other perverted stories?"

"Nah, it's all the same shit. Just one thing, Linda. Watch out for those rap stars. They never check in without a posse. Those guys are gang. They are a disaster in the making. Mark my words."

After lunch, I couldn't keep my eyes open. Oxtail stew had that tryptophan effect on me. Tryptophan is the chemical in turkey meat as well as in certain other meats that makes you feel sleepy after pigging out on Thanksgiving. I read that claptrap in the 'papers, where it's the synthesis of melatonin in the intestines that causes the chemical reaction, yada yada yada. Anyhow, I had in–suite dining bring up a mega carafe of espresso to my desk so I could revive a bit. I was in the midst of guzzling this high–octane witches' brew when I received a phone call from Carole, two days after we had last spoke.

"Babycakes, found your lost pen. Anything new?"

"No, the usual. Just firming things up for the impending deal. Do you intend to continue with your trip?" I hoped she understood what I attempted to say in code as the walls have ears in this place.

"Yeah, it's going down."

"Do you think you may change your mind?"

"To answer your question, no, I'm not gonna change my mind."

"Are you sure? Is that your final answer?" I felt uneasy about this development.

"Yes, and yes. Nothing changed since we last spoke. Don't fret yourself."
She hung up.

I realized that I couldn't worry for everyone. Carole was her own woman and this was the path she had chosen. I had my own worries to contend with.

Chapter 25

A pre–dawn electrolysis session left my chin feeling raw. Nevertheless, I was radiant. The process removed over 200 hairs. At a dollar per hair that made for two hundred bucks. "What a great investment," I extolled as I arrived very early at the office. My chin now resembled a plucked porcupine but I was happy. The phone rang.

"Morning, beautiful lady," said the disembodied voice on the phone.

"Isn't it like the middle of the night there?"

He laughed. "Guess I'm still on New York time."

I guess the guy is still interested! "So, how was your flight?"

"Linda, that was the longest flight of my life. Don't know how he did it! Steven Koneman grabbed a seat next to me. That schmuck didn't stop talking for five hours. I almost jumped out over the Grand Canyon."

I chuckled. "I know you'll find this hard to believe: I knew about it. Or at least I knew that Koneman arranged it."

"You didn't warn me?"

"I couldn't. It was one of those situations, Jay."

My accidental slippage of Jay's name registered on Mr. Ganiff's antenna. He yelled out from his office, "Hey, is that Jay Krieger on the line?"

"Yeah, it's him," I hollered in Mr. Ganiff's direction.

"What does he want?"

I raised my voice for effect, "Jay, thanks for calling. Yes, Mr. Ganiff is available to speak to you." Despite Jay's protestations on the other end of the line, I transferred the call.

Mr. Ganiff picked up his phone and in an upbeat manner said, "A very good morning to you, Jay Krieger."

With that sewn in place, I closed the door, and within seconds the bolt slid in from the other side.

At the staff meeting, Mr. Ganiff made the announcement that the entire executive team could've anticipated, "Nikrovetch won the contract. It should be signed today. So, we scheduled construction to start at the end of the month."

Looking at my colleagues, I witnessed their various states of fatigue, boredom and restlessness. Ms. Djorak stifled a jaw–opened yawn and Cappy pulled threads from his sweater. Murlise separated her split ends.

Mr. Ganiff—oblivious to the indifferent reactions—went on to tell us how he managed to get the contract signed.

"I made an impromptu visit to the hospital to see Miss Suijii late last night. She was laid up with a few broken ribs. I brought along a dozen bouquets of roses in all shades, even maroon!" He tugged on his mustache for emphasis. "Mr. Shitsu was overwhelmed. So much so, in fact, that he finally admitted he received several weeks ago the go–ahead for Nikrovetch. I guess the poor bastard felt compelled to continue his competition to see how much longer I could hold out. Must be a cultural thing. No matter, Mr. Shitsu folded. Signed the contract on the spot." Mr. Ganiff chuckled. "It was only good luck that she fell off that damn horse." He pointed at Mr. Dorck. "Have the first check issued this afternoon."

Next, he pointed at Ronny, our Banquets Manager who had recently returned from another round at an expensive rehab clinic paid for in full by the Supreme Superior. I wondered whether his reaction towards the last set–up for Ganiff's bible meeting contributed to that setback. "Ronny, have you contacted your corporate clientele to ensure that all catering events in the upcoming two months have been postponed?"

Joe Smith, Ronny's boss, protested. "So much for advance notice! Mr. Ganiff, with all due respect, we've got more than twenty jobs to reschedule."

Mr. Ganiff stood up from his chair. "Joe, what the hell do you do for a living? Do I have to do your job for you? What the fuck do you think we discuss every day? Do you mean that you haven't taken the initiative to inform our banquets manager?"

"I… um…" Joe stuttered.

Mr. Ganiff leveled his good eye at him. Abruptly, he swung his head to the side and did a double–take. He definitely caught sight of something right outside his window because he almost keeled over.

"Joe, before I stroke out in front of all you professionals, what flag is hanging in front of my office?"

The Supreme Superior, like many major New York City hotels, exhibited around fifty flags in front of the hotel, representing the diverse nationalities of our guests.

Joe stood up from the foldable chair and peered out. "The Israeli flag, sir."

Mr. Ganiff almost choked. "Murlise, could you kindly review for us again who is visiting this esteemed establishment?" He flopped down onto his chair, arms and legs spread–eagle.

Murlise stared down at her clipboard. She smiled, content because someone else took the heat this meeting. "Yes sir. It's Mr. Abdul el–Rahman, senior government official from Libya. I should add, a dignitary with a notable repute of anti–Zionism."

"Joe, do you have a brain in your head? Why didn't you change the flag? Or is it customary to insult our guests? After all, do we really need clients?"

Cappy trembled in his chair. He wheezed as he spoke up, "Mr. Ganiff, Mr. Ganiff."

"Not now, Cappy. You're out of turn."

"But that's my responsibility, sir. I put up the flags."

Thunderstruck, Mr. Ganiff placed his hand to his chest. "Cappy, you're even stupider than Joe. Joe, at least doesn't admit to his fuck–ups! He'll sacrifice his mother, or gnaw off his arm rather than fess up. I just don't get you. You volunteer—"

"Mr. Ganiff, Mr. Ganiff," pleaded Cappy, "I'll have my guys change the flag immediately."

"Cappy, do it now. Or you can head on home and don't bother coming back. Got it?"

Cappy shoved his way out of Mr. Ganiff's office and used my phone to call his staff. At the same time, Mr. Ganiff continued to rant, foam pouring out of his mouth. Both of his eyes rolled up in his skull. His mustache stood at attention. Like a volcano, he erupted, with smoke and flames emitting from all orifices, even his derrière. No one was excluded from blame. Except for Ms. Djorak. With a grin on her face, she enjoyed the show.

The executive staff didn't know whether to cover their ears or their noses. Hans from Marketing tried a diversionary tactic. "Mr. Ganiff, I have here a draft of our current newsletter. It has the latest hotel rates." He proceeded to pass around copies for everyone in the room.

I reached for a copy and leafed through the pages. Anything to distract myself from the toxic atmosphere and the inhalation thereof. I discovered a glaring error. "Um, Hans, I think there's a mistake on page two."

Hans flashed me a look of uncertainty. "Linda, what do you mean? I proofed this thing twice over before sending it out to the printers."

"Your rate card is showing the discounted off–peak winter rates from last year. Shouldn't it have the current rates for summer?"

"Oh shit! I think you're right." Hans bolted out of his seat, heading to the door. "I've gotta stop the circulation. I can't believe they picked up the wrong rate card!"

Out of the blue, we heard a thunk against the window; a ladder, long enough to extend three floors. We were all riveted. One of Cappy's guys climbed the rungs to remove the Israeli flag.

"For crying out loud," snarled Mr. Ganiff, "they're supposed to lower the flag from the street. I can't watch this. Can someone close the blinds and spare me the agony?"

Mr. Dorck, Joe Smith and Seebok, closest to the window, leapt in unison. Anything to move away from Ganiff. As one, they closed the blinds.

"I can't bear this anymore. Meeting is adjourned, and under pain of death, I am not to be disturbed." Mr. Ganiff rose from his chair. He shoved Seebok and Cappy out of his office and bellowed, "No one is allowed near me today!" He slammed the door behind us. That was followed by the click of the lock, the shift of the bolt and the thud of a chair pushed against the doorknob. Everyone dispersed out of my office.

Oblivious to the goings–on inside, Calvin sauntered into the vestibule whistling. "Hey, Linda. You're not a liar."

I arched my eyebrows. "Huh?"

"Didn't you hear Howard Stern this morning?"

"I didn't. No. Why? What happened?" I usually set my alarm to go off in time for the popular morning radio show. The shock–jock often proved more effective in rousing me from my slumber than the alarm. This morning, however, I awoke long before dawn and went to the gym to get into shape for Jay's return.

Unlike me, Calvin was an inveterate Howard Stern fan. In private, on our one date, I had told him that I met Fred Norris, one of Howard's radio show gang; Calvin hadn't been that impressed with my disclosure.

"Yeah, I kinda met Howard on the streets a few days ago and he invited me on his show for one of his 'Stump Fred' contests," said Calvin.

"No way! That's so cool! Incidentally, what contest is that?"

"It's the one where they ask Fred and a guest, this time me, ten questions, and then whoever gets more right wins. As usual, Fred won. Get this, Linda," he puffed out his chest and plunged on, "Howard interviewed me live on radio. Right before the contest, I got to say my name, where I live and the name of my company. I tried to make a joke but he totally insulted me. Said something like: Don't be such a genius! Then after the contest, he said: 'Hard to believe that you own your own company because you're about as smart as cardboard.'"

Calvin was proud of being dissed in front of millions of listeners. *Go figure.*

"Congratulations! Sounds pretty funny to me, in a way. I gather you got to talk to Fred off the air?"

"I did. That's why I'm here! I mentioned your name and Fred asked about you. You were right, he does know you."

"Of course I know him. Calvin, why would I lie about knowing Fred? If I were to lie, it'd be about someone you would never meet!"

"So, I guess you were also honest when you said you were a banker. That's one thing around here that no one could believe."

I folded my arms and locked eyes with him. "Why in the world would I lie about that? That's what I did for years."

195

Mystified, he asked, "So what're you doing working here? In the hotel business?"

Before I could spit out something clever he interrupted my introspective moment. "By the way, I mentioned the Supreme Superior on the air. Won't Mr. Ganiff be thrilled? Free publicity."

"I don't think now's the time to tell Mr. Ganiff about that!" I unfolded my arms. "He's not having the best of days."

Calvin flourished a check from his coat pocket. "Well, he'll be happy once this is in his paws."

"What's that for?" I leaned forward to read what it said. The check was issued to Ignatius Elmer Ganiff to the tune of $375,000.

"His cut." Calvin gave a broad smile.

My mouth dropped wide open. "What?"

"C'mon, Linda, get with the program. You, of all people, should know this. Hey, after all, you do handle the papers."

"Obviously, not all of them."

Calvin, exasperated, sighed. "Yeah, you did work in finance. Listen, he receives his fee, that's 25% of every major contract that he signs on behalf of the hotel. You know, the fee for his construction project."

"Wait, that money came outta your pocket! How do you get that back?"

"Through the Supreme Superior, of course. All the contracts are inflated to take care of his cut. They just don't know it."

"Oh." I switched gears into supersonic hyper–drive. Calvin had an open and nonchalant attitude about this. Could this be the way business was conducted in all hotels? Not likely, but…

He dangled the check in front of me, taunting me. *What did he think I was— a cat?* Then he tucked it back in his pocket. "He doesn't get his until I get mine."

"Well, I'm guessing José Dorck'll issue your check a little later. The Gang of Three already signed off on your first invoice. Ganiff'll sign it in a few hours." I narrowed my eyes. "I guess the bigger question is: What does Ganiff do with all these kickbacks?"

He laughed. "Linda, he's supporting fifteen people. C'mon, his kids, their spouses, their kids. That whole family is a bunch of losers. His daughters never worked and some of them married bums twice over! He's paying alimony for three ex–husbands. Why do you think he bought Baldwin Laundry? Between Clod and that fucked up loser of an ex–brother–in–law of mine, they'll screw up the whole investment."

My head spun. I couldn't dismiss what I now knew as truth. About Ganiff.

Baldwin Laundry. Fees. Kickbacks. I needed to find a place to think this one through.

"Hey, there's a joke around here that whatever is not nailed down will find itself in Ganiff's coffers." Calvin chuckled.

All along, I wanted to believe that I was mistaken about Ganiff. Now, I had no choice other than to accept that I had irrefutable proof.

"I think you've said enough. I don't want to get involved any more with this."

"Ah, you already are, my sweet," he said in a low voice, "and now there's no turning back."

I felt my face turn a ghostly white.

"Oh, Linda. Remember, it was your spreadsheets that provided the detailed adjustments to those construction figures. Without your hard work, the Japanese group would've been hauling in their own trucks later this month."

I froze in my chair, lost in contemplation.

So now I'm trapped. Caught by the scruff of my neck in Ganiff's mandibles. I felt that familiar knot of dread grab hold of my belly. *Should this information ever be found beyond this office, all fingers will point to me!*

What was it that my friend Monica had said during our lunch a few months ago? Something to the effect that circumstances in my job would be doomed to repeat? *Well, if I'm going to have any say in this matter, I better cover my ass before it gets burned again in the corporate frying pan.*

197

Chapter 26

Ganiff had an illustrious past. He was the consummate hospitality professional. All his past successes were linked to the five–star hotels he represented. Even so, as impressive as was his past, he still held high aspirations for the future. From my vantage point, I noticed his many fingers in so many different pots, paving the way for that very future.

One day, an extremely attractive woman, the human equivalent of Jessica Rabbit, a "toon" character from a movie, visited with me at the office. Ganiff spotted her from his desk, and within seconds, sidled over, salivating for an introduction. As it turned out, Veronica was one of Tony Tenneb's agents. She dropped by, en route to an appointment, with free concert tickets for Mr. Ganiff and his family. A generous thank you gesture for the Penthouse suite rental.

Later that day, Mr. Ganiff called to me with a veneer of kindness. "How friendly are you with that Veronica?" He probably remembered her name from all his frequent calls to Tony Tenneb's office requesting free tickets.

"We talk from time to time."

"Well, I have an idea. Perhaps you can help me out with this. Might even be a little something in it for you."

Mr. Ganiff leant back in his upholstered chair, crossing his arms behind his head. "A few years ago, I came up with an idea for a television talk show. It's a terrific concept, different from any other. Most importantly, it features the Supreme Superior. You know, free advertising for the hotel. My friend, Walter Cronkite, was the host for the pilot." He stopped, reached behind his desk and pulled out a videotape which he handed to me. "I hired one of those old time New York public relations agents, you know that old man, Beedy MacReilly."

Beedy MacReilly was the same age as Mr. Ganiff. However, a dissipated lifestyle had aged Beedy by more than a few decades. Besides the rheumy eyes, he was bent almost in half with osteoporosis. When Mr. Ganiff had returned from his retirement, he had brought Beedy on–board. Beedy worked at the Supreme Superior as a public relations consultant. To tell the God's honest truth, I never saw his work. Since I came on–board, I handled almost all of the public relations material. And, I worked closely with Hans Holook. Insofar as the PR aspect with Beedy, we never met, conversed or even corresponded.

As for Beedy, he received $2,000 a month merely by showing up for his check.

"Hey Linda," said the troglodyte as he trudged that folded body into my office. "Heh heh heh, ya got money to help out my boy–os!" he gleefully chortled open–mouthed showing off his gap–spaced yellowed fangs. For my edification, he rubbed his crotch with one wrinkled claw. With his other hand, he grabbed the check from my desk using his long, curled and yellowed nails. "I got me enough now to buy me a few ladies for the night." Total revulsion crossed my face. He sneered, "What are you, a prude? A little girl? Sex is natural." To be kind, or politically correct, natural would not necessarily be the word that I would associate with Beedy.

During my initial interaction with the slogging half–dead, I handed over the check by its furthest corner. He still managed to caress my hand which made my skin crawl. It also soured my stomach as well as my disposition. Knowing he was a personal and close friend of Mr. Ganiff, I refrained from saying a word during this initial as well as each subsequent distasteful encounter. Right after he clumped out of my office, I waited a few seconds to ensure he no longer was in the corridor, then ran like a bandit into the ladies' room. I washed my hand until the first seven layers of flesh were sloughed off.

This time Ganiff moseyed out of his office and told me outright, "You have to hand it to Beedy. He's a genius. He's been a key element in launching the television pilot."

Such a genius! Funny thing though, Beedy never had a nibble with the pilot. That, ladies and gentlemen, was the reason for Ganiff's hard sell.

"Take the tape home tonight, Linda. Watch it. You'll see. Tomorrow you can call Veronica and get that tape to Tony. Tony would be a marvelous host. Even better than Cronkite."

With reluctance, I took the tape. Sherwin phoned. A little too late to be saved by the bell.

"Hi, Linda. I know it's a long shot: is Murlise in your office? Can't find her anywhere."

"Oh, hi Sherwin. No, she's not here. Anything I can help with?"

"Well, it's just… we have a problem. It's about our check–in/check–out."

We always had a problem when it concerned the check–in/check–out period. We attributed this on–going situation to two major problems occurring concurrently. The first entailed our housekeeping staff. They had a very limited and finite window of time to turn over the rooms, thanks to Murlise. She staunchly believed that three hours were more than adequate to clean and clear hundreds of rooms in five–star fashion to accommodate our new clientele. Given the ridiculous ratio of rooms to housekeepers, one of the many ways in which Mr. Ganiff kept expenses down, the result was a daily race at breakneck speed. In fact, the housekeepers were rarely able to meet their quotas in the limited allotted time. That didn't deter Murlise; she would staunchly defend her position to the death.

The second major problem rested once again with Murlise. Schedules for her staff violated the Geneva Convention. Front desk customarily worked three consecutive fourteen–hour shifts followed by three eight–hour shifts, then three days off. Sometimes she placed the shifts back–to–back so that the staff never went home. This resulted in severe sleep deprivation. It tended to negatively affect the effectiveness of our clerks. They were either punch happy from fatigue, or went off the deep end from seeing multitudes of spiders emerging from the cracks in the marble walls. Oftentimes, at the end of these long shifts, Sherwin resembled an owl. Large black concentric circles looped around his eyes. Security received calls numerous times from our more religious and superstitious guests with reports of zombies; we found several front desk staff, in their exhaustion, lurching toward the exit like the undead. It became a quotidian event.

Generally, these two potent and lethal situations often combusted. Usually, when a celebrity was involved.

Sherwin laid it on thick. "Mr. Reynolds is trying to check in and there are no rooms available."

"Burt Reynolds?" I guessed.

"Yes, Linda. Burt Reynolds. He's been here a while and he's getting impatient, especially with gawkers plaguing him for autographs. What do you suggest?"

"Is he in front of you now, Sherwin?"

"Yes," came the reply.

Oh man, this is all I need to top off my day. An unhappy celebrity to appease! "Do you want me to try and stall him while Housekeeping is readying his room? Is Housekeeping almost done?" I asked.

"Yes to both questions. Can you?"

"Okay, pass him on to me. I'll deal with him."

A recognizable voice grumbled, "Is this the manager's office? I'm told you can fix this."

"Mr. Reynolds. It's nice to know you're in town and patronizing our esteemed hotel," I said in a professional voice.

"Yes, Ma'am. Good to be here, other than all these room delays."

"Sir, my name is Linda. I apologize for the delay in checking you into our hotel, and thank you for your patience. We do have a room which is currently being prepared specifically for you in mind. It should only take a few more minutes."

"Well, it's about time. Is this part of that Sublime experience everyone's talking about? I've been standing here for ages," he peevishly said.

"Again, my apologies, sir. As a goodwill gesture, we'll be sure to send up a bottle of one of our finest wines featured at our *Bliss* restaurant as well as some of our specialty chocolates. Our compliments."

"Yeah, whatever," he said and dropped the phone to the counter top. *Incontestably not swayed at all by our freebees. You rock, Burt!*

At the same time, Murlise ran up, breathless. "Is Mr. Ganiff here?" she asked.

I pointed at his closed doors. Taped to the mirrored panel was a "Do Not Disturb" sign ornamented with little multi–colored skull and cross bones.

"Does that mean he won't open the door for an emergency?"

"Would you like to find out?" I responded.

She changed tactics. "Who's he in there with?"

"Honestly, I don't know." I shrugged. "I turned my back for two seconds… and you know this place!"

"What are we going to do?" wailed Murlise. "Iggy Two is rollerblading in the Lobby. It's totally packed. Check–in/check–out time. He almost knocked over Burt Reynolds. And he smacked into a stack of boxes filled with photo equipment for a movie junket."

"Oh, c'mon Murlise. He's a kid. Can't Security stop him?"

"Big Guy tried. He collared him, but Iggy Two laughed at him and told him, as the General Manager's son, he could do anything he wants. It sounded like a threat so Big Guy let him go."

"Kid's got a point although I think I may have a solution." With the utmost discretion, I tried to peer over the profile of Murlise's immense jaw to see if BeeBee were there.

Murlise noticed the empty desk and smiled. "Don't bother, just pass the phones to the operators."

We descended to the Lobby. There were over a hundred people in flux. Iggy Two finished his moonwalk on someone's luggage and pirouetted around three guests. He paused the moment he spotted me.

"Hey, Linda! Look at me!" his voice echoed off the marble interior.

All motion, chatter and arguing stopped. Even the piano in the Lounge went silent, for once. Everyone stared at the boy on skates.

"Iggy Two, can you come here?" I gestured toward a spot by the elevator banks.

"Don't ya wanna see my latest moves?" He proceeded to spin around a pile of luggage and two bellhops. Burt Reynolds ducked behind the front desk.

"You know I'd love to. Hey, I heard that Howard Stern is making a movie."

Iggy Two stopped. "No way! You're not saying that to make me stop?" he pouted.

"Iggy Two, have I ever lied to you?"

"Big deal. My parents'll never let me see it." Once again, he bladed between Big Guy and Murlise. Neither would dare apprehend him.

"If you come over here, Iggy Two, and take off the skates, I promise you that we'll sneak off and watch it together."

201

Iggy Two hesitated for a moment. Then, he glided up right beside me. Without saying a word, he extracted a pair of Nikes from his backpack. Rapidly, he removed his skates, tied the shoelaces to each other and strung them around his neck. After he put on his Nikes, the Lobby exploded in applause.

"Hey," he smiled, "they like my blading!"

"I'm certain," I said dryly.

"I should do it again!" He reached over to lift the rollerblades from his neck but I prevented him from removing them with a simple arm block. Something I had learned from one too many Bruce Lee movies.

"Iggy Two, something tells me that your father wouldn't be proud of your actions," I whispered.

His face darkened. A deep scowl, reminiscent of his father, contorted his fine features. Then he broke into a grin, swung his arm around my shoulder and asked, "Do you think we can meet Howard Stern? When is the movie coming out?"

When I returned home late that night, I reluctantly set up Mr. Ganiff's videotape and sat on the sofa, remote control in-hand. The talk show was a train wreck. Horrible, abysmal and downright boring. Those were the good points.

The theme of the pilot was simple—celebrity meets celebrity, ambush-style. The execution—needlessly complex.

The show began with the hotel's very own Barby, our public relations executive, talking on her telephone with the press agent of the celebrity scheduled to stay at the Supreme Superior. The premise was that our celebrity guest would soon arrive, and then would be introduced to another celebrity who he/she had always wanted to meet but never did. The audience was apprised of all the reasons why our celebrity would want to meet celebrity #2. Barby then phoned the press agent of celebrity #2 and made all the arrangements.

Surprise surprise. Fireworks. A long shot of the Supreme Superior. An advertisement for the much-extolled *Bliss* restaurant.

Then came the big twist which was not in the original scenario. It was a horrid oversight. The press agent of our celebrity #1 failed to notify him of the surprise encounter. Plus, he forgot to mention the camera and live footage that would be taken from inside the star's airport limo.

Our unsuspecting celebrity had spent more than eighteen hours on a flight from Perth, Australia to New York after wrapping up a six-month shoot. All he wanted was a warm bed and possessed no thoughts whatsoever of checking in for a Sublime experience. His hair was spiked and unruly. His clothes rumpled. His eyes ringed from lack of sleep. Not exactly the face to present to millions of adoring fans. Nor to a fellow actor he had always coveted and wanted to impress.

And most definitely not to Walter Cronkite who was hosting this historic event, movie camera on shoulder.

The footage grew tiresome. Five unedited minutes of an agitated movie star pounding on the glass divider imploring the chauffeur to drive faster.

I drifted off to sleep well before the ending, two hours later. With utter certainty, I knew that Tony Tenneb would not be entertained by this project let alone interested in hosting the show.

The following morning, I handed Mr. Ganiff the tape. He beamed ear to ear. "Now Linda, is this a winner or what?"

"Or what!" I answered in a hushed tone, so as not to offend him. I don't think he heard me.

"Great premise for a show, huh? Tony Tenneb is gonna be doing back flips when he sees this."

I immediately thought, *oh, that's not the only thing he'll do!*

Ganiff continued, "Do me a favor and call Veronica now. Then rush the tape to his office."

Against my better judgment, I called Veronica. Only after Ganiff had locked himself in his office.

"Hi Veronica, it's Linda at the Supreme Superior. Are you free?"

"Hello Linda. Tony's in Vegas this week, so things are pretty quiet here. Why? What's on your mind?" She figured another request for Ganiff's family. I knew she would not be prepared for what was coming.

"You gotta help me out," I whispered into the receiver.

"Sure, shoot."

"O–kay. Mr. Ganiff made a pilot for a television show. A celebrity ambush talk show based here at the hotel. He thinks it's a winner. Trust me, it's dreadful."

Veronica laughed nervously. "Oh boy. Lemme guess. He wants Tony to be in it?"

"No, he wants Tony to host it!" I had to remove the receiver from my ear while Veronica loudly groaned. After a few moments I continued, "I know there's no way. The pilot is unwatchable. The premise is offensive. What should we do? You know Ganiff'll drive both of us crazy. Once he gets these ideas in his head, he's relentless."

Veronica grew quiet for a moment. "Okay, let me get back to you. I'm sure there's a way to resolve this without hurting his feelings. Meanwhile, send me the tape by messenger. I could use a good laugh this morning."

Ganiff intercommed right after I hung up. More than likely he had observed the light for my phone extension go dark.

"So, what did she say? Will he do it?"

"Tony's in Vegas. She'll get back to me."

He chuckled. "Good, job, Linda. Good girl."

Dorck and Wapiti met with Mr. Ganiff to review the inventory conducted for the eighth or fourteenth time. I had lost count. Ganiff's door was surprisingly left wide open. The results remained consistent. Still dissatisfied that he wasn't able to catch any fault with the caliber of the massive inventory effort, Mr. Ganiff must've realized that he reached an impasse. He needed a fall guy, a stooge, a scapegoat to take the blame. And he had a perfect victim—his son–in–law, the shell–less turtle, Clyde.

A few days passed. Mr. Ganiff came to many conclusions and provided me with a legal–sized yellow pad filled with his scrawled handwriting.

"What is this?" I asked.

"It's a contract for you to type up," he responded.

"Mr. Ganiff, shouldn't Harry, our corporate attorney, be handling this? It's a legal document."

He made a noise that resembled a cleared throat. "Harry isn't involved in this. I have another attorney who helped me iron out this agreement." He stayed silent for a moment. "Linda, just type the damn thing up and stop asking so many questions."

As I loaded paper into the printer, I wondered why Ganiff would burden me with such a task. Perhaps he thought I wouldn't understand what I was typing. Or behind Door #2, the option I didn't want to face: I was so involved in his felonious activities that it no longer mattered what I knew. I was in over my head.

The contract was a tri–party agreement between the Supreme Superior, Clyde Hammergesundschmidt and Baldwin Laundry LLC. Mr. Ganiff acted as the representative for both the Supreme Superior and Baldwin Laundry. In the particulars of this contract, Clyde Hammergesundschmidt would forfeit his salary for five consecutive years and the monies would be upstreamed to the Supreme Superior Hotel as partial reimbursement of the purloined linens. Furthermore, Baldwin Laundry would provide a significantly lesser amount of additional remuneration to the Supreme Superior over the same period of time. Reading between the lines, I could see how this arrangement would benefit Ganiff: there was no admission of guilt whatsoever and it wouldn't financially cripple his personal laundry company.

The document also put into place the reimbursement mechanism for all parties; Baldwin Laundry would keep on receiving its weekly paycheck which averaged $25,000. In return, Baldwin Laundry would send a weekly check, once the reimbursement tallies were mutually agreed upon. Baldwin Laundry was given a flexible repayment schedule toward the reimbursement of sheets, towels, napkins, coverlets, duvets, pillowcases and tablecloths in the form of their monies commingled with those of Clyde Hammergesundschmidt's.

I did not receive a final tally on the replacement value of the lost items. All allusions to monetary figures within this legal instrument were simply referred to as "Exhibit A." Except for one glitch: there was no "Exhibit A" attached to these pages. I found it strange. While I was typing, Ganiff hopped on a conference call via speakerphone with Ms. Wapiti and Mr. Dorck, leaving the door open. I knew then that I was involved.

"Miss Wapiti, I need to know what the final tally is for the contract."

Ms. Wapiti coughed. "Mr. Ganiff, I already provided you with our cost estimates."

"Miss Wapiti, and note here Dorck, those are for brand new sheets and towels. What are you trying to do to me? You guys know that these things radically depreciate after usage. After you remove the plastic covers, they depreciate almost in half!" Mr. Ganiff's voice rose an octave.

Ms. Wapiti screamed, "Sir, we provided you at least a hundred spreadsheets containing replacement costs, comparable costs, depreciation costs, costs of the same products produced in Malaysia and/or China in different colors, sizes, shapes, cotton/percale mixtures and in different threads per square inch." She gasped for breath.

"Please let me intervene," Mr. Dorck's voice was more relaxed, "sir, pick any costs on any of the spreadsheets for each of the items."

Mr. Dorck, albeit a professional, nonetheless knew on which side his bread was buttered.

Mollified, Mr. Ganiff hung up on the less than dynamic duet. He chuckled. Then he phoned Clyde.

"Clod, I'm having my girl type up the contract." His voice became terse. "No, you're still punished." He hesitated. "You don't know why? Well, how about for fucking up? By getting too greedy. Yeah, you. Now shut the fuck up and listen." His chair squeaked as he settled in. "I feel confident that I can delay the schedule for a few more months before repayment. Perhaps, after I belabor the point even further for several more weeks, I can buy us even more time," he snickered, "perhaps enough time in which Baldwin Laundry could then suspend payment and no one would be the wiser."

I took it all in while typing. More than anything, I now understood why things here were the way they were. I frenetically formulated an outline of how to extricate myself from this disingenuous dilemma. Inspiration struck. While Ganiff busied himself in his office, I swiveled my chair and made a copy of the handwritten pages using the fax machine behind me, displacing a little dust. Just as swiftly, I stuffed the copies in my handbag.

★ ★ ★ ★ ★

A few hours later, Veronica returned my call.

"Okay, Linda, you were right. That tape is appalling! I couldn't tolerate more than the first twenty minutes." She continued to vent, "The whole concept is in such bad taste. I could never show this to Tony! He'd cringe, to say the least."

"Well, what now? I obviously can't tell Ganiff the truth."

"No worries, Linda. I got a plan. We're gonna have to do the brush–off."

"Brush–off? How? You know Ganiff. He'll have me calling your office every hour until Tony personally calls him back to say no."

Veronica laughed. "Nah, it won't come to that. Let's set up a ten–minute meeting between Ganiff and myself. He'll do his pitch. I'll run out of there, then stall him for the next century. I figure he'll eventually get the hint."

"Are you sure that this'll work? Do you have any idea who you're dealing with?"

"Well, if not, we'll use the contingency plan."

I laughed nervously. "Yeah, what's that?"

"I don't have one. I'll change my phone number and if that doesn't work, I'm leaving town. I'd suggest you do the same."

Chapter 27

I couldn't wait for Jay's return. He went for the gusto and booked a Sublime suite at the full corporate price. Now, that's love.

My chin had healed nicely and I spent the days dreaming about rubbing my face all over his rugged body. My daydreams were much nicer than my reality in the office.

Ganiff was in a good mood since the check exchange with Calvin. I guess three hundred seventy–five thousand bucks in your pocket will have that effect on even the most venal and coldhearted of men.

As it was Friday, a Clyde visit to pick up Baldwin Laundry's weekly paycheck was expected. Sometimes, when he couldn't get to the city, Mrs. Ganiff would waddle down to the executive office, take the check and deposit it to her husband's account at Marine Midland Bank. Keith Robenstine used to do the weekly check deposits but he was no longer trusted.

Calvin bopped up one day singing my name, "Hey, Linda, you'll never guess who's permanently persona non grata!"

"Who?"

"My brother–in–law! Can you believe he never paid back the twenty–five grand to Clod? Ganiff is pissed." Calvin grabbed a guest chair, sat down and, with the chair glued to his butt, moved right up to the lip of my desk so he could whisper, "I think Keith is blackmailing Ganiff."

"You serious? How do you know?" I leaned in closer.

"Wouldn't be the first time." Calvin winked. "Too bad that Keith isn't en route to jail in handcuffs. Well, we still have a chance because he didn't run off yet to Costa Rica."

His words "en route to jail in handcuffs" struck a wedge of fear that landed in the more vulnerable spots inside my body. It also torpedoed the happiness I felt awaiting Jay's arrival. My constant moral quagmire weighed me down, as did the dilemma of possessing knowledge of the curious financial goings–on in the executive office. Even more so, I was preoccupied with what I should do about it. I became terrified about my role in all of this chicanery. Unlike the situation at GermBank where I was busy uncovering illicit activities, here I was busy abetting illicit activities. No matter how innocent my involvement was at first, I recognized that the continuation of these duties would strip me of the ability to plead innocent. I dwelled upon this and whether it would translate to prison time should the crime be uncovered.

I pretty much gathered that almost no one else had grasped the entire extent of Mr. Ganiff's web of thievery. With the exception of two people: Mr. Dorck and Seebok. I perceived Mr. Dorck as an accomplice because he was responsible for covering up Ganiff's expenses for over five years. And please don't get me started on Seebok's role in all this! The other senior hotel executives were myopic vis-à-vis the larger picture because their focus was strictly on micromanaging their respective departments. For example, Ms. Wapiti, according to Carole, knew about the inventories. Murlise was well aware of the comped rooms for the weddings and conventions. I was certain Joe Smith was intimately acquainted with the copious consumption of food and booze. Remarkably, despite these peculiar extracurricular activities, the hotel executives continued to perceive Ganiff as their prestigious General Manager.

The situation brought to mind a parable my mother loved to recount throughout my life. The one about twelve blind men touching an elephant. The way she told it, each one had drawn a different description of an elephant depending upon their location—some thought an elephant was a large ear, others a trunk, some a tail and a few a leg. In my current situation, I saw the mammoth and the mammoth saw me.

And, of all the people I interacted with, only Calvin knew everything. Then again, I knew that both his oars weren't in the water at the same time. Sometimes Calvin acted a tad insane. Sometimes I discredited what he said: it couldn't all be true. Or, I didn't want to admit it. The real issue here concerned culpability. Also fear of consequences. This morass kept me in limbo. Then the phone rang, interrupting my train of thought.

"Linda, you gotta help me out!" Clyde sounded distressed.

Deep in my bones, I had a feeling as to what he was about to request.

"You're never gonna believe what happened to me this morning." While I deliberated whether to hang up, he ploughed on. "Early today I went to work. As I backed out of the laundry parking lot because I had to go to the Long Island Railroad to take the train to come to the City to pick up the check, all of a sudden I heard a giant clunk. So, I got out of the car—"

I cut short this long-winded excuse and went to the punch line, "Okay, okay, enough! I can't take it anymore! I'll deposit the check at your bank. Give me the account number." *If I were going to be involved, might as well go all the way.* I ran out of the office, informing BeeBee while exiting that I'd return momentarily.

The transaction took less than ten minutes and I jotted the account number on a slip of paper in my handbag. When I returned, Mr. Ganiff was in one of the most congenial moods I had witnessed in a very long time.

"Hey, Linda, do you have a few minutes? Come sit with me. I have something to show you."

Finally, he was going to commend me for my instrumental role in capturing that dangerous armed criminal. Notions of a twenty-grand reward and all the things I could spend it on fluttered around my head like little butterflies with green dollar–sign wings.

"Mr. Ganiff, is this about my commendation?" I grabbed a chair facing his desk.

He almost scowled. Almost. But he corrected himself. "No. Miss Djorak didn't agree to that. Anyhow, that's not what I called you in here for."

"Wait a second! Why not? Big Guy showed me a copy of the letter of commendation he wrote and sent to you and Ms. Djorak."

Ganiff slumped back in his chair and sighed. "Miss Djorak feels that there may be a conflict of interest since you're the representative of the General Manager. Surely you'll agree that I need to protect my spotless reputation."

The man had to be kidding me.

"Mr. Ganiff, since I got here Seebok's been boasting about a commendation he received two years ago."

Ganiff drew in a deep breath, then let it out slowly. His breath smelled like distilled wine mixed with smoked oysters. "Linda, I'll make it up to you. I promise. You have my word on it. The word of the General Manager of the Supreme Superior Hotel."

I wanted to press on, not let it go when Ganiff changed gears.

"I called you in here to show you something. Do you want to see my portfolio?"

See his portfolio? What a self–centered bastard. No, what I really wanted to do was strangle him with the power cord of my fax machine. I tried to maintain my cool, performing tantric mental exercises. I recalled a recent conversation with my father. Something he told me when I was blue and discouraged.

"Linda, do you know what you're gonna do yet with the job?"

"Not yet, Dad. I'm still not clear."

"Sweetheart, if you're that unhappy, then quit. Move on to something else. You've already proved you can make it in this field."

I scoffed at the idea. "Not right now, Dad. Let me tell you, I'm beginning to realize that there're some funny things going on."

"What do you mean?" my father's high–pitched tone relayed his concern.

"Well, at first, I thought the way things're done here with Ganiff were standard industry practice…" I hesitated, afraid to voice how I felt. "Dad, I believe I'm a bit over my head. I don't need your help cause I'm gonna find a way out. Right now I need your support."

"Remember, your mother and I are behind you no matter what you do. Just keep in mind: it was a hotelier who turned down Joseph and Mary when they needed a room."

I was now mulling over what to do next. Just in case, I had some ammunition.

Even so, I was up once more against an industry leader. That old disco song, *Instant Reply* kept playing. Breaking into my reverie was that insistent, nagging, pervasively oily voice.

"Linda, oh Linda. Do you want to see my portfolio," cooed Mr. Ganiff coyly, like a neighborhood pedophile who asks a child if she wants a piece of candy.

I shrugged without any resistance. "Sure, why not?" I moved in closer to his desk.

He flipped open a leather–bound folder with some papers inside. Then he pushed it across the desk. I reached to grab it and proceeded to read his current statement.

The printout showed the current market value of his bonds and their performance over the past year. Most of the bonds were concentrated in various Latin American companies. Companies that had experienced problems over the past two decades. The remainder of the bonds were invested in what I euphemistically call "dog" companies. Overall, the quality of the portfolio was sub–par, and the estimated current market value degraded over 60%. In essence, the portfolio had fallen from $5 million to less than $2 million in a year's time.

"Well, Miss Linda, what do you think?"

"Your broker should be shot." I kept a perfectly straight face.

He pouted back at me. "That wasn't my broker's fault. I thought those bonds would do well. The recent implementation of NAFTA, you know?"

His logic was so wrong. I didn't even know where to begin.

I looked at him. He squinted back at me. "Linda, I have a proposal for you," he said without a trace of malice, "how about I give you a few thousand dollars and you invest it for me? Just for fun."

That statement gave me room for serious pause. On many different levels. All this time, he had questioned the authenticity of my prior work experience. Now he's asking me to invest his money. Which is it? Am I a fraud or a professional? Also, how much of a professional did he think I was that I would invest his money and open myself wide to potential litigation?

"I have a proposal for you, Mr. Ganiff." I snapped the folder shut. "How about you sign a legal document indemnifying me from any and all potential losses and lawsuits? If you're looking to capitalize on my former professional expertise, you're gonna have to do it above board. Otherwise…" I let the words hang.

Once again, he stared at me intently with his right eye. At long last, he spoke in a low voice, "Fine. Have it your way. Here I thought I was being friendly. Very well, never mind. Give that folder back to me and get the hell out of my office."

Obviously, the man didn't accept playing by the rules. What a stunning revelation!

Chapter 28

It was the start of another work week. While I shoveled the papers on my desk, Doreen dashed into Mr. Ganiff's office, out of breath. I didn't bother to try and stop her. I did, though, waltz in moments later as I wanted to see what the commotion was all about.

"Mithter Ganiff! You gotta hear thith one! That Theebok, he'th done it again!" She giggled uncontrollably.

Ganiff lifted his head from his *Daily Post* and smiled. "Miss Doreen, what a pleasure. Who did what again?"

Before she could compose herself sufficiently to respond, Doreen was knocked aside by Selena, tears of laughter streaming down her cheeks.

"Hello there, Selena. Now, ladies, please tell me. What is it?"

Both women exchanged glances, then doubled over in mirth.

"Mithter Ganiff, you jutht have to lithten to thith."

Doreen picked up the phone, dialed a few numbers and placed the receiver against his ear.

Ganiff's good eye widened. Then, a smile like a beacon swept across his face from chin to upper proboscis. "What in the world—"

"Theebok," Doreen tried to explain between bouts of whooping gales of laughter that she could no longer suppress, "he wath tethting out hith new voithe mail thythtem. The one he'th been talking about for monthth."

"Yeah, I know the one." Ganiff nodded, fighting off a smile. "The system with call forwarding, three way calling," he chuckled, "oh, and that hook–up to the MIR satellite." Now he dissembled; he barked and snorted in glee.

The struggle not to laugh was a foregone conclusion. Their laughter was contagious and I found myself giggling like the village idiot without even understanding the underlying cause.

I should note here that Standard atelier guests were oftentimes used as guinea pigs for the testing of new hotel equipment without their consent nor knowledge. In this case, they were subjected to Seebok's new telephone and voicemail system. The feedback received from those irate guests was disheartening. I knew that this new venture was a failure. Atrocious. Similar to the new televisions, barely functional.

But that didn't deter Seebok. Not when a particular vendor paying for a one-year lease on a brand new BMW was at stake. Another little tidbit I picked up from Trish, his assistant.

"Hey, give that back to me!" With good humor, Ganiff grabbed the receiver from Doreen's hand and placed it back on the console. He could no longer restrain himself. Emanating from the man's mouth was the honking, hooting and cackling that bore his distinctive trademark. A semblance of laughter that up till now I had not been privy. "Hallelujah! Now we know what Seebok's been doing all these weeks. No wonder the jerk's always missing in action."

Doreen chortled with delight. "Well, it wathn't vendorth meetingth!"

Trish ran in, panting and tittering. Followed by Big Guy, Ms. Wapiti, Joe Smith and Edwing from Concierge. We now had assembled in the office a fair representation of several departments within the hotel. Doreen pressed the speakerphone button for everyone's benefit and redialed the voicemail to replay the message.

"Oh, Seebok," said a sultry Jamaican accented voice. One that was categorically not that of the Southern Mrs. Murray. "Yesterday was amazing. Even better than last Friday. Ah, hmmmmmmmmmm. Three times in one hour. You stud, you beast, you! Can't wait to see you tonight at my place. Hmmmmmmmmmm. Oh, and this time you wear the thong. As I said to you, tit for tat. I'll wear your favorite strap–on."

"I can't get enough of thith!" said Doreen, redialing the voicemail again to replay the message.

The communal merriment had all of us cracking up; a few were rolling on the floor in convulsions. Some of us knelt with our midsections wrapped by our arms, others bent indecently over chairs, in paroxysms of breathing.

"Why is this on the voicemail?" I asked, wiping my watering eyes with my fingertips.

At that moment, Murlise entered the office, got a load of the decadent state of the people inside and burst out in a deep laugh, realizing that the word was out about Seebok.

"He must have pressed the wrong button," said Murlise, tears rolling down her over–sized lantern jaw, "and copied the message to everyone's voicemail boxes."

"You mean, just the hotel admin offices?" I wanted to know.

"No. Every phone in the hotel, even the guests!" Murlise held onto her sides. "We've been fielding calls from our conscientious customers who want to make sure that Seebok gets to see some action tonight."

"Full house tonight?" Ganiff kept on sighing and trying to regain his composure, but Doreen kept on redialing the voicemail saying, "I thwear, tith'll nefer get old!" At the onset of each replay of the message, Ganiff would start the bark that would ignite the laugh that would orchestrate his subordinates to join him in concurrence.

"Of course," Murlise affirmed through her laughter.

Never could I have imagined such a raucous scene in such an otherwise miserable environment. I guess the humiliation of an incompetent and detested co–worker is what it took to bring the Supreme Superior personnel together. All the more so because it was Seebok.

Mr. Ganiff guffawed so hard that he squealed in amusement. "What a lying, cheating piece of crap he is." For my benefit, he pressed his nose to the side in reference to the Alletti garbage fiasco that nearly jeopardized his and Seebok's very lives. "So now he's cheating on his wife too. Helluva way to keep it discreet, huh?"

All at once, I recalled the tape of Seebok in the elevator cab. *Ah,* I realized. *So that explains what the little bugger was up to!*

"Do you think he'll show his face?" asked Selena above the hilarity.

Doreen had to stick in her two cents. Unintentionally, she spoiled our magic moment. "I remember my hubby went away to our thummer houthe upthtate for a golfing weekend without me. When I did hith laundry, I found a pair of my pantieth. I thought they were mine even though they were too thmall for me!"

Everyone stopped laughing and stared at her. A little too late, she recognized that the story did not fit the occasion.

Ganiff sat back in his seat and straightened his tie. "Well, don't we all have work to do now? I know I do." With a wave of his hand, he shooed everyone out of the office.

After everyone exited, Seebok strolled in without a care in the world. "Is Mr. Ganiff available?" he asked.

With the best straight face I could muster, I pointed towards the office, fearing a stroke from holding in my laughter.

He entered Ganiff's office. The moment the door shut, I let loose with a howl. It took me a minute to compose myself sufficiently to pick up the intercom. I was thrilled to see that it remained functional in its non–functional way.

"Boss, I gotta talk to you."

I thought that now was the appropriate time to be the proverbial fly on the wall. I poured a cup of coffee from the carafe on my desk and reflected, *it's showtime.*

"And I, you," replied Ganiff who chortled.

"Is there something wrong, sir?" Seebok said, apparently unaware of the uproar he had caused.

"Ah, Seebok, what am I gonna do with you?" sighed Ganiff dramatically.

I picked up the cup and took a sip.

"Listen, Boss, I was doing some research on the porn industry. Did you have any idea that it is a billion dollar industry?"

I almost gagged on my coffee.

"So?" Ganiff tapped his knuckles on his desktop.

"I was thinking, sir, that, considering we're into this industry, how about we—" Seebok hesitated for a moment and then plunged ahead, "how about we put our money where our mouths are?"

What? What the fuck was he saying? I thought.

"What?" asked Ganiff, "Seebok, what the fuck are you saying?"

"Sir, please, let me clarify. I think we should invest in this industry. We can put money into a company, and in a short period of time make a fortune. I have some funds set aside—"

"Stop right there, Seebok. I have a reputation to maintain. I am a family man and a pillar to my community. My re–li–gious community. Something like that would destroy me."

Seebok panted in heat. "Sir, that is precisely why I'm talking to you. We can be silent investors, get in strong and hard, then pull out fast after a movie is made. I've been researching for days and look here."

Papers spilled on the table.

"Seebok, watch it with those papers, you're gonna knock over my tea." After a beat, "Oh damn you, Seebok! Go get some paper towels."

Knocking, thumping, a few curses and Seebok from afar asking, "Where are they?" After a while, more thumps, groans and, from close up, "Oh shit, Seebok! It's all over the place. Damn, it's everywhere."

A few moments passed in silence. At long last Ganiff spoke. "Hmmmm. I think you have a point, Seebok. Whom should we invest with?"

This was getting interesting.

"Well, sir, here's the thing. Your friend, Steven Koneman, is situated in Los Angeles. That's the capital of the porn industry, and I think he might know companies because…" Seebok faltered for a second. "Well, because, I noticed from my, ahem, um," and then a strange gargling noise, "my research, that some of these companies do their advertising with KKK."

For some reason, it all made sense to me.

"Capital idea, Seebok. I was beginning to get worried about you, you know, losing your edge a bit with the recent marriage and… the girlfriend!"

Seebok let out a moan. "What? Oh my God! How did you find out?"

Ganiff sounded almost paternal. "Oh Seebok, I'm not going to judge or criticize you. Get rid of her. It isn't right to be a married man and cheat on your wife. That's what porn is all about." He sighed and repeated the phrase like a drowning man, "That's what porn is all about." A silence until the intercom rang.

Without thinking, I said, "Yes sir," and realized that there was an echo.

"Linda, what is wrong with the phone?" asked Ganiff.

214

"Oh, it's something to do with the trunk line, sir." I lied through my teeth. "Maybe it has something to do with Seebok's testing of the phones."

Mollified, Ganiff said, "Get me Steven Koneman."

A few minutes later I patched Steven Koneman through as a conference call and clandestinely included myself as well. After the typical introductions, Ganiff cleared his throat. "Steven, I have an interesting proposition for you. My man Seebok has done some research. And, well, we want to invest in blue movies for the short term if you get my drift. Do you know of any companies?"

"Ganiff baby, you came to the right man. I knew you'd go blue!" responded Steven. I could envision him sitting at his desk rubbing his hands in delight. "Hey, let me pony up a few companies. It's an excellent idea and I think I'm gonna go in with you guys. I'll keep you posted."

I hung up. Reflecting on my past and possible future, *I think I may have found a solution.*

Chapter 29

The big day arrived. The scheduled hotel union strike.

As per Ganiff's instructions, I had distributed internal memos over several days warning our staff that participation in the strike at the other New York City hotels would lead to immediate termination of employment.

The Supreme Superior anticipated a backlash from the Housekeeping staff, headed by Carole Carlson who no longer responded to my calls or missing pens in toilet stalls. Ms. "highest paid" Wapiti had held meetings over the previous week with her staff to ensure compliance. Big Guy beefed up his security team for the big day with overtime blessed by Ms. Djorak. The morning meeting consisted of a checklist of contingencies; Mr. Ganiff was reassured that his executive staff knew what to do.

The strike couldn't have come at a worse time. Peak season.

Peak season is the time that makes or breaks hotels. Peak season in the hospitality industry in New York City at that time usually fell from October through December, up to and not including Christmas. It started up again in mid–February and ran through mid–April. Once every several years, there would be a surge in occupancy in July or August, depending on several factors, e.g., the economy, the weather, the Olympics, etc. In other words, every day counted in the hospitality industry. There were only six reliable months of the year where the hotel had the opportunity to achieve 100% occupancy.

At the time of the strike we were in the latter part of March and overbooked. The conference rooms on the second floor, untouched by the construction on the top floors, had five banquet functions running concurrently. Ford Motor Company had even booked *Bliss* for a sales manager luncheon. Joe Smith contributed wine and bar drinks at minimal cost to the sales managers. This was an effort to disguise the poor quality of cuisine in *Bliss*. He hoped that if they were drunk, they wouldn't notice or care.

Doreen had managed to grab junket work from Miramax. This was extremely lucrative as Miramax had to book at least a dozen Sublime suites for its high profile actors. Kim Bassinger, Sophia Loren and Marcello Mastroianni were in town to promote the new Robert Altman film, *Prêt à Porter*. Also booked was the Mae West Suite on the top Sublime floor at $3,000 a day for a three–day blow–out media frenzy. As a result, these Sublime floors were riddled with cables, cameras, light machines and engineers.

Due to peak occupancy, Ms. Wapiti had requests for at least three–dozen cots for families who couldn't book additional rooms for their children. She rented them from a local furniture supplier. The loading dock was crammed between construction material, food deliveries, recyclable garbage and soiled linens stockpiled for pick up the following day from Baldwin Laundry.

Screw the strike. I'd much rather think about Jay. He was due for a late afternoon check–in. We kept in touch daily; Jay even called me at home when he commuted. I felt like I had known him for years due to all the hours we spoke on the phone. I touched my chin. It was kissable soft. In preparation for the evening's festivities, I pulled my hair back into a loose chignon and wore a short skirt showing off my calves. My focus shifted once again and my thoughts touched upon Carole and her plight, knowing that she would join the demonstrators outside. I convinced myself not to worry. After all, there were a few thousand people rallying outside. She should be safe.

Mr. Ganiff was annoyed. He gathered that I was up to something, however, he couldn't put his finger on it. Earlier that day, I had strong–armed him into signing a $5,000 check to Donald Silverberg with an air of smug self–satisfaction.

"You should have listened to me," I muttered to his left eye as I took the check from his hands and placed it into a Federal Express pouch.

I could see he wanted to slap me. Instead, he stomped off to see his wife for lord–knows–what reason. At least he left me alone for a little while.

Regrettably, he left only for a very little while, no more than an hour. Upon his return, I greeted him with a very dark look.

"We have problems, Mr. Ganiff." That announcement stopped him in his tracks.

Big Guy stood in the middle of the room, walkie–talkies squalling, arms folded. "Mr. Ganiff, sorry to bother you. We have a situation here that we have to stop immediately."

"What is it, Big Guy?"

"Look out your window."

They stared out the window. Hundreds of protestors amassed in front of the entrance to the Hilton Hotel. There was one NYPD patrol car parked in front.

"It looks controlled," Ganiff said.

Big Guy shifted weight to his other side and cleared his throat. "Half our busboys and housekeeping joined forces."

"That's our people? What the… Linda, get Miss Djorak," hollered Ganiff.

Big Guy shifted his bulk once more. I reached for the phone and perfunctorily made a series of calls without any luck. "Mr. Ganiff, I can't seem to find her. She's MIA." Upon this proclamation, I felt the blood literally freeze in my veins.

"What do you mean, MIA?"

"Missing in action. We're not the only ones looking for her. The Front Desk's been paging her for over an hour. They had Security search all the subbasements."

Big Guy nodded his head in agreement. "We looked everywhere. No way a woman that size could simply blend into the background."

"They even interrogated BeeBee," I added, "with no luck. Djorak's nowhere to be found." I felt those little hairs on the back of my neck rise. *Act cool*, I thought. I said brightly, "Oh, but we do know she must be somewhere on–property—she left her cigarettes on her desk."

Murlise and Ms. Wapiti burst onto the scene. "Mr. Ganiff, we have a problem," said Murlise, panting from the exertion of running.

Ms. Wapiti, usually soft–spoken, raised her voice, "I have over three hundred check–ins scheduled in one hour and hardly any staff down there. Plus, there are still twenty–two cots that have to be delivered. I'm so screwed!"

Joe Smith walked in behind them. "Mr. Ganiff, there's no one here to set up for the luncheons. We have over a hundred drunk and hungry people grumbling!"

The phone rang. I decided to answer it back at my desk where I could hear myself think.

"Hey Linda, it's Marie at William Morris."

"Marie, we're a little busy. Let me get back to you later." I could barely make out what she was saying over the shouting din piercing through the walls of my office combined with the chanting that had just begun from outside.

"Wait! Don't hang up," she implored at top volume, "Linda, there's someone on your balcony. We think it's the twenty–seventh floor. A man with long, silver hair wearing a beret. He's got a cigarette in his mouth." After a slight pause, Marie said, "Linda, we're trying to focus in with the binoculars." The phone rattled on her end. "Okay, let's see." Marie gasped, "Oh my God, he has a rifle!"

I had a feeling I knew exactly who that man was. And it wasn't a man at all.

"Okay, thanks Marie. I'll run now and deal with it."

I hung up the phone, ran back into Ganiff's office and shouted over the cacophony of blame, "Mr. Ganiff, there's been a sighting—Ms. Djorak is on the balcony. Twenty–seventh floor. And she's armed!"

Big Guy whipped out his walkie–talkies from his vest and shouted, "May Day! May Day!"

Mr. Ganiff screamed, "No police. Please no cops."

"We'll handle it, don't worry." Big Guy heaved his heft out of the office, barking orders into the walkie–talkies, "Johnny, grab two men and go to the balcony on the twenty–seventh floor. Copy?"

An electronic scritch. "Front and center? Copy," replied Johnny.

"Add an additional man to each side of the balcony. Got that? Don't use guns but use force. Copy." Big Guy flourished under pressure.

"Got that. Will get back at ya when done. Copy," said Johnny.

Mr. Ganiff stared at his stricken staff, summoning his superior executive decision–making talent. He remained calm while he commandeered his subordinates. "Murlise, pull your admin people. Gather your reservations clerks. Place all the wagons in a tight circle." He pointed at Joe and ordered, "Pull your junior level chefs, waiters and dining staff. Start the set–ups now."

Everyone scrambled out of the office, falling over each other.

"Linda, get me my doctor."

"Huh?" I said, befuddled.

"Set up an appointment for tomorrow morning."

"Um, okay." I didn't understand what that had to do with the situation at hand, but then again, at this stage, nothing else seemed pertinent.

"Get Sam Hammer on the line." Another conundrum.

Sam Hammer owned a large travel agency, Hammer Travel. Mr. Ganiff had recently met him in the Lounge and they had struck some sort of a lucrative deal. I'd gathered this from reading notes on a yellow pad that Mr. Ganiff had tossed haphazardly onto the conference table.

The Supreme Superior sales/marketing team traveled extensively in order to rope in corporate clients. Hammer's agency offered to give the Supreme Superior the cheapest corporate rates in town on the proviso that the hotel used them exclusively for booking flights. This pertained to the Supreme Superior staff in addition to hotel guests whose flights were booked through the concierge. Our guests took advantage of our concierge as their ad hoc travel agent. In return for this arrangement with Hammer, Mr. Ganiff would receive first class tickets— gratis, of course—for him and his wife to any destination, any time.

I dialed his doctor numerous times but the line was busy. Instead, I got Mr. Hammer on the phone. I passed the call to Ganiff so I could redial the doctor. The line stayed busy. I took a break from dialing to lend an ear to Ganiff's conversation.

"Mr. Hammer, hello. What a pleasant day." He listened for a while. "Is it possible to arrange a weekend trip for the little missus and myself? Yes, San Juan." He paused for a few seconds. "Now, Sam, I know that this is a busy time for you, but I'm sure you will work wonders."

After he hung up, he paged me again.

"Linda, now get me the General Manager of the Sands Hotel in San Juan."

What the hell is he up to? I wondered. *What's this fascination with the Sands Hotel? Seebok and now him?* I pondered. *Could it be that there are no extradition treaties with Puerto Rico?*

I resorted to the rolodex for the direct dial number of the Sands Hotel's General Manager. Once he was on the line, I put him on hold and intercommed Ganiff. He picked up and requested a complimentary suite for the weekend with hardly any preamble.

One benefit of the General Manager's position at the Supreme Superior was the ability to call up your counterparts in any hotel in the world and get royal treatment. Many General Managers of five–star hotels enjoy this perk. It could also be interpreted as another form of industry bonding. Not to mention the poor man's version of corporate espionage.

At this point, I simmered with resentment and fury. My vocabulary does not contain a singular word to describe how I felt about Mr. Ganiff's actions. No matter what occurred at the Supreme Superior, Ganiff was more preoccupied with his personal life than the situation in–house. Nor the fact that this was the largest crisis that the hotel experienced since I came on board—Ganiff planned to skip town that weekend. *The man has a big set of cojones.*

When Ganiff hung up the phone, Big Guy entered the office with his head down. He seemed to be crying. "Sir, we had no choice. We took her down."

"Took her down?" repeated Mr. Ganiff.

We gaped in astonishment. *Was Djorak dead?*

Big Guy noticed our faces. "No, she's not dead." He explained to Ganiff, "She allegedly had her rifle pointed at Carole from Housekeeping, the union rep. She even fired a shot and killed a parking meter."

I gasped. Ganiff looked at me strangely.

Unruffled, Big Guy went on with his story, "Have to hand it to Djorak—she does have superb aim." He observed our reactions. "Anyhow, Carole from Housekeeping headed up one of the picket lines. She's an easy target you know, wearing that white sable full–length coat. All the same, we caught Djorak with her finger on the trigger. She was going to shoot again when my guys tackled her." He sat down heavily on one of Ganiff's plush chairs. "That was after a knock and drag 'em out fight."

"How many out of commission?" Mr. Ganiff's right eye grew red and glossy. His left traveled further north.

"Twelve men. They're all on their way to the hospital. Arm injuries, ribs, legs. Several lost teeth and probably one concussion so far." He shrugged. Moments later he brightened, "On a positive note, Mr. Ganiff, we didn't lose a single guy from Security! On the other hand, Engineering might be understaffed for a while."

Ganiff fanned himself with a few loose papers from his desk. "Where is Djorak now?"

I interjected, "What about Carole? Is she all right?"

"Say, what's with the sudden interest in that woman?" Mr. Ganiff turned my way.

"Aren't you in the least bit concerned about one of your staff who was shot at by the head of your human resources?" I asked.

Big Guy interrupted, "I phoned my man at NYPD. They whisked Carole away to a safe house. They want to be certain that Djorak acted alone; that she didn't use any of her former... ahem, friends, and that she won't use them."

Ganiff yelled, "Enough with Carole." He shot me another pointed glance. Turning to Big Guy he asked, "So, where's Djorak now?"

Big Guy cracked a lopsided smile. "Oh, we took care of her. After we got her off the balcony, we shoved a king–sized pillow in her mouth and duct–taped her arms to her sides. Edwing is accompanying her with the police to Bellevue."

"Bellevue? The police?!?" His mustache sagged along with his jaw.

"Sir, we had to report this to the police. I'm sorry. She had several rounds of ammo. She had a rifle. She was aiming to kill."

Mr. Ganiff tsked in mock sorrow. "That poor poor unhinged woman. How did she think she could get away with this?" I could've sworn I heard him murmur, "I hope to God on my blackened, twisted, warped and perverted soul she didn't think I gave her the go ahead."

Abruptly, the tune of *ding dong, the gorgon's gone, the gorgon's gone* popped into my head.

Big Guy stood up and exhaled. "Anyway, now that Djorak's dealt with, I'm off to the cafeteria for lunch. All this drama can really work up a big time appetite. Hmm, you think they have oxtail stew today?" Once again, he turned around and said, "Oh, I'll forward the police reports to you later on."

"Uh, wait a second." Ganiff displayed his worried face. "Does the hotel have any legal liability?"

"Sir, am I a lawyer?" With that statement, Big Guy turned back once more and exited.

"Don't look at me," I exclaimed, "remember, finance is my background."

Chapter 30

"They had to sedate her in the ambulance because she bit the EMTs."
I laughed whole–heartedly. "Oh, I can't believe that bitch is finally history."

Jay smiled back from across the table. This time we dined in my neighborhood at a local restaurant, *La Tormentia*. Guess I have a certain penchant for Italian cuisine.

He described the convoluted tactics employed to thwart Steven Koneman from picking up his scent to New York.

"You wouldn't believe what I went through!" Jay laughed. "I had my secretary concoct a business trip so convoluted... I plotted the original trip from Jack Kerouac's novel, *On the Road*. We combined that with maps from Lewis and Clark. I had her fax the itinerary to Steven's girl. I figured that would keep him from finding me!" He paused, introspective for a moment. "By now, he should be en route to Hawaii."

"Not a bad destination. Why not downtown Detroit?"

"Ah, too close. That would make it way too easy for him to get to New York. This way, I have two full days sans a Koneman interruption." He took a sip of white wine. "Say, did I ever tell you how he swings his golf club?" He stood up from his chair to simulate someone swinging a five iron. Out of nowhere, he squatted down to do a few push–ups and then jumped right back up again to swing away. A few surrounding diners glanced askew at him.

I didn't get the point of that demonstration although I enjoyed the confident way Jay moved. I imagined his body against mine, to paraphrase an e e cummings poem. Throughout dinner, I felt the electricity between us, and ate an entire meal without tasting the food.

The discussion kept turning back to the Supreme Superior. I described my disillusionment with the executive staff and the hotel operations. "You know, Jay, most of the people believe I lied about my background. You know, being a banker and all."

His eyes flapped open. "You were a banker? So why the hell are you working at the Supreme Superior?"

I sighed. The perennial question.

After dinner, I led Jay to my lair where I felt more comfortable: a typical, small New York City one–bedroom apartment. The moment I turned on the hallway light, I removed the pins holding my chignon, allowing my hair to cascade down my back. I removed my shoes, then made a trail of tossed clothing leading to the bedroom. Blouse. Skirt. Bra. Panties. Holster. Jay followed, loosening his tie, kicking off his shoes and socks, slipping out of his suit jacket and shirt.

"Come here, tiger," I purred, while lounging fully nude on the bed.

Jay sat next to me and cupped my chin. It felt smooth. He leant forward and kissed me. In response, my arms surrounded him and my toes curled.

My fingers caressed the thick white hair on his back and slid forward and down, past his distended love handles and around his protuberant belly to his small, yet fully erect penis. I had assumed he had a rugged body by the way his suits fitted around him. It goes to show—never judge a book by its cover.

"Oh babe, I've dreamt of this every night," he moaned in my hair.

"Same here," I gently said, as I pushed him on his back.

While he writhed like a fish pulled out of water, I slid on top of him, mounted my thighs around his chin and rode my way to ecstasy.

"Oh my God, that was amazing," I said as I flopped down next to him.

"Yeah, sure was worth the wait, I guess," he replied, caressing the small of my back, his member standing at full mast.

We cuddled for several minutes. Then Jay propped himself up on his elbow and brushed a hand across my cheek. "Linda, I have to talk to you."

"About?"

"My wife," he replied in a tone more serious than pillow talk.

"Your wife? Koneman told me you guys were legally separated. Aren't you?"

"Oh man! Did you have to mention that asshole while we're naked in bed like this?"

I reached for the covers and pulled them over my naked lower half. "Oh, sorry for the buzz kill, but I'm not the one involved in a committed relationship. I mean, I thought you were free and single. You never told me differently."

"Not exactly. It's like, we're together but… we're not… I mean, I had a girlfriend for ten years—don't worry, Linda, that's over." Jay droned on about the lack of passion in his marriage. "Linda, she doesn't understand me. We never talk anymore. She's just no more fun. Forget about the sex. I mean, I had to go out of the relationship to get laid."

Now I understood what hell was about: the repetition of the same ol' shit one hears on the soaps. I brooded. How trite. What a stereotype! No fucking integrity. Then it struck me. *What is it with these guys? First Calvin, now Jay?* My brain moved out of hyper–drive and back to reality. Curious, I examined the body next to mine.

For the first time I saw with clarity the wrinkles etched on Jay's face. The thatch of white, thinning hair on his head. The black hair sticking out of his ears. The flab on his arms, waist and stomach. The very small penis, remaining erect, and enormous scrotal sag. How true that old saying: a few words can change a mood.

"So, I'm really crazy about you." He nuzzled my neck. "Linda, baby, everything's cool. I'm raring to go. Come, roll over on top of me. Let's finish what we started, shall we?"

Repulsed, I turned over to my side of the mattress. And almost fell off the bed, if it weren't for the three smallest toes on my left foot. I decided to get up and swung my right leg over the side. "Jay, I just remembered, I have to be in before dawn tomorrow. It's getting late."

"It's only nine–thirty. It's still early."

I leapt out of bed and bent down to pick up his clothes. I didn't need to have a man in my life. Especially a philandering caricature. I wanted a real man, not a buffoon.

Jay scooched over to my side of the bed. I thrust his pants at him. He lay there for a while, staring at the ceiling. He dressed hastily, grunting in frustration as he did. Then I shoved him down the hallway. By the reflection of the mirror, I stood at least a foot taller than him in bare feet. Out of politeness, I bent down to give him a peck on the cheek.

"What about tomorrow night?" He backed away from my door. The guy refused to give up.

"I'm busy. Got a date with someone who's truly single."

On that note I booted him out, slammed the door and headed back to my bedroom alone.

"A selfish jerk," I said to myself, "a waste of my time and energy." Then a thought struck me. It was my turn to grunt from frustration. *Please don't tell me that this will be my karmic path with men as well!*

Chapter 31

As predicted, I awoke at sunrise and dressed carefully. True to my word, I arrived at work extra early. Too early. The terrible sight I encountered was permanently and disturbingly engraved in my memory.

Splayed naked in my chair, head thrown back, was another swollen, hairy and flabby belly hanging over, in this instance, a tweezer–thin penis and mouse–sized testicles. Another man, this one clothed in a dark suit, hovered over him.

"Ohmigod," I screamed and turned my head away, afraid that I would turn into a pillar of salt. *Too many flabby bellies, too many small dicks in too short a time! How can a girl manage?*

"Oh my God," shouted Mr. Ganiff. He used three fingers to cup his privates. The strange man whirled around.

I shot up the corridor, took the rear stairwell, went down four flights to the employees' cafeteria in subbasement No. 2. Thankfully, the room was empty save for one of the banquet staff stirring eggs. He wore an oversized white apron.

"Breakfast, Miss Linda?"

I never felt so nauseous. *How could I eat after what I witnessed?* I took time to calm my racing heart. It hammered like a jackrabbit and my feet ached. I had seen a sight that would render mere mortals blind. I needed to interact with another human being who wasn't naked.

"What's in that container next to the eggs?"

"Oxtail stew."

"What else do you have?"

"Sara Lee cake."

"How about some cake and coffee?"

Listlessly, I picked at the cake. Once I felt sufficiently recovered, I headed into the separate smoking room and pulled out a pack of cigarettes. Twelve cigarettes later, the cafeteria filled up.

A deep, grating voice bellowed my name.

"Linda, you all right?" BeeBee slid into the seat across from me, genuine concern crossing her face.

If I weren't already totally grossed out by Ganiff, I would've been equally shocked by BeeBee's volte–face after having been victimized by her for such a long time. I replied, "Yeah, I'm all right, I guess. Why?"

"You missed the morning meeting."

I checked my watch. The little hand almost touched eleven. That meant nearly five hours had passed me by.

"Oh." In my shell–shocked mind, BeeBee reminded me of a character out of a fairy tale released on probation and thereby reverting to whatever shape, or personality she had prior to being enslaved by mystical powers, or the prisons of New York. There was not that much of a transformation; I felt that BeeBee, stripped of her guardian gorgon, had no alternative but to appear appallingly nice. Then again, I had undergone severe visual trauma.

Alarmed, BeeBee asked, "Are you coming upstairs?"

"Uh, yeah. In a minute."

I did a double–take. Everyone in the smoking lounge wore large smiles. There was an air of festivity and goodwill. Like that time when the house fell on the evil witch.

BeeBee led the way to the rear elevator. Word must've spread fast about Ms. Djorak's demise because busboys and housekeepers greeted us with warmth. All over the hotel, Supreme Superior staff slapped high fives. Front desk employees greeted guests with more than their customary smiles. Hotel employees who were notorious for being surly, glowed.

I was reluctant to enter my office. BeeBee gave me encouragement in the form of a good, hard shove in my kidneys. Hey, she is from da Bronx after all.

Ganiff's office door was closed. I sighed with relief. No way in hell would I ever sit on my desk chair again. I reached to pull out one of the guest chairs when I noticed the multiple bouquets of flowers. On my desk. On my credenza unit. On top of the cobwebbed fax machine. The room burst with color.

They were all from Jay.

"Linda, you have quite a few messages here," said BeeBee, curiously helpful, "mostly from Mr. Jay Krieger, Suite 4812."

"Thanks, BeeBee." I was too stunned, too frazzled and too overwhelmed to deal with him.

"You want me to handle it?"

"Oh, no, that's okay. I'll get back to him. Oh, and thanks a lot for taking the messages."

"No problem, Linda. Anytime."

What the hell have they done with the uncooperative BeeBee? I wondered. *She hasn't reverted to form... yet. I guess this is a major change... for the better. Now with dental care and a few rounds of Smokers Anonymous...*

Mr. Ganiff intercommed. The moment I dreaded. "Um, about this morning—"

"I didn't see a thing," I said. Not that there was much to see anyway.

"It wasn't what you think it was, I swear. I'm a good church–going man. I was

226

just getting examined by my doctor."

"In the early morning? In the office? In *my* office? In my *chair?*"

"He comes here early for me. We go way back."

I murmured, "I can only imagine."

"Linda, please don't tell anyone. It was truly on the level."

"Yeah, fine," I replied. *I'm not the homophobe—he is.* "I am ordering myself a new chair."

"Yeah, sure. Now, moving along, I need a favor this morning. I'm interviewing Miss Djorak's replacement in half an hour or so. Can you take her on a tour of the hotel?"

"Yeah, sure. Whatever." I tossed the receiver back on its hook.

According to the front–page article in my morning edition of the *Daily Post*, Ms. Djorak had already been arraigned for illegal possession of a stolen weapon and attempted manslaughter. Out of the corner of my eye, I detected movement and looked up from the newspaper. I almost jumped through the ceiling when BeeBee popped up like a jack–in–the–box in front of my desk.

"You're awfully jittery," she remarked. Apologetically, she said, "I dropped an invoice for Mr. Ganiff to sign." She fanned the paper under my nose, then proceeded to drop it again in the in–box. She almost turned away when suddenly her head swiveled to a halt. I followed her line of vision. It rested upon the article about Ms. Djorak.

She heaved a deep sigh and whispered, "You know, she tried to contact Mr. Ganiff last night, but he had instructed the operators to divert all calls to Big Guy. Since Big Guy didn't answer the call either, Ms. Djorak had to spend the evening in Rikers Island."

For some inexplicable reason, I found it difficult to conjure up any sympathy.

BeeBee continued in a hushed voice, "While you were downstairs, Mr. Ganiff placed a special call to the prosecutor." She trembled. "His begging, crying and carrying on rattled the entire building!"

"What did he say?"

"Oh, he used all his pull and title as General Manager so that Ms. Djorak would be locked up until her court date." She swallowed with difficulty. Suddenly, she began to sniffle. "Would you believe he also informed the prosecutor of Ms. Djorak's past?" Tears welled in her eyes. This display of weakness embarrassed her, so she turned around and ran into the operators' room.

A few seconds later, Ms. Djorak entered my office. My mouth dropped. I fumbled around for the emergency button wired to three police precincts that Security had installed overnight under my desk for dire situations.

The woman then spoke in a falsetto. "Hi, my name is Élan Vared. Sorry, I'm early. I have an appointment with Mr. Ganiff." She flashed a bright smile at me.

I stopped seeking the button and regained my composure. I tapped on Ganiff's door. The lock unbolted and I slipped in. He was seated behind his desk.

"Mr. Ganiff, have a look outside. It's your appointment. Do you know this woman?"

"Why are you whispering?" he nonchalantly inquired.

"Seriously, have a peek. Have you ever met this woman?"

"No, I didn't." He explained patiently, "Linda, I called an employment agency. I even found the card on Djorak's desk."

I ran behind his desk. With all the force I could muster, I tipped his chair and then bodily prodded, kicked and pushed him to the door. "Take a look," I grunted from the exertion.

Ganiff peered out the crack of the open door. He spied the woman who flashed her molars back at him. Quickly, he withdrew his head. "How did she get out of prison? Did she escape?"

I shrugged. "Supposedly this is Élan Vared. Your appointment this morning."

He opened the door a sliver and peered again. "Uncanny resemblance!" Ms. Vared grinned at him once more. He whirled around and peered at me. "Does she have a twin?"

"You'd think I know? What should I do about her?"

"Give her the tour. And afterwards, do not, absolutely do not bring her back here."

I was nervous as hell. Tentatively, I escorted Ms. Vared down to the Lobby. Not too far away, Supreme Superior employees scraped the corridor walls in their desire to jump out of our way.

"Awful nervous staff you have here," remarked Ms. Vared.

"Well, we've been through a lot in a short period of time."

At the end of the tour, Ms. Vared thanked me. I took a step back and studied her very closely. In the dim light from the corridor sconces, I noticed the thick layer of pancake make-up with the trace of a five o'clock shadow. It was right at that moment when I realized that Ms. Vared was not a woman. She was a man. Not really a man; now a woman, who was once a little boy.

"Pardon me, are you Donna the Dominatrix?"

In a bass voice Ms. Vared asked, "Have we met before?"

"Oh, Donna, I think we have. On the cross-town bus years ago."

Ms. Vared flashed a grin. "I vaguely recall. In the middle of the night, in the meatpacking district?"

I nodded.

"Around two or three o'clock in the morning?"

I kept nodding.

"Ah yes. I remember it well," she said, "that brilliant sky."

"It was night," I corrected.

"It was raining," she conceded.

"No, it was clear," I corrected her once more.

"It was in the middle of winter."

"No, it was in July."

"Ah, yes. I remember it well. I was wearing purple."

"No, you were wearing red."

"Yes, yes. I remember it well."

"So it was you!" I was flabbergasted. "It warms my heart to know that you remember it still the way you do." The two of us women, or rather the one woman and the shemale embraced. "Élan or Donna, I'm thrilled that we met up again. Let me talk to the General Manager and we shall get back to you soon, okay?"

"My dear, it was a pleasure after all this time." He/she shook my proffered hand.

Soon, I was back in Ganiff's office. "She seems rather nice. Also, her physical similarity to Djorak would provide the staff with some sort of continuity."

He looked askance... and reconsidered. There was merit to my remark. Besides, there were benefits of hiring a doppelganger. It would maintain fear and order. Otherwise, the employees might enjoy their work. Lord knows where that might lead.

"Set it up," he commanded, "I need no more convincing."

Chapter 32
June 1995

Three months later the hotel was a–humming. Construction was in full force. Guests called from the top five floors of the high caliber Sublime ateliers complaining about the early morning racket. Ganiff stated, "It's nine in the morning. Who the hell do they think they are?"

"Movie stars," Murlise dryly replied.

The hotel staff resumed a quieter, albeit busier pace. Mr. Ganiff did hire Ms. Vared who was the good witch. She dropped the falsetto and maintained her low–pitched voice. No one even suspected that she was once a little boy.

Meanwhile, Ganiff stalled the final linen inventory replacement list until he had put into place a depreciation and amortization schedule that would be almost half of what Ms. Wapiti and Mr. Dorck had assessed. Even though he couldn't evict the anonymous tenant, he focused his energies into an enjoyable hobby, that of terrorizing the man. He allowed the construction crew to utilize the entire building as a factory. All day. All night. And, as the song went, he'd only just begun.

At my desk, I was in the process of organizing some papers when the phone rang. Before I could turn to get it, BeeBee yelled on my intercom with an announcement: "Linda, it's Veronica from Tony Tenneb's office. Line one."

Veronica couldn't put it off any longer. At long last she met with Ganiff. "I have to tell you, Linda, how excruciating that was. More importantly, I have to thank you for the tape because it cured my chronic insomnia. Every time I couldn't get to sleep, I'd pop it into the VCR and like a charm, it always knocked me out. Did Ganiff ever consider selling it on QVC as an insomnia cure–all?"

"Don't give him that idea! With my luck, he'll get rich from it! So what happened during the meeting?" I asked with bated breath.

"Well, I put into place a new countermeasure. Now that Ganiff's phoning me daily, he first has to go through my secretary's secretary. Then her secretary's secretary. And so on. In this way, I can buy us some breathing time. I do have to let you know, Linda, that judging by his messages, he fully believes that in a matter of time Tony's gonna be throwing himself into this project."

We both had a good laugh. Mr. Ganiff's delusion never felt so sweet.

I remained unhappy with my position and still dreaded the future, not knowing when the sword of Damocles would ritualistically behead me. For the moment, I had found a plateau of complacency and a false sense of security. This was fortified by Ms. Vared's goodwill gesture: she extended a generous blanket clemency to all those employees who attended the strike. As a result, no one was fired. Instead, they were docked for the time spent away from their duties.

I was under the impression that the drama surrounding me, for the most part, had evaporated and all the bad things went bye–bye. I guess this is what the professionals call "denial" or "delusion."

It took several weeks but Jay Krieger stopped sending flowers. In good time, too. The senior level managers complained that my office smelt like a mortuary. And miracle of miracles, my relationship with BeeBee strengthened. I found BeeBee—although coarse and vulgar—more supportive, when not absent from her desk. Maybe without Djorak as her primary ally, she felt vulnerable. Whatever the reason, I wasn't about to complain.

On the other hand, Ms. Djorak faced a ten–year sentence with no chance of parole. The newspapers, fascinated by her sordid past, reported that she was fortunate to face such a small term after having hired former colleagues from her wide mercenary organization to harass and scare the jury. Sometimes, I received phone calls from prison. Religiously, I hung up. I also received calls from reporters, and hung up as well. Carole was still nowhere to be found and I assumed she had no alternative, as a potential victim, other than to enter the witness protection program.

And whatever rift I had with Mr. Ganiff seemed to mend… or, at least, so I thought. He continued to be volatile, almost as mercurial as New York City weather. As the old joke goes, if you don't like the weather, wait a minute. One day he slammed the door in my face, the next he confided in me. I rather dreaded his congenial moments and preferred the monster, because, if nothing else, the monster stayed locked in his office.

I received a letter from Iggy Two on which he wrote the same sentence over and over, "It sucks here." He ended the letter with a plea, "Please don't show my parents this note. PS: Say hi to Howard Stern for me."

True to Iggy Two's prophecy, the retaliation for shaving his head and piercing his ears was harsh. His parents shipped him off to a specialized school for children suffering from attention deficit syndrome. In all likelihood, the interactions between the Ganiffs and their son had produced a maladroit. As they say: the apple doesn't fall far from the tree.

I contended that Iggy Two was a normal kid, albeit dumb and spoiled—a lethal combination for someone who had no aspirations in life other than to be dressed in all things Ralph Lauren.

Mr. Ganiff, with his innate radar, strolled out of his office. Out of the hundreds of letters on my desk, he zoomed in on the envelope from Iggy Two. He snatched it off my desk and looked it over. "Linda, is this a letter from my son?"

"Yep. I believe it is. Got it just this minute." What I didn't tell him was that the letter was safely tucked in my handbag.

He put the envelope in his pocket and locked himself back in his office. Minutes later, an enraged Mrs. Ganiff hefted her bulk into my office and stood in front of my desk, quivering. A magnificent as well as a mind–altering sight to behold.

Breathing forcefully and heavily, she managed to wheeze, "Linda, did my son write to you?" I feared a heart attack was moments away. If that occurred, she was shit out of luck as I had failed the CPR exam for the second time.

"Yes, Mrs. Ganiff."

"What did he say?"

"Nothing much." Which was true as he had filled a page with the words, "It sucks here."

"Do you know that Mr. Ganiff and I phone him daily? He refuses to speak to us. He'll call his sister, Reba, to get money but he won't talk to us, nor write back to us."

Mr. Ganiff joined his wife in front of my desk. "Linda, may we have the letter?"

Mrs. Ganiff stretched her hand out and imperiously said, "Please."

Even though I knew that that word must have been inordinately difficult for her to pronounce, I couldn't do it. "No." I was adamant.

Her voice raised an octave. "What do you mean by no? He's our son. We have that right—"

I was in no mood for this. And I owed it to the kid to maintain his confidentiality. "No is a complete sentence, Mrs. Ganiff. And you do not have that right. He asked that I keep it to myself. Privacy, you know? He's entitled. So am I."

My blatant brazenness traumatized the Ganiffs. Mrs. Ganiff's massive bosom heaved up and down, causing a shock wave that distorted time and space. Her lips alternated between sneering and flapping, threatening to topple the tilt of the earth's axis. Mr. Ganiff tried his utmost to control his rage. His mustache tips first zigged then zagged. His hands formed fists.

"What did he write?" pleaded Mrs. Ganiff, "and has he written you before?"

"He's obviously not happy. He doesn't think he belongs at that place. That's pretty much it. If he were in any kind of trouble, I'd surely tell you. Rest assured, he's not. And no, this is the only time he's written me."

The truth was, I had never received any other written communications from Iggy Two. What I didn't disclose to the Ganiffs were the daily collect calls I had been receiving from the troubled teen. I'd become something of his confidant. Though I wasn't about to volunteer this information either.

Mrs. Ganiff shot a furious look at her husband, turned around and waddled out of the office.

"Thanks a lot for meddling in my personal affairs." Ganiff's tone was full of sarcasm. I tuned him out completely while he ranted and raged back in his office. I felt unaffected because I had become inured and immune to his temper. Funny how people can adjust to almost anything when subjected long enough.

Later that day, Ganiff ordered me into his office. I expected the worst—another tongue–lashing about my refusal to part with the correspondence from his son. His face didn't hold that kind of enmity. It held his usual demeanor—a dollop of nasty with a side of condescension. I entered the dungeon with my customary dread, knowing that perhaps he would disclose some deep, dark secret from his twisted psyche better left moldering inside him.

"Linda, I received the results of my physical."

Oh shit, I thought, *lucky me.*

"Anyway, it seems my Hungarian reflexologist was not off base. Blood tests say that I have an enlarged prostate." He held his hands a foot apart. "Severely enlarged."

He rambled on endlessly, absently twisting his mustache ends. All about the quantity of bran he ate, the amount of time he spent in the bathroom and the quality, frequency and nature of his stools. I couldn't believe my ears.

After subjecting me to this TMI (too much information)—which surpassed that of his belabored family tales—he belatedly became aware of the inappropriateness of the conversation. Which also explained why I wasn't rendered unconscious during this moderately evocative and appallingly indecent discussion. He lamely finished his diatribe. "Don't let Mrs. Ganiff know. You hear me? She'll castrate us both… um, you know what I mean!"

I was pissed that he had confided in me and not his wife. At the very least, his wife tolerated him. "Don't you want your wife to know that you might have prostate cancer?"

"Well, we don't know for sure. Let me see what happens. I'll have to go for additional tests. And, of course, I'll check with other doctors."

"Mr. Ganiff, this is not one of your contracts. It's your health. Delaying those tests won't make the problem go away."

He groaned with distaste. "Aw, Linda, leave me alone. Please, on your way out, close the door."

Oh, I was more than willing to submit to that request. *That man has some nerve! And here I expressed genuine concern for his well–being. What a lout!*

As usual, I eavesdropped on the intercom while taking notes. Seebok presented the results of his latest research on pornography.

"Sir, Steven Koneman gave me the name and contact number of a terrific video start–up company that's looking for capital. Their name is, let me see…"

Papers fanned in accompaniment to Mr. Ganiff's shouts, "Seebok, why are you always so disorganized?"

"Boss, I have it right here. It's called 'Hamsterland Productions.' Steven said there are two guys who run it. They used to work at other companies. You know one of them: VixenChix. The videos with terrific three–ways."

"Go on," Ganiff crisply said.

"Well, if we give them at least $750,000, that's $250,000 apiece, within the next six month period, not only will we recoup our money, but we should see a profit of forty–five percent. That comes to $337,500 in total, or $112,500 for each of us. Boss, there's no way we could ever make that kind of guaranteed profit in such a short term elsewhere. This can be our trial run to bigger and better things."

For quite a few seconds there was silence on the other side. I felt transported to the racetrack. *C'mon number one. C'mon number one.* I not only crossed my fingers, I crossed my toes and eyes as well.

"Fine. Set it up with Steven. Get all the info from him. Listen up, I want you to handle all the finances and contracts. Keep my name out of it. I need to keep my hands clean."

I felt as if I had won the trifecta. I stood up for a mini–chicken happy dance. I finished writing on a piece of paper all the information I had overheard and placed it in my handbag to add to all the others on my desk at home. My "cover–my–ass" plan was now in full force.

★ ★ ★ ★ ★

I met my father for dinner that evening while my mother and her girlfriends went out. We decided to eat at a wonderful Chinatown restaurant, *Hung Wun*. My father picked me up at work and we took a cab downtown.

While the taxi driver navigated through traffic, my father's curiosity won out. "So what's going on with you and that damn job?"

"Dad, I think I got myself covered. All I need is a little more time to learn a little more. Then I'll flesh out my resume."

We exited the cab and found the restaurant easily enough. After we ordered our meals, I told my father the latest dirt on Mr. Ganiff and his enlarged prostate.

"Dad, here's the weird thing about this man. His health scare doesn't have much impact on him." I picked up the chopsticks, removed them from their package and separated them. "You'd think he would change his habits. Not Ganiff!"

My father unfolded a red linen napkin. He placed it on his lap. "Really? How so? Maybe I can learn something from this idiot."

"Well, for starters, he didn't alter his drinking any. It's wine during lunch, before and after dinner. The diagnosis didn't change his diet, or his love of eating rare and endangered species. In addition, he always has both paws dipped into snacks whenever I'm around. Pretzels, cookies, whatever." I sighed and threw my hands up, knocking over the waiter serving us our dinner. "Sorry about that," I said to him and continued with my train of thought, "and his exercise program practically consists of taking elevators to and from his office."

My father chuckled. I passed the rice over to him and kept myself occupied by taking heaping spoonfuls of lobster in ginger sauce. My father poured rice onto his plate and fought me for the last morsels of the lobster. He asked a very intuitive question, "Do you care about his health?"

"Hell no! The man's a misery." I nibbled on the spicy food and used the chopsticks for emphasis between bites. "Let me tell you: the positive effect from his medical problems is that he limits his time with his staff more than ever before. Oh, and he spends even more time in the bathroom, if that's possible." I took a few more bites and swallowed. "He isolated himself and rarely ventures out of his office now. And, he admits a select few in there." I hesitated and then plunged forth. "Dad, the man has no conscience. He's extremely innovative when it comes to ripping off the hotel."

My father's chopsticks stopped in mid–air. I eyed the succulent piece of lobster held in between the utensils. "Linda, first off, get your eyes off my food. You have some on your own plate. Secondly, how about you run that last sentence by me again?"

I put down my chopsticks. "Yeah, Dad. Well… part of the problem I have working there is that I'm kinda witnessing my boss pulling all these little financial stunts to spruce up his wallet." I shrugged with my hands in the air for emphasis. I purposely omitted my participation in his schemes as well as the fact that the sound of women moaning from Seebok's video collection constantly serenaded me through the locked doors of Ganiff's office. My father eyed me incredulously.

"Linda, how could you continue to work in such an environment? I'm surprised." The devolution of my job astonished my father. It no longer astonished me; I was way beyond that now.

"Don't be, Dad. I've come to terms with what's been happening around me. And I'm going to resolve it once and for all. I just need a little more time." *If he only knew what really was going on!* I thought. *Thank the gods, I never told him about my peripheral involvement in Ganiff's schemes. Those same schemes from which I intended to extricate myself. All I needed was a little more time and ingenuity.*

235

Chapter 33

"RAP GANG THUGS SOUGHT IN HOTEL STABBING"

Daily Post June 17, 1995

Two hotel security guards are reported in critical condition after a late–night stabbing incident at the Supreme Superior Hotel. According to several eyewitnesses, the incident began around 3:00 a.m. That's when the posse for rap sensation U–Tool was confronted by hotel security guards.

U–Tool was said to be in town for an album release party. He was registered in the Supreme Superior's penthouse suite. Sources say that around 2:45 a.m. the front desk became inundated with calls of a disturbance. There were reports of excessive screaming, loud music and breaking glass. An unidentified hotel employee said a security guard attempted to evict the rowdy group on the top floor. That's when a member of U–Tool's posse allegedly stabbed the man in the chest with a Swiss Army Knife.

"It was crazy, man!" said one eyewitness who refused to be identified. "The guy was just doing his job and one of U–Tool's boys cut him open. It was sick. Blood and guts everywhere."

Witnesses say that the security guard activated a panic switch on his walkie–talkie before he collapsed onto the corridor floor. A second security guard later confronted the group as they fled through the hotel lobby. Another gang member allegedly stabbed him in the abdomen.

Both suspects fled the scene. U–Tool and his entourage were later held for questioning by police. The two security guards are in intensive care at Roosevelt Hospital and are reported to be in critical condition. Management at the Supreme Superior Hotel declined to comment.

I read the article at my desk on Monday morning. I was angry beyond belief. If not for Mr. Ganiff's policy of maintaining a thinly staffed crew, this could have been avoided. Now, two men were severely and needlessly injured. And to think of all the kickback money that Ganiff had pocketed which could have paid for extra security…

All three New York City newspapers railed against the Supreme Superior with screaming headlines:

U–TOOL TOOL BEHIND SUPREME BOO–BOO

SUPREME SUPERIOR STABBINGS SCANDAL

FIVE–STAR STABBING FIASCO

The story had all the ingredients for sensationalism: a luxury hotel, a rap star, violence and questionable hotel management. Not to mention that all this happened on the heels of the brouhaha surrounding Ms. Djorak. As expected, the journalists had a field day resurrecting those stories as well.

Ganiff shunned the limelight for two consecutive weeks. He locked himself away in his office, refusing all calls and visitors. He even avoided the executive staff and blew off our morning meetings. Instead, he had Murlise and Doreen handle the proceedings. Too bad it couldn't have lasted longer!

One morning, he emerged from his office. "Staff meeting now. Pronto! Linda, round up all our glorious fuck–ups and bring 'em in here."

All the executives quickly gathered in my office. There was quite a flurry when Big Guy entered the room. And like the Red Sea, the executive team parted to let him approach my desk.

Ms. Vared pulled on his sleeve. "Did you recently visit our guys at the hospital? How's Tito and Carmine doing? Any new prognosis on their condition?"

The room went silent.

Big Guy was somber. "They took Tito off life support last night but he's still listed as critical. His wife told me that he moved his hand."

Murlise gasped. Ms. Wapiti cried.

Big Guy continued, "And Carmine, well…" He stopped himself from tearing up. "I saw him and it's bad. A lot of damage in his stomach, intestines, even his pancreas was nicked. He's in a lot of pain. They have him on a morphine drip."

Joe Smith and Hans dropped their heads down. Even Seebok appeared upset.

"I don't know what to tell all of you," Big Guy said, "due to the severity of their injuries, they may be in the hospital for months. Maybe years to fully recuperate." He shook his head in resignation and whispered, "The doctor on call at the hospital confided in me that they'll never work again. Their careers are over for sure."

While we absorbed this daunting news, Ganiff poked his head into my office and displayed those infamous and highly touted executive managerial skills that made him the most solicited man in hotel management. "Enough blathering! Everyone get your butts in here, now!"

Without preamble or reference to the tragedy that had befallen the Supreme Superior, Mr. Ganiff took the reins. "In light of recent events," he deliberately paused for a second, "I found that I have no other recourse but to put into place a new corporate policy, effective immediately."

Big Guy and Ms. Vared sighed in relief. This avoidable tragedy had weighed them down. With the pronouncement of Mr. Ganiff's words, a spark of interest ignited in the formerly listless attitude among the staff. I could smell the anticipation. Finally, the General Manager would step up to the plate, banish his former stance and hire additional security staff. Collectively, we all straightened up and waited for what was to come.

"As you may be aware, I've been sitting in my office and thinking."

I groaned with foreboding while Murlise whispered, "Enough with the preamble. Get on with it."

"And I've been doing some analysis of my own." He paused again. "As it turns out, all of you in this room are guilty. Guilty as sin."

At this point, we all stared among ourselves, astonished.

Ganiff took time to smooth his mustache and tug at his forelock. "By my calculations, all of you are spending far too much money and costing the hotel a fortune."

I was stupefied. Huh? We're spending too much money? On what? What does that have to do with the recent tragedy that destroyed the health of two of our comrades?

The change in the pronouncement shocked Big Guy and Ms. Vared. Quickly losing all interest, Seebok knocked at the window, trying to gain the attention of the pigeons outside. Doreen kicked at Seebok's chair. "Knock it off, you moron tho we can finish up and get outta here!"

Mr. Ganiff harrumphed. "Therefore…"

Here it comes! We were biting our nails now.

"No more free dry cleaning." He pounded on his desk to punctuate his statement.

Startled by the proclamation, we were all jolted out of our chairs in unison.

"No more free limos." Pow went his fist. Once more, up went our bodies. Then down. "No more free *Bliss* lunches, or room–service, or brunches, unless for business and approved by me." Bam! Bam! Bam! Bam! Ten bodies, all as one, again defied gravity. As usual, gravity won out and we plopped right back down. "And no more free rooms." Smack. Exhausted by this display, he wiped his sweaty forehead with his breast pocket hanky and fell back into his chair. "This would save the hotel at least a few hundred thou. You all hear me?"

Everyone in the room nodded dejectedly. We stood up to leave.

"Wait, there's more!" said Ganiff. We sat down again. He picked up a yellow legal sized pad and perused his notes.

"Joe, I figured out how to get reimbursement for the employees' food. Dorck, listen up. Effective immediately, we charge all staff who are not managers at least five bucks a week for employee cafeteria privileges. Supervisors, assistants and managers pay fifteen bucks. And all of you here will pay twenty. That'll add up to at least $200,000 a year."

Joe kept mute; given his track record with Ganiff, he did not want to be in the cross–hairs of any missile or projectile, verbal or otherwise. Cappy and Ms. "highest paid" Wapiti played a silent game of footsie, trying to suppress their giggles. Hans straightened the cuffs to his shirt. Mr. Dorck didn't move a muscle.

Everyone got up to leave again when Ganiff growled, "No, don't go yet, I have even more." We took our seats. He pointed to Murlise. "From here on forward, have Edwing and the other concierges use Hammer Travel Agency exclusively."

Murlise flashed a puzzled look, yet I understood what he wanted. I recalled Ganiff's deal with Hammer that would entitle them to have sole rights for all travel arrangements the hotel made. In return, Ganiff would get free airline tickets. I guess Edwing didn't cotton to the original mandate and continued to do business with other travel agencies.

Mr. Ganiff regarded his team with an expression of accomplishment. He somehow anticipated gratitude. How pathetic. The shocked faces in front of him annihilated his expression. A dark, sinister scowl replaced his formerly benevolent smile.

Ms. Vared posed the question that must have been racing through all of our minds the duration of this meeting, "What are we going to do about Security? We have only three men left."

Mr. Ganiff gnashed his teeth. "Vared, you know we gotta keep expenses down, especially now, when we have an extensive, and might I add, expensive construction project. Didn't you pay attention to what I have been saying this entire time? What do you think I'm doing? I'm saving us almost half a million dollars a year right now!"

"Mr. Ganiff, the hotel association is tenacious about conflicts with the contract, especially with understaffing. And since the hotel strike, they've been investigating a shopping list of grievances." Ms. Vared took a deep breath. She didn't even know that they'd come from my friend, Carole.

Ganiff's face was impassive. Ms. Vared plunged on, "Mr. Ganiff, I think it behooves us to meet with them instead of making our relationship even more adversarial. They're at the point of fining us, or putting sanctions on the hotel. Look, all they want to do is discuss renegotiating the current arrangement. They're not looking to sue us or even close us down outright."

"Vared, the hotel association would not close this hotel. Not ever! They'd lose all those union dues." He sighed and said, "Go ahead, do what you have to." He fluttered his hand dismissively. "I want you to handle the lawyers for the stabbing lawsuit as well." He examined each and every one of us. "And, as for the rest of you, why are you staying here? Don't you all have jobs to do? Now go!"

Later that day, I received a furious call from the chief concierge. Edwing was livid. "Linda, is this man out to ruin me? How am I supposed to conduct my business? Hammer is the worst travel agency—no one wants to be booked on Amelia Earhart flights!"

Edwing was very concerned that he would lose a large part of his contacts within the intricate system of favors that lined his pockets. Services such as florists, spas, boutiques, escorts, restaurants, car rentals and airlines, to name a few, royally compensated concierges for recommending them to the clientele. This is the way of the world. I didn't blame him. But I couldn't suffer through any more of his whining; I had some to do of my own.

The latest Ganiff mandate frustrated me as well. I ran to Doreen's office and sat down by her desk to vent. Doreen also looked glum.

"Hey, Doreen. Helluva meeting this morning, huh?"

"Yeah, sure wath. I couldn't wait to be outta there either. Mithter Ganiff wath pretty mad."

"You mean mad like a crazy, or do you mean angry?" She shot me a dirty look which I overlooked. "What do you think about Mr. Ganiff taking away all our perks? You must be as thrilled as the rest of us."

She shrugged. "Oh, it thuckth. What am I going to do? Have the guy arrethted? I mean, he'th thtill the big kahuna here."

"Well, funny you should mention the arrest part." I laughed. "Doreen, how would you feel if you knew that Mr. Ganiff had done other things here at the hotel? Things that are, let's say, a tad illegal?"

She shrugged once more. "Look, Linda. I'fe been here for almotht five yearth. I earn thikth figureth a year. And I get a bonuth. My huthband doethn't have a thteady thalary. We own a condo and I pay all the billth. I don't have the freedom to thpeak my mind. Tho I jutht pretend like everyfing'th fine, you know?"

"Well, sort of. I also believe in doing things the right way. So much has happened around here. The stabbings. The Djorak incident. The disappearing linens." At the mention of the linens, Doreen looked askance at me. I could tell she was unaware of that shady situation. I continued, "I think I've reached my saturation point. It's bad enough he's doing some really weird shit here but man, now he's gouging it out of us and we're paying for him!"

Doreen didn't have much to say. She twitched a bit and gave me a noncommittal smile.

Even for Doreen, her reaction was a bit off, I thought. As far as I was concerned, she owed me a little co-worker empathy. I should never have allowed her to physically strong-arm me from entering Seebok's office.

Disgusted and discouraged, I left early that day, the first time since I had joined the Supreme Superior. I was at an impasse.

★ ★ ★ ★ ★

I arrived at my office early the next morning. So early, in fact, that sunlight had yet to shine through the windows. To clarify, sunlight never actually shone through those windows. The building across the street that housed the William Morris Agency blocked all sunlight to the lower floors. The executive offices were in perpetual gloom, appropriately so.

I switched on the overhead fluorescents, went to my desk and turned on the computer. I could tell by the flickering lights from under Ganiff's office door that he was huddled in there. Probably enjoying another all–night marathon from the best of his pornographic video collection.

For some odd reason, I could not log onto the computer. I repeatedly re–entered my name and password and repeatedly received a system error. I wanted to call the computer guys, but no one would be in at this hour. So, I headed downstairs to my favorite area in the entire hotel, the delectables bin at the back of the restaurant by the loading dock. This time, a conventional pain–au–chocolat and a small carafe of designer coffee did the trick. I then returned upstairs via the back elevators.

The *New York Times* crossword puzzle was difficult which was peculiar given the fact that it was a Tuesday puzzle. Tapping my pen, I racked my brain for answers to the clues, accompanied by the sounds of muffled groans as well as discordant canned disco music pulsating from Ganiff's office. I had just taken the first bite of my pastry when Big Guy arrived at my door.

"Hey Big Guy, whatchya doin here so bright and early?" He couldn't bring himself to look at me. He stood there, dawdling, rubbing the toe of his right boot into the carpeting.

"Big Guy, are you okay?"

Abruptly, the large man wept, the likes of which I'd never seen in my life. I put my croissant down on top of my crossword puzzle, wiped my hands on a linen napkin and got up from my desk to console him.

"Oh, what's the matter? Did someone die? Oh My God! Please don't tell me it's one of our security guys!"

Big Guy reached out, grabbed me and pulled me close to his chest in a bear hug. He squeezed the breath out of me while lifting me off the ground. His tears poured down my neck. The pressure from his arms and chest made it difficult for me to gasp in air. Futilely, I tried to break out of this death–like embrace, except my arms were clamped down at my sides. It felt like Sasquatch had grasped me although I confess that I've never had that experience firsthand. Conserving what little air remained in my lungs, I flailed my legs and fingers. Feeling faint, I succumbed to the inevitable. The struggle was over.

Next thing I knew, I was on the ground and Big Guy's lips were on mine.

241

"What the hell!" My head bolted up and slammed against his bottom lip, splitting it instantly. Big Guy jumped up. This time, his tears mixed with blood and poured in rivulets down his chin. "Linda, it's not what you think! I was giving you mouth–to–mouth!" *If that was what it was, no wonder I failed all those CPR exams.*

Right then, BeeBee entered. At first, she noticed a bloody and tear–laden Big Guy. Then, she turned to see me splayed out on the floor. She said, "Holy shit! I can't believe this!" and rapidly retraced her steps to flee out of the office.

I pushed myself up to a sitting position. Big Guy was on his knees, still weeping.

"Hey, what the fuck is going on?" Gingerly, I stood up from the ground and checked my body for any kind of entry points.

Between sobs, hiccups—and the noise that someone makes when they're inhaling their phlegm while trying to hide it—he said, "Ms. Vared wants me to… to…" and he burst out crying again.

I reached over my desk to get the linen napkin that I used to wipe my hands and handed it to Big Guy. He blew his nose in it and then he wiped his lips. Gross was the word that came to mind. He tidied up a little more, quieted down and finally completed his sentence. "I have to escort you to human resources." And then he mumbled, "Yer frd."

"I'm what?"

"You're frd," he mumbled again.

"I'm fried?" The way he reacted and the downfall of tears clarified my confusion about what he said. "Oh, I'm fired!" Just then, I felt relieved. I felt invincible. I felt the chains that had been constricting me drop away. Moments later, though, I got in touch with my feelings. I was pissed!

And then I took two steps towards Mr. Ganiff's office door. Big Guy scooped me up before I could get there.

"Not a chance, Linda! Sorry, I can't let you."

We heard Ganiff bolting his door from the inside. Next, he grunted aloud as he pushed some furniture to fortify his secure position. Big Guy put me down like a giant releasing a rag doll. He folded his arms across his chest. He'd gotten his mojo back.

"Linda, from what Ms. Vared told me, Mr. Ganiff fired you. Please come with us, we'll escort you downstairs to human resources."

"Who's us?" I peered around his bulk but could not discern anyone hiding behind the potted plants.

"Oh, um, sorry. Got used to having extra men with me. I figured I could handle you alone." He wiped his face with his sleeve and then beckoned with a crook of a finger. "C'mon. I guess you'll know more when you get there."

The meaning behind the words "yer frd" finally registered in my brain. I felt the impact as if the local Mayan Chieftain had reached in and tore out my beating heart. This was the first time that I was ever fired. And Ganiff didn't even have the guts to do it himself!

Big Guy helped get my handbag and croissant. Blood flowed abundantly from his lip. Silently, he escorted me down to the bowels of the Supreme Superior. We walked side–by–side along the concrete subbasement hallways to the human resources antechamber of horror. Not another soul witnessed this event.

Big Guy patted my back in consolation when we arrived. "Sorry, Linda. Not my call." And right before I left him, he picked me up again and through the linen napkin now draped over the lower quadrant of his face he said, "Good luck."

Ms. Vared gestured for me to enter. "Linda, please take a seat, my dear."

I took a seat on the rickety foldout chair in front of her desk which was empty except for a manila envelope. "What is this? I'm fired?"

"Yes. Unfortunately, my dear. You were doing very well here. We liked you a lot, so we were truly shocked when Mr. Ganiff brought it to our attention late last night. He said that you've been stealing linens from the hotel. Quite a lot of them."

My eyes crossed. "I did what? Wait one fucking minute!" Ganiff went overboard this time. There was no fucking way that he was going to pin his thievery on me in order to weasel out of repaying the hotel. "I want to know right here right now. Do you have evidence? Security cameras, pictures? Anything to support these allegations?" I pounded the desk in disgust. "And what the fuck would I do with all those soiled hotel linens? Did that thought cross anyone's minds here? Or did anyone consider how I'm gonna store them in my tiny one–bedroom apartment?"

Ms. Vared flicked her wrist at me, conveying her dismissal of what I had to say. He/she opened the file on the desk and picked up a handful of papers. She inspected them, then me. "My predecessor, before her untimely departure from sanity and freedom in that order, compiled some information on a select few individuals through her extensive network of paranoid mercenaries. She forwarded this information to Mr. Ganiff."

I lurched forward to pluck the papers out of her hand. The sly tranny was quicker than me and moved the papers out of my reach. "As per her sources, yes, you were indeed a banker. It says here that you left prior to some dubious occurrences."

Whoa! I had no idea what had ensued after I had resigned from GermBank. Intrigued, I asked, "What do you mean by dubious?"

"According to this report which was based on innuendos, interviews and documentation, your former boss was investigated for fraudulent activities by Federal banking authorities. Before this investigation was concluded, he ran off to…" she read from the papers, "ah, Berlin. Hmm. It says here that there were

243

memos uncovered by a routine audit from same authorities that cast a negative light on your former boss. As reported by one of the sources, you were the author of these memos. It just so happens that you provided details of his corporate skullduggery."

Sitting at the edge of the folding chair, perilous in and of itself, I clenched my fists and refrained from jumping up and down. *They worked! Hallelujah! The memos got that heinous former boss out of the way. The scorecard now read: Linda—1, Heinous Ex–Boss—0. Yet, was there more?* "And what does that have to do with your accusation of theft?"

"We drew parallels."

She spoke to me as if I were a retarded mongrel dog.

"Linda, you have to understand our position." Ms. Vared held out the palms of her massive knuckle–laden hands as if they were scales to weigh fish; they were big enough. She shook her left palm. "There was theft at the bank where you worked and," she indicated with her right palm, "there's theft here." Again she indicated with her left palm, "You stated to a colleague that you believed that Mr. Ganiff stole from the hotel and," again her right palm, "you wrote memos about your former boss stealing money from the bank." She made a production of folding her hands on top of the desk. "It appears to us that you're the key. The conduit. The catalyst. The thief."

First off, I wanted to show her my hands. Next, I'd join my palms together, using her face as the focal point. Secondly, on a less aggressive basis, I wanted to let her know that in both instances those thefts occurred way before I joined those institutions. The moment I opened my mouth, she gave me the stop sign.

"Let me tell you, Mr. Ganiff is a gracious and kind man. You should thank him. It was upon his insistence that we decided not to press charges." I held myself back from blurting comments that would serve to ignite an already inflammatory situation for me. She continued, "We'll pay you for a few sick days and accumulated vacation time. I think it all totals to about three weeks."

I recognized the futility of pursuing any further conversation in this vein. However, I had to address another matter of unfinished business and reckoned that now would be the last opportunity to ask. After all, I had nothing else to lose. "What about my commendation?"

"For what?"

"I was supposed to receive a check for helping the hotel. I know this is corporate policy—it's in the manual—and also because quite a few other employees have received this benefit. Mr. Ganiff told me he would make it up to me. He promised and gave me his word as General Manager of the hotel—"

"Ah, let me get this clear. You want us to reward you for capturing a thief, yet you don't want to be punished for stealing hotel property?" Ms. Vared said.

At that moment, I realized the worth of his word. I guess, in his perverse and retaliatory view of the world, firing me was his warm and fuzzy way of making it up to me… My head almost exploded. I had to change the topic out of fear of losing my cool beyond the legal limit. "Are there any papers that you want me to sign?" I had had enough of this shit and wanted documentary evidence of these allegations for my own legal protection.

"Linda, we decided that with all that's happening at the hotel, we're going to make a clean break with you. There are no papers, nothing."

Of course there were no papers, I fumed.

She continued, "We wish you the best of luck. And make sure to stay out of prison."

Big Guy waited for me outside of Ms. Vared's office. Oh, he knew exactly what went on because he treated me like I had leprosy. He couldn't even look me in the eye.

I returned back to my apartment by nine in the morning. I stripped out of my monkey suit and put on my worn out pjs and bunny slippers that my mother attempted to trash during each of her visits. I phoned my local deli for the mandatory junk food delivery and made a nest on the living room sofa. Then, I turned up the air conditioning unit to full blast.

I had at my disposal a full day ahead to wallow in my misery. A much–needed day to rail at the universe and to curse at the gods who had thrown me once more to the wolves. A day to weep tears aplenty into my array of delivered comfort foods now surrounding me on my sofa, floor and end tables. My dwindling good friends—a devoured pint of Häagen–Dazs, a mostly empty bag of Butterfingers, several strips of teriyaki beef jerky and three remaining malted milk balls—were there for me… At least for another twenty minutes, or so. They didn't malign, nor berate me. They gave me the succor required to collect my thoughts. To figure out what to do with the rest of my life… or at least the next chapter.

I surveyed my current landscape and felt even more disgusted with myself. I sat cross–legged on the sofa surrounded by junk food wrappers, empty containers and crumpled napkins. Repulsed, I tried to feast my eyes elsewhere, impeded by my distended belly. With my remote, I flicked through my all–time favorite television shows: *Soul Train* reruns and Bollywood musicals. Not even they distracted me from my misery and self–repugnance.

When a person knows they are on the verge of losing their job, they plan ahead for the inevitable search. This might include stocking up on resume paper, envelopes and labels as well as making phone calls to the placement agencies. I was naïve to believe that my job at the Supreme Superior was secure. With all the goods I had on Ganiff, I never expected this to happen so soon. I was unprepared. On every level imaginable.

When I moved into this apartment years ago, I designated the corner area of my living room as my home office. It started with an IBM computer that I used from time to time. Next came the addition of a small antique wooden desk that Mom gave me two years before and then, the previous year, a telephone with a new digital answering machine from Dad. Truth was, I hadn't been working from home over the past ten months because of all the hours I put in at the hotel. Now, this small, disheveled and dusty area in my living room was about to become headquarters for… Well, I wasn't sure just yet.

I allowed myself to celebrate my pity party until the sugar coursed through my veins. The very second my digital clock flipped to twelve, I jumped up, showered and changed. I cleaned up the mess in the living room. Then I stopped at my local Staples store and invested in a fax machine and two reams of paper. I also grabbed the *New York Times* at my corner newsstand, figuring I'd have a peek at the Employment section. Nevertheless, the bitterness of this abrupt end to my run at the Supreme Superior left me in no mood to scan through the classifieds. Instead, I hooked up the fax machine, ate a nutritious salad and downed an even more nutritious shot of vodka or four and went to bed.

The next morning I awoke with a severe stomach–ache. That should teach me a lesson! I guess next time, heaven forbid should there be a next time, I gotta lay off those malted milk balls—they're deadly. I selected a nice business suit that would cover my bloated stomach, and prior to leaving my apartment, looked up the address to the unemployment office in the yellow pages.

Just my luck! The damn building was cross–town and down the street, a half a block from… yes, the Supreme Superior Hotel. I skirted the hotel by using a circuitous route and arrived at the Department of Labor office in time to stand in a line. The wait was not that untenable because Wednesdays were off–peak for unemployment issues.

"Before you can file for unemployment, you have to watch a demonstration," the dour Department of Labor laborer behind the counter informed me.

"When does it start?" I asked, less than enthusiastic.

"In twenty minutes." He pointed to a door.

The room quickly filled up, and we were subjected to an hour–long remedial introduction to unemployment. Afterwards, we were given little pencils to fill in the circles on questionnaires that were distributed to each one of us. *At least I'll have some money coming in to tide me over,* I thought.

I had an urgent task to complete when I returned home. Namely what the professionals today call "closure." It took me a few minutes to channel my inner child before I worked up the nerve to call Ganiff's private number. A woman's voice answered.

"Um, yes, may I speak with Mr. Ganiff, please?"

"And may I tell him who's calling?"

"Yes, um, tell him it's Linda, his assistant."

She chuckled. "Very funny. I'm Linda. Linda Luppner, Mr. Ganiff's assistant."

He had plotted my termination of employment well in advance. He didn't even wait for the body to get cold. Linda Luppner was back.

"Linda, this is Linda Lane. Is Mr. Ganiff there?"

Linda sniffed into the phone. "Linda, um… he doesn't want to speak to you now. Please address all your concerns to Ms. Vared." With that, she hung up.

Several times I called, even on his private numbers, to no avail.

Then Ms. Vared called. "Linda, please leave Mr. Ganiff alone. Any further attempts will find you charged with harassment. Now, we've been overly generous in not having you prosecuted in the first place. Do you want us to change our minds?"

I hung up.

That night, I called Monica, my composer friend and recounted all that had occurred. I needed to talk to a clear thinker. Someone who could cut away at the bullshit.

"Look, Linda, he got the upper hand on you before you could retaliate. C'mon, he had this planned, maybe as a contingency plan. Probably thought he'd better get rid of you now before you ratted him out."

Monica had a point. I did confess to Doreen—that yellow–bellied bitch—my suspicions that Ganiff was involved in illegal activities. Whatever possessed me to do that? Why did I trust that backstabber? More than likely those comments I shared with her were, in turn, shared with that gutless criminal, Ganiff. In essence, they had triggered my firing. "That damn, prickless wonder!" I shouted, "he got rid of me before I could do anything to him. And now he's trying to pin all his shit on me. For all I know, he pocketed the money from my commendation!"

I could envision my dear friend rolling her eyes in simulated disgust while suppressing a yawn. Perhaps she even simulated putting her fingers down her throat. "What did you expect?" she said.

"He's a thief, Monica. In more ways than one. I bet you, if he did this at the Supreme Superior, he did this at other hotels. He's a career thief. And not only that, he's been getting away with this for over thirty–five years!"

She sighed. "You gotta put it in perspective. What he has is arrogance, Linda. The way you described him, he never held an iota of respect for you. And, more than likely, he thinks that now you're bluffing. After all, you never said or did anything all those months. And that's despite all you've witnessed."

She was right. "How am I ever going to extricate myself from this guy and his dealings?" I could feel the onset of a panic attack arising from the quickening of my pulse. "He already demonstrated that he could do whatever he wants, whenever he wants to whomever he wants." I held back my tears from fears and frustration.

"Linda, if anybody can take that monster down, it's you and no one else. Think about it. You spent how many years in a trading room?"

It was at that moment when I clued her in about the downfall of my ex–boss at GermBank. In the process, I felt a ray of hope.

She laughed on the other side of the line. "And you're worried? Linda, you go girl! You got what it takes."

I thought about what she said. *If all it took was a solitary piece of paper to bring down one heinous bastard, imagine all those pieces of papers, all those copies of papers that I had brought home and what they could do to another heinous bastard.* Then my mind switched back to how Ganiff played me. It chafed me to think that I had bought into his perception of me—that of a weak, sniveling victim.

Well, he was definitely fucking with the wrong woman. He put me in a compromising position and no fucking way will I take it passively lying on my back! He had the audacity to fire me when he should be in prison eating tinned generic cat food!

"What was that saying about a scorned woman? He bruised my ego by underestimating my intelligence. Now it's time to fight back. Time to systematically bring him down."

"I totally agree," she said, "but to do that, you'll need evidence. Something to prove what a lying, thieving weasel he is."

"Oh, don't worry about that," I said. *I'll get even more than ample documentation to bring Satan down,* I thought, *although it may be harder to collect now that I'm an outsider. Then again, maybe not as hard as some might imagine.*

Chapter 34

It was unavoidable. I had to do it. I had to see Mom and Dad. I had some explaining to do.

My father appeared happy to see me when he opened the front door. "Linda, it's Thursday. Why aren't you at work?"

"Hi Dad, how are you?" I asked when I entered the house, walking past my father who stood immobile at the entrance. I flung myself on the couch. "You know how worried you were about that job at the hotel? Well, you don't need to be worried no more."

"Okay kiddo, let's backtrack. Do you want to tell me now and I can translate for your mother later?" My father plunked right down into a nearby chair.

"Where's Mom?"

"White sale at Macy's. Need I say more?" My father and I laughed, sharing our inside joke about my mother's proclivity for shopping on certain sale days. I wryly thought that if I'd stolen all those linens that I'd been accused of stealing, my mom would never partake in another white sale again. She'd never get to leave her laundry room either.

"Well, Dad. This one's a doozy." I recounted the events of the better part of ten months' service at the Supreme Superior. "Hey, I didn't even make it to a year. Damn, I missed out on the Annual Born Again Convention! And I guess I won't be invited to Ganiff's daughter Reba's upcoming wedding. Life can be so cruel."

My father ran his hand through his full head of hair. My poor dad. I gave him endless grief, not as a child, nor as a teen–ager but as an adult. Several times he attempted to say something, though he couldn't find the words. Several times he lifted his finger to lecture me; his hand fell to the chair. He tried to get up, but then didn't.

"Dad?" I inquired.

He looked into my eyes. "I am honestly confounded. I can't believe that you actually outdid yourself!" He shook his head and muttered, "I don't know what to say, Linda. I'm floored."

I wanted to calm him down and admitted, "Well, I don't know what to say either, Dad. I'm hurting. Angry too. I'm only now beginning to gain a little perspective. My friend Monica, you know her? The composer? She said to me a while back something to the effect that if you don't remedy a situation, it'll keep on recurring. She said it's karmic."

"Linda, I don't subscribe to that Buddhist stuff as you know," my father interjected, "wrong religion. And what does that have to do with what's going on?"

I ignored his comments. "Anyhow, it was the head of human resources, incidentally, who pointed out the parallel between what happened to me at GermBank and tied it into what was going on at the hotel."

"And?"

I sat up straight. I had a glimmer of prescient knowledge. "Dad, I'm getting an idea."

A groan came from the occupant in the chair.

"Dad, please don't start in."

"Earth to Linda. Don't mess with these people. You're way out of your league." He clenched his head in his hands. "I don't understand why you didn't leave them when you had your first suspicions."

I felt my blood pressure rise. "And do what? Run away again? Dad, it's becoming more and more evident that there's corruption all over the place. I mean, give me a break—how much more disparate can banking be from hospitality? And I stumbled over this shit again! What does that say about corporate America?" I was on a roll. "I have a funny feeling that these dishonest acts are here to stay. Or, perhaps they were always here. But now, due to the size of these abhorrent deeds and how they destroy people, families, jobs and lives, they can no longer be hidden from the public. So, what should I do for the rest of my life? Run at the slightest indication of something unsavory? Or perhaps…" At last, everything came together for me. "Perhaps, my dear ol' dad, I should take a stand against corruption. What is it you always told me? Or was that Mom?"

My dad lifted his head from his hands and said, "Your mother. She loves saying: 'It takes the squeaky wheel to get the grease.'"

"Yes! I should've noticed it before now. Not Mom saying that, but who I am. Or was. Or—" My father shot me a quizzical look. I revved up. "Let me tell you something about those people at the hotel: they knew I was the squeaky wheel!" *Probably when I mouthed off to Doreen,* I realized. "I never understood that the power was in my hands. They fired me out of fear and tried to pin something illegal on me that I didn't do. Just to shut me up. They hoped that I would slink off like I did at the bank, and that rat bastard otherwise known as Ganiff would get off free and clear." I was excited. "I got the power!" I rushed over to my father and gave him a massive hug. "I love these father/daughter conversations, Dad. You help me out all the time."

My father had that shell–shocked look about him. "Okay, Linda. I gather you found out how to resolve this?"

"Dad, I have the ammunition. Now it's time to get all my ducks in a row."

"What is that supposed to mean?"

"Oh, I have to compile evidence. Get witnesses. Affidavits. You know, all the stuff it takes to make an unbreakable case." I hugged my father again and gave him a big kiss on the forehead. "I'll let you and Mom know when it's over. And then we're gonna celebrate!"

I put on one of my more corporate outfits and brought along a yellow legal pad. It took forever to get down to City Hall on the Lexington Avenue subway. But, hey, I didn't have a fixed schedule or a job that would compel me to rush.

I disembarked from the train, trudged up the steps and found my way to the New York State Department of Corporate Filings located on the first floor. I submitted my requests at a reference desk, and then grabbed a seat. It took three and a half hours. I spent my time twiddling my thumbs and fidgeting on a broken plastic chair amidst assorted clerks, until… "Ms. Lane, I think this is the file you're seeking."

A woman in a tan cardigan sweater handed me a thick manila folder. I let out a low peep of excitement while reading the contents.

Back home, I peeled off the suit and stepped into a pair of jeans. Then I cleaned off my desk, just like the way I cleaned Ganiff's desk. Same effort, energy and efficiency. At least I wasn't as bad as him. It didn't take much time for me to go through my amassed papers and place them by topic into folders. I put everything in order.

Pulling out another yellow pad of paper, I sat at my desk and wrote an outline to my budding plan. I felt grateful for having possessed the foresight to bring home ample information as a starting point. I needed a few additional things to put the plan into action, namely inside help. And I had to move fast. Fast because of the old adage: out of sight, out of mind. The longer I stayed out of contact with my friends at the hotel, the harder it would be to persuade them to assist me.

My first call had to be to Big Guy. When I last laid eyes on that mug, it was in front of the employee entrance right by the loading dock. He couldn't bring himself to look at me after having witnessed my exit interview with Vared. And afterwards, when I turned around mid–way down the block, I caught him staring at the ground, forlorn and lost like a bioengineered mutant six–foot five–inch puppy. It had almost broke my heart. Now, with reluctance, I dialed his direct extension.

"Hello. Security," said Big Guy.

"Big Guy? Please don't hang up. It's me, Linda." He did not respond. I thought I'd break the ice. "How's the lip?" No response except for the sound of his breathing, a firm indication that he didn't hang up. "Hey, I know what you heard—"

"Can't talk to you," he spoke in a hushed tone, "and decidedly not from here. I'm on duty in the Lobby. Tons of people around. How about calling back some other time?"

"Wait, wait, wait! Don't hang up. Please, one minute. Don't go yet."

"It's not safe. Not here. Not now. Murlise... she's down here scrutinizing everyone."

"Okay, fine. I've another idea." Thinking quickly now. "Do you have a mobile phone on you? A personal phone, one not from the hotel?"

"Yeah, I got one. I still can't talk to you now. How 'bout giving me your number? I'll call you later."

We exchanged numbers. I was about to hang up when Big Guy's mood brightened. "Okay, the coast is clear. Murlise entered the elevator. Talk fast."

"All right. I'll talk fast. Or better yet, let me call you on the mobile."
I disconnected the call and dialed the ten digits he provided. The phone rang twice. He laughed as he picked up.

"You are something. Nothing changes, business as usual."

"C'mon, Big Guy. Talking about... we did have some funny lip–locking business going—"

"Very funny, if you want to know!" He spoke like a little boy, "Five stitches and it now passes for a harelip."

"Oh, my! Sorry about that. Do you think it'll change your CPR technique?"
I laughed, then quieted myself. *What was I, suicidal? I needed this man!* With a little coyness I added, "Should I give you a kiss to make it better?"

Big Guy laughed. "Don't threaten me! I'm gonna have to wear protective headgear to accept one of your kisses!"

"If you feel that way, the threat's on! I do need your help, though."

"As long as you don't kiss me," he suggested again with merriment.

"All right, all right, enough with the kisses. Here's the deal: I know you know I didn't steal the sheets and towels. Ganiff and Vared used that as an excuse to can me. I can prove it. Seriously."

"You can?" He sounded as though he were prepared to give me the benefit of the doubt. "I don't know about this. If you can really prove that they lied about the theft, then yeah, I'm listening."

I pumped my fist in the air. Coming through the line was his walkie–talkie with a muffled announcement. "Copy that," he replied to another party. Then he refocused on me.

"Hey, I've been thinking about this since I last saw you, Linda. What's so strange about the whole thing is that this was the first time I ever heard of stolen sheets and towels. You'd think they'd contact me as head of Security, right? I mean, if they thought something of that magnitude was being stolen..."

"Well, for what it's worth, I believe that Vared's innocent in all of this. It's Ganiff who's behind it all. The one–eyed mastermind."

"Can you prove it?"

I laughed. "Big Guy, I have one question: Is there paper in your fax machine?"

He dropped his mobile with a clunk and fumbled around before he picked the phone back up. "Yes, for once."

"Do not, I repeat, do not let what I'm going to fax you in the next five minutes get into anyone's hands at the hotel. Read it and shred it. Capisce?"

"Understood."

"Okay. You have my home number now, so I'm gonna hang up and fax you some papers. Call me back after you read them." I disconnected and turned around to my mini–home office and faxed the copies of Ganiff's handwritten tri–party contract I had typed up a few weeks before. *Thank goodness I had the foresight to copy these documents while I still worked there.* I was completing the *New York Times* crossword puzzle when my phone rang.

"Unfuckingbelievable," said Big Guy, enraged. "The fucker blamed you when it was his son–in–law! I think, that's the gist of it, right?"

I coughed. "Trust me, Big Guy, it wasn't even his son–in–law. It was him."

"What? Are you sure? Do you have proof?"

I patted the separate manila folders neatly stacked on my desk. "Some. I'm working on getting more."

"Linda, I knew you didn't do it. How could you be a thief? You're too anal to do stuff like that. Plus, you don't seem like the type to steal sheets. Not your style. But… Certainly chocolates or cakes. Conceivably cookies and croissants. Definitely donuts… Perhaps pastries…"

Before he could continue through the rest of the dessert alphabet, I cut him off at the pass. "Okay, okay, why, thanks. Had no idea you monitored my eating habits. Now, let's get back to the situation at hand, the Ganiff theft thing? I've still a long way to go to nail the bastard. I may need to rely on you for a few favors. Quite a few, as a matter of fact."

He lapsed into silence for a few moments. "Depends on what I have to do. I'm kinda getting a bad feeling here." The wheels turned in his head. He said, "That Ganiff, he jeopardized my men by keeping a small security staff. He fired you and ripped off his own hotel. Not in that order, but I'm wondering what else that man did. I mean, I didn't know about the thefts and… and…"

I did a mental countdown, and by the time I hit "one, blast–off," Big Guy exploded with rage. "That fucker! I knew something was up with him, I mean, who in their right mind would hire a South African ex–mercenary for the head of human resources?"

I spoke softly to calm him, "Big Guy, I have a plan to take him down. Are you with me, or what?"

"Shit, I dunno. Would it involve anything illegal?"

"Of course. Well, sort of. Just not with us. We're the good guys. Here's what I need: a one–time pass into the hotel and a little cloak and dagger from you. I gave you the fun part."

"Sounds risky." He exhaled. "Go on. Tell me more."

"Hey, rumor has it that you still have contacts with the FBI. Is that right? I'm talking The FBI, not the Food and Beverage Institute."

"Funny you should ask. I'm still in touch with this one FeeBee, Wilson. We recently met up at a reunion lunch. We go way back when we served together in Lebanon in '84. Pretty cool cat, when he has the time for me."

"Oh, you do know someone! A great start. Do you think he'd like to do a sting on Ganiff? Investigate illegally gotten gains from the sale of the stolen linens and other shady activities?"

"Wait a sec, Linda. You want me to phone a FeeBee about short sheeting? Give me a break. Stolen linens aren't that huge a deal. Certainly not a federal crime."

"Yeah, well how about Ganiff's involvement in a porno company?"

"Say what?" The phone hit the floor. Half a minute later he spoke again. "You telling me Mr. Bible Man is dabbling in skin flicks? You're shitting me!"

"Big Guy, I'm not. I can prove it."

"Yeah, well, porn is more like it. It's more Wilson's style. Sheets, shit! That'll make me a laughingstock. Let me call you back, Linda. This is gonna be sweet… if you can pull it off. You know, for my two men who got hurt."

Satisfied, I hung up the phone.

Step One falling in place.

★ ★ ★ ★ ★

"Hi, Trish. Remember me?"

"Oh my God!" Trish's voice dropped a few decibels. "What happened, Linda? You okay?"

"Yeah, I'm hanging in there. Am I getting you at a good time?"

Her chair squeaked. More than likely, Trish spun around to survey her surroundings. "We can talk now, Linda. If I have to go, I'm just gonna hang up. Don't take it personally, okay?"

"No problem. So tell me what's been happening since I have been gone."

"Oh, Linda, there's rumors all over the place. That horrible woman, the other Linda, took over your spot. All sorts of craziness. Murlise is drowning in her bad occupancy stats. Seebok and Ganiff are forever tied up in meetings."

Meetings? I had to laugh. I informed her, "Trish, I was fired."

254

She gasped, "I knew it!"

"Hey, don't listen to gossip. Trust me on this one. My firing was a sham."

"Yeah, I figured," she said.

I had to tread on eggshells. "My pal, I have to ask a favor from you. I know that it may jeopardize your job but we're close and you'd help out a friend, right?" Before she could get a word in, I added, "Who was the one who carried you out during the Seebok slaughterhouse; kept you from being trampled by rubberneckers? Who was the one who backed you up during the burn and slash revenge by Alletti? What about when Doreen and Seebok were murdering each other? Huh? Have you ever had a better friend at the hotel?" I held my breath.

Trish laughed. "We had our share of fun, didn't we? Yeah, no one else here's done so much for me." Without warning her voice choked up, "I miss you so much. Seebok's so dreadful. He won't even talk to me or give me any work. I know he's looking to fire me." She raggedly inhaled. "What do you want me to do?"

"A few things, but we'll do them together, just like old times."

"Really? Gee, Linda. Sounds like fun. Something I don't have much of these days. Okay, I'll give you my home number. Phone me when you need me."

"Trish, thanks for being there for me! You're a good friend. Oh, one last request…" I hesitated for a moment, not knowing how she would react when I dropped the bombshell. "I'd appreciate that you befriend the bad witch, Linda."

"What?" she cried in revulsion.

"Trust me, my dear. It'll pay off. You'll see!" I said in an upbeat manner. Shit, I couldn't even convince myself.

After what seemed an eternity, Trish reluctantly agreed. "What I do in the name of friendship."

Step Two in place.

My back was killing me. I'd spent too much time contorting my spine into a question mark from slouching in front of my home office. I decided to go for a little walk around the block, or as my father would call it, "a constitutional."

I enjoy New York City summer weather. If I'd still been at the hotel, I would've been insulated from the experience. Even in the late afternoon when the heat had relented a wee bit, the 'hood retained its native Manhattan odors: fried food, vomit, urine and garbage. I inhaled this indigenous perfume deeply. It cleared out the cobwebs in my mind, and effectively suppressed hunger pangs. I stretched my back one last time in front of my building and reentered, ready to continue my war games fully engaged.

Back upstairs, I sat down again at my desk and dialed a very special number on my phone. "Veronica! Hi, it's Linda!"

"Linda! The good Linda, I presume? What you up to, girl? Where've you been?" Veronica sounded happy to hear from me.

"Well, before I get to the purpose of this call, let me get you up to speed on current events. As you gathered, I'm no longer at the Supreme Superior. Ganiff fired me to get me out of the way."

"Whoa, Linda! Sorry about your job, I feel terrible."

"Don't. Trust me, I'm better off being far from there. Something big's going to go down with Ganiff, and I don't want Tony's reputation to be tarnished by association. Giving you a sneak preview because Tony's a real nice guy."

"Say no more, Linda," she said, "let's put it this way, Ganiff abused his so–called friendship one too many times. That crazy videotape business was the last straw for all of us. He phoned so often that he fried our lines. And before that, he was bugging the crap outta us for forty free front row tickets at Carnegie Hall. That's the entire front row! Let me amend that statement—it exceeds the front row!"

I let out a good laugh. *Typical Ganiff.*

Veronica said with disgust, "Who the fuck does he think he is? He's not an old friend of Tony's! They knew each other eons ago, but friends, hell no. You know what? I'm glad you gave me the heads up. It's a great excuse for us to sever ties with him. Don't you worry, I'll tell Tony that something's up."

"Well, this is a nice segue," I said. "I need a little favor."

"No problem, Linda. After what you told me, I'll help out as best I can."

"Veronica, all I need you to do, with Tony's permission if you can get it, is to make one phone call for me."

"Just make a phone call? That's it? No sweat. Isn't that what friends are for? Give me the details."

"I'm setting it up. Let me get back to you a little later."

Phase Three in progress.

★ ★ ★ ★ ★

It took me six hours and eight versions to perfect it. Voilà, a mini–masterpiece. I addressed a five–page letter to the attention of the five Board members representing Japanese senior management. Someone had to advise them of the fact that their hand–picked General Manager was ripping them off. There was always the possibility that they may already have known about it and had not gotten around to remedying the situation. In that event, my letter might sufficiently incite them to action.

At the closing of the letter, I debated on–and–off whether I should provide my name as author. Something told me that there might be severe penalties should

I go down that road. I phoned my father who knew a thing or two.

"Oh, Linda," he said, "if I were you, I would keep my name out of this and off that letter. You have no idea what might be in store for you. There could possibly be horrendous legal ramifications. Unless you want to wing it and let the chips fall..."

Dad had a point. Why bother going down that avenue with forecasted dire consequences? Not putting my name on the letter might protect me from legal worries. I could always be "Anona Miss." Though I wondered whether my nameless allegations would be discarded as frivolous and unfounded. In addition, they might be looked upon as the rantings of an unhinged former employee with a chainsaw to grind. I then decided upon an amalgamation of the two options.

At the onset of my illustrious career at the hotel, I had carried to my apartment a box of Supreme Superior letterhead in case I had to do correspondence from home. I never had the occasion to use the stationary. Too many long hours spent on premises. The box rested in the bottom drawer of my desk. I pulled it out and added twenty–five sheets to my printer. I made the assumption that Japanese management might not readily discard a letter from an anonymous malcontent former employee when printed on their very own embossed stationary.

The letter, in essence, described intimate details of the whole laundry morass, the costs that the hotel absorbed for the Ganiff weddings plus bible conventions as well as the alteration of the contractor's bids. I topped it off with the kickbacks that Ganiff had received from Nikrovetch along with the bank account information.

I made certain that the letter contained serious insider details such as:

"... upon the recommendation by Mr. Ganiff who strongly urged you to use a laundry contractor... Baldwin Laundry LLC was awarded an exclusive laundry arrangement with the Supreme Superior Hotel. What you were not informed of was that this company is ultimately 100% owned by Mr. Ganiff as per the New York State Department of Corporate Filings. This clearly constitutes a conflict of interest. On a weekly basis, Mr. Ganiff's company receives on or about $25,000 payable by hotel check that is then deposited into Mr. Ganiff's personal demand deposit account at Marine Midland Bank, #374000810293. This can easily be verified by reviewing the back of any of the cashed checks where you will see the endorsement in Mr. Ganiff's name and handwriting... Also, please note that there is in place a tri–party arrangement between the Supreme Superior, Baldwin Laundry LLC and Clyde Hammergesundschmidt which dictates the reimbursement for 'lost' linens. As of the date of this letter, no reimbursement has ever occurred. There is conjecture whether there shall be any reimbursements whatsoever..."

Knowing these executives, not even an ocean half a world away would impede them from getting back their money if they concurred with my allegations. I also wondered what they might do to the Gang of Three. Those guys knew absolutely nothing. Of this I was certain. Sadly, this situation could only result in the death knell of their careers. *Perhaps*, I rationalized, *if they spent more time questioning what was taking place at the hotel instead of perfecting the New York Times crossword puzzle... Then again, who was I to judge?*

Along with the hotel stationary, I had also brought home a copy of the confidential directory containing phone and fax numbers of the executives in Japan. I bent down under my desk, where I had placed my fax machine, and fed it the five pages which I faxed five times—once for each of the Board members in Japan. Then, in case they didn't receive my faxes, I placed the printed hard copies into airmail envelopes and went for a stroll to the post office.

Let's see the efficiency of my letter writing campaign. It may end up even more impressive than my save–your–ass memo at GermBank.

Step Four completed. Now I had to pull it together. Maybe even have a little fun in the process.

Chapter 35
July 1995

Big Guy and I met at a bar on the Upper East Side. He brought along his friend, introduced as "Bob," and the three of us squeezed into a booth for six. Both Big Guy and Bob were oversized hunks of macho and muscle. I sat across from them. I was feeling the love instantly.

After the waitress served us our draft beers, Bob took the lead. "So, Big Guy told me what transpired. Let me see if I got it right. This Ganiff guy set up a dummy company that washes hotel linens and towels. You're also telling me that his company has an exclusive arrangement, right?" Bob's eyes pierced right through me.

Big Guy and I assented. I reached for my handbag which bulged from the manila folders containing documentation. I had at my fingertips the papers obtained from the New York State Department of Corporate Filings. "Yeah, I have a copy of the ownership status of his company right here with me." I thumped the top of my handbag for emphasis.

Bob sighed. "You two are aware that this constitutes a serious conflict of interest, right?"

Big Guy and I exchanged glances. *Of course we knew!*

Bob rolled his eyes. "O–kay." He shrugged, then took a sip of his beer. "Now, what I deduced is that this company has been stealing linens and towels for the secondary market, right?"

Once again, Big Guy and I nodded.

"This so–called evidence… If your claim is true, you're gonna need to prove it beyond the he–said, she–said scenario. Otherwise, it's your word against his. He's still the boss, while you're a former employee with an ax to grind."

"Well, I have a copy of Mr. Ganiff's handwritten contract here. It is an admission of theft as well as an indication that he intends to further his laundry scam." I reached forward and handed Bob the manila folder containing the incriminating papers.

Bob studied the pages carefully, his face giving nothing away. "Interesting." He took another sip of his beer. "Mind if I hold onto this for now?"

Out of the corner of my eye, I looked over at Big Guy. He shook his head in approval, as if to say: *sure, you can trust this guy, no problem.*

"Um, sure. I mean, I've copies of it at home."

"It's safe with me." He tucked the paper inside a cellophane folder and stashed it in his briefcase. "Okay, moving on, so we've got illicit income. Ganiff's company steals linens and towels for, I gather, resale and makes money on it. That's not where he has his illegal gains. Or rather, that's a small part of the equation."

"Correct," I answered, flashing Big Guy a smile, "it's the tip of the iceberg."

"Well, good." Bob looked fortified. "Because, while the linen thing is pretty serious, it's not by itself a crime for the Feds to handle. So tell me about this construction thing." Bob pointed his thumb at Big Guy. "My buddy here gave me the gist, but he doesn't know what you know."

I leaned forward and brushed an errant strand of hair from my face. "Ganiff gets kickbacks from all big contracts conducted at the hotel. The most recent one is from Nikrovetch Contractors. They're doing the current upstairs renovation on the hotel. Ganiff had me personally deposit the check into his account at the Bank of the Cape. Incidentally, I believe he uses that account for all his kickbacks."

"Do you still have this account information? How do you know it was a kickback?" Bob replied.

"Well, for starters, Calvin Nikrovetch, owner of Nikrovetch Contractors, told me the whole arrangement. The man has no stop or pause button when it comes to disseminating information. You know, what they say in the banking business, follow the paper trail? Now, as for the account number, I have it right here." I pulled a single yellow Post–It note from another manila folder readily at my disposal, and placed the note in front of Bob.

Bob raised his mug in salute. "Hmmm. Sounds like we're getting warmer." He took a sip of beer, lowered the mug, then reached into his rear pocket, displacing Big Guy who almost fell out of the booth. "Sorry there, Big Guy."

He pulled out a tiny pad of lined paper and pen. "Gotta let the IRS know about that, because that's capital gain, illicit, or not. Either way, he's gotta pay taxes."

While he jotted down notes, his little pink tongue stuck out of his mouth. Captivated, I failed to drink my beer. Big Guy, ever observant, kicked me under the table, almost breaking my shinbone in half. I shot up in the air knocking over everyone's beers. Big Guy signaled the waitress and motioned for another round. I mopped the excess beer off the table with the napkins from the canister.

Bob ignored the surrounding action. He was all business. He took the Post–It, stuffed his mini–notepad in his breast pocket, and peered at me. "Moving forward, you say Ganiff was also aligning himself with two other partners to invest in a video porn company to launder his money?" Bob glanced over to Big Guy, then at me. "Money laundering. Now that's illegal. Investing in porn, while it may offend some, is not."

Big Guy and I shrugged. *Damn! Here I took for granted that the porn thing might be the juiciest charge in my arsenal.*

The waitress served us another round. Bob took a sip from his frothy mug. After that, he pointed at me. "Laundering non–disclosed capital gains from unlawful activities is illegal. Think Al Capone. Remember, it wasn't Elliott Ness that brought him down. It was the IRS." He reached for a napkin and wiped the foam off his upper lip. "I'm thinking here. I shouldn't be telling you guys this..." He reconsidered. "Hell, I believe you guys're trustworthy." His voice dropped to a husky whisper and we had to lean into him to hear what he had to say.

"Right now we're working a major new case involving a video company specializing in kiddie porn. It would be terrific, and a helluva lot more fun to combine this case with your Ganiff one." He became contemplative and said, "I don't want to throw any monkey wrenches into this major case—it's too big and we want it to go down kosher. Let's see what you have on Ganiff's video company and then maybe we can do something, preferably above board."

That sounded like a good idea, though not necessarily what I wanted to hear. Well, it's a start.

Bob explained further, "Lemme put some thought into this." He paused. "Here's how I see it. Hypothetically speaking... Let's say we were able to nail him, or rather implicate him on something sordid. He wouldn't be able to wiggle out of those charges. Even if he does, his reputation will be shot to hell. It's a win–win situation for us."

Big Guy and I clanked our mugs. Bob turned to Big Guy and said, "This is the guy who pared your staff down to nothing and caused two good men to be maimed for life?"

Big Guy confirmed via a succinct nod. Bob looked back at me. "You don't fuck with us people in law enforcement. We're a brotherhood, thicker than blood." He gulped back his remaining glass of beer, then swiped mine for good measure and polished it off. "Okay guys, I'll be in touch. See if you can get your hands on a little more hard evidence."

"Wait!" I said, "one more thing." Both macho men stared at me. "One of the last things I did at the hotel was book a stay for the Ganiffs at the Sands in Puerto Rico. The timing was highly unusual, and moreover, the Ganiffs rarely travel anywhere. Bob, do you think Ganiff might use this trip as an escape route for the future? I mean, are there extradition treaties in force between Puerto Rico and the U.S.?"

"Possibly, Linda, it could be," Bob responded, "he might want to squirrel some of his money there, but isn't Puerto Rico part of the U.S.? Let me play devil's advocate: perhaps he and his wife were truly vacationing there." He sighed. "Well, I gotta check it out anyway because it may be another deal he's involved with. I'll be sure to get back to you on it."

Big Guy slid out of the booth to let Bob pass. I stood up to shake Bob's hand and he tossed a twenty dollar bill on the table.

We sat back down again when Bob departed, briefcase in hand. Big Guy had tears in his eyes. "Linda, thank you!"

"For what?"

He clasped my hands, leaned forward and gazed into my eyes. "For this magic

261

moment, and…" he noticed me cringing because he leaned back and said, "the opportunity to get back at that fucker."

I extricated my hands from his paws and we both shared an intimate smile. I whispered, "Call me when Bob reaches out." I stood up, leaned forward and gave him a peck on the cheek. Not the kiss I promised. Then again, he didn't wear protective headgear. All the same, he looked satisfied.

★ ★ ★ ★ ★

Kenin was next on my list.

I knew that Kenin frequently worked late hours. When I returned home, I called his direct extension in the room service department. He sounded pleased to hear my voice.

"Oh wow! Linda, how's it going? Anything's gotta be better than slaving here at the good ship SS."

We gossiped for a few minutes about the latest hotel news. Then I got down to business.

"Have a little favor to ask. More like a prank, really."

"You naughty little minx! I'm all ears, Mary."

I wasn't about to volunteer any more than this small part of my plan. The part where I get to disintegrate Ganiff's mental and financial well–being. Well, my hat was off to Ganiff—he taught me well. Now I intended to employ his tactics… on him. As I heard from him many times: "Imitation is the greatest form of flattery." Hope he will be sufficiently flattered.

Kenin's enthusiasm demonstrated that he eagerly wanted to play along.

"Remember that ordeal with the busboy that Ganiff fired for chucking out a piece of old junk?"

"Oh, Gary Yong. How could I forget? Man, did he ever get a raw deal!"

"Yeah, well how 'bout a little poetic justice for him? As well as for me, too?"

"Wouldn't that be sweet? You know the Indonesian bible boy who Ganiff brought in to replace Gary? Not that you'll be surprised, Ganiff managed to get his hooks into the kid's first year's salary. He quit last Friday when he figured it out— with a little help from Ronny," Kenin laughed out loud, "who was pissed because he didn't get his cut."

All of a sudden, that angry feeling took hold again. Not that I felt any particular affection for the bible busboy, but still… "Wow! Same shit, different day. It never ends, huh?"

"Linda, what're you thinking? What's your little trick–or–treat gimmick?"

"Okay, here's the deal." I drew in a deep breath. "After the whole fiasco with Gary Yong and Koneman went down, Ganiff asked me to dispose of that piece of shit. You know what I mean, the cigar holder. I decided not to toss it. For some reason, I kinda knew it might be valuable one day, so it ended up with Lydia, the cold chef, for safekeeping. Sure as hell didn't want to store that turd in my desk drawer."

Kenin chuckled. "Like I blame you. That thing is Nasty with a capital 'N.' Where is it now? What on earth do you want me to do with it?"

"You need to ask Lydia. I know she kept it in a safe place, lord knows why. I want you to get it from her and stick it in one of Ganiff's brisket sandwiches. The ones you bring up to him what, three times a week for lunch? A little extra gravy that day and he'll never know the difference."

Kenin laughed. "Oh, Linda, you sick woman! You want the guy to eat that piece of shit? Literally?"

"Well, maybe not eat it. I don't want him to choke and die, or anything." *He better not die because I have much better things in store for him.* "It's to gross him out. Besides, he'll never be able to chew it. He'll spit it out as soon as he bites into something leathery."

"I don't know. I mean, sure it would be funny, but someone's bound to get fired for a stunt like that. Shit, Ganiff's so paranoid, he might fire the whole kitchen and room–service staff just to retaliate."

"No way, Kenin! Not these days. He won't be able to fire anyone with the way the hotel union is breathing down his neck. They'd make his life a living hell. The last thing I heard before they fired my ass was that the union's already threatening sanctions over housekeeping violations. Unless he can directly prove who did it, he's basically powerless on personnel moves. Trust me."

"What if he traces it back to me? Linda, I can't lose my job over this. I don't know about you, but I need the paycheck." Kenin sounded a mite frantic.

"Kenin, there's not a chance he'll think it's you. First off, you're his one shining star out of the whole food services staff. Second, he's never had a beef with you— other than those brisket sandwiches. It's not like you'd have any motive to get at him. Plus, as far as he knows, that piece of turd was thrown out for the second time. The last time he saw it, it was carried out of his office with ice tongs."

He sounded skeptical at best. "I don't know, Linda."

"Well, do what you think is best. Weigh the risks versus the rewards. Just let me know your decision. However, please take into account the most important ingredient—the legend factor..."

Kenin laughed as I hung up the phone.

I wanted to visit my parents although I wasn't ready yet. We spoke on the phone a few times, yet I demurred when my father suggested that I stop by.

263

"Linda, honey, your mother and I don't understand why you don't want to come over," said my father who sounded hurt.

"Dad, it's not that I don't want to come over. I want to wait until all this stuff is done."

"What stuff are you talking about?" he asked, now sounding upset. "Wait, did you put your name on that letter?"

"No, Dad. What I'm doing is putting my life back together. It's about retaliating at the hotel."

My father exhaled on the other end. "Forget about that place, Linda. Why don't you use your time productively, like getting a new job?"

"Dad!" I shouted, "remember the conversation we had about GermBank? About how you told me that I should've done more?"

Dad gulped. "Yessssssssss? I didn't forget."

"Well, this time I am doing more. I'm no longer anybody's patsy. I have to stand up to my fears. I want to stop that karmic thing of repeating my mistakes." I stopped and inhaled. "Dad, this time around I'm gonna win. Going forward, I'll never have to go through this ever again."

My father sighed; this time he sounded frustrated. "Linda, I love you and I support you in whatever you do to push your life forward. Now listen, kiddo, I don't agree with what you're doing. However, just because I don't agree with what you're doing doesn't mean that this is not the best thing you can do."

"Huh?" I asked. Too many dos, don'ts and double negatives.

My father sighed again. "What I mean is, go for it. When you get it out of your system, I'm sure you'll be up to bigger and better things."

Well, it wasn't the vote of confidence I wanted. As the song goes, *"you can't always get what you want... you get what you need!"* And with my parents behind me, I got what I needed.

★ ★ ★ ★ ★

With some free time on my hands, I needed to do something different. Something I had experimented with once. A terrific splurge and an excellent way to spend an afternoon.

I had to get rid of the toxins within myself. All those repressed emotions, all that stress carried inside, all ten months' worth. It had to be sweated out, pummeled out, shredded out. What would be better than a Korean spa experience?

I don't recall who had originally introduced me to Korean spas. Nevertheless, this was one of the most potent activities I had ever endured. When I entered the spa, the head matron remembered me from the previous time although it must've been well over a year. I guess they hadn't yet recuperated from my shrieks of pain.

"Ms. Lane, welcome again," said the petite Korean woman dressed in a beautifully tailored uniform. "Correct me if I'm wrong: weren't you comfortable being naked?" she congenially asked.

I smiled back. "Yes, only indoors with women." *That didn't sound right,* I reflected and then let it go. I paid the fee up–front and she escorted me to the dressing room. I proceeded to strip.

The spa in itself was gorgeous. It took up the space of an entire floor, the length and breadth of a city block. Located in a nondescript office building in the "Korea Town" neighborhood of Manhattan, the entire room was tiled in exquisite colors ranging from gold to rosy pink to aquamarine blue. It was empty except for the women who worked there; they were naked as well. The head matron followed me into the spa area and gestured to a shower where I rinsed off. She then accompanied me to a small tub the size of a suburban backyard pool.

"Today's selection is a green tea bath. Normally we prefer a mango one but too many people kept siphoning it. Enjoy!" She left me to my own devices.

The water was scalding! Every inch of me smoldered as I lowered myself into the tub. A layer of my flesh peeled off in one fell swoop, moderately alarming me. Several analogies about the hotel then came to mind. Mostly thoughts about purging the filth associated with that place from my body. While my eyes were closed, someone placed a tray on the lip of the tiled bath. I looked over to see displayed on top half a sliced pineapple, mangoes, papayas and bottled water. Partake I did.

At long last, another woman nudged my body to the sauna. The room bore a resemblance to a tiled igloo from the outside. Inside, the heat took my breath away. At this point, I wondered what I found so wonderful about this whole spa scene. The door swung open and the same woman gestured for me to take another shower. I washed and she brought me this time to a glass enclosed circular steam room. I struggled to breathe within the moist scented mist. It may've been jasmine, though I wanted much–needed oxygen.

At that moment, I must've started to hallucinate. Oxygen–starved, I became convinced that Ganiff paid off the women at the spa to kill me, to finish the job he began with that first lunch at the hotel. I couldn't see anything through the thick steam and was just about to succumb to my paranoia when a door opened, parting the billows of steam. A soft woman's voice said, "Please follow me, Ms. Lane."

While in this limp and weakened state, I was escorted to a table, where still another naked woman wearing loofah gloves exfoliated my entire body except for two sensitive areas. Twice. She poured tubs of water all over my body to cleanse me off. Finally, she massaged me—the highlight of my afternoon. It felt good when she walked on my back even though that, as well, resurfaced vivid images of the previous ten months. So many analogies, such limited time! After a few facials, my hair shampooed and conditioned, I was done.

Three and a half hours after entering this lavish den of equity, I dressed in my clothes. I felt refreshed like a new woman whose past had been scoured both from the inside as well as the outside.

★ ★ ★ ★ ★

I woke up the next day, sat up in my bed and couldn't arch my back or straighten my limbs. I threw off the bed covers and examined my arms and legs. They were black and blue. I crawled out of bed, and hobbled to the bathroom mirror. My entire back had blood specks from the exfoliation. *Oh damn! It happened again just like the last time.* Healing would occur in a few days, as per past experience.

Two hours later, armed with a massive cup of coffee, I hunched over my command post in the corner of the living room. And then my back gave out. I had to get up for a few minutes to stretch. After I sat down again, I pulled out my yellow revenge tablet and reviewed the checklist for today's activities.

Trish phoned, hysterical with laughter. She sang, "I know what you did!"

"Trish? Hey, thanks for calling. Did I do something?" My rueful laugh betrayed me. My fingers were crossed that Kenin delivered.

She was giddy. "The sacrifices I make in the name of our friendship!"

Now I wasn't sure where she intended to go with this. "Um, Trish, what's the good word?"

"Okay, I did as you asked. I befriended Linda Luppner. Or at least I tried to like you asked. I gotta tell you that she's no fun at all. She just spends the day on the phone gossiping, running errands, getting manicures, pedicures, facials, massages—"

I intentionally coughed, interrupting the shopping list.

"Oh, sorry, Linda, where was I? Oh yeah. I stopped by her office around ten minutes ago. We heard a high-pitched shriek from behind Ganiff's closed doors." She giggled. "You shoulda seen him. He ran out with this piece of shit in his hand, gagging, trying not to throw up. He kept saying: 'What the hell is this?' Later, he made Linda phone Security."

"What happened next?" I was curious, on pins and needles. At the same time, I had a twinge of guilt that someone could've gotten in serious trouble.

"Big Guy and Johnny came upstairs. Ganiff was flashing this piece of shit; screaming about how it was in his lunch, and that someone was out to poison him. Turns out it wasn't shit. It was plastic. Anyhow, he was acting all weird. He said that until we find the perpetrator, he can't eat food in the hotel again."

Ah, so far so good!

"Then Big Guy started asking questions." Trish deepened her voice and said, "Who do you think would have the motivation to do this to you?" She switched back to talking like herself. "Then Ganiff started listing tons of names. A few I recognized: Koneman, Housekeeping Carole, Nick Alletti, Iggy Two, the Missus, the hotel union, Clyde, his son–in–law, Keith Robenstine, Calvin Nikrovetch, Joe Smith, Donald Silverberg, Elizabeth Taylor, Mortimer Wilbur and the guy who lives on the top floor of the apartment building."

So many names. I had to shift position on the chair because my back ached. "Wow! That's some cast of characters. You sure that's all of 'em?"

She laughed. "Big Guy left Johnny to write it all down. He's still there."

"What about me? Did you hear my name?"

"Not by the time I left. Isn't that extraordinary?" said Trish with jocularity, "you're probably small potatoes compared to all the people he screwed over the years."

Damn, I didn't even merit enemy status. *Well*, I thought, *I'm getting warm.* "Say, could you do me one more small favor, Trish?"

"Depends. Is it gonna be as much fun as what you did today? I mean, you were right about befriending the bad Linda. What a nice pay off! I don't know if I can handle all the excitement."

I chuckled. "Can't promise it but we aim to please."

"Tell me what you have in mind and I'll let you know if I'm up for it."

"Okay, here's the deal. I need the dates for Ganiff's annual Born Again function. Also for Reba's wedding, you know, Ganiff's daughter. I need to know how many rooms are booked for each, and the amenities he ordered. I have an idea." I heard her pounding on the keyboard. I said, "Not too terrible a chore, right?"

"Aye, aye, capitain. I'll do my best although it's gonna be a little hard."

"Why is that?"

"Murlise has been having fits about the convention, it's no secret. I'm kinda scared that if I start asking her questions, it'll get back to Seebok and then he'll get suspicious and then I'm gonna get fired."

"What about Luppner?"

"Forget about her. It's always all about her." She quieted for a moment. "You know what, I'll work my magic with the guys in banquets. Believe I should be able to pin it down. Call you back as soon as I get it."

"One last thing. Seebok has a file somewhere in his office. Your office. I don't know if it would be in his computer or in a cabinet. It may be labeled 'Hamsterland Productions.' Think you can find it?"

She put me on speakerphone. I heard her spin around in her chair. She opened the metal filing cabinet. For my benefit, she read aloud in alphabetical order, "Let's see here… Alletti, Big Screen TVs, Catering, Doreen, Djorak… no, nothing under 'H.' Could it be under another name?"

"Yeah, try under porn! It's gotta be there somewhere."

"Damn!" cried Trish with revulsion, "he's got a porno file! This is so gross, he has a file and it has those nasty old dirty magazines inside. I think they're... used. Is that what you're looking for?"

"No, no. There must be a Hamsterland file somewhere. Keep looking if you can."

She rifled through more file folders and gave me a running commentary for each and every piece of paper. Finally, she let out a whistle and I almost dropped the phone receiver.

"Ah, here it is! Hamsterland. Had it filed in a folder labeled 'Generation X." Now what?"

"Okay, when it's safe for a few minutes, fax the contents here to my home. Presuming the pages aren't all stuck to each other."

"That's gross! Damn, the things you make me do. Seriously, it's no problem." She fiddled with the papers. "Give me a few minutes to fax it all, okay? Seebok's down in Ganiff's office. Something about a double feature."

I padded away from my desk and stretched. Despite my aches and pain, my skin felt taut which, I guess, was a good thing. I already placed the faxed papers on Hamsterland in a manila folder. A little light reading for later on in the day. Trish, true to her word, sent me another fax, this time with the other info I requested. She did have friends in good places. Time to place another phone call.

"Hey Veronica. About that favor we talked about?"

Those precise words had been uttered often enough when I worked for Ganiff. Odds were that there wasn't a Tony Tenneb concert that a Ganiff family member didn't attend. I phoned not because I was looking for tickets or backstage passes. I hunted much bigger game. I wanted to bag me a prized Ganiff.

"You must mean a favor as in payback's a bitch?" Veronica burst out in laughter. "You know, Linda, you have extraordinary timing. Would you believe that Ganiff's new Linda just called me for like the twelfth time this week? She's been plaguing me to ask Tony to sing at Ganiff's daughter's wedding. I keep ignoring her."

"Hmmm, how predictable! That's precisely why I phoned. I have the info. All I need is for you to make that call that we talked about. To request reservations for the 14th and 15th." I filled her in with the salient details that I had gotten from Trish.

Veronica pondered for a moment. "I'm okay with it. Let me talk to Tony to get his green light, or at the very least to warn him. Incidentally, I advised Tony about what you said the other day concerning Ganiff. He sends his thanks for looking out for him. Hey, we all look out for him here. In that vein, it'll be a good thing to disassociate him from your former boss. I gotta discuss this with him, but you know Tony, nice to a fault, not willing to hurt the man's feelings. Oh, wait, he just came in. Hold for a few minutes."

With the phone to my ear, I was serenaded by a tinny muzak version of *Best is Yet to Come.*

Veronica picked up as the song faded out. She sounded thrilled. "Sorry to keep you waiting, the other lines were ringing. Oh no! I forgot to speak to him about the phone call. I don't think it's a problem at all! When should we do it? How 'bout right now?"

I would've jumped out of my seat if my back weren't so damn sore. "Can I be placed on the conference line? I want to hear it go down." I gripped the phone even tighter with anticipation, not exactly the same adrenaline jolt that I had gotten accustomed to in my months at the hotel.

"That's the easy part. The hard part is not to laugh out loud. Or better yet, keep your finger on the mute button."

"Veronica, I love you for doing this! Don't you worry, I'll keep perfectly silent. I'll do my laughing on the inside."

"Okay, let me do one thing in between. I'll call you back in ten minutes. Do me a favor, don't say a word when I patch you in, okay?"

After I hung up, I quickly phoned Trish. She answered at once.

"Seebok Murray's office. Can I help you?"

"Trish, sorry with all the phoning today, but you have to find some excuse to hang out with Linda Luppner in the next few minutes."

"Hey, Linda. This better be good. I was about to head downstairs for lunch. Thought this time I'll have some Sara Lee cake."

"Oh, it should be worth your while. Just get yourself to Linda's office. You'll see."

"Wait a second. Is this something about his lunch?" Her question and subsequent laugh set off alarm bells in my head. Maybe sending an eyewitness wasn't the best idea.

"Trish, please act with discretion. Don't let them know you're onto this."

She took a deep breath, then let it out slowly "Okay. I'm fine. I'm better now. Okay, okay, I'm heading down. Let's talk later so I can give you the post–game recap."

Moments later my phone rang again. My caller ID box displayed Veronica's number. I picked up the receiver and stayed perfectly silent. She spoke to Linda Luppner.

"Linda, I'd like to speak with Mr. Ganiff. It's about the request for his daughter's wedding."

A half–minute later, Ganiff's slick voice greeted us. "Ah, Miss Veronica! So pleased to hear from you so soon."

Ganiff had always been great with conversational foreplay. The chronic problem for him remained his inability to sustain it.

"So, will Tony be available to sing at my daughter's wedding?" Typical Ganiff, going straight for the jugular.

Veronica sighed. "Mr. Ganiff, Tony would love to, however, his schedule precludes any engagements during that time." She lapsed into silence for several seconds. "Maybe… No. I don't think I can get him out of it. It may not work."

Ganiff grabbed at the bait. "What's the problem? Perhaps I can assist."

"Oh, Mr. Ganiff, if you could help me out, you would be a godsend, and maybe then…" She let the sentence hang.

Ganiff practically achieved orgasm. "Anything, sweetheart. Let me know what I can do."

Veronica dropped all friendly pretense and launched into her professional demeanor. "Well, as you know, Tony contributes to many charities. A few of them want to come together and honor him in New York, his hometown. They don't have enough money for the rooms, the food, conference rooms and cars because all their money goes to their good works. These companies are not–for–profit. Do you think the Supreme Superior could sponsor them?" She dropped the professional voice and simpered, "He'd be so indebted to you." I had to hold back from roaring in laughter when I heard her speak like that.

Ganiff said, "I don't see any problem. How many people? What are the dates?"

"Oh, figure around 175 rooms," she said in a matter–of–fact way. "Sorry for the short notice. It should be in two weeks, the 14th and 15th. Reba's wedding is when? In a month and a half, right?"

"Wait a second, Veronica. You said, 175 rooms on the 14th and the 15th?" His voice sounded slightly nervous, his enthusiasm wilting, as probably was his organ.

"Yes, and if they can have at least three conference rooms for those two days and nights as well? I know it's last second, and I heard that there's on–going construction… This is for a good cause. And Tony'd be so pleased."

The silence on Ganiff's end of the line was magical. Or neurochemical. After a while, he spoke. "Can you give me a little while to sort things out here?"

"Yes, please, Mr. Ganiff. Please try to get back to us as soon as possible. Tony's rather anxious for all this to be resolved."

After Ganiff hung up, Veronica made sure to disconnect that line for our snickering session.

"You are evil, Veronica. I believe you enjoyed it as much I as did listening!"

"You think? Oh, by the way, I made sure to put aside two front row tickets for us at his next Carnegie Hall concert. Of course you're invited backstage and to the dinner."

"Thanks. Send my best to him, okay? Let me know what goes down."

"Will do!"

I hung up and clumsily danced the funky chicken for about ten minutes in my living room, trying to overcome the constant back pain. Then my phone rang, interrupting the electric slide portion of the dance.

"Linda, what the hell's going on? What did you do?" asked Trish, "Ganiff is freaking out!"

"What happened?" *Damn, too bad I'm not a fly on the wall. Double damn. Is there no way to connect Ganiff's conference table intercom to my home phone?*

Trish provided her on–scene commentary. "After Ganiff hung up the phone, he made the other Linda get Joe Smith and Murlise. Something about a request for a hundred and seventy–five comp rooms on the same nights as his bible freebees! They're still going at it."

"How so?"

She couldn't stop giggling. "You're way too bad. I know your style. Here goes. If Ganiff bumps an additional 175 paying guests on those two nights and uses all the remaining conference rooms, well, that's like 25% occupancy for two nights during one of the busiest non–seasonal periods to hit us in five years, according to Murlise. She's screaming bloody murder about her occupancy runs and how to justify this to the Gang of Three."

"Is that it?"

"No, there's more. Give me a sec. I scribbled it all down." She rifled pages in the background while humming. Finally she said, "Joe Smith is flipping out because all his revenues are already crippled by the construction project. He said that with the feeding frenzy from both groups, he'll have zippo. Losses for two straight days. It's bad enough he's paying for a full staff with half the work. Having in place a full staff, losses and no tips, that's rock bottom."

Ganiff found himself faced with a choice: either get rid of his annual religious group, or say no to his idol, Tony Tenneb.

"You are a bad girl," Trish said, and then hiccupped.

"Ah, you have no idea how bad. Stay posted, okay?"

As luck would have it, I received a surprise phone call the following day. Too late, I picked up before checking my caller ID. The number on the machine belonged to Jay Krieger.

"Linda, I'm sorry to hear about everything."

"How did you find out? Wait. Fucking Steven Koneman, right?" I was furious that Koneman would be sharing my plight with Jay. Not that I expected anything less.

"Yeah, the lowlife was euphoric that he got his Linda babe back again. The two of them are conspiring, I'm certain." His voice turned sharp, "Say, why did you ignore me, Linda? Why did you chase me away? What did I do wrong?"

I felt deflated. "Jay, it wasn't you. It was—"

He said tersely, "Linda, don't give me that shit." He mimicked me, "Oh, it wasn't you baby, it was me." Then he said, "Shit, I'm old enough to handle whatever you have to say."

Old enough? Oh, yes. Like an LSD–induced nightmare, the vision of Jay's wrinkled body splayed on my bed flashed before my eyes. I shuddered. "Jay, I want a man who's free and clear of his past, not with one foot mired in it. I want a man who has the strength to make a commitment and keep it strong. I don't think you have it in you to do that. It's a deal breaker for me."

Jay sighed in frustration, not unlike the sound he made when I rolled away from him in bed. "Linda, I understand that. I wasn't exactly an exemplary husband both times nor a good father. I get it. Even so, a man can change, right?"

I coughed. "Usually after a near death experience like getting struck by lightening." I paused. "Twice."

"Or, by finally meeting the right woman."

That shut me up. I tepidly laughed to dispel the tension. "Okay, Jay. You got me good."

He cracked up on the other side. "That should teach you to fuck with the master."

"The master–bator?" I ventured, "I'm guessing after you left my apartment that time…"

We both laughed. The sun shone once more and happiness was restored in the kingdom.

"Knowing you, Linda, I bet you haven't left that hotel all that quietly."

"Moi?" I asked innocently.

"Well, if you ever wanna get back at anybody especially that asshole, Koneman, I'm at your disposal," he paused for effect, then softly added, "even if not, honey, please know that I'm here for you should you ever need me."

I smiled at the fortuitous possibility. "Thanks, Jay. I'm sure we'll be in touch down the road."

I didn't know how soon.

★ ★ ★ ★ ★

Dinnertime was rapidly approaching. I was trying to decide on whether to phone in Chinese takeout, or to go for a walk and pick up some malted milk balls when Bob gave me a call.

"No fucking way, just no fucking way."

"Give me a clue, Bob. What are you talking about?"

"You know those Hamsterland papers you faxed me?"

Before I could get in a word, Bob was off and running. "My sources tell me that they are exactly one of the companies we've had an eye on!"

I thought, *how the hell did Seebok do that one?* Out loud I asked, "How the hell did that happen?"

"Linda, hear me out. Okay, what probably went down was this: instead of phoning Hamsterland, a quasi–soft porn video company, your pal Seecrock—"

"Seebok," I interjected.

"Whatever… Let me explain, please. Your pal Seecock contacted and established a relationship with the elusive man–boy video porn enterprise: Hamsterfish."

"Huh?" I said. Now this was an interesting turn of events if not downright scary.

Bob continued, "Now, everything I'm gonna tell you has to be confidential, okay?"

"Okay."

"It's about this guy in L.A., this Koneman. He happens to be one of those guys who plays it a little too much on the edge. I mean, he's a bona fide PR guy although we know for a fact that he reps several porn companies." Bob stopped for a moment. "Sorry, let me look at my files." Paper rustled in the background. Bob then said, "My take on it is that this Koneman guy must've accidentally given Seebop the wrong phone number, probably from a list. I'm gonna make a professional intuitive leap here: Koneman must've misread the contact info from his roster of clients. Think about it: Hamsterfish, Hamsterland. Freaky, huh? At least this eliminated some clandestine operation on my side to get them involved." Bob chuckled. "What're the odds?"

"Well, the odds are favorably on your side when my buddy–boy Seebok's involved." Then I laughed. "Bob, it's absolutely amazing what a genius that guy is in fucking up. It's like he steps in it! Wait a sec! All those documents I sent you are in the name of Hamsterland. What the fuck is wrong with that guy? Did he bother to check the name of the company he's dealing with?" I laughed some more. "Even more amazing is that Ganiff would put him in charge of all of this." I felt that this may be a death wish on Ganiff's part.

"Here's something weird, as if it could get any weirder," said Bob, rifling through paperwork. "We hunted for this company for years without success. Now lo–and–behold, we're finally able to pinpoint them because of the size of the wire transfers into a known laundered account. Your man Ganiff or Seeclock, or whatever the fuck his name is, stepped up our investigation. They perpetrated their own sting!"

"I'm just... blown away. Do you think Ganiff will get jail time? What else, if anything, do you need from me?"

"As a matter of fact, yes to both questions. Both Ganiff and Seecrok and their trusted associate, Koneman, could face hard time. It's not yet a slam–dunk. If we want to make these charges stick, we have to prove guilt beyond a reasonable doubt. Still some key papers missing."

Bob proceeded to give me a few more details. All came together even better than I could've imagined.

I went to bed early that night and dreamed of sugar plum fairies.

Chapter 36
August 1995

Big Guy woke me with an early morning phone call. He had explicit instructions from Bob.

"Got something for you, a package that you need to pick up. Put on your best disguise and get on over here. How about in an hour? I'll meet you at the loading dock."

"Whoa there, boyfriend. You can't be serious."

"Oh, I'm totally serious. Sorry for short notice but Bob called me—"

"Wait! There's no way I'm going back there with all the shit that's about to go down. Plus, everyone knows me at the hotel. Remember, I'm persona–non–grata. If I even come on the premises for a drink I'm as good as arrested. You know the deal!" This proposition terrified me.

"Linda, you have to disguise yourself well. It's not all that complicated. I'll help you with the rest. And don't worry about being arrested. I'm still in charge of Security."

"Big Guy, this doesn't make sense. Why can't you have the package dropped at my apartment, whatever it is? Have Trish bring it up here on her lunch hour. I'll even pay for the cab fare."

"You need to come here for more than just the package," he said. He was adamant. "Bob needs other Ganiff stuff to dredge up. You alone know where to find it. I wouldn't know where to begin."

I checked my bedside clock. 7:45 a.m. "If it's that crucial, I guess... I don't know. I mean, what if someone catches me? And why do I have to do this during business hours? Isn't it safer if I came by later at night? Or on Saturday?"

Big Guy yawned. "Look, I'm sorry to make you do this. I know how nervous you'll be. The reason you need to come during daytime is because Ganiff's office is usually unlocked even when he's not in it, like during lunch or during his drinking binges. On the weekends or at night... it's the only room in the place that I don't have the key for."

I sat up on the edge of my bed. My neck cradled the receiver. I stretched my hands over my head. *Great, no more stiffness. I'm almost good as new.* The way Big Guy laid it out, I couldn't avoid this return trip to my personal house of horrors. Not if we intended to finish the job we started. "Okay, I'll see what I can do. Hey, I'm not even dressed for the day. I need some time to shower and to pull myself together. If I have to get into Ganiff's office, guess I should sneak in during lunch hour? Might be fewer people wandering around."

"Yeah, I guess that makes sense. All right, let's say twelve–thirty. Call me on

275

my mobile phone before you get here so I can meet you round back."

I lay down again in bed, long after Big Guy had hung up. Everything in my plan thus far had gone swimmingly well. However, the idea of breaking into my former boss's office had me feeling like I was the criminal. I could even feel my heart accelerating with each passing moment, something that had not occurred very often in the weeks since I was fired.

Well, at least I have the perfect disguise, I reminded myself. Years before, I purchased a wig as part of my Morticia Adams of the Adams Family costume for Halloween. At the last moment I chickened out. I remembered stashing it in a hatbox at the top of my bedroom closet. I pulled it out, knocked the dust off and tried it on in front of the mirror. I pondered, *whatever possessed me to purchase this?!*

Later, after I showered, I put on the wig and cut bangs straight across, then added black–rimmed glasses and caked on layers of pale make–up. Next, I stepped into a pair of tight jeans, threw on a décolleté black top, and slid into a rarely worn pair of black butch boots. I was the picture of a freaky gothic lipstick dyke. So many mixed signals that would dissuade people from getting too curious. Not even my mother would recognize me in this get–up!

I arrived at the hotel at a quarter past twelve and phoned Big Guy from a payphone on the corner.

"Okay, I'm here. Black wig. Lots of face paint. See you soon."

I arrived at the loading dock and walked right up the concrete steps unmolested. Based on the foul odor emanating from the nearby bins, it was laundry pick–up day. Or the later–than–usually–scheduled Alletti garbage pick–up day. Scarily enough, the odors were identical.

"Hey, I thought you were coming in disguise!" Big Guy called to me from a side entrance. He laughed as he stepped near me.

"What? You can tell it's me?" What the hell was his problem? Why couldn't he see a difference between my natural blond hair and this jet–black wig? Was the man blind? Or had my disguise already failed me?

"The tits, my girl. The tits say it all."

I looked down. *Damn.* I turned my back to him, pulled my shirt free and rummaged underneath to remove my bra. My breasts, freed from fabric and underwire, moved down an inch or three. "Well?" I asked when I turned around, bra in hand.

Big Guy licked his lips. "Much better. Maybe I can assist a little more." He moved forward, his two hands extended towards my chest.

"Get away from me, you freak!" I shrieked, then giggled. I turned around again to put my bra back on when he said, "No. Keep it off. Trust me on this."

He handed me a small package wrapped in brown paper which I placed in my plastic Duane Reade shopping bag along with the bra.

"Linda," he whispered, "this is from my guy, Bob. He's got a little gift for us. Something that'll help him keep closer tabs on our pornographers. While you're in there, I'm gonna need you to plant them."

I nodded as we walked slowly into the building through the service entrance. All at once, I turned to him and asked, "Well, why not you, Big Guy? Why me? I mean, you're here. You have access."

Big Guy raised a paw in self–defense. "There's a limit, Linda. Bob knows that. In my capacity, I've already surpassed the parameters of my contribution." He gazed at me with indulgence. "This is after all your war, Linda."

We went up the back stairwell to the fourth floor. I felt sweat pouring down my forehead, ruining my already horrible make–up job. I knew we would never encounter Ganiff here. The man probably hadn't walked up a flight of stairs in two or more decades.

Big Guy stopped me on the landing between the third and fourth floors. "Wait here! I have to check if the coast is clear. Be right back. Oh, and here's a little something in case of an emergency." He handed me a small walkie–talkie. "Just in case I need to warn you, or if you urgently need to reach me."

I tucked the device in my shopping bag and stood alone on the landing, wondering how I had gotten involved with this madness. There was no question in my mind that I had to take Ganiff down. My only concern was the method. This clandestine operation left me feeling a bit out of my league.

I reflected over the past two years. *What a radical change in my life! More like a downward spiral from banking executive to where I was now: fired, unemployed, standing braless in a concrete stairwell wearing a Dawn of the Dead faux lesbian outfit, waiting to gain entry into my former boss's office to do lord–knows–what under a quasi–legal guise. What if I get caught? Arrested even? How do I parlay that into my resume? Would it demonstrate my resourcefulness, creativity, out–of–the–box thinking and initiative?* I shook myself out of my reverie. No time to lose focus now.

Big Guy poked his head through the doorway to give me the thumbs–up. Must be hitting Seebok's cage first, I guessed. Side–by–side we walked down the corridor to the designated office. Trish opened the door and drew me inside. Big Guy pulled the door shut and remained stationed outside.

"Linda! Love the look!" she squealed. Soon, she had her arms around me in a warm embrace and said, "So good to see you again, you devil."

I extricated myself from her octopi arms after a few moments. "All right, Trish. Love the hugging but we don't have much time."

From the shopping bag, I pulled out my bra. She seemed confused and inquired, "Are you planting your bra so Seebok's wife will find out that he's been cheating on her?"

I laughed. "Good guess. No, I took it off because of Big Guy."

"What? You wanna run that one back for me?" I could tell that her initial elation had worn off.

"Feggedaboudit." I pulled out the envelope that Big Guy had given me. Inside was a small piece of paper with the following instructions:

> *Should you elect to undertake this mission, and trust me you have no fucking choice, take the three bugs and place one in the first office and then phone: 595–6755 to notify us that this has been done. If there is any additional info lying around pertaining to the company in question, secure it for us. Likewise, do the same with the two bugs in the second office. Also, while you're in the second office, secure blank checks from the two banks in question along with any recent statements. After this mission is completed, eat this piece of paper. It's edible and the paper and ink are made of rice. It's sugar–free too.*

From the envelope, I pulled out a small metal disk, this one no larger than a watch battery. I removed an adhesive tab from the back and stuck it on the bottom of Seebok's phone base. Then I looked up to find Trish staring at me.

"Let me make a phone call."

I picked up Seebok's receiver and dialed the number on the paper. A man answered. "Hello," said Bob's contact.

"Hi, I'm calling from Seebok Murray's office. All clear?"

"Yeah. We're receiving right now. Thank you Ms. Lane."

"Gotchya."

I hung up. Trish couldn't wait to get me out of the office.

"What's next, Linda?" she said with an edge.

"One more pit stop. Ganiff's office."

Right at that point, Big Guy poked his head in. "You two ladies done yet?"

Inspiration struck. "Give us a few more minutes." He turned around and closed the door behind him. I pulled out a floppy disc from Seebok's desk and placed it in his computer. I crossed my fingers when the password icon was prompted.

"Trish, do you know his password for this?"

She did not answer. Instead, she leaned over me, typed in the word "boobs" and hit the enter button.

"You know, Linda, you were right. He treats me as invisible. The thought never even crossed his mind that I'm monitoring his every move. Arrogant prick."

I rifled through Seebok's file directory until I came across the specific folders concerning Hamsterland, Deviant and for good measure, Alletti. I hit the save button and waited thirty seconds until the disc drive stopped humming. Then I tapped the eject button and pocketed the disc. "Stuff for me and insurance policy for you, Trish."

She smiled back at me with a knowing look. Once more we hugged and she appeared relieved. I opened the door into Big Guy's back. "Okay to go?" He grabbed my elbow and we walked double–time back to the employee staircase where we raced down one flight. "Okay, Big Guy, this is the hard part. Are you sure that no one's at the executive office?"

He nodded. "Linda left for her daily waxing appointment."

Wow, must be a lot of hair going on down there. Any relation to Yeti? I wondered.

"Ganiff is down in the Lounge binge drinking which he's done every day since you were fired. Even more so now that he refuses to eat the hotel food. It'll take a sec. Be right back."

He left me once more at the stairwell. I stood there thinking back on all the time I'd spent in this miserable place. I wondered, *what would Ganiff's reaction be if he caught me here? Hopefully, he'd call hotel security and not the actual police. Or, I might be the one who will have to call the police 'cause if that man ever found out that I was the wizard behind the curtain who had been orchestrating his demise, he'd strangle me!*

Minutes later, Big Guy returned. This time he arrived with a second set of footsteps behind him. My heart skipped a beat. BeeBee entered the stairwell.

"What the fuck?" BeeBee and I said in unison.

I almost fainted. I grabbed onto the metal railing for support.

Big Guy spoke, "BeeBee was there. I couldn't get rid of her."

"So you just included her in this?" I was incredulous.

"No, it's not like that. Seriously, she's on board with us. Got some heavy–duty issues with Ganiff because of Djorak."

BeeBee bobbed her head as acknowledgement. "She was my friend no matter what you all thought of her."

I wasn't sold yet. After all, she still merited an award as the most unreliable, uncooperative secretary ever known to modern day business. I turned to Big Guy. "Since when are you making the decisions?" My anger replaced my nervousness.

"Since I started risking my job for you," he responded.

"Point well taken," I conceded, "but I don't have to like it." Then I turned to BeeBee. "How did you know it was me?"

"The girls, Linda." She pointed to my chest. "Love that braless look!"

I glared at Big Guy. He pointed his walkie–talkie in my direction.

"The emergency word is 'Ganiff.' Our safe word is 'Vared.' Keep your unit on, but keep the volume low so no one else can hear me. Got it?"

I nodded.

The three of us peered out of the stairwell and swiftly tiptoed down the hall to the General Manager's office. My heart pounded with each step. BeeBee and Big Guy took sentry positions flanking the doorpost. *Discretion. Ah, you gotta love it.* As if what they were doing didn't look peculiar enough by itself.

I walked through the open outer door and entered my office—now Linda Luppner's office—and scoped around. Not much had changed since Big Guy had last escorted me out of there except for the mess in front of me. Linda's desk could not be seen due to the clutter of files and loose papers. Plus a few printed vouchers for an assortment of goods and services that she'd more than likely bartered in exchange for hotel suites.

It was now Ganiff time. I had never been so nervous to enter the room to my left, even on my worst day as his assistant. The mirrored door to Ganiff's inner sanctum was ajar. I inhaled and stepped inside.

This room was far messier than I had remembered it ever having been. Piles of papers strewn helter-skelter. I could tell that Seebok had spent quite some time there. He left his mark: dried out puddles of tea-stained papers stuck to the glass table. On top of Ganiff's desk were mounds of unopened envelopes competing for space against room-service trays, take-out cardboard containers with congealed food rotting inside and empty videotape cases. I couldn't help but smirk at the mess. Even in my wildest imagination, I could never have conjured up the scene before me; it was that bad.

Bob's note instructed me to get blank checks from each of Ganiff's three checkbooks representing his personal and commercial accounts at Marine Midland as well as his personal one at Bank of the Cape. That was easy enough. I opened his top drawer on the left and sure enough… I tore off the bottom two in each stack, so as not to raise immediate suspicion. Then I stuffed them in my shopping bag. Similarly, I rummaged through his desk drawers until I found the bank statements for the past three months for each of his accounts. They were loosely jammed in his bottom right drawer. Those, too, I tossed into the bag.

My next step was to bug Ganiff's office. Reaching inside the package from Bob, I pulled out another of the recording devices. I unscrewed the mouthpiece of Ganiff's old-fashioned phone receiver, slid in one of the bugs, then twisted the piece back on. I stuck the second bug on the bottom of the conference room phone. *Funny,* I thought, *all I needed before to eavesdrop on Ganiff was a faulty intercom system.*

I hadn't heard from Big Guy since entering the room. I checked my watch. 1:17 p.m. I figured I had at least twenty more minutes before Ganiff returned from the bar. *No harm in snooping a little more. Never know what one might find.*

Across from Ganiff's desk stood a metal cart on wheels holding a television on the top level and a VCR on the bottom. A videotape hung out of the deck. I ran over, snatched it from the machine and glanced at the title. Just my luck, his favorite: *Three's a Crowd and Tigger Too*. Talk about striking gold! I had just dropped the tape in my bag when I heard a commotion coming from the corridor. It was heading my way. I froze.

"Sir, I said you can't go in there. We're running a security check to make sure the new alarm system is working. Please come back in five minutes." Big Guy was doing his best to keep someone out of the office.

"What new alarm system? How come I wasn't told anything about this?" *Ohmigod, it was Ganiff's voice! He's here! So much for the walkie–talkie warning!*

Like a chicken without a head, I scrambled around the room for a place to hide. I eyeballed the piles of magazines next to the conference table and considered their height. Then I observed the crown molding over an archway to my left. It could be either a coat closet or Ganiff's private bathroom—a place no one had ever dared to enter other than the puppet master himself. His footsteps came closer. It seemed like my last resort, so I ducked inside and closed the door behind me.

Indeed, it was a bathroom. A small, simple bathroom at that. With a standard toilet, two towel racks, an overhead light fixture and, on one side, a sink resting on a vanity cabinet. Across from the toilet, a towel cupboard abutted the bathtub. In front of the toilet lay randomly scattered porn magazines. There were no windows to break out.

With both arms, I leaned against the sink, racking my brains to figure out an escape route. Big Guy's voice faintly emerged from my shopping bag. "Linda, he's coming your way."

Oh shit! I thought. *I'm so dead.* I resorted to my last ditch option: the towel cupboard. In a frenzy, I pulled open the double doors. The cupboard seemed barren on the bottom portion. The top shelves were filled with toilet paper and all sorts of Supreme Superior promotional paraphernalia, e.g., baseball caps, pens, Tiffany's keychains, items I never saw the entire time I worked there. I first stashed my Duane Reade bag on the bottom. Then, I ducked down into a deep squat and wiggled inside, leading with my left leg. At the same time, I contorted my upper body to fit right under the shelf above. That meant I had to bend my head against my chest. I carefully reached forward to close the doors. And almost had a stroke when a spare roll of toilet paper fell from above and toppled out as the doors snapped shut.

It was dark and claustrophobic inside the cabinet. Oxygen was at a premium. After a few seconds, a door slammed and footsteps walked nearby. I felt my heart thumping out of my chest, out of control. I felt close to fainting. The footsteps stopped by the closet and I realized with a deep, sinking feeling that he intended to use the toilet across from me.

I squeezed the handles of my shopping bag to my chest and closed my eyes. All of a sudden, there was this tremendous noise like someone tuning a tuba, and then an odor assailed my nostrils. An odor so rancid that it would make raw sewage smell sweet. I couldn't breathe and reached for a small washcloth pinned under my foot with one hand. Somehow I corralled it and lifted it to my face without making any noise.

He panted in pain from outside. "Sweet Jesus," he squealed, then trumpeted into the toilet. That was followed by, "Shoulda eaten my Wheaties!" which was punctuated by another blast from the sphincter. Seconds later he shrieked, "Damn, I forgot my V–8!" with the loudest sounding flatulence to which I had ever been subjected. *Damn,* I thought, *if he utters one more platitude, I might be blown to smithereens!*

This was way too much for me. Bringing him down for all the shit he did was one thing. Being subjected to this... he should be garroted.

The toilet flushed. Ganiff had left the bathroom. Without washing his hands. I spent the next few seconds dry–heaving. *Where the hell are BeeBee and Big Guy? Why didn't they save me from this ordeal? If they don't get me outta here now, I may perish. Then they will be obligated to honor my last request, that of a Viking funeral!*

They must've known I was thinking of them because my plastic bag talked. Or rather, it was Big Guy who spoke into the walkie–talkie, "Linda, can you hear me? I think he's out of the bathroom. Linda, come in."

I pushed open the cupboard doors with one hand. I filled my lungs with the foulest smelling air I had ever inhaled, outside of the time I visited sheep farms in New Zealand. To my dismay, sheep methane smelt considerably better. I finished gagging as quietly as I could. Then I untangled my body from the small enclosure one limb at a time and somehow silently crawled free to the tiled floor. I reached for the walkie–talkie in my bag.

"Hi, I'm still alive, but barely," I whispered. "Help! I'm stuck in his bathroom. Where the hell are you guys?" I gasped for air, but finding none, continued gagging. "Please help! I may die here from the fumes!" Once again, I stifled my gacking.

"Copy that," answered Big Guy, "just lemme think of something."

The intercom on Ganiff's desk buzzed. "Sir, I need to see you urgently for a minute."

"What are you doing on my intercom, Big Guy? What is this nonsense? Go away! Let me work in peace." He grumbled to himself, "What the hell is with these people here? Don't they have better things to do than to constantly annoy me?"

I peeked out through a slight opening in the bathroom door and got a view of Ganiff's profile. Desperate for fresh air, I placed my lips against the sliver of space. There was the sound of frantic knocking at Ganiff's office door. At first, he ignored the noise. Then, the door swung open while he sat at his desk. *How does he do that?*

I wondered for hopefully the last time in my life. Big Guy and BeeBee shouted from his doorway, trying to get him out of the office. It wasn't working.

I poked my head out of the bathroom. Big Guy stepped into the office and peered around in all directions until he spotted me.

"Mr. Ganiff, we may have a situation outside. A bomb threat next door. Can you come with me for a few minutes? It's a precaution for your safety."

I could see Ganiff behind his desk. "Bomb threat. Are we evacuating at the orders of the police?"

"No sir. Not the police. Just a precaution like I said. Might very well be nothing, but I'd rather be safe than sorry."

BeeBee made her grand entrance. She walked straight up to Ganiff's desk, blocking my view of him as well as his view of the rest of the room. "Sir, it's no big deal. Staying put is fine until we hear otherwise from the fire department. Now that I have your attention, can we go over a few things about your bible group's needs for this upcoming event?"

"Yes, BeeBee. What is it you need to know?"

While she peppered Ganiff with questions, Big Guy made eye contact with me and smiled. He headed for the office door and gestured for me to follow.

I rolled up the plastic shopping bag, stuffed it in my shirt and went down on all fours. I counted to five and then crawled across the floor as quickly as I knew how.

"So, from what church do you need me to order the bibles this time?" BeeBee did her best to distract Ganiff. "In the past you always had Linda do it. I figured I should get those details now. Oh, and what about the whore's divorce? Do you think we should go with egg rolls this time?"

I paused in mid–crawl. *Whore's divorce? What the fuck? Oh*, I realized, *she meant hors d'oeuvres*. Quickly, I picked up the pace.

"What the—? Whore's divorce?" Ganiff must've gotten it as well because he said, "BeeBee, since when do you get involved with these details?" He shouted, "Let's leave catering decisions to the banquet staff, and the rest of it to Linda. Now, don't you have a pack of Marlboros to smoke, or something?"

She had stalled him long enough. As I scrambled through his doorway, he bellowed, "What the hell is with you people lately? Don't you have better things to do than to disturb me all day long?"

When I had made it partway into my former office, Big Guy reached for me. He pulled me up by my arms and swung me like a rag doll towards the outer doorway, tucking me under his left arm. In the process, my Duane Reade bag slipped out from under my shirt; Big Guy bent down to grab it for me. He paused in mid–movement when an unfamiliar young woman walked into the office.

"Oh, hi Big Guy. Who's inside with Mr. Ganiff?" She looked at me. "Say, who's

283

that tucked in your armpit?"

"BeeBee's with Mr. G," Big Guy muttered as he tucked the bag into my receptive arms, "something about the bible convention. This here's… um…" He released me to stand on my feet, sliding one arm up the back of my shirt to keep me from toppling over. "Linda, meet hmmm…"

"Nice to meet you," said Linda Luppner who extended her hand.

Even in my frazzled state, I was perplexed or rather stunned not only by the lack of creativity exhibited by Big Guy in supplying me with an identity, but further by the unquestioning acceptance of his apparent lack of clarity by that nitwit, Ms. Luppner.

I refused to shake her hand or even to say a word. I pulled a Mrs. Ganiff and stared at the proffered hand. She did not appear miffed in the least. I ventured to guess that she was accustomed to a lack of manners given her association with the Ganiff family. Still trembling from my close encounter with Ganiff, I felt literally as well as metaphysically shat upon. In so many different and bad ways.

"Oh, um, she's from Czechoslovakia," Big Guy interjected. "She doesn't speak a word of English. My um…" He reached for my free arm and yanked me out of the office like a marionette. "Whew! That was close," he said as we headed into the stairwell. Without thinking, he picked me up to carry me down the steps. "Girl, you stink! What the hell were you rolling in back there?"

"It was Ganiff. He took a dump while I hid in his bathroom closet, and—"

Big Guy released me to cover his ears. "Say no more, Linda. Let's get you outta here."

We stopped as we hit the ground floor. I decided to double–check my shopping bag to make sure I still had everything I had come for.

"Let's see. Blank checks. Bank statements. Let's not forget those extra tidbits: My bra. Disc from Seebok's office. The videotape. Here's your walkie–talkie." I handed him the apparatus. "Talk about ineffective use of equipment. Okay, from what I can see, all is done." I put the piece of rice paper in my mouth, chewed twice and swallowed. After this ordeal, it didn't taste all that bad.

"Okay, you got it all? Let's go!" Big Guy patted me on the back. "I'd kiss you now, but first of all, I don't know what you just ate." He reflected for a moment. "You know, I don't want to know what you ate. Also, you must shower, or something."

"Why should it stop you now?" I smiled and proceeded to open the fire door at the bottom of the stairs. Big Guy stepped out first and I followed behind. "At least you can consider it unforgettable—"

A familiar voice stopped us in our tracks. Karen from Security. "Hold up there, cowboys and cowgirls. Where do you two think you're going?" She approached us only to grab me by the arm. "You walk by me and don't say hello, Linda?"

"How did you know it was me?" I asked her, dissembling again.

Karen took my hands and steadied them. "The tits, lady. The tits. Remember, if you ever need a good woman, the offer still stands."

I glared up at Big Guy who had a silly grin on his face. He threw his arms up in the air and gave an innocent shrug. "Sue me! Except that sexual harassment only applies to people you still work with."

Karen giggled too. "So, aren't you gonna give your friend a hug for old times' sake?"

I went to embrace my former colleague except for one problem: I reeked.

Big Guy whirled me around and said, "You didn't see Linda and you didn't see me. Now we gotta go. Save the hugs for another time."

Karen gave him a two–finger salute. "Gotchya." She winked at me. "Stay cool, Linda. By the way, Gothic is a good look for you."

There are a wide variety of home remedies to remove odors from people and/or dogs who have been "skunkified." In my case, I had been "Ganiffied."

I spent the next two days immersed in at least half a dozen ritual tomato juice baths alternating with milk baths, trying to rid myself of the horrid smell. Also to recondition my hair. Above all, I needed some introspective time to consider my options now that I joined the ranks of the gainfully unemployed. I had no idea what to do with myself. Every time I flipped open the *New York Times* job section, angry memories of my departure from the Supreme Superior broke my concentration. I couldn't get back on track, and knew deep in my bones that I would be sidetracked until the chief criminal was out of commission.

Then it hit me. Dealing with this smelly stuff. Olfactory and otherwise. The missing link, the ingredient that I had inadvertently put aside: Steven Koneman. A stinker in his own right. I had to get him directly involved on the receiving end of this. How?

My bath–time was cut short as the phone rang.

"Linda? It's Murlise. How are you?"

Murlise, I thought, *how the hell did she get my home number? I'm certain I didn't supply it.*

"With Doreen."

"And Edwing too."

Oh Shit! What the hell do these people want from me? It's time to change my home number.

"Hi guys," I tentatively said.

"We know you're up to something," said Murlise, always to the point.

"We want in," piped up Doreen.

"Wait a second! What're you crazy kids talking about? How are things back at the hotel?" I tittered. I felt naked. I was naked. I grabbed a bath towel and wrapped it around myself. Now, back to the topic at hand. While I trusted Big Guy with my very life and BeeBee was a necessary evil who had proved her worth back in Ganiff's office during my hands–and–knees escape, Murlise and I were not even close. And I didn't know Edwing all that well. Let's not mention Doreen, that backstabbing, thinging canary. *Great, this is just what I needed!*

Murlise spoke, "It's no secret that you're behind the turd–burger, even though Ganiff doesn't know it."

I denied the accusation but Doreen's voice overrode mine.

"Furthermore, Linda, it hath become more and more efident that he'th up to thinithter thingth. I'm thorry I ratted on you."

My temper flared. "Oh, Doreen, so it was you who cost me my job! Well, thanks for being trustworthy. All I was trying to do was vent a little and—"

"Linda," Edwing said, "the man wants to kill my rep in the marketplace. He keeps insisting I use this horrid travel agent. So it's either me or him."

Murlise followed. "It's all about him now. He wants to take over three–quarters of the hotel for two non–paying functions. I'm putting my foot down. It's either me or him."

Doreen didn't say a thing.

"Oh, Doreen, for heaven's sake, tell Linda why you joined forces with us," nudged Murlise.

"Oh, all right. For the patht year Ganiff'th been ruining my corporate blockth for hith perthonal gainth. I lotht out on my commithionth. Theferal of my corporate clienth aren't coming back." Doreen sounded almost convincing; she should've been an actor.

"Enough of the bullshit, Doreen, tell her the real reason why you're joining forces." Murlise called it, all right.

"Fucking Theebok ith acting like the big kahuna now. He hath Ganiff'th earth. Probably hith ballth too!"

Oh, I figured it out. The hotel cartel. The variable political factions had shifted again. Since my departure, all the diversified interests now merged into two camps: the department heads vs. Seebok and Ganiff.

To allow these untrustworthy people into my plan—a plan that already included a Federal kiddie porn sting, Federal tax evasion and money laundering—seemed both overkill and completely unnecessary. Plus, involving them in any shape or form would compromise my revenge should someone change sides which was almost a given.

"You know what, guys? I appreciate you calling to check on me and all. Honestly, I'm through with the hotel. I'm moving on with my life. So, I thank you for your call. I appreciate it. Maybe we can do lunch one day once I get settled in whatever my next job may be."

Doreen shouted, "Linda, you're tho full of shit."

Murlise chimed in. "You're keeping all the fun and glory to yourself!" Each voice clamored and overlapped the other: "You're thelfish!" "Don't come running to us when it backfires."

I quickly hung up the phone and marveled.

What presumption to contact me in order to help them out! Where were they when I suffered all those miserable months? Not a single helping hand. To quote Big Guy: Unfuckingbelievable.

I proceeded to disconnect my phone line.

★ ★ ★ ★ ★

The next morning, I found a note shoved under my apartment door. It read:

Linda—In the future, don't disconnect your phone without advising me first. Meet me at corner of 53rd Street and 7th Avenue. 2 pm today. Black cargo van. Knock on the back—Bob PS. This paper is NOT edible. Do NOT eat as you will choke and die.

I found the van parked alongside a fire hydrant. I knew that this was my FeeBee vehicle because of the specially tinted windows. What really gave it away was the small sign displayed on the driver's dashboard with the words, "Federal Bureau of Investigation."

Since Big Guy was on duty at the hotel this particular afternoon, I arrived solo at the prearranged time and pounded on the rear doors of the van.

"Who is it?" sang a male voice in falsetto.

"It's Big Guy," I replied in a brutally deep voice.

Bob unlocked the back door, poked his head out. "Okay, great. Come inside. Did you bring the package?"

I stepped on board and scanned the interior. The rear of the van was set up like a movie set. Outfitted with a desk and laptop computers as well as the mandatory team of three, all wearing headphones. I handed Bob the sealed envelope.

Bob ripped off the top flap of the package. "What have we got?"

"It's the blank checks from Marine Midland and the Bank of the Cape. I didn't forget to bring the statements for all the accounts. I also have in there a printout from a disc which includes all the Hamsterland documents, plus other deals that they did in the past."

Bob rummaged through the contents.

The whole operation made me curious. "How's the sound with those bugs I planted? As per your instructions, I stuck them in highly accessed areas so you should be able to rock and roll."

Bob moved to the front of the van. With a jerk of his head, he motioned for me to follow. We sat in the two bucket seats up front. Bob tapped the envelope edge against the steering wheel, impatient to move on.

"We started to record last night. This Ganiff guy went ballistic for a few hours because he couldn't find a videotape. The screaming almost short–circuited our equipment in the back." He gestured at the rear of the van with his thumb. "Let's say this: he certainly loves his porn."

I let that last remark pass me by. "One request, Bob. You know the third party to this, Steven Koneman. It's all in the envelope. The guy's frequently in New York. Any chance we can nab him as well?"

Bob scratched his head. "Ah, the PR guy from L.A. Yeah, he's a slippery one. We're looking at him too. Real close… Let me tell you what's been going down." He peered outside of the van window to make sure no one was too close by. "According to my sources, Ganiff and friends were the ones who initiated this whole sting. We've got them on quite a few things. I'm working the IRS angle as well. Just hold your horses, all right? We have to run through this evidence," he said as he whacked the end of the envelope again against the steering wheel, "to prove ownership and tie everything up in a nice, neat package." He leaned over me to open the passenger door. "Linda, you're doing good work. Don't worry. Hang tight, we're almost there."

★ ★ ★ ★ ★

The phone rang the moment my key released the lock to my front door. Just my luck—Calvin Nikrovetch was at the other end of the line.

"Linda, what the fuck are you up to? Why didn't you warn me?"

Great, I thought, *another unscrupulous voice from the past got my home number. I better get this changed to unlisted, and fast!*

"Calvin? How pleasant it is to hear your voice. What's going on?" By his tone and volume, I knew that my anonymous letter to the Japanese management had had the desired effect.

"Do you have any idea what you did to me?"

"No," I casually replied, "I don't exactly work at the Supreme Superior anymore. You could say that I'm kinda out of touch."

"Linda, I was called into Ganiff's office last Thursday. He had a faxed copy of a letter that someone sent to the head office in Japan. Ganiff is clueless, but you and I know that it was you. Right in front of me, he ripped the construction contract in half. He wants to sue me. Even told me he contacted the IRS." Calvin stopped for a moment to switch gears into hyper–drive.

I used the small window of opportunity to say something. "Calvin, I don't know what letter you're talking about. I'm no longer an employee of the hotel. I'm out of the picture. Do you get that? Out of it!"

He didn't pay me any heed because he wound himself up and fired away. "Well, that rat fink can't cancel the arrangement. It's a legal document. I did everything above board. Well, almost everything. Don't worry, I'll come out ahead in this. Maybe a few problems with the IRS, but I'll have my accountant handle it." He pounded whatever surface was closest to him. "Let me tell you, Ganiff has his hands full, thanks to you. He confessed that the hotel owners in Japan don't want to press charges, they just want their money back. It runs into the millions. That's not even including his Born Again social event which they know all about!" He paused to catch his breath. "You know, he's relieved that he's not going to jail. But he firmly believes he can still pull out of repaying them. Exactly what he tried to do with the laundry situation, trying to pin it on you. But you nipped that in the bud."

I thought, *Glad I sent that letter!*

Calvin quieted for a moment. "Well, I wanted to kill you for this…" He paused for a moment. "You know what? It's okay. I'm a big boy. Kudos to you, Linda. Didn't know you had it in you." That was reassuring of sorts. Furthermore, the call wasn't a waste of my time because now I knew that the letter had produced results.

After Calvin hung up, I decided to contact NYNEX about changing my phone number. Getting a live person on the line was a major challenge. I had been sitting on hold for more than twenty minutes when my call waiting beeped.

This better be important, I thought as I clicked over to the other call.

"Linda, okay, let's call this 'quid pro quo' time," said Veronica from Tony Tenneb's office.

"What do you mean by 'quid pro quo?'"

She laughed. "Tit for tat."

I groaned, "I know what quid pro quo means!"

She replied with humor, "But not in this context! For the past several days, I've been tormenting Ganiff, having people from my office call him every half hour, just like what he does to me. So far he hasn't returned a single call."

With glee I asked, "Isn't there a deadline?"

"You got it! You wanna listen in again?"

Minutes later, Ganiff answered. His voice was a shell of its robustness while maintaining its pervasively slimy trademark. "Oh, I thought it was Tony on the line.

Miss Veronica, I apologize for not getting back to you."

Veronica spoke firmly, "Mr. Ganiff, my people have been calling for days. Tony's getting impatient. We need a response and we need it now!"

Ganiff faintly whispered something.

"What?" asked Veronica, "speak up, sir, I can't hear you."

"Please convey to Tony my utmost apologies," he said weakly.

"What?" asked Veronica again, "I still can't hear you!"

Ganiff emitted a heavy sigh of resignation. "Please tell Tony I'm sorry to let him down." There was a long silence before Ganiff said in a world–weary voice, "So, I gather that he's not going to sing at Reba's wedding?"

"You guessed right, Mr. Ganiff. Oh, about those ticket requests, sorry to let you down. Don't even consider calling here about the pilot television show. You screwed Tony, Mr. Ganiff. This is most unforgivable." With that pronouncement, she hung up.

Seconds later she phoned back. "How was that performance?"

"Not as good as Reba's will be when she finds out that her dear old dad screwed up! Now Tony won't sing at her wedding like he did at her sister's. Wouldn't you love to hear that one?"

After I finished my call with Veronica, my thoughts returned to Calvin and the likelihood that this guy could potentially harm me. He was not exactly mentally balanced. In all probability, he counted as the first fallout of my actions. After all, I cost him hundreds of thousands of dollars on the construction project. Calvin admitted that he had already considered plotting my demise, so I could only wonder how the rest of them would react when everything went down. Before I could spin wheels about the future, I had to handle the Calvin situation. How do I get this resolved and fast?

Bob answered his mobile phone from inside the surveillance van. Quickly as I could, I filled him in on what had transpired, up to and including the recent exchange between Calvin and myself. Before he could get a word in edgewise, I concurred that I had acted like a Wild West character by sending that anonymous letter to the Japanese executive management. I even fessed up to my slight fear that Calvin might change his mind again and chainsaw me into fish bait.

"What the fuck, Linda? What was going through your mind when you sent out that letter? You coulda jeopardized this whole operation! Why the fuck didn't you tell me this at the beginning?" Bob ranted, and not surprisingly, I found myself accustomed to this kind of behavior.

"Hey, I'm sorry. I didn't expect anything of it. In truth, I'm kinda freaked that it worked!" I said to dampen the screaming.

Bob quieted and said in a conciliatory tone of voice, "All right. I hear you.

We can't have you in harm's way, now can we? I wish you had told me about this earlier. It now kinda explains what's been going on there." He paused for a moment. "You stirred up a wasp's nest, all right. You have them all running around and fighting amongst each other… On second thought, it works out even better for us. We can help this Calvin out with the kickback situation if he's willing to testify for us. That could be the final piece to put us over the top."

"Yeah, I think he'll cooperate. The guy sounded kinda angry but—"

"Well, thanks for the info," said Bob curtly, "I'm in the middle of listening in on Ganiff. It's very juicy. I'll call this Calvin when I'm done, then will get back to you."

Hours later, the voice of a human customer service representative interrupted the drone of muzaked classical music. "Hello, this is NYNEX. May we help you?"

I provided her with all my pertinent information so that she could access my records. "What I'd like to do is change my current phone number immediately to a new, private one. Is this something I could do within twenty–four hours?"

"Ms. Lane, we could get it done within one to two business days. Though we do need you to put the request in writing. It would allow us to charge your account an additional monthly surcharge of five dollars for an unlisted number. Do you want to proceed?"

Hell yeah! I thought, *rather inexpensive for peace of mind.* "Well, considering I'm out of work at the moment, there's no reason why I can't do it right now. Can you fax the form to my home? I need one minute to switch over to the fax machine."

I was in the middle of filling out the request form when my phone rang again.

"Linda, is this guy a maniac?" asked Bob. He had lost his cool.

"Which guy are you referring to?" I played coy.

"This Calvin character. He's out of control. Would you believe he won't budge unless he goes into the witness protection program?" Bob was nonplussed. "It's a simple testimony. No one's out to kill him. Well, almost no one if you exclude me." Calvin Nikrovetch, in less than five minutes, had accomplished what no one else had been able to over the course of Bob's years as an unflappable FBI veteran: he had unraveled the man.

"Sorry, Bob. Did I mention that he's a bit of an eccentric? Throw him a valium. He'll call you back a little bit later when he kinda gets himself under control."

"Linda, I don't know what kind of testimony I can get from the man if he acts like this. He's unreliable."

"No, trust me, Bob. He has some pretty valuable information and the motive to put the final nail in Ganiff's coffin. He's worth the trouble."

Bob exhaled in a huff. "Okay, fine. I'll get written testimony for now.

The thought of putting him on the stand…" Then he switched gears. "While we're at it, I want to have a few words with you, missy." He sounded like he was about to deliver a stern lecture.

"Yes?"

"Look, Linda, I know you're playing every angle on your own. That's fine, as long as you don't interfere with my sting. No more of these surprises, got it? Keep me informed of any more left–fielders here in the ninth inning."

The phone company form was easy enough to complete now that I had a bit of quiet time. Seated comfortably at my desk, I compiled a list of all the things I'd already accomplished in my retribution plot against Ganiff:

★ Scared Ganiff from eating the food in the hotel. Probably Mrs. Ganiff too!

★ Worsened his drinking problem, a nasty side effect of my actions.

★ Enhanced his paranoia over the disappearance of his favorite porno videotape.

★ Cost him his friendship with his idol, Tony Tenneb.

★ Compromised his relationship with his daughter, Reba over the Tony Tenneb fallout.

★ Cost him a potential fortune, should he have to reimburse the hotel for unauthorized expenses.

★ Soon to come: IRS woes over unreported taxes.

Not bad for starters, I concluded. Even though there was still so much more to rectify. Needless to say, there were Ganiff's other outstanding problems that didn't even require my interference or nudging. They were of his own making:

★ The hotel association was seeking a renegotiation of the union contract for increased staff. If successful, it would surely minimize Ganiff's ability to steal, should he somehow manage to hold onto his job.

★ As per Big Guy, a major litigation was in the works against the hotel due to the security guard stabbing. The injured guards planned to sue their attackers, the Supreme Superior and even Ganiff personally.

Just a few more finishing touches and he'll feel the full wrath and vengeance of all the people he had wronged! Provided everything went according to plan.

Chapter 37

The following day passed by in a flash. I asked Big Guy to try and locate Carole for me. He couldn't find her through conventional means, though we both knew she was up and about because of some very unusual goings–on at the hotel.

Trish was the first to phone me with the news. It was obvious that I now had viable rivals in making Ganiff's life miserable.

"This is too rich," she said, "with what happened to the Ganiffs' suite!"

"Ah, let me guess. Did excess methane cause the place to combust?" Having had firsthand experience, I was all too familiar with this intimate aspect of Ganiff.

Trish giggled. "Along those lines. Bedbugs. Trillions of them. In the Ganiffs' marital bed and nowhere else in the hotel! You outdid yourself this time, Linda. How—"

"Hey, I swear, it wasn't me! Not this time."

It wasn't.

Trish still marveled at the deed. "The lady doth protest too much. You should see Mrs. Ganiff's face—it's blotchy and purple. She didn't do too well with the bedbugs, not as well as Mr. Ganiff who was bitten only on his arms. Such a fuss she's making! Mrs. G is upset because her friends at the Born Again shindig are coming and she said something like how she's no longer photogenic with the welts on her face!"

That should be the least of her worries. "That's all she's concerned about?" We both crowed over this episode of delightful misfortune.

"No, no, there's more. The Ganiffs have to move out of their suite while it's being fumigated, but the thing is, we're sold out because of his bible convention. There's no way we can bump anyone without major pushback from Murlise. So, Murlise arranged for them to stay at the Four Seasons! Can you believe it?"

I chuckled. "How deliciously ironic!"

"Yeah, Ganiff got very strange and refused to stay at the competition. He stopped her from making the reservation and then had her book them rooms under a fake name at the Howard Johnson's down the street!"

"Amazing!" This had the earmarks of Carole. More than likely, she had worked behind–the–scenes with Murlise. Another convoluted twist of office political bedfellows. *Poor Ganiff, he's getting it on all ends. Deservedly so.*

"Yeah. This is fun. You're so creative, Linda."

"Wait a sec. I didn't have anything to do with this. By the way, the other day Doreen, Murlise and Edwing phoned. Sounds like everyone's coming out of the woodwork and sticking it to the old fart. Guess I better get innovative, you know, with all the competition."

"So, you're not done with him yet?"

"Hell no! Not by a long shot."

Later that afternoon, I received a phone call from Bob. He sounded calm again.

"Linda, we need your help. We'd like to take down all the perpetrators in one shot. Maybe even catch 'em red–handed together. I'm talking Ganiff, that Seecrock and that Koneman character from L.A." All of a sudden, he sounded anxious. "Any chance that L.A. guy's coming here, like real soon?"

"You know, I've this friend who might be able to lure him to New York and—"

"That would be ideal. Set it up! If he comes here with his buddy, then he wouldn't be suspicious. He's a real slippery one. I'd prefer we do it in public so we have witnesses. Also to limit them from using weapons."

Weapons? Did I hear right? "Uh, Bob, we're talking about crooked hotel managers and one social misfit." *Or perhaps three,* I reconsidered.

"In my book, Linda, they're dangerous. They invested in child pornography. They wired illegal funds into a bank account with intent to launder money through a porn company that we've been trying to indict for years. They've threatened anyone who finds out with the loss of their livelihood, like you."

I laughed nervously. "Okay, you convinced me. Go for it. Use muscle. Lots of it. Don't be surprised, though, by a lack of resistance."

"So, we're thinking a few days from now. Linda, I do need your help. This could only go down on the proviso that you get the Hollywood guy to come here."

I glanced down at my desk calendar. Ganiff's Born Again get–together was coming up next week. "Well, thanks, Bob, for the additional pressure. How 'bout we aim for the 15th? That is, if I can get Koneman to come east."

"The 15th? That would be perfect. The sooner the better. Just get him here. I have faith in you, Linda. And call me the second you have it set up and I'll get my team in place."

I had a few last arrangements to make.

With my usual reluctance, I phoned Jay Krieger, seeking to cash in on my one and only standing favor with him. It wasn't easy. After our successful conversation the other day, he had followed up with a late night call for a little "pillow talk." I tried my best to ignore his allusions but he refused to take the hint. He had every intention to capitalize on my need for his assistance. In other words, a platonic friendship was not on the table for him. As my mother used to say: "It's like inviting the cock into the henhouse." My situation was more like inviting the cock in—

period—and I didn't like where it wanted to go.

"How may I help my sweet damsel in distress?" he said, perfectly amenable. "You calling to apologize about the other night?"

The hairs on the back of my neck stood straight up. "Apologize for what?"

He purred. "I was just trying to find a way to finish what we started back at your place."

Damn it! I laughed in spite of myself. "Jay, let's save the socializing for later. I'm calling about our good buddy, Koneman." I knew that would rattle his cage and divert his attention.

"Shit, not that bastard again. You know, that guy showed up at my office the other day with no appointment. He refused to leave for over three hours until I came out to meet with him. Just for a frigging photo–op. Pushy bastard! I can't believe Sinatra would've ever enjoyed his company."

I thought back to the report I'd gotten from the William Morris office and laughed. "While we're talking about that asshole, there's something you should know. This guy's not nearly all he's cracked up to be."

"What do you mean? The guy's an asshole but everyone knows him as the self–proclaimed king of PR."

"Jay, the fucker lied about his past. I have papers here to prove it. He was not nor has he ever been an agent at William Morris. Ergo, he never repped Mis–ter Sinatra! Never even carried his bags!" I was thrilled to finally pull that rabbit out of the hat by the ears. "The guy was a gofer for less than a year before he got canned... some thirty years ago."

"Oh, no way!" Jay laughed. I was crestfallen. "You're telling me the ruthless bastard lied his way to the top? That's pretty impressive in some sick, twisted way. I mean, he is pretty good at what he does—"

"And amazingly effective 'cause he got something from you with minimal energy. It doesn't take a lot of effort simulating a planter in your office, you know. Look what you gave him. I bet you got nothing in return!"

Jay hesitated. "Eh, you got that right," he said. "Damn! Did I tell you that he's very good at what he does?"

"Yup. If I count previous conversations, quite a few times, in fact."

Jay vented, "He didn't even have to spend a dime and I gave him a photo–op on a fucking silver platter for five of his clients!"

I gave him a moment to vent. "Jay, well, hate to pull a Koneman on you, but guess what? I need you as bait."

"How overly romantic of you, dear," Jay responded.

I refused to dignify his overtures. "Can you work it so that Steven will come here for say, the 14th and 15th? I know it's short notice and all. Let's say it'll be worth your while as well."

He wavered for a moment and then made another futile attempt at romance. "Worth my while, huh? Like the two of us hot, sweaty and nekkid on a private tropical beach somewhere?"

"Doesn't that sound nice?" I lied. "No, when I say worth your while, I mean getting Koneman out of your hair, possibly for good."

"Holy shit! You gonna have the guy whacked? What are you up to, Linda?"

"War!" I laughed. "No bloodshed, I promise. Just make the call. Then phone me back, okay? I know you can do it, baby!"

Two hours later, my machine spewed out a fax. It had a cover sheet from Jay's MGM office and a travel itinerary from an agency. Both Jay Krieger and Steven Koneman had been booked first class from LAX to JFK airports to arrive on the evening of August 14th.

When I saw Jay's name on the document, I groaned and picked up the phone. He took my call straight away.

"Jay, when I said 'bait,' I meant that figuratively. You're not supposed to come here. You're supposed to misdirect the man."

"Hey, it was the only way to set it up with that guy. Besides, I'm curious. I want to see what'll go down. Promise me that Linda, and I'll be your man forever."

"Forever is not a word in your vocabulary, Jay," I chided him. "I do promise you that it'll be worth your trouble… sweetheart." I found that last word difficult to get out let alone say, however, given what he had done for me, mandatory.

I disconnected Jay, waited for a dial tone and called Bob's mobile phone.

"It's Linda. We've a done deal. The 15th it is."

"Okay. Hold on a sec." Bob shuffled papers. "Wait a sec. Did you say the 15th?"

"Uh, yes."

"Damn, I don't know. I'll have to get my team assembled. Give me another sec." Objects were tossed in the background.

"Now you change your mind?" I groused, "Bob, you have no idea what I did to set this up! Let's just say I compromised my body and soul just to get that Koneman here! And, a little reminder: Ganiff will have his Born Again gathering there, which makes it perfect. Should be plenty of witnesses."

Bob muttered, "All right, the 15th it is, but I won't have my full team. Only eleven men. Damn, let me schedule them to get there by ten in the morning for the grand finale."

"Whew! Good! Too bad I won't be able to see this go down."

Bob cleared his throat. "You have to be there."

"What? Are you serious?" My mouth dropped to the floor. "I was under the impression that my involvement with this investigation was done after this."

"I need you on–site to make sure everyone's together for the bust."

I gasped. "Really? I mean, okay. I would hate to miss all the excitement. Thing is, if Ganiff spots me on the premises, he might somehow suspect something. Or he could call the cops and mess everything up."

"Don't worry," Bob said with confidence, "everything's arranged. Just got Big Guy up to speed. We'll have you wired and disguised."

Arranged. Hmmm. Perhaps they'll serve free popcorn, or even better, malted milk balls at the front row.

Chapter 38

Seated at my command central, I finished reading a form letter from the New York State Department of Labor. It stated that I was denied benefits because I was fired for insubordination. *No surprise but absolutely galling.*

I was livid. They had pushed the envelope now. My anger stoked my creative juices because out of nowhere I had another brainstorm.

I dialed a number I never considered calling before.

"Hello, Calvin—I'm gonna make this short and sweet. You're gonna give me $25,000. There's something I need to do. Something you don't need to know anything about."

Calvin laughed. "Oh, um… Linda. So, you want $25,000? May I ask why?"

I didn't respond.

"With an offer like that, how could I say no? How 'bout I do one better? What would you say if I gave you my credit card number?"

"Wait a sec, Calvin. You gave up that quickly? Are you truly not the least bit interested in what I'm up to?" I was stunned that he didn't express his customary curiosity, quite unlike the Calvin of a thousand questions. He seemed rather subdued.

"Listen, Linda. I know you're the catalyst behind all this shit. I did read that 'Anona Miss' letter. Stole a copy off Ganiff's desk. It had to be you."

I laughed. Pursuant to Bob's instructions, I wasn't permitted to talk about my efforts in that scheme. Inasmuch as I wanted to confirm Calvin's suspicions, I had no choice other than to let him continue talking.

"Anyhow, in an indirect way you're gonna save me a fortune in legal bills. So, what's $25,000 in the scheme of things? Consider this my way to repay you for your kindness."

At least he's repaying me with money, I thought, *and not with a bloody horse's head in my bed! I thanked the gods for blessing me.*

He forged on. "FYI, I won't be facing jail time either. In a way, you jumpstarted my new life. So, do what you have to do and we'll call it even. My little thank you." He proceeded to read off the numbers and expiration date and then hung up.

I reached for the GermBank nerf ball that I found wedged in the back of my desk drawer. Tossing it from hand to hand, I reflected about clueing Bob in on this new course of action so that there would not be any unscripted surprises. I put the nerf ball down, picked up the phone and made the call.

Chapter 39

Morning. 8:00 a.m. August 15th. On the corner of West 54th Street, a hulk of a man approached me. My savior, Big Guy. He tossed a gray blanket over my head, threw me over his shoulder and carried my body like a sack of potatoes down the street. All at once, he stopped and threw open a door. It was the rarely used side entrance of the hotel that led into a small office behind the banquets area.

When he put me down and removed the blanket, a familiar, friendly face was before mine.

"Ta da!" he sang, "hello gorgeous!"

"Kenin! Good to see you. Are you in on this too?"

"Whaddaya mean by that?" He laughed. "I'm always in. Never one to be left out of the in–crowd. You know that!"

I was happy to have another ally on board.

"Okay, time for me to tend to other matters," Big Guy announced as he headed in the direction of the Lobby. Right before he shut the door, he shot out "see you guys later."

Kenin opened a bag and proceeded to place an array of cosmetics on a nearby table. As per Bob's instructions, I dressed in the typical *Bliss* waiter uniform: Starched white shirt. Black pants. Black bowtie and black Reebok sneakers.

Kenin ordered me to sit on top of a room–service cart. He proceeded to release my hair from the ponytail. Rummaging through his bag of utensils, he selected a pair of nose–hair clippers. Brows furrowed deep in concentration, he gave a few short snips on both sides of my head and collected two longish, thin strands of hair. "So far, so good," he declared.

He gently applied a dab of adhesive liquid to the tips. Then he glued the tips to my upper lip. With smaller scissors, he trimmed the ends so that they trailed to my shoulders. "Voilà," he said, showing off my reflection with the back of a faux silver serving tray.

Horrified, I exclaimed, "Kenin, what the hell is this—you call this a disguise? It looks like I glued my hair to my lip! Oh my! It itches like crazy!"

"You don't like your Fu Manchu? You'll see. Let's tie your hair back into a low ponytail. Nobody'll know it's you."

With major misgivings, I allowed him to play cosmetician to the stars. He added black eyeliner to the lower outer corners of my eyes, dabbed my nose with powder and wiped off my lipstick. I resembled Joel Grey in *Cabaret*.

Bob poked his head into the room. He was dressed in a dark blue suit and a tan overcoat. "Psst, say, do you know where Linda is?" he asked Kenin.

"Right here, Bob, in front of you," I said. "Now, stop with the comedy!"

"You gotta be kidding. You're really Linda?" said Bob, in total sincerity.

"Yeah, it's me." Right at that moment, I felt somehow that we had slipped between the cracks and were now living in a parallel universe where clocks run backwards and the lunatics from the asylums were allowed to run amok with the local citizenry.

"Hey, there. You did a magnificent job!" waxed Bob enthusiastically to Kenin, thumping him on the back. Bob said, "Big Guy highly endorsed Kenin's skills as a practitioner of cosmetics. I was not misled." Bob nodded his head at Kenin, "We met last night."

Kenin bowed in appreciation, saluted and said, "Good luck." He stepped out, leaving Bob and me to talk strategy.

I jumped off the room–service cart. "So, what's next on the program?"

"As I said before, you need to lurk around for about an hour. That's more than ample time for you to put into place your strange little party, okay?" Bob peered into my eyes. Abruptly he said, "Let's synchronize our watches. I have 9:46 a.m."

I checked my digital watch. It displayed the same time. "Right on."

"Your task is to hang around the second floor. Pretend to perform waiter work, like carry a drink, or two. Blend into the background. You'll have ample time to do your final swan song, or whatever the hell... Just make sure you don't deviate from what you described to me on the phone. And don't wait last second to do it! Once again, Linda, please stay below radar when you see the Ganiffs."

Now nervous, I asked, "What about the bible get–together? They're still on the second floor, right?"

"They are. Don't worry, nothing changed," Bob confirmed. "Right now, the Ganiffs are mixing between the two conference rooms. We have to get him away from his wife and into the Lounge along with Seebok and Koneman. Hey, don't worry, my people will assist in getting this done. You're pretty much the fallback guy." Bob placed a wire on the inside of my tie and set me up with an earpiece and battery pack. He shook his head in admiration. "That guy, Kenin, is definitely talented. He truly missed his calling."

I rolled my eyes in exasperation. "One major question. It seems to me like you're running a shoestring operation here. I mean, what's with using Kenin and me for the bust?"

Bob cackled. "You're right on the mark! Thought I'd show my superiors that I could orchestrate a big sting, and do it under budget. That's why I deputized you and some of your cohorts. All of you are doing good work."

He was about to leave when he swung back to say to me. "Incidentally, about those trips Ganiff took to San Juan? It may be hard to believe that they were real

300

vacations. Like who goes to Puerto Rico in the summer? Sometimes, with these criminal types, it gets difficult to tell what they're up to because of their ulterior motives. In this regard, you were absolutely right to check with us."

"Oh, okay." I was disheartened that we couldn't get Ganiff on more. On the other hand, what we had was more than necessary if everything went as planned. We left the small office to enter the corridor where Bob handed me off to Kenin who lovingly shoved me in my kidneys.

"Okay, time to head upstairs. You're on!"

This was it. Showtime. My heart thrashed against my ribs. I trudged up three flights using the employee staircase and entered the second floor. Directly in front of me were banners strewn from the ceiling welcoming the Born Agains. Tables lined both sides of the hallway, piled with heaps of food and drinks. The guests picked and gorged. The food, not each other. On both sides of each doorway were stacks of bibles.

I walked around the perimeter of the first room. There were clusters of well-dressed and happy people mingling, citing obscure Scripture and gobbling free food, bibles tucked under their arms. I kept staring at these good people. They surely knew their gospel. Everything for them was about God and their very own personal relationship with Jesus. Their moon, pallid faces and bland appearances combined with the fact that they never possessed one creative thought in their lives captivated me. I had formed that impression from my—thankfully— limited interactions with Mrs. Ganiff.

One of the more impressive soliloquies to which I had been subjected outside of theatre had occurred two weeks before my termination. The Missus tucked in her chin and rolled downstairs to ask Mr. Ganiff a question. As usual, he was locked in the john. While waiting imperiously in front of my desk like an immutable mountain, she had initiated a discourse about the sexual goings–on between her friends, Abraham and Sarah and their maid, Hagar.

"Because Sarah was barren, Abraham had no choice but to bed Hagar."

Simultaneously rendered speechless and perversely intrigued, I listened with jaw agape.

"Hagar gave Abraham a child, Ishmael—"

The door to the inner office opened and Ganiff dashed out during the last snippet. "Mabel, darling, please don't waste your breath explaining Scripture…"

That was Scripture? I felt educated, of sorts. All this time, I had assumed these were scandalous neighbors at Cape Cod. It sounded juicy enough although a tad familiar. Like stories that had been branded across my childhood mind from old catechism classes.

I shook myself out of this flashback. Waitstaff bustled between clumps of conventioneers, furiously busy picking up discarded plates, glasses, cups, napkins and dropped food. Once again, I found it difficult to reconcile these normal, banal–looking people—who radiated innocence and sincerity—with their infamous close–mindedness. The typical remarks were, "Hi, how're the kids?" The response invariably intoned, "Fine." This trite ritual, repeated over–and–over in the room, almost compelled me to contemplate suicide, taking a page from Hitsuhana–san. Luckily, there were no samurai swords nor tatami mats lying around.

All at once, I spotted the Ganiff.

He strolled into the room, wearing one of his favorite pin–striped Armani suits and took center stage among his fellow worshipers. I must've caught his eye because he signaled for me to come over. *Shit,* I thought, *my cover was already blown?*

He placed his empty glass on my tray and said in a loud voice, "Kindly get me another glass of water." When I turned around, he pulled me back by the elbow. "Let me guess, you're Croatian?"

Numbly, I dipped my head. I felt sweat cascading down my back. *Was he toying with me? Or, perhaps, he hadn't figured it out!*

"Aha! Guessed right again!" He turned to his audience and boasted, "Here at the Supreme Superior we employ people from all over the world. More than 135 languages are spoken here!" He pointed at me, never once releasing my elbow. "This young man is an example of the kind of people our hotel attracts as employees. They come to this country poverty–stricken, seeking the American dream. Some of them find God through our efforts." He paused for effect. "If they do well here, we have a program that assists them in moving up the corporate ladder." He let go of me. "My good man, please get me my water, pronto!" With that, he turned around and started up another conversation with his adoring fan club.

Close call. I exhaled once more.

I departed from the room, found another waiter and motioned him over. "Hey, I need a favor."

"Um, okay," the young man said.

I handed him Ganiff's empty glass. "You know who Mr. Ganiff is, right?"

The waiter nodded in recognition.

"Good, well he's asked me to bring him another glass of water. Can I ask you to do the honors? Gotta make a quick pit stop."

He smiled up at me and nodded again. Clearly, he didn't seem to speak much English. Perhaps he was from Croatia. He took the glass and departed from the area.

I scoped the rooms for a trio of conservatively dressed women: a blonde, a redhead and a brunette. It was almost ten–thirty. Till now, I hadn't had a moment to seek them out.

The hallway outside this area was crowded, comprised of bible thumpers and hotel staff. At last, I spotted them exiting the ladies' room. I recognized them because all three were very skinny and exceedingly "well–endowed." They wore knee–length skirts and buttoned–up blouses covered by dark collared jackets. They seemed tired from their red-eye flight. I ran over to them and introduced myself.

"Hi, I'm Linda. You guys must be the cast from that movie."

"Three's A Crowd and Tigger Too," replied the blonde, the tallest of the women. She flashed a toothy smile. "I'm Vinnie, as you can see by the name tag." She tapped the hotel–generated self–adhesive label on her blouse with a long, French–manicured fingernail.

The trio looked me up and down. "Are you a tranny?" asked the redhead. The tag on her lapel read "Vidi."

"No, just in disguise." I pointed to my ridiculous pasted–on mustache. "Glad you guys could make it. Feel free to mingle. Your Number One Fan is around here somewhere. How about starting in there?" I pointed to the big conference room. "Go ahead—roam and eat. Enjoy!"

The brunette, "Vicki" as per her badge, smiled at me. "For the money you're paying us just to say hi to this fellow... you're the boss."

The trio made it up to the doorway where they skidded to a standstill. I figured they had noticed the wall–to–wall screens with Billy Graham's face superimposed on top because Vidi stepped back and nudged me. "Hey, are those born agains inside?"

"Why, yes they are." I grinned.

The redhead groaned. "Oh no, I'm sorry. We can't do this. We'll refund the money, less flights and incidentals. No way are we gonna mix with these people."

"Why not?" I threw my hands up in disgust. "I mean, you've come all this way. What's the big deal? You don't have to seduce anyone, or anything." I couldn't imagine that these actresses would back out. They weren't part of the sting operation but my very own contribution to the collective effort. This unforeseen reluctance to participate felt like a lost opportunity for me to perform my last Ganiff kerplunk. My personal way of saying thanks for the memories.

The other two women walked over to join us. Vicki said, "We were invited last year to one of these gatherings by a really creepy guy."

My first thought was, *you gotta be kidding me!*

Her colleagues nodded, serious. "He splurged for the flights and a hotel room in Hoboken. Then, he invited us to attend this same conference somewhere in Jersey." While Vidi recounted her story, the four of us casually strolled into another room. "The weird thing was we didn't have his name. Or anything. He went by the moniker, 'Number One Fan.'"

Oy vey, I thought. *Another Number One Fan? What're the odds that there's another one involved with this religious organization?*

Vinnie spoke, "So, we decided to go. We were having an okay time but there was this one guy—"

Vicki chimed in. "We would've preferred to hear the words of their Lord, but..." she shrugged, "things kinda got strange."

"What are you talking about?" I said, preoccupied with this turn of events. We'd walked almost to the front of the room.

Directly ahead of us stood a five–foot high platform, adorned with a row of chairs. The stage was also graced with the mandatory towering stacks of bibles. Suspended from above was a large screen playing selected video highlights from previous conferences. We paused in front of the stairway that led to the stage.

Vinnie kept on. "This older guy came up to us. He was drooling. Gross! He kept whispering lewd comments. When we wouldn't react, he pinched our asses from behind. We tried to blow him off, but he kept circling us. It was eerie. I even heard that music from *Jaws,*" to which she made a deep–throated noise, "da da, da da, da da." Then she said, "The guy was weird. He had one eye that worked and one that didn't."

Fucking surreal! It had to be Ganiff. Who else? What was the probability? I pinched myself to make sure I wasn't dreaming. At this point, I wondered about Ganiff's state of mind—to invite porn stars to a religious convention? I mean, sure, I did the same for a vastly different reason. Beyond a doubt, they had introduced me to a new level of Ganiff perversity.

While they chattered away, I surveyed the room for a Ganiff sighting and strategized how to introduce him to the three ladies. I didn't pay any mind to what they said until all three women began to choke. That grabbed my attention.

Vidi frowned. "Yeah, we're porn stars and we're used to having sex with different men. But—"

"But we are actors not hookers!" Vicki vehemently stressed. "These men think that we do this all the time for or with anyone! We don't!"

"You had to be there. The guy had blood oozing outta his head," said Vinnie animatedly.

My head whipped from one woman to the next. *What were they talking about? Who the hell were they talking about? Could it be Ganiff?*

Vinnie continued, "His arm was dangling out of its socket, and he still wanted us to watch him whack off with that lame arm! And then he cried, begging us to recreate a scene from one of our videos!" She blanched.

Even I blanched. That was nasty! Definitely deviant! *Who the fuck were they talking about? Cause it sure sounded like Ganiff!*

Vicki said, "No way we're going through that again!"

I thought, *Huh?*

Without any warning, a strangled yelp came from behind us. We turned around as one. It emanated from Ganiff. His left eye bulged from its socket. He stood stock–still and pointed his arm straight at us. With his other arm, he grabbed at his chest. My three professionals were also in shock. One of them whispered, "Is he the one from last year?"

"I can't tell 'cause there's no blood on him… Oh wait! It's him—check out those eyes!" said the redheaded porn starlet. She then spat out, "Sick bastard!"

For me, the moment proved predictable and anti–climatic, given what I knew about Ganiff. For them, it was that Eureka moment of discovery. Fear registered on their faces. *What should I do?* I had to weigh between getting discovered and blowing the bust, or protecting these women. After all, we had three against one, so they didn't need my assistance. Or did they? On the other hand, this was a room full of religious people. I made my decision.

I quickly scampered away. I found an alcove with a great view of the entire room. Ganiff was still pointing at the porn trio. They, in turn, stood frozen like statues in front of the platform. So far, none of the milling crowd was aware of the unfolding events.

I spotted Mrs. Ganiff, the event hostess who commandeered the far left of the room. She sported an orange muumuu dress that flowed freely over her bulk. Regrettably, her outfit clashed with her face that had achieved an almost purple hue. Probably from the exertion of her forced smile plus the after–effects of the bedbug bites. Her eyes followed her husband's every move.

Perhaps Mr. Ganiff was aware that his every move was monitored by Mabel because he suddenly spoke exceedingly loud, causing heads to turn everywhere, "You! I know all of you. So good to see you!" His chuckle sounded forced.

I looked back over to where I had left my hired girls. Vinnie stepped forward and said, "Yes, intimately."

"Not in the biblical sense," Ganiff rapidly riposted.

Due to the distance, Mrs. Ganiff couldn't effectively snoop. She was curious as to why her dear Iggy was shouting. Even more curious as to whom he was shouting. She slowly sidled over to him, feigning that she hadn't noticed the triplets beforehand. "Hi, I'm Mabel. Are you friends of my husband?" She extended a hand. Mr. Ganiff grabbed her by the arm and yanked her away.

"You don't want to know these people, Mabel. Trust me on this. They are not God–fearing, good people… or anyone on the guest list."

Vicki scowled at Mr. Ganiff and pointed. "As if you would know about fearing God—after what happened in Hoboken? You sick fuck!"

I leaned forward to see better. Just as things got good, a short man with a head full of abundant, thick, curly hair blocked my bird's eye view.

"Excuse me, sir." I tapped him on the shoulder. Calvin whipped around. My heart stopped for a moment. Before he could react, I placed my hand over his mouth and whispered, "Shhh. Don't say a word. It's me, Linda, in disguise."

"Wow! I'd never have guessed." He laughed and reached to touch my mustache. I slapped his hand away.

"Look what your twenty–five grand bought you!" I said, indicating with a nod toward the scene transpiring in the front of the room.

"Ah, great investment." He pivoted and pointed at the porn trio. "At least I know it's money well spent… I guess?"

"Yeah, I believe the party's just starting. What are you doing here?" I asked in a low voice.

Before Calvin could reply, one of the actresses said something to Mrs. Ganiff who followed up with a scream, "Oh my! Oh my!"

Something told me that the Missus didn't like what she had heard. Her shrieks shattered the room's ambiance. People murmured.

Without warning, a tiny old lady wearing trifocals tottered up to Mrs. Ganiff and hit her repeatedly on the head with her handbag. It had a bible sticking out of the unzipped top. "Shut up you rhino! I want to hear what they have to say! I've had it with you, you pushy broad!"

My attention was diverted towards the other performance in progress. It was almost like a two ring circus. Each time the threesome attempted to get away, Ganiff went out of his way to body–block them while hurling vile insults.

The women tried their damnedest to escape. They even walked in reverse to avoid him until the heel of Vinnie's shoe got caught on the first step to the platform. Falling backwards onto the staircase, she accidentally knocked over a pile of bibles that were precariously perched on the penultimate step.

"Ohmilord!" Mrs. Ganiff shouted while fielding blows to her head from the little old lady. "Iggy, what did you do?"

Vidi and Vicki ran over to lift their fallen friend from the steps. The poor woman had the wind knocked out of her. As they bent forward, their skirts rode upward, revealing a little too much information. These women were not wearing panties.

There were gasps and quick whispers exchanged among the church members. One–by–one, people stopped talking to follow the action. Now all three women were up on the platform. Vinnie sat on the stage, gulping in air while Vicki tried to calm her down. Vidi rushed to restack the bibles on the steps, only for them to topple over again. Not unlike the myth of Sisyphus.

"Wow, I can't believe that Mr. Ganiff would do such a thing," commented one of the bystanders to my left, "who is this monster, shoving these skinny, top–heavy women for no reason?"

Mr. Ganiff, in any event, was impervious to anyone else in the room. He persisted in shouting at his favorite video trio from below the stage, "What the hell are you wenches doing here? Who invited you to my hotel?"

Vinnie revived sufficiently to shoo Vicki away. She stood up, dusted herself off and bent down to pick up her earring lying on a lower step. It had fallen off during her tumble. Unintentionally, in the process of bending, she thrust her buttocks almost inches from Mr. Ganiff's face. He stumbled backwards.

It took him a minute to regain his balance. "Are you people trying to destroy me? How dare you!" he shouted. He ran up the steps to the stage, kicking bibles out of his way. Like a bull in a china shop, he knocked over the stacks that Vidi had completed.

A collective gasp went up in the audience. Ganiff had everyone's attention now.

The spectators were stunned. First by Mr. Ganiff's temper. Second of all, by his yelling and carrying on. Tertiary, by the visible fact that none of the trio onstage were natural blonds and redheads.

There was a buzzing in the air. The murmuring grew louder.

Part of the crowd turned their focus away from the main event toward the one unfolding in front of the stage. Mrs. Ganiff's heated exchange with the bespectacled older woman had escalated. The white–haired woman grew tired of propelling her handbag upward. Inspired by her second wind, she swung her cane at Mrs. Ganiff's knees. It connected solidly, knocking the mastodon to the ground. I felt a slight tremor in the underpinnings of the building. Clumsily, Mrs. Ganiff quickly scrambled to her feet—a feat incredibly executed given her bulk. With all her summoned strength, she hauled back and slapped the geriatric lady across the face.

The slap sounded as loud as a gunshot. As resounding as a rifle shot. As damaging as a cannon. As detonating as a nuclear bomb. And with that much impact. Stunned by the reaction of one simple, yet violent move, the Ganiffs stopped in their tracks. Jaws dropped across the room, mine included.

Suddenly, a couple dozen mobile phones were whipped out. Like electronic cicadas, the room filled with the repeated dialed equivalent of the numbers "911." Almost all of the people who had witnessed the debacle were horrified. What callous and un–Christian behavior from these supposed pillars of their community!

Iggy and Mabel's eyes met. I could see Master Ganiff shaken to the very core of his hollowed corporal soul. People shouted among themselves, "You call them the bedrock of our society?" followed by "How could he? How could she?" and, "They lead by example—what example are they?"

307

I was closely examining Mr. Ganiff's reaction. After having spent the better part of ten months reading the nuances of his body language, I easily picked up on his guilt and shame. Especially in the way he surveyed the angry crowd. Realization finally crept in. He had subjected his very own people to degradation. He had brought filth into his congregation. His standing in the community had been compromised. His reputation was now in shreds. In other words, he was majorly screwed.

Calvin took the initiative and ran up the steps. "Psst, Iggy, let me get you outta here. It's dangerous!"

Unaccustomed to being the center of enmity, Mr. Ganiff became confused. He passively allowed Calvin to lead him out, leaving his sweet Mabel to her own devices within the angry mob. As they passed me by, Calvin winked and lip–synced, "Destination Lobby."

With Mr. Ganiff out of the way, the disgruntled conventioneers focused their attention on Mrs. Ganiff. Several members from her community questioned her ethics. "Is it Christian to slap an old lady? Shouldn't it be more like 'turn the other cheek'?"

During this turn of events, I signaled to my three traumatized specialists. The sympathetic born agains helped the actresses stumble through the crowd. I caught their attention once more and pointed to the employee staircase exit. The brunette, Vicki, stopped to flash a thumbs–up to several of the people in the room. Vinnie blew kisses. Vidi swiped a bible off one of the stacks by the doorway. They exited stage left.

Meanwhile, Mrs. Ganiff was taking a beating. A short bandy–legged man with no teeth nabbed her from behind. An elderly lady elbowed her in the ribs. With each blow, Mrs. Ganiff's eyes bulged and her mouth pursed into a perfect "O."

I stepped into the hallway and bowed my head to whisper into my wire, "Bob, this is Linda. Calvin took Ganiff to the Lobby. Do you copy?" A crinkling noise in my earpiece greeted me.

"I copy, Linda. We have a bit of a problem here. No one can find Seebok anywhere. It's been quite a while."

"Define how long a while," I said.

"A while meaning, from what people are saying, since last night. The guy's gone AWOL."

I laughed. "Nothing unusual about that. He has perfected the knack of disappearing, but let me check."

I had a hunch. I remembered viewing a certain elevator videotape which Johnny from Security had further researched. It involved Suite 1515 on the 15th floor. That was the room where Seebok had had a rendezvous with his mistress. My instinct might've been an intuitive stretch even though I didn't think so.

One thing I knew about Seebok was his consistency—if anything, he always returned to the scene of his crimes.

I took the employee elevator and furtively prowled down the hallway of the 15th floor. In front of each doorway, I executed a perfect forward roll, a technique used to avoid exposure in Bruce Lee movies. One of the housekeeping staff lumbered by, arms laden with towels. She spotted me hugging the walls. I gave her the international silence gesture, the finger in front of the mouth. Wide–eyed, she dropped the towels, turned around and bolted down the corridor. I crawled up to Suite 1515 on my forearms, another method gleaned from the movies, this time to avoid detection from the doorway peephole. Gingerly, I placed my ear to the door and heard muffled gurglings, followed by the sound of Trish's voice.

Pay dirt!

"Trish? Trish, come on, let me in!" I stood up and pounded on the door.

"Who is it?" asked Trish.

"It's me, Linda. Open the door."

Trish poked her head out. Her dilated eyes astounded me. I said, "Damn, are you okay?"

"Shhh." She placed an index finger on her lips. "Everything's okay, young man."

"Then let me in," I said as I kicked the door wide open.

The sight behind Trish was the scariest I'd witnessed in this hostelry of horrors.

Seebok was seated across the room in front of open windows. Duct–taped to his chair, the one with the roller wheels. It had all the hallmarks of a scene in a horror film. Trish must have pushed him like this from his office. Probably used the rear elevator. *How did she get away with it?*

That's when I had a flash of clarity. Even if there had been witnesses, Seebok's earlier antics afforded Trish the best invisibility. Ever since the sacrificial animals escapade, no hotel employee would've raised an eyebrow if they had seen Seebok duct–taped and bound to a chair pushed by a subordinate. I'm certain that many would've been grateful that there were no blood and guts this round.

A whiff of a foul odor drifted into my nose. Suite 1515 reeked of urine.

"How long has he been like this?" I asked.

"Since last night. He threatened to fire me once he left the office, so I decided that I'll have this job for as long as he's here."

I could see the stress of the past several weeks had completely worn Trish down. Way down! The woman was broken.

"All right, Trish. This is a little too creepy, even for me. We need to let him go."

Trish cried. I patted her on the shoulder, helped her over to sit at the foot of the bed and whispered in her ear, "Don't you worry. It's all over now. Trust me—you won't be fired for this. Institutionalized, perhaps, but not fired."

I located a small pair of scissors in the credenza unit. I grabbed them and headed over to Seebok. His face turned scarlet, his eyes protruded from their sockets and he emitted some violent deep–throated noises. His entire body strained. He heaved and bucked against the duct–tape. Inasmuch as I enjoyed the performance, I had to calm him lest his struggle might cause a massive coronary or seizure. Perhaps I also worried about the legality of the situation because in the event of a massive coronary or seizure I couldn't help him. Yep, I had failed the CPR test one final time before I was fired.

"Don't worry, Seebok, I won't stab you to death. Although I'm awfully tempted. Well, perhaps a slight nick or two."

Relieved, his eyes—resembling those of a little cartoon puppy dog—pleaded with me to release him.

The duct–tape was applied everywhere. I had to cut off part of his pants and the top of his hair to get him out of the chair. Trish stood up and paced the floor behind us while she watched my every move.

Finally, I cut Seebok's legs free. Weakly, he leaned against the wall and used his remaining energy to unsuccessfully pull the duct–tape from his wrists. That was after he plucked the duct–tape out of the residual skeins of hair that I hadn't chopped up. It left huge bald swatches across his scalp. He would've screamed, if not for the fact that his mouth was still covered. I decided to share a farewell one–way powwow with the man before setting him altogether free.

"Seebok, you lowlife, whatever you did to make Trish snap like this must've been downright sickening. Then again, that's typical you, ain't it?"

Seebok bobbed his head up and down.

Right before I went to remove the last piece of tape off his lips, I brandished the scissors under his nose, "Don't even think of saying a word, or I'll be back to finish the job." Seebok's nostrils flared. I then proceeded to rip the tape off in one fell swoop. He let out a whimper. After a few seconds, he drew in a long, deep breath. Tears streamed down his reddened and blotchy face.

He couldn't restrain himself from asking, "Who the fuck are you?"

I smiled with malicious mirth. "I'm the new Montenegrin waiter. For your information, half the hotel is looking for you. Mr. Ganiff is down in the Lounge right now. He requires your immediate presence."

I stared at his soiled and patchwork suit. "Don't worry, Seebok, I'm sure he wouldn't care how you look, or how bad you smell. Just get down there."

Seebok staggered backward and landed in his chair anew. He was thoroughly sapped and powerless to do any physical damage to anyone. "Please, don't leave me alone in here with this woman another minute," he implored.

I picked up the phone closest to us on the credenza unit and dialed the hotel operator. "Please page Big Guy and tell him to come to Suite 1515. ASAP."

I turned my back to Seebok and whispered into my tie, "Seebok located. Getting Big Guy to assist. Copy?" Again, there was static on the line.

Bob said, "Copy that. We have twenty minutes."

Then I turned to Trish and stepped back in her direction. "You poor, deranged young lady."

She reached out to hug me.

"Don't worry, you'll be well taken care of." I took from my pocket the disc that we had copied from Seebok's computer a few weeks earlier and placed it in her hands. I repeated, "Don't worry. Now you have the means to take care of yourself, okay?" I peered into her eyes. "Do you understand?"

Trish grabbed hold of the disc and stuck it in her pocket. A swift knock on the door interrupted our tender moment. Big Guy poked his head in.

"Everyone all right in here?"

"Seebok's here. He's all yours." I informed him.

Big Guy entered the room and lifted Seebok from his chair. "Damn, Seebok, you stink! What the fuck is your problem?"

"I was tied up since yesterday," he mumbled.

Trish nodded vehemently.

"C'mon, Ganiff's waiting. He's in no mood, Seebok, for your monkey business. Before you go, you gotta clean up."

I looked at Big Guy and pointed at Trish as if to ask what we should do about her. Misunderstanding my gesture, he said, "I don't need her help. I'll handle him myself."

I then crooked a come hither finger in Big Guy's direction. He deposited Seebok back onto the chair and sidled up to me. "You called?"

In sotto voce I said, "Thanks, Big Guy, for the lead time to get things set up. See you downstairs." I gave him a slight buss on the cheek, rubbing his nose in the process.

Big Guy turned red and rushed over to lift Seebok from his chair. Seebok, misinterpreting my kiss and Big Guy's intentions, moaned.

"Shut up, Seebok," yelled Big Guy as he tucked him under his arm, "I'm carrying you to the bathroom. I'll help you undress, but you have to do the rest." Seebok let out another moan.

311

I raced down to the Lobby to witness a rare occurrence—a large gathering of people in the Lounge before noontime. Teddie, the bartender, was busy serving up drinks and counting his tips. I felt that he was the sole safe harbor in all this madness. After a few minutes, I grabbed his attention.

"Oh, you're that new Albanian waiter?"

"No, Teddie, it's me, Linda, in disguise."

Teddie barked in laughter. "That's funny! You're Linda! What a kidder!"

I walked right up to him and touched his cheek. "No, it's me! Linda the crossword lady."

He clapped me on the shoulder, "Whatever, my man, you are truly funny." He wiped his tearing eyes with a bar napkin.

The pandemonium, one story above, did not taint business in the Lounge. I spotted Ganiff drinking a trough of something alcoholic at the corner table. Calvin sat next to him. Then, Steven Koneman joined them with Jay Krieger. I did a double–take. *Fucking Jay Krieger! He's not supposed to be there. What am I gonna do with this guy?*

I grabbed a towel, placed it over my right forearm and went to the table. "May I help you gentlemen?"

Jay almost fell off his chair.

"Oh, you speak English," said an inebriated Ganiff. He opened his arms wide. To his audience, he said, "This is that new Lithuanian waiter." To me, he said, "Get these men anything they want," and dipped his head in his trough to suction in more fluid.

Steven Koneman went first. "Teddie knows what I like."

Calvin gave me a signal indicating he didn't want anything to drink.

I ignored Jay.

Back at the bar, I grabbed Teddie's attention once more. "Give Koneman what he wants, okay?"

Jay Krieger snuck up from behind and pulled me to the side.

"Perhaps I'm the only sane person on the planet, but do you know that nobody realizes you're you?" he said, his eyebrows raised in astonishment.

"Fucking amazing, huh?" I nodded back. "Jay, what are you doing here?"

"Curiosity. I'm gonna go hide behind a potted plant now. Steven's been giving me none too discreet signals to vamoose because he wants to talk to Ganiff."

"Then do me a favor, heed his advice and go away. Take Calvin with you."

Jay walked back to his table. I turned to face the corner and whispered into my wire. "We're getting in place. Seebok due momentarily."

Bob spoke in my earpiece. "Big Guy is finished cleaning him up. We're almost in position. Let me know when he gets there because there was an incident on the second floor. We want to get this done before the police come."

A battalion of NYPD's finest stampeded the Lobby, followed by members of the EMT with stretcher in tow. Murlise directed them to the second floor.

"Too late, Bob, much too late."

The moment I uttered those words, Big Guy delivered Seebok to the bar. Seebok squeezed in at the table with Ganiff and Steven Koneman. No one noticed he was missing almost all his hair. Or that his suit was tattered. Or that he smelled like piss.

Jay and Calvin left the table and moved towards Bliss. My heart rate accelerated into overdrive. I spoke into my lapel, "Everyone in place."

And then I counted to ten.

Eleven federal agents surrounded the table with guns outstretched, wearing black outfits with the letters "FBI" emblazoned in orange on their chests. "No one make a move," said Bob.

The three men seated at the table didn't seem to react at all. I could tell that the situation didn't completely register in any of their brains. Despite the eleven heavily armed men standing not even three feet away. Ganiff was polluted, with both eyes crossed—as opposed to one. Seebok didn't have the strength to move a muscle. Koneman... well, Koneman stared at the cigar between his fingers with a wry grin. He moved his head infinitesimally from side to side.

A commotion in the adjoining Lobby echoed through the Lounge. Four policemen alternately dragged and were dragged by Mrs. Ganiff due to her constant pulling and bucking. She stopped short in the Lobby causing all four NYPD to bump into each other. Then she let out a shriek that broke windows in the top floors of high-rises across the Upper West Side. One word encapsulated it all:

"Iggy!"

In the adjoining room, Mr. Ganiff snapped to attention. He tried to rise from the table, yet couldn't, impeded by the weight of his beverage. Not to mention the guns aimed at him. Drunkenly he yelled back, "Mabel!" The bellowing of the two names concurrently had the same effect as that scratch noise when a record needle is shoved across vinyl grooves. Pigeons throughout the five boroughs lifted as one entity from their perches on electric wires and flew in a tornado formation high in the sky. Apartment buildings in Astoria shook as violently as if an earthquake registering a 2.0 had just occurred. In the Supreme Superior Hotel, the two discordant and dissonant voices disrupted time so that everyone froze in mid-step for at least twenty-seven seconds. If the Romeo and Juliet duet weren't so pathetic, it would've struck me as romantic in a very dysfunctional and besotted way.

Right then, Iggy Two skate-boarded into the Lobby from outside. He stopped in front of his mother, now handcuffed and a model of tameness and resignation. She was surrounded by NYPD's finest. He followed her line of vision, and then turned to see his father in the Lounge. Men with guns also surrounded père Ganiff, yet unlike the men surrounding his mother, these men were FBI agents. Son of Ganiff couldn't figure it out. Bewildered, his eyes darted first to his mother, then to his father and back–and–forth several times in succession.

Finally, he shrugged. With a modicum of comprehension, he said to his mother, "Something tells me, Mom, that you and Dad won't be around tonight to stop me from seeing Howard Stern's movie." He jumped back on the skateboard and made a beeline to the elevator banks. The NYPD officers yanked on Mrs. Ganiff's handcuffs. She screamed, "Iggy Two, hell no! You better not! You have to do your homework. Don't forget your bible study!" Once again, the officers tugged on her handcuffs, forcibly propelling her outside to a waiting patrol car.

In the other arena, the team of Feds moved in closer. "Now stand up, away from the table. Spread your legs and put your hands behind your head." All three men staggered to their feet, still oblivious as to the full situation. Soon, they were handcuffed. Ankle–cuffed too.

Bob stepped into the circle of agents and read the men their rights. "All three of youse are under arrest in violation of the following federal laws…"

When Bob announced the kiddie porn charges, Ganiff tried to break loose in Seebok's direction. "Seebok, you moron, what the fuck did you do this time? You're fired! Oh, I'm gonna kill you, you jackass!" Although he couldn't quite break free from the grasp of two FBI agents, Ganiff did manage to kick Seebok's shins a few times, a considerable victory given the lack of slack in his ankle–cuffs. He even managed to sneak in a head–butt. The agents politely waited until Ganiff had finished. Then they pounced on him.

I waited for them to get the man upright again. A team of six surrounded Ganiff and marched him toward the main entrance. Everyone in the Lobby stopped and stared. Some of the front desk staff even clapped.

I ran ahead of the group, skidding to a full stop at the revolving doors and waited. Ordinarily, I wouldn't have gotten anywhere near Ganiff, but Bob recognized me and signaled to his men to halt. This was my big chance to ultimately unload on the man who had tortured me and so many others for so long.

"What the hell is this? You're bringing me a drink now?" Even though he misunderstood my intentions, Ganiff, true to form, stayed belligerent to the very bitter end. I walked right up to him and yanked off my glued Fu Manchu which hurt like hell.

He gasped, "Oh my God! You're not the Belarusian waiter. You're… you're Linda! What the hell are you doing back here in my hotel? I'll have you arrested!"

I slapped him hard across the face. *What a jubilant feeling!* "That's for Gary

Yong, for Carole Carlson, for the wounded security guards and for everyone else who you fucked over."

All around me was applause and cheering.

While Ganiff was whipped around by his FBI companions, Rory, the teatime pianist, launched into a rendition of *Happy Days Are Here Again*. I imagined confetti flying and balloons floating by. Members of the bible convention joined in with a Glory, Glory chorus, their arms encircling each others' shoulders. It was New Year's Eve all over again.

Jay and Calvin rushed over to join me near the front entrance. I was too caught up with the festive atmosphere to stop Jay from cupping my ass. Out of the corner of my eyes, I caught Calvin observing what Jay had done out of the corner of his eyes. When I looked up at Jay, he smiled back at me. "Hey sweet–cheeks, did I deliver as promised, or what?" He pointed at four heavily armed agents who escorted Steven Koneman. "You did," I smiled back at him, "one commitment that you were finally able to keep. It's a start." I felt Calvin's hand removing Jay's from my butt.

Kenin soon found me and ran over. "Hey, gorgeous, what happened to the 'stache? You know, you were totally convincing as a man. Damn, you were almost my type."

Before I could respond, Trish came running over and threw her arms out to hug me again. She revived from her quasi–breakdown the moment Seebok was placed in handcuffs.

Big Guy managed to push through the crowds of fundamentalists entering the Lobby. He came right up to me and grabbed my hand. "If it weren't for you, Linda… Thanks!" He pointed at Bob, "Now, he's a happy camper."

I followed his finger. One beaming FeeBee. Behind him, a smiling BeeBee, cigarette tucked behind one ear. Other Supreme Superior Hotel employees emerged, eager to watch the demise of their beloved leader.

Things became too hectic in the Lobby. The horde of Federal agents had to turn around and take the little–used *Bliss* exit where Big Guy had brought me in not quite three hours earlier. From there, they frog–marched Ganiff and Seebok toward the line–up of parked black cargo vans. Koneman was escorted behind them, separately. Flashbulbs popped nearby as the paparazzi were getting eyewitness scoops.

I threw my arms around Big Guy and planted a big, wet kiss on his lips. He was stunned by the development and reached for his walkie–talkie, just in case.

"Linda, did that just happen?"

I laughed. "Did you think it was mouth–to–mouth resuscitation? Hey, just like you, I deliver on all my promises."

Jay Krieger disagreed. "Don't believe her," he shouted to Big Guy, "she's bound to change her mind at the oddest of moments."

We followed the crowd outside the hotel onto the sidewalk and found it full with the crush of NYPD's finest, Federal agents, gawkers, conventioneers, paparazzi and pedestrians. As well as Supreme Superior guests. Despite the wild clamor, Ganiff roared at Seebok, "You idiot! They better put us in separate cars, or else I'm gonna strangle you with these cuffs. I can't believe it. You fucked up again!"

Seebok cried out, "Mr. Ganiff, I don't understand. I don't know how this happened."

The Federal agents had to stop the procession for a few minutes. Emergency medical workers wheeled the injured old bible lady into an ambulance at the curb, cutting off easy access to the FBI vans. Thankfully, the old lady appeared alert. "That fucking rhino," she said, "if I had a longer cane…"

Mrs. Ganiff shrieked in a nearby police car, "Iggy, what the hell have you done? Get us out of this!"

Crocodile tears welled up in Mr. Ganiff's eyes. He may have suddenly realized that he and his beloved Mabel would be separated for a long time.

Steven Koneman walked quietly along with the agents, trying to maintain a dignified silence. More than likely, he was conniving some sort of plea bargain or plotting to toss his pals to the wolves. Or, perhaps he realized that of all the devious things he had done in his life, he had gotten nabbed for the least notorious of his dastardly deeds. He had the usual smirk plastered on his face until the agents marched him right up to the same van that held Ganiff and Seebok. That was when he let loose with a keen of thinly veiled panic. They placed him between his two conspirators in the back of the van. As it sped off behind a motorcade, Koneman's face was smashed against the window. Ganiff's shrieking was still audible long after the vehicle was no longer in sight.

"And let this be a lesson to you," whispered a voice behind me. I turned around, but no one else was there other than a few curious busboys and non–English speaking housekeeping staff. I looked above, noticed the sun and cloudless sky. I smiled. My job here was done.

Epilogue
Summer 2008

I was seated next to Veronica in the front row, dead center at the sold–out Tony Tenneb concert. The last time I had seen him perform was thirteen years ago. As usual, he delivered a bang–up show.

Veronica caught my eye and we both smiled. It was like old times again. I was plunged back into my memories while he sang and spoke to the audience about his past.

After the show, we headed backstage. "You know, Veronica, I always imagined that Ganiff, while he was in prison, was going to produce a musical. You know, like the Supreme Superior version of *Springtime with Hitler.*"

"You are so funny!"

"You know what is funnier? The fact that Ganiff was pretty much on target about reality television!"

"Well, visionary or not, c'mon, that pilot show was horrid. Not even the passing years can make that tape good!" Veronica laughed. "Oh, by the way, would you believe that when he was released out of prison, he sent Tony a postcard? He's back at Cape Cod. Have you ever heard from the rest of those bozos?"

"Not really. Although the doormen said that when Mrs. Ganiff moved out of the hotel for good, she left with her arms filled with Supreme Superior towels and sheets. Not only that, she even removed fixtures including pipes and electrical wires!"

After we had a good laugh, Veronica leaned over and whispered, "What about Calvin? Anything recently?"

"Heaven forbid no!" Right after the big bang of a showdown, Calvin closed his construction company. His wife left him. Then he hunted me down. "You know, I was pretty scared of him before I realized that all those impromptu phone calls were his way of courting me. What a putz! He didn't get my subtle messages. You know, changing my phone number again, buying a Doberman and getting a court order of protection."

Veronica nodded in recognition. "That's right, I vaguely remember you telling me. That's also when your karma with men turned around. It's been so long, I'd almost forgotten."

"So, how 'bout you, Veronica. Do you miss the limelight?"

Veronica shrugged and smiled. She had made headlines a decade earlier for dating a world famous movie star. After a relatively modest wedding by Hollywood standards, she popped out three children in succession. The paparazzis' interest soon waned as her marriage and lifestyle were way too pedestrian. Around that time, she also made the difficult decision to resign from her full time position in the music industry. "It'll always be there for me when the kids are old enough," she said.

We entered the cordoned off backstage area. Veronica explained to me the ins and outs of the meet–and–greet function. "Please, Linda, do not under any circumstance mention Ganiff or the Supreme Superior to Tony. He never liked that man. Bad memories."

We were seated at a table on the outside veranda, when Tony walked up to us. He noticed Veronica and gave her a big kiss on the cheek. "Hey sweetheart, how's the family?"

"Oh, we're doing great. The little one's started second grade. Can you believe my baby's that old already?"

Tony smiled at her and crooned, *"Fairy tales can come true, it can happen to you if you're young at heart."* He flashed me a curious look. "I apologize, do I know you from somewhere? You look familiar." Tony squinted at me as he gently shook my hand.

"Oh, it has been many years, Mr. Tenneb. My name is Linda and you knew me when I worked at the Supreme Superior Hotel."

The words had barely left my mouth when Tony grimaced, dropped my hand like a rock and turned his back on me to greet other well–wishers.

Veronica hissed into my ear, "Linda, whatever got into you? I told you not to mention it."

I had no idea why I did it. "Maybe it slipped out. I don't know." I couldn't help but smile as Tony continued to greet his adoring fans. "Veronica, it was so long ago and far away from who we are today. Very few people remember what we did. Even what I did. In a strange way, Tony's reaction was a validation that it did occur, and it had been that bad."

I began to laugh and then couldn't stop. In retrospect, it struck me as comical all the things I did to Ganiff and his band of criminals.

Who was that woman, I wondered, *who pulled off this caper? How did I come up with those ideas? From where did I get the courage to tangle with the Feds, let alone confront all those people? From what fountain of strength did I sip to do the things I did?* Then my thoughts returned to Ganiff.

I wondered if that man had ever taken the time to reflect upon what had happened to him and why it had gone down the way it did. Had he ever taken responsibility for his actions? Ha! A leopard rarely changes his stripes. I'm certain that he continued to blame me, the one who devised his downfall, for all his woes, even up to today. Which reminded me of a movie I once saw where the characters were never accountable for their actions; as a result, they went through hell to avoid being responsible. It was hysterical.

But getting back to Ganiff, knowing his lack of integrity and negative outlook towards the integrity of others, I had an inkling of what had probably run through his mind over the years. I could envision him sitting even now on the deck of his house at Cape Cod and grousing to his sweet Mabel, "You know, none of this would've happened if I had just given her that damn commendation!"

THE END

Acknowledgements

When I embarked on this journey around fourteen years ago, I had no idea that the manuscript I was working on would ultimately become this novel. It took a lot of faith and assistance to make this reclusive hobby into what it is now. And I want to take this opportunity to show my appreciation to several people for helping me keep the vision and not abandon this project which had consumed me for such a long time.

My thanks to Thelma Medida, my bastion for almost thirty years. She ran to meet me at a hotel bar for happy hour in order to discuss my mid–life crisis that transmogrified into the production of this novel. To my dear friend and sister, Trish Bleier who provided unlimited and unconditional support, especially through the constant re–writes. Not to mention those bleak periods when I questioned my mentation. To my editor, Lonnie Ostrow for his clear mind, wit and dedication to the initial manuscript and for providing guidance and structure to produce this end result. To my buddy, Laslo Cheffolway for all his hard work in creating the excellent graphics and design, especially the gorgeous book cover and Supreme Superior logo. To Armando da Silva for the magnificent website and unparalleled sense of humor in three major languages.

A deep and heartfelt thank you to my cousin and moral compass, Nate Silva, especially for keeping family tradition alive. And, a few special shout–outs to the White Lake crowd, the gang at Commack High School North, the gals in HR, Jill Lopano, Benji & Jakes, Arnaldo Carrera, Ajit Sahgal, Lindy and Jeremy Lilley, Greg Else, Leonardo Stivelman, Lucilia Amador, Yanna Darilis, Sheldon Kirsh, Mark and Sharon Usefof, Matt Stone and Jim Daly.

Lastly, a postscript. Never let anyone diminish your dreams.